REVENGE OF THE PUPPET MASTER

TALES OF IRON AND SMOKE, BOOK 3

JOSEPH TRUITT

For my father, Larry, of whom I used to steal science fiction books from under his bed and read late into the night in my bedroom.

ACKNOWLEDGMENTS

Thanks again to my wife Holly for her continued support of my writing. I couldn't do it without you.

CONNECT WITH THE AUTHOR

My name is Joseph Truitt and I would like to welcome you to the Tales of Iron and Smoke book series.

For updates on this series you can sign up for my email list. Those who subscribe to the email list will be notified of giveaways, new releases, and receive updates from behind the scenes.

I am thrilled you've chosen to continue the journey through this epic fantasy world with me and I look forward to having you join me for many more "Tales of Iron and Smoke".

For more information go to JosephTruitt.com

PROLOGUE

Hans Kloppenheimer
(The Puppet Master)

*M*y dearest Emilia,

IT IS WITH THE DEEPEST AND MOST SINCERE REGRET THAT I HAVE chosen to strike a bargain with evil for the restoration of your life. Though I have been able to repair our precious sons to the best of my ability, I have failed at every turn in my efforts to bring you back to us. During these many years, my soul has been consumed with a tempest of hatred for that vile, half-breed tunnel troll, even to the fracturing of blood vessels in my body. Even to the fracturing of my mind. My anger for Angus Grand burned within me so strong that I lost myself in the madness of darkness. Many nights I wandered the dreary streets of Gabriel's Harbor, searching out the forgotten souls of this dead world that I might enact my vengeance upon them in pretense they were Angus Grand. It was only by the blood of those poor, wretched souls that my lust for vengeance was sated, but fear not, my love, I only chose the dregs of this world. Although, sometimes I chose the Black Mist infected souls out of pure pity, but the guilt was too heavy for me to bear, and it did not satisfy the devil within me.

For years I was tortured by the hideous visions of those poor souls begging for mercy as I struck them down with blood-covered hands. It was more than I could stand, but I dared not try and cage the monster inside of me for fear I would take out my anger on James or Victor. In desperation to quench my blood lust for Angus, I sought out our old enemies in Karl's Labyrinth, and soon the tunnels echoed with the icy shrieks of my wicked deeds. It was there that the labyrinth people learned to fear me as their stories about me turned to legend. I even became a monster to the children of labyrinth monsters. It seems that, in my efforts to save you from the evil of this world, I had mistakenly become a greater darkness than the darkness itself. So, I fled from everyone, even our sons, and spent most of my days and nights sulking at the base of your watery grave with only my mindless servants to keep me company. I had lost my direction and singular purpose in life—to bring you back to us at all costs.

My life was now forfeit, and my soul had become lost in a world of madness and blood lust for an enemy I could not lay my hands upon. As I was about to smash your protective container and destroy our every hope, in walked an enemy, as broken and sorrowful as I was the night our ship went down. At first I wanted to kill them. Crush them! Make them pay for all my years of hurt. But somehow, in a fit of rage, I came to myself and regained my deepest desire—the restoration of your life. It became very clear to me that my enemy needed me, as much as we needed them, and so I have likely doomed my soul for you, my beloved Emilia.

My dearest, wife, I beg of you not to hate me for what I have done and am about to do. I do not suppose any man, with such a broken heart as I, would do any less for the one he loves, but I ask your forgiveness in advance for the deeds I am now blood-bound to fulfill. It is for the restoration of your life that I have pledged myself to their dark demands, and in doing so, I have betrayed the world for you. For love.

FOREVER YOURS, EVEN INTO DARKNESS,
Hans

1

THE DREAM SLAYER

*T*hrough the hazy, lamp-lit streets of Grand Fortune City, a scruffy messenger boy gripped his hat tight to his head as he fled the ever-encroaching shadows behind him. His lungs filled with the cool, wet air that pushed the chimney smoke back down into the city streets, nearly blocking his view. He didn't need to see where he was going, anyway. He could have run these streets without eyes, and he knew if he didn't stay ahead of the shadows, he might just have to. Besides, it was his job. Henry was a messenger rascal for the Jackboot.

If you were orphaned, or just plain poor, you might take a job as a messenger rascal for the Jackboot, and you would be well-clothed and protected. Rascals were given the best food, the best water, the best lodging and most importantly, the best shoes for running. It was a good job that, for the most part, was fairly simple—get the message to the Jackboot as fast as you can and hope that he is pleased with your speed. Of course, no one dared block the path of a messenger rascal or thought to stop them mid-run out of fear they might incur the Jackboot's wrath. Maybe someone who'd gone completely mad would consider it.

Someone with different rules, different thoughts. Something primal. Something rotten, perhaps.

He pushed himself harder, block after block, toward the Iron Weaver's warehouse. Toward the Jackboot. Toward safety. The only sounds echoing in his ears were that of his own shoes clapping hard beneath him and his heart pounding like a rapid-fire cannon in his small chest. *Breathe! Don't forget to breathe!* His breath was hot with fear, and the soles of his feet burned inside his shoes with every hard step. His suit jacket was slowing him down, holding him back. He needed to get rid of it, but he didn't want to let go of his new hat. *Run faster, or die for a hat?* He quickly let go of his hat as he turned hard down Station Street. Out of the corner of his eye he saw it roll off into the darkness, then he tore off his suit jacket and cast it aside. *I'll get new ones! Yeah, new ones!*

He ran harder. So hard, he thought his heart would explode in his chest. He wanted to look back and see if he was gaining ground, but he knew how costly the error of curiosity could be. *Never look back! Never look back!* The shadows from the streets lamps almost seemed to bow down to the smoke as, one by one, their lights were snuffed out behind him. *Never look back! Never look back!* He pushed himself harder as his thoughts drew back to the moments before he was given his message.

He stood silent in the place where laughter roared over the heartache of deep wounds. It was the place where hardened men could drop their guard and breathe the smoke-filled air with ease. It was the place where short stories grew into tall tales, and ale flowed as freely as it was sloshed onto the floor. It was where honesty was as cold and harsh as it was true and faithful. It was the place where the Jackboot's men traded the sweetness of victory for the bitterness of cold brew. It was called The Wooden Leg, and it was the favorite pub of the Jack-boot's seven Mighty Men.

The Jackboot's men had never called him by name, though he'd introduced himself to them countless times. *Hi, my name's Henry! Hello, Henry's the name. Henry here, how's the weather today? Top of the morning to ya, sir! Just let Henry get the door for you. By the way, name's Henry. Good day, sir, Henry here, thank you very much. Henry thanks you for the tip, kind sir.* Indeed, Henry knew his job well—stand by the door and wait for any message from the barkeep. Mostly, of late, his messages had to do with the normal problems warriors without a battle faced, like creating their own battles for the simple, joyful remembrance of pain. Or so it seemed to this rascal. One would accuse the other of cheating, knowing full well that no cheating had taken place, then words would be exchanged and fists would fly. The barkeep would send Henry on a run for the Jackboot, who would arrive and break up the fight. Although, Henry believed it to be the only way the men could get the Jackboot out of his office to join them for some ale.

For the most part, Henry enjoyed watching the men tell tall tales and laugh. He even enjoyed the fighting, but this night was different. This night, the mood of the room shifted from laughter and song to somber and silent as the men were reminiscing about one of their own. The one they called Big Bobby "The Kitchen" was gone, and the loss weighed heavy on the men.

With a clink from their glasses, ale sloshed out on to the circular table as the men raised mechanical mod-arms in a toast to their old friend. It was about that time that a strange darkness fell over the pub, and the cedar door creaked open. A wisp of smoke preceded a cloaked man that calmly entered and softly closed the door behind him. The man quietly slid the latch bolt on the door, but his deed didn't go unnoticed by Henry. His face was entirely hidden, making it difficult to tell exactly who or what he was looking at. Henry naturally assumed the man was looking at the floor as his head seemed to be drooping down inside his hood. It was clear to Henry that the man's boots were very heavy, because the cedar floor boards popped against each other fiercely as the man passed him by without tipping. This careless act caught the attention of the Jackboot's men, who normally considered Henry nothing more than a ghostly apparition they flipped coins to as they entered the pub. Henry knew this wouldn't go well for the traveler as he'd witnessed the men's fury on other fools who forgot to tip. *Jackboot's rules, always tip the rascals.*

"You forgetting something, mister?" one of the men asked. The cloaked man took one more step, and the boards beneath his boot let out a loud crack and pop as they snapped under his weight.

Henry clinched his teeth and gripped the Jackboot's seal he carried in his right pocket. Every rascal carried one as proof they were a runner, and whenever Henry was afraid, he gripped it tightly to bolster his courage. As the man stood motionless in front of him, Henry's courage began to fade. He squeezed the Jackboot's seal tighter in hopes the man dare not strike him. The man took a step back toward him, reached into his cloak, and fumbled around for a moment. Henry held his breath. Then the stranger pulled his arm out of the cloak and extended it out toward Henry's tip jar. A gold coin dropped into it with a triple clank, and for a split-second Henry caught a glimpse of the man's hand. The stranger's fingers were large and gnarled with dirty nails to complement the gruesomeness of it all. Henry sensed a cold chill run down the base of his neck then down the back of his legs, and his toes quickly froze inside his shoes.

"That's more like it," the Jackboot's men said as they went back to their reminiscing of The Kitchen.

Henry released his anxiety with a loud breath that he didn't even realize he was holding. He knew everyone in the pub heard it, but he tried to cover it up by clearing his throat. Whether the stranger was friendly or not, Henry decided to keep his hand on the Jackboot's seal for the time being as he watched the man. The stranger made his way over to the bar but never ordered anything, even after the barkeep asked several times for the man's order. Finally, the barkeep gave up and went back to wiping down his bar. Then, after a long bit of silence the man took a seat and began to speak.

"I was wondering if I might trouble the Jackboot's *Mighty Men* with a bit of sport this dark evening," the cloaked stranger asked.

A painfully hard swallow echoed through the pub when the only other patron in The Wooden Leg that night quickly gulped down the rest of his ale. He knocked over his chair as he popped up and scurried out the back door, nearly forgetting to tip Henry. Henry reasoned the man was a good block away by the time the coin landed inside his cup, and the only evidence the man had tipped him was the sound of a coin tingling in Henry's jar until it warbled to a stop.

The stranger's smooth, sarcastic tone took Henry by surprise, and oddly, his voice didn't seem to match his gnarled hands in the least. Henry kept his eyes on the cloaked man as his challenge was largely ignored by the war-seasoned veterans who, themselves, were no strangers to stranger's challenges. Besides, this night was not a night for fighting. This night, they were remembering their friend, and so they pushed aside the dark stranger's request—but the man continued.

"Barkeep, am I in the right pub? Isn't this the pub of the Jackboot's Mighty Men?" the man asked. The barkeep said nothing but looked over at the warriors sipping their ale, then he went back to wiping down his bar. "Maybe I stumbled into the wrong pub," the man said aloud to himself. "Barkeep, is this The Wooden Leg?"

"It is, sir," the barkeep answered.

"And isn't The Wooden Leg the pub of the Jackboot's Mighty Men?"

The barkeep held his breath as he looked over at the Jackboot's men for some sort of affirmation or acknowledgment in hopes that his bar would not be left in tatters that evening. One of them raised his head, took a deep draw on his fat stogie, then gave the barkeep a gentle nod of approval. The barkeep let out a big sigh of relief. "I believe it is, sir," he answered.

"Good! Great! Fantastic! I was hoping you would say that, because I was beginning to think this was the pub for that worthless, fat dead man. Now, what was it they called him? Was it "The Oven?" No wait…wait… it was the "Sink" … No, that's not it. What was it?" The barkeep's hand began to tremble, and the Jackboot's men sat up straight in their chairs. Their glass mugs groaned under the pressure of their angry mod-hands as they held back their fury.

The barkeep leaned in toward the man and whispered, "Surely you don't mean "The Kitchen," do you, sir?"

"THE KITCHEN!" the man shouted and slapped his gnarled hand down on the bar with a loud smack. "That's the one! That fat glob of a brute with more belly than brains. Yes, indeed, that's the one I'm talking about. Didn't someone kill that slob under the monument?"

Suddenly, all six ale mugs shattered against the crushing force of angry metal hands, and the Jackboot's men stood to their feet. The man let out a joyful chuckle as he had finally achieved his goal. "That's more like it," he said in a gruff but relieved voice then stood to his feet. He was still facing the barkeep with his back toward the Mighty Men, and he didn't seem concerned about giving them the advantage. He just stood there and waited patiently for their response.

Billy Bloodbath was the first to step up behind the dark figure. "Look here, bub, I don't know who you think you are, but no one and I mean NO ONE comes in to our pub and talks about our friend that way."

"Well, let me introduce myself then," the man said confidently. "I'm the Dream Slayer."

"You're the what?"

"I'm a Life Taker," the man added as he adjusted his hooded cloak.

"A what?"

"A Neck Breaker!"

A confused Billy placed his hand on the man's shoulder and started to speak, but the man swiftly turned and grabbed Billy's mod-arm. The shock on Billy's face seemed to last a lifetime, but in reality, it was mere seconds. The man's gnarled, green hands were now very visible and terrifying to Henry, but the confused tone in Billy's voice caught everyone off guard.

"You? But... but how? Why?" Billy stuttered out. Deep from within the hooded cloak came a terrifying laughter that released clouds of Black Mist into the room. His filthy arms pulsed green blood through their veins as he gripped Billy's mod-arm hard enough for the metal to groan. Suddenly, Billy looked back at Henry with the cold stare of a man who'd seen death before, but it wasn't the look in Billy's eyes that changed Henry forever. It was his words.

"Henry... run!"

It all happened so fast, and at first Henry didn't know what to do. He'd finally received the acknowledgement he'd so desperately desired for so long from the mightiest men he'd ever known, but at the worst possible time.

"HENRY... RUN!" Billy screamed.

It was in that moment that Henry knew he'd been accepted, and so Henry ran, and he ran swiftly. He didn't need a detailed message to take to the Jackboot this time, because the look in Billy's eyes was enough. It was the look of death and pain, and it was the first time Henry had ever heard panic in Billy's voice.

Hearing Billy call out his name stirred the fires of confidence deep in Henry's belly that sent his feet swiftly through the city streets as fast as they would move him. As Henry ran, his ears were filled with the echoing screams from the pub, and he desperately wanted to know what was happening, but Henry kept his head forward and pushed himself harder. *Never look back! Never look back!*

Henry had only gone a couple of city blocks when he sensed something was following him. Dark shadows passed through alleys and up the sides of buildings all around him. Soon a putrid odor began to fill his nostrils. He'd smelled this stench before, but he dared not look back now for fear he would stumble. Instead, Henry repeated in his mind his own personal motto that had made him the Jackboot's fastest rascal. *Never look back! Never look back!*

Suddenly, Henry's thoughts were transported back to his present circumstances when he rounded the corner of a building on Baker's Boulevard. He crashed hard into a finely dressed business man who was in the process of locking up his shop for night and hit the man with such force they both tumbled out into the street. The man quickly got to his feet and jerked Henry up by the arm, then he proceeded to scold him for his foolish act of carelessness.

"GET UP HERE, BOY! Now, just what the devil are you doing out, running about the streets in the middle of the night?" The man snapped out his frustration as he squeezed Henry's arm so hard Henry nearly passed out from the pain. He was certain the man had pulled his arm completely out of socket, but Henry pushed the pain to the back of his mind.

"M-my pocket, i-in my pocket," Henry groaned out as he

tried to explain to the man that he was carrying the Jackboot's seal.

"Oh, I see – trying to rob me, are you?" The man lifted Henry up by his arm.

Through the terrible pain, Henry managed to groan out one word. "Rascal!"

"What's that?"

"Ras-cal," an exhausted Henry eked out again.

"Liar!"

"Right p-pocket. In my right pocket."

The man dropped Henry, who tried to reach into his pocket and pull out the seal, but his arm was on fire from the man's hard grip. "I-I can't reach it," Henry said, pointing to his pocket.

Begrudgingly, the man reached down into Henry's pocket and pull out a gear shaped wheel then softly read it out loud. "Jackboot - Official Messenger." The man's face suddenly lost all color, and he quickly brushed the dirt off Henry's shirt and tried to straighten his arm.

"Ouch!" Henry cried out.

"Oh blimey, what have I done? Please, I beg you; please don't mention this to the Jackboot. Please, son. I own one of the finest chocolate shops in town. I'll make sure you have whatever you please anytime you want. Just stop by and I'll give you whatever you like. I promise, just please, please don't tell the Jackboot." The man pleaded with Henry, but Henry's attention was drawn away from the man's efforts to save himself from a crime.

From the tops of the buildings to the bottoms of the dark alleyways, a sea of beady green eyes glowed like ghoulish stars blinking in the night. Henry glanced down at his gear-shaped emblem still in the man's hand. "Mister, can I have my runner's seal back?"

"Yes. Yes, of course," the man said placing it into Henry's left hand.

Henry looked up at the man and said, "I'm sorry, Mister!"

"Sorry? Well, whatever for, son? I'm the one that should be apologizing."

"I have to deliver my message, sir. I have to. I'm sorry. I really am sorry," Henry said. Taking a deep breath and favoring his injured shoulder, Henry burst forth into the man as hard as he could with his left shoulder, knocking him down. The man hit the road hard as Henry's feet exploded down the center of the street.

"HEY! What the... why did you do that for? This is an outrage! I demand to..."

Henry tried to get far enough away from the man so he wouldn't have to hear him, but the man's screams and cries of horror echoed perfectly through the empty streets. He blocked it out of his mind. *Never look back! Never look back!* A small tear slid down Henry's cheek as he ran. The man had been cruel and foolish, but he didn't deserve to die that way. The cost of delivering his message weighed heavily on him, but if he didn't reach the Jackboot in time, that poor man would be the first of many to perish before the night was over. Henry pushed harder. Only two blocks away now and he could see the light of the Iron Weaver's station. The large doors were open and he had a clear path to the Jackboot. *Never look back! Never look back!*

FOR THE JACKBOOT, THE EVENING HAD BEEN QUITE STRESSFUL. Flit had just returned that morning with news of the Whisper crew's safe arrival at the Petinon's mountain and that the king had not been very receptive to them. Though his comfort level with the city's repairs was not what he would have preferred, he decided to depart Grand Fortune City early the next morning and leave Hans in charge.

"Bosarus, did you pack my hat? You know, the tall black one with the silver band?"

"Yes, sir, and the matching suit you requested is also in the suitcase as well as your favorite eye patches. I also made sure there are plenty of pressed shirts, and your best pocket watches are stored in the smaller wooden case. The gifts have already been loaded onto the ship, and the ship is fueled according to Isabella's specifications for the journey."

"Fantastic, Bosarus! Fantastic! I'm glad to know you're on top of things, as usual," the Jackboot said as he sat back in his chair and placed his hands behind his head in a relaxed fashion.

"Thank you, sir. I'm happy to be of service," Bosarus said and took a slight bow at the door of the Jackboot's office then turned and headed back through the Iron Weaver's cars. He only got to the third car when he heard the Jackboot cry out.

"BOSARUS! Where's my pipe? I can't find my blasted pipe," the Jackboot bellowed out as he smashed his fist against his desktop.

Bosarus peered back into the Jackboot's office and with a slight grin said, "I do believe it's in your mouth, Mr. Jackboot, sir."

The Jackboot looked down the bridge of his nose and spotted his large, bullhead pipe, glowing a soft red at the top. He let out a loud, boisterous laugh, "HA! HA! I do believe your right, Bosarus."

"Indeed, sir," Bosarus nodded and headed back through the train.

The Jackboot placed his hands behind his head and leaned back in his chair. He pursed gently on his pipe for a moment and smiled at the thought of seeing his children soon. He released a large puff of smoke into the air and watched it climb to the ceiling, then, all of a sudden, a shout came from outside the Iron Weaver.

"WE GOT A RUNNER!" Iron Jaw cried out.

"Send him in," the Jackboot calmly replied.

"HE'S TWO BLOCKS OUT, MR. JACKBOOT, SIR, AND SOMETHING'S AFTER HIM!"

The Jackboot sat up in his chair. "WHAT DID YOU SAY?"

"SOMETHING IS AFTER HIM! LOTS OF SOMETHINGS, FROM MY ESTIMATION!"

"CHASING MY RUNNER?" An angry scowl slid across his face.

"THAT'S RIGHT, SIR!"

The Jackboot got up from his chair and quickly made his way through the cars and out of the Iron Weaver. Furiously stomping over to the large open doors of the train station, he then peered out into the dark streets. A single rascal was running toward them, and thousands of green glowing eyes were gaining on him.

"He's never going to make it, sir," Iron Jaw clacked out, but the Jackboot was way ahead of his old friend and had already hopped on his Ever-Wheel. The Jackboot fired it up and shot out of the station in a fiery blast of black smoke as he headed straight for the rascal.

"I'LL COVER YOU, SIR!" Iron Jaw hollered out and reached behind his back for his sawed off shot guns. Both of them, however, were missing from his holsters. His ears caught the sound of thunder, and he looked up to see his commander blasting away at the ghoulish eyes as he headed toward the runner.

HENRY WAS NEARLY OUT OF BREATH, AND TWO OF THE BEASTS were only a single missed step away from him. It was then he spotted something rolling through a thick cloud of black smoke, and with two bright flashes of orange the beasts fell dead behind him. Henry knew now the Jackboot was coming. *Never look back! Never look back!*

Suddenly, Henry tripped and hit the street hard. He rolled several feet until a light pole stopped him. Five of the beasts quickly surrounded him. He knew what they were all along. Their nasty smell had given them away. Tunnel rats—and big ones. The city had been overrun with them. The rats stood around Henry with hunger in their eyes. Hot saliva dripped from their steaming mouths, and they were clearly ready for a feast. The biggest one leaned its head down and prepared for the first bite, when suddenly its head disappeared in a cloud of red mist. The others quickly looked up, and two more exploded over him, sending the rest fleeing for the safety of darkness.

"You alright, boy?" the Jackboot asked as the sound of scurrying rats echoed around them.

"Name's... H-H-Henry, sir and I-I don't know, sir," Henry replied. The Jackboot reached down and picked him up. He sat Henry on the back of a monster Ever-Wheel and quickly blasted two more rats off the side of a building.

"HANG ON, HENRY! WE'RE GETTING OUT OF HERE!" The Jackboot hammered down on the throttle, and the Ever-Wheel spun around with a screech. Like a bullet, they shot back into the Iron Weaver's station, and Iron Jaw closed the doors behind them.

The Jackboot lifted Henry off the Ever-Wheel and stood him up. "Well, I can only assume by that mess of tunnel rats out there that that's what your message is. Am I correct?" the Jackboot asked with a grin.

"N-No sir. I mean...well...yes, that would be another message as well, sir," Henry said, holding his shoulder tight.

"Let me have a look at that, would you, son?" The Jackboot knelt down beside Henry, but Henry pulled away from him.

"No sir! I have to give you my message." Henry grimaced in pain.

"Well, alright then. What's your message, boy?"

"A man came into The Wooden Leg tonight, and he... he challenged your Mighty Men." A tear slid down Henry's cheek.

"HA! Poor fool!" Iron Jaw said, laughing.

"NO!" Henry cried out. The Jackboot cocked his head slightly and gritted his teeth.

Henry realized he was being disrespectful, but they weren't getting the message correctly. He closed his eyes and thought about the look on Billy's face. "Billy, sir, Billy looked at me. The man was powerful strong, sir. Billy looked at me, sir. He looked at me and called me Henry."

"Well, that is your name, isn't it, son?" the Jackboot questioned with a dumbstruck look toward Iron Jaw as if maybe Henry had been severely traumatized by the tunnel rats chasing him through the city.

Then Henry grabbed the Jackboot by the coat and said, "They never call me Henry! The look in Billy's eyes, sir. The look in his eyes!" Finally, the weight of his pain was too great, and Henry collapsed to his knees in tears. "They're all dead, sir, I just know it now. The Mighty Men are all dead... but I didn't look back, sir. I didn't look back. I ran as fast as I could. I didn't look back."

The Jackboot knelt down beside him and lifted Henry's head. "You did good, Henry. You did real good."

Iron Jaw gave an approving nod to the Jackboot's words. "A right good job, son," he clacked.

The Jackboot stood Henry to his feet and took him by the hand. "Henry, your arm is out of socket. It needs to be put back in place. That's what I going to do for you right now. Okay?" Before Henry had a chance to think things through, the Jackboot popped his arm back in with a snap, and Henry passed out.

"IRON JAW, READY MY TRAIN FOR BATTLE," THE JACKBOOT ordered.

"What should I do with the boy, sir?"

"Have Bosarus hide him in the tower-escape until this is over."

"What are you going to do, commander?"

"I'm going to go kill some tunnel rats."

"YES SIR, MR. JACKBOOT! YES SIR!" Iron Jaw replied with a twinkle in his eye.

The Jackboot lit a thick cigar and hopped back on his Ever-Wheel. With the flick of a switch the beast rumbled to a start. Black smoke filled the Iron Weaver's station as he fixed a tight leather cap to the top of his head. He gave a thumbs up to Iron Jaw, who opened a small side door, then he shot back out into the rat invested streets of Grand Fortune City.

Wriggling rodent shadows crawled down the buildings and across the sidewalks like lumpy slime poured from a bucket while the street lights fought back an uncommon darkness gripping the night. Green eyes floated from roof tops down into the path of his Ever-Wheel. The Jackboot pulled a lever under his seat, and two large Gatling guns rose up on each side of his iron horse. In seconds, the city streets were filled with the glorious illumination of flames erupting from hot iron barrels as he cleared the rodents from his path with their spitting death. He slaughtered them with maddening fury, but where one fell, three more took its place. At first the Jackboot found it comical as he failed at every turn to simply cut their numbers. He laughed as his Ever-Wheel barreled through the streets of GFC and nearly lost his stogie in the processes. But soon the Jackboot began to wonder where Iron Jaw was with the Iron Weaver, and why he couldn't hear its whistle wailing on the wind.

Bedroom lights burst on from everywhere as citizens awoke to the sounds of war-filled streets and screams soon followed as their rodent infestation became clear. Some barred their doors, while others grabbed their guns and headed out into the streets to help the Jackboot do some damage, but the tunnel rats were too numerous and too crafty. Grand Fortune City wasn't simply being invested with tunnel rats. It was being invaded.

The Jackboot had finally spent all the rounds from his Gatling guns and had begun using his massive Ever-Wheel to run them down. It was messy work, but for the most part effective until his wheel became so covered in rodent guts he could barely keep it upright. He roared through the streets with an army of rats to the left and to the right of him. They clawed, scraped and scratched at his arms and legs. Several rats jumped from roof tops directly onto the fast moving Ever-Wheel only to be flung down in front of him and plowed over like crunchy speed bumps. Foul teeth gnashed and snapped at him with every turn as he hopped sidewalks and weaved around street lamps. In all the slaughtering confusion, the Jackboot noticed something very peculiar about these tunnel rats that he hadn't noticed before. As one dove through the center of the wheel, nearly knocking him off his ride, he spotted a familiar looking brain mod snapped to the top of the rat's head. *Maybe they overpowered him? Maybe a major malfunction?* He pushed his questions to the back of his mind and tried to focus on the task at hand, killing rats.

The light from the pub was now visible as he rounded the corner, and from the looks of things, it was now completely overrun. As his Ever-Wheel roared past the open door, he looked for signs of hope that his men might have survived the battle with their challenger. However, the shining glare of mod-arms and legs strung out into the street proved otherwise. His heart sank in his chest, if only for a moment, when suddenly a glimmer of hope echoed in his ears.

"COMMANDER!"

It was Billy Bloodbath, and he was buried under a pile of

dead rats in an alleyway. A goodly sized one was on top of the pile, gnashing its teeth at his face. All but one of his mods was missing, and he was doing his best to keep the beast from gnawing off his nose. The Jackboot slammed his brakes hard, causing a pileup of rats behind him that pushed his Ever-Wheel down the slippery street even further until he lost control and slammed into a streetlamp. The rats nearly overtook him, but he got to his feet quickly and launched himself into the night sky with his magnetic boots. He hovered over the street for a moment and got his bearings, then brought his boots down on the neck of Billy's hungry rat with loud crunch.

"What took you so long?" Billy asked with a painful chuckle.

"Well, you might not believe this, but I think we have a rat problem," the Jackboot retorted with a snarky grin. He dragged Billy out from underneath the pile of dead rats and tried hopelessly to launch them both into the air as rats quickly filled the alley. Many rats began lining the tops of the buildings around them, while others swiftly removed their dead brothers that were blocking the alleyway.

"Leave me, Commander!" Billy demanded.

The Jackboot pulled Billy to the back wall of the dead end alley and leaned him against it. Staring out into the sea of green tunnel rat eyes, he spoke. "That's not my style, Billy, and you know it. Besides, you bled for me in the war, how could I ever abandon you and face my daughter again?"

"I'm dead already, sir." Billy lifted his shirt to reveal a terrible wound in his side. "The Dream Slayer, sir. At least that's what he called himself."

"What do you mean, Dream Slayer?"

Billy let out a blood-filled coughed and reached for his side with his bent mod-arm. "H-He called himself t-the Dream Slayer."

"But, Billy, these are Hans' rats," the Jackboot said as the rats closed in on them.

"RIGHT YOU ARE!" Suddenly, the tunnel rats let out a unified squeal, as if they were terrified of something, then quickly drew back away from them. A dark, cloaked figure stepped through the sea of parting rodents and into the alley. "These are the Puppet Master's rats, but I am not Hans. I'm the Dream Slayer."

"If you hurt Hans, I'll make you suffer," the Jackboot warned the shadowy figure.

"Relax! Relax! I didn't do anything to your friend. In fact, he's the one who employed me to take down your Mighty Men. He worried that all of you together would pose too great a threat to his plan," the Dream Slayer said with subtle grin. "To be right honest, I can't figure out what he was so worried about. Your Mighty Men weren't so mighty after all."

"Liar!"

"Hey, if you don't believe me, why don't you ask him yourself." The Dream Slayer stepped off to the side, and soon the sound a clacking cane echoed into the dark alley. In the light of a greenish, mist-filled moon a tall, thin shadow of a man emerged from the chaos of the night, wearing a ghoulish top hat. A bright green glow of smoke slowly rose from its crown. And though his face was different now and covered in fire berry metal, the unmistakable hands of Hans Kloppenheimer, gripping a dragon's head cane, was enough to send an exhausted Jackboot collapsing to the ground next to Billy.

"HANS? Why?" the Jackboot begged.

"I knew you would ask this question of me, my dear friend and savior from the flames. At first, I struggled to answer this question in my own mind, but it soon came to me...that one thing that drove me to madness...that one lost piece of her that led me to betray all that is good, even my most loyal of friends." His leather gloves scrunched against his cane as he gripped it tighter.

"And what was that?" the Jackboot sneered.

"I had forgotten the gentle sound of her voice… and that was more than my fragile soul could bear."

"But, Hans, how is killing me going to bring Emilia back?"

"Your life is not to be taken. That was part of our agreement. Since your last attack on the Labyrinth, they've desperately been searching for a way to get their hands on you. It took some work, but I convinced her that selling you to the Labyrinth would go a long way in brokering peace with her people," Hans said, pointing to the sky above them.

"Her?" a confused Jackboot asked as he looked up to see dark figure floating down into the alley with a black umbrella.

"My dear, sweet Owen, you look simply awful."

"CASSANDRA!"

2

ARRIVAL

*W*hispers filled the early morning skies as heavy clouds washed over Elias' face. Walking out onto the forward deck, he winced as the cool air rushed over the large scar on his chest. The irritating itch of his scar was a constant reminder of his new heart, but sometimes he felt as if the heart mod was still mounted there. In his mind he could hear its generator pumping, chugging and pulsing away, keeping him alive. Every now and then forgetfulness would get the best of him, and he would quickly look down to see if he'd forgotten to refuel the generator, but not today. Today the scar seemed terribly irritated. Perhaps by the weather or something else, but it was enough to wake him and force him to seek the cool morning air for comfort. He paused for a moment and slid his fingers down the scar. If only the morning sun would rise up and soothe the irritation, but there'd be no morning sun to greet him this morning. Nothing but gray damp clouds and the comfort of an old friend, perched out on the railing.

As far as he knew, today was his thirteenth birthday, unless of course Sunago and his mother had lied about that as well. He kept it to himself and decided he would make up a different day to call his own, something that wouldn't remind him of his past. He might not be able to run or hide from his past, but at least now he could alter his future enough to create new memories, and he planned to do just that.

He continued across the deck and stopped next to Casper, who was looking out into the passing clouds at the gray nothingness ahead of them. Elias stared out into the sky with him for a brief moment, pondering his reoccurring dream of flying with Prince Enupnion. What once had been a blessed comfort had now become a haunting reminder of the death of his dear friend and a mockery of his inability to fly. It bothered Elias deeply, but he spoke nothing of it to his friends or Epekneia or even his beloved sister. *Why burden them with my heartache? They've endured enough at my expense.*

Out of the corner of his eye, Elias noticed Casper had turned toward him. Casper was gazing directly at him, so Elias turned and peered into the bird's deep yellow eyes with a curious wonder as to the creatures own thoughts. After a short time, Elias raised his hand and brushed it over the owl's head and down the back of his damp wings. He flicked the water back onto the deck several times.

"What a nasty way to start the..." Suddenly, Casper shook his feathered body vigorously, splattering the remaining droplets of water all over Elias' bare chest and face. Elias closed his eyes and scrunched his nose, "Ugh, thanks a lot, Casper." He chuckled a little bit, but before he could reopen his eyes, he heard Casper flutter away, and instantly two clawed hands covered his view.

"Guess who?" a gentle voice asked.

"Oh, this is going to be a hard one. I'm going to go with Bogan," Elias playfully replied.

"Oh, you are way off, mister."

"Well, I'm sure it's not Jimmy or Merlin, and I certainly hope it's not Gideon." Elias snickered.

"HEY! I don't sound anything like those guys."

"I should think not. You sound more like Izzy when she's trying to mother me. Only Izzy doesn't have claws. So maybe it's that wonderful Petinon girl with two brilliant red wings and dark red hair. What was her name again?" Elias joked.

"Really! It's not that hard to pronounce. I can't believe you're still having trouble with it," Epekneia complained as she uncovered his eyes and spun him around.

"I know, I know. I should have it down by now. I promise I'm going to get it right... before we arrive, I hope," Elias said with a smile.

"Well, you better hurry. We're very close now."

"Seriously! How close?"

"Turn around and put your nose in the air," Epekneia said with smile.

"Come on! No more games," he complained.

"It's not a game. Just close your eyes and tell me what you smell."

Reluctantly, Elias turned around, took several deep sniffs into the air and pondered. "It smells... kind of like burning cinnamon."

"Does that remind you of anything?"

"FIRE BERRIES!" Elias blurted out.

"Exactly! The land in front of our mountain is covered in fire berries."

"We should wake the others right away." His heart skipped with excitement.

Epekneia squinted her piercing eyes and demanded, "Not so fast. First, tell me why you come out here every morning and stare out into the sky."

"We don't have time for that." Elias said, trying to maneuver around her, but she quickly flared out her wings and blocked his path on either side.

"Ugh, seriously!" he scoffed. "You really overuse that wing blocking maneuver."

"Just a hint."

"Some other time."

"No! I care about you, and I want to know why you're so troubled."

Elias could see the resolve in her eyes as she held her ground. He didn't want to explain his dreams of flying with the prince, but he had to give her some kind of answer, so he blurted out the first epiphany that entered his mind. "I think this heart wants to fly, but I don't have wings." Suddenly, Elias realized that he'd solved the riddle of his dream with an accidental honesty.

She smiled. "I wondered as much. Wingless Petinon are prone to depression and madness. I've worried about this for some time, but I think maybe we can trick your heart to help you deal with that problem."

"What do you mean?"

"Turn around and face the sky."

A bewildered look slid across his face.

"Trust me. Just turn around, silly." A gentle smile brightened her face. "Come on, turn around."

Elias slowly turned around and faced the sky. "You've been hanging out with Isabella too much."

"Why's that?"

"You're starting to sound like her."

"GOOD! I like her," Epekneia said, slipping her arms up underneath his arms and wrapping them around his chest. "Here we go."

"HEY! WHAT ARE YOU DOING?" Elias yelled.

"Trust me," she said as her wings beat the air hard, lifting them off the deck of the Whisper. "How does this feel?"

"I... I-it feels weird. I mean... not weird, but... I-I don't know." Elias' legs dangled below him as she held him in the air.

"Close your eyes. Pretend my wings are yours, and concentrate on what your heart feels."

At first, Elias felt weak and almost ashamed, but he took her advice and closed his eyes, concentrating on the pounding in his chest. It didn't take long until joy filled his heart, and a giant smile rose on his face. He enjoyed the wind from her wings as they beat the air around him. He stretched out his arms and opened his eyes. Much to his surprise, in front of him, about fifty yards out, a young Petinon boy appeared through the clouds in mid-flight. Shock filled the boy's face as the two of them stared each other down for what seemed like an eternity. Epekneia was so busy trying to carry Elias that she couldn't see the boy in front of them, and her entire body was hidden behind him, making it appear as though her bright, red wings, belonged to him. Elias reached out his hand to the boy and startled him so bad he cried out then dove into the clouds below.

The sound of the voice alarmed Epekneia so much she nearly dropped Elias. "Did you say that?"

"WHAT? It wasn't me. There was a boy flying out in front of us. I think he said, 'Ouranos' or something like that."

"THAT'S EXACTLY WHAT HE SAID!" Epekneia seemed shaken as they landed hard on the Whisper's forward deck.

"What's it mean?" Elias asked, pulling one of her feathers from his mouth.

"I'll tell you later. Right now, we need to wake the crew." Epekneia got to her feet and shook her wings a bit before pulling them snuggly back into place on her back.

Suddenly, Izzy and Bogan burst through the door onto the deck. Bogan was trying to pull his boot onto his mod-leg as he came out of the door and tripped, knocking Izzy to the ground in front of him.

"BOGAN, YOU LUNK!" Izzy cried out as she tumbled to a stop at the feet of Elias and Epekneia. She looked up at them both and asked, "What's going on out here?"

"We've arrived." Epekneia answered.

"Oh! Good, I was worried I was going to have to pry you two apart or something." Izzy winked.

THROUGH DARK AND MYSTERIOUS LANDS, THE WHISPER CREW HAD traveled. Over glorious mountains, through hopeless valleys, they pressed onward. Onward, into terrible storms that pulled, twisted, scraped and clawed at their tiny ship as they soared toward clearer skies. Toward something strange but fascinating beyond their imagination, and no one was more pleased to have finally arrived than Epekneia.

For her part, the trip back home had been filled with a constant bombardment of questions from Elias and her strange, new mechanically-modified friends. So much so that she had become weary of speaking about her home and her own people. Deep down, she knew she'd given her own kind more grace than what they deserved, but she hoped they had changed. Hope was more than just a pretty word to her. It was the foundation she and her father clung to during their captivity at Gabriel's Harbor. When everyone was gone. When they had nothing left, nothing but that little word shining like a light in the darkness of her mind. *Hope works. I know it.* Maybe they had set aside their old, judgmental ways. She desperately hoped so, especially in regards to humans with mods. But what concerned her even more was how they would treat Elias. Even though he was of Petinon blood, he had no wings. She knew this would be a major sticking point for most Petinons, even the more accepting ones. What's more, it bothered her that Elias had wanted to bury his old, black heart with the prince. *Why didn't they just destroy the black heart? It serves no purpose now. Once the king finds out the prince's heart is in Elias' chest, what then?* She trembled every time the thought entered her mind. Whoever had cried out in the sky had no doubt already taken the message back to the city, and the expectation of their arrival was now set to the highest of standards. Something she had preferred to explain on her own was now being handled by someone else. Not that she felt they would have believed her in the first place, but she had hoped to have some time to make her case. *Oh well, what's done is done. It's out now. They'll either believe it or they won't. Then Elias will just have to show them and that will be the end of it.* She hoped.

Epekneia watched the crew scramble about the ship, trying to deal with the surprise the morning had brought them. Their ill-prepared confusion brought a slight smile to her face as she watched her friends' chaotically joyful dress rehearsal. She didn't have the heart to tell them their choice of clothes wasn't anywhere near what would be acceptable in the king's court, or anywhere else in the city for that matter. She knew her people would be staring at their mods right from the start, but she enjoyed watching their efforts none-the-less.

"BOGAN! GIVE ME BACK MY HAT!" Merlin snapped.

"Ah, come on, mate. You'll make a much better impression without it." Bogan passed the hat around his back, circling himself one hand to the next as Merlin reached for it.

"I completely agree with Bogan on this one," Izzy said, sneaking up behind Merlin and placing her hands over his green, glowing glass dome. "Why would you want to hide such a beautiful brain from them?"

Merlin blushed as Bogan tossed the hat over to Gideon, but it was quickly intercepted by Jimmy.

"This is Merlin's hat. Why are you stealing it from him, Bogan?"

"I-I'm not stealing it, Jimmy. I'm just trying to... I was... ah, forget it. Jimmy, you always manage to take the fun out of everything," Bogan scoffed.

Suddenly, Ava stepped out of her room with a terrified look on her face and screamed.

"AVA! What's wrong?" Izzy asked as everyone's faces were smashed with befuddle wonder.

"I CAN'T FIND IT! I can't find it anywhere," Ava cried out.

"Find what?" Gideon asked with a gentle voice, hoping to help calm her down.

Ava buried her face into her hands and sobbed as her muffled voice blubbered out, "M-m-my lip gloss... I-I can't find my lip gloss. I-It was Charlie's favorite."

Izzy ran over to Ava and wrapped her arms around her, "OH, you poor thing."

"WHAT!" Bogan blurted out. "You nearly gave me a heart attack for a stinkin tube of lip gloss!"

"WAIT! Where's my art pad?" Ava instantly broke free from Izzy's embrace. "Where did I put it? I can't forget to take it with us." She grabbed Izzy by the shoulders and looked her square in the eyes. *"I have to show Charlie everything that happened. What did I do with it?"*

Bogan shook his head. "SHE'S CRACKED! Completely lost it."

"I think it was in the control room," Epekneia said softly and watched as Ava's face lit up, seemingly forgetting all about her missing lip gloss.

"THANK YOU! Thank you so much," Ava said, running into the control room.

"Look. We all just need to get a grip for a minute. Okay? Can we do that?" Gideon said firmly.

"Gideon is right," Epekneia said, speaking louder and clearer than before. "My people might not be so eager to accept you. As I explained several times before, they might even be a little hostile toward you." Epekneia looked to Elias. "I've had some time to think about this and... I think it might be best if Elias walks ahead of us all—after he eats some fire berries. It might break the ice easier if they are confused by a wingless boy."

But Izzy forcefully disagreed. "WHAT! NO WAY, SISTER! You are not putting him in direct danger like that."

"No, Isabella. She's right," Elias said.

"B-But..." Izzy stammered.

Epekneia had only heard Elias call Izzy by her full name a few times, but the impact it had on Izzy was profoundly affective. Elias never seemed to abuse it to his advantage, even though he could have several times during their journey.

"Izzy, whoever spotted Elias this morning has already spoken a word that no one dare speak unless...unless the chosen one has arrived. When we land, their expectations will be high, and well, Elias not having wings is already going to be a problem for them. They must, at the very least, be surprised by his ability to eat the berries. Let's hope that is enough." Epekneia looked toward Elias with uncertainty in her eyes. "I honestly don't know what they will do or how they will view you."

"Wait, are you saying we need to go in there armed?" Bogan asked.

"No. No weapons. They will already see your mods as a grave threat to their way of life," Epekneia explained.

"Sorry, but not sorry. I'm taking my baton with me," Izzy said, looking to Elias as if she was waiting for him to try his "Isabella" trick again, but she was surprised when he gave a nod of approval. "Good!" Izzy winked.

Suddenly, the Whisper shook and stopped with a hard bump. "We have landed," Jimmy said plainly.

"Elias, come with me." Epekneia motioned with her claw. "I'll tell you what you need to say when they first see you."

33

Makarios tucked his wings tight around his body as he punctured holes through the clouds like a falling star rocketing toward the earth. His heart thumped heavy in his chest, and his mind raced circles around what his eyes had seen. Though he was merely a boy, he knew the law and the consequences for speaking that word if he were wrong, but it burned in his mouth so hot he could barely contain himself. He knew what he'd seen and it felt right to him. The word was screaming inside his head louder than the wind around his ears as it sought freedom from the captivity of his mouth. Suddenly, he broke through the last cloud and spotted the great city below him. In that moment he set free the name his people had desired to hear for so many years.

"OURANOS! OURANOS!" At first no one noticed, but he persisted in his efforts.

"OURANOS! OURANOS!" Soon, several of his fellow Petinons began to look toward the sky as he flared out his wings with barely enough time to slow his descent. "OURANOS! OURANIO!" he hit the ground hard and tumbled through the city streets, landing at the foot of an old Petinon. "OURANOS! He is here. He has come."

The old Petinon looked down at the boy for a moment then burst into laughter. Makarios was instantly offended by the old one's mockery. "It's true! I've seen him. In the sky, I've seen him with my own eyes."

"And I'm the Lord Commander of the Convocation." The old one laughed again, only frustrating Makarios all the more.

"I know what I've seen. You'll see. He's coming," Makarios said, picking himself up off the white cobblestone road. "He's here and with fiery red wings to show for it."

"Keep that up and you'll end up in the cages for the rest of your days," the old one sneered.

Makarios glared into the eyes of the old one and then shouted with all his might, "OURANOS! OURANOS! OURA-

NOS! OURANOS!" It didn't take long before the royal guards appeared from every direction. Some dropped out of trees and others swooped through crowded streets. In an instant, Makarios was surrounded.

The royal guards donned dark leather shirts with four straps around their chest. In the center of the four straps was a golden emblem with a red flower. Their helmets were also made of gold and were so small they seemed to be more of a uniform than something to protect their heads. Their boots were leather and cross strapped all the way up to the top of their knees with gold buckles to lock them in place. Some carried spears with bright steel tips, and others carried long, double-edged blades at their side. A strong warrior stepped up from among them and removed his helmet. He wiped his claw over his brow and down the back of his feathered neck, then he spoke.

"Boy, what do you think you're doing?" he asked.

"I-I've seen him. For sure, I have," Makarios said with a good deal of confidence.

"Have you really, now?" the warrior asked as the others around him chuckled softly.

"I have!" Makarios' eyes fixed hard on the warrior's golden name plate stretched across his helmet. It was a powerful name and one that every Petinon knew. A name that carried weight among his people, and Makarios took a deep breath, hoping his eyes had not deceived him. "Y-Your Thumacheo?"

"I am. And what's your name, boy?" Thumacheo asked.

"I-I'm Makarios."

"Ah, that's a good name. So are you living up to its meaning? Are you happy and blessed?"

"Y-Yes, I mean, I think so," Makarios stuttered out.

"Well, Makarios, if you would like to remain happy then you better not go fluttering about crying out that name, or you're going to end up in the cages for the rest of your life."

"But why? Why can't we say it?"

Thumacheo knelt down on one knee to face the boy as he spoke with a whisper. "Because it gives people false hope, and false hope creates fanatical behavior, and that makes my job of maintaining the peace very, very difficult. Now, you don't want my job to be difficult... do you, Makarios?"

"Well, but... I know I saw him. I just know it."

Thumacheo glared his haunting gaze into Makarios' eyes, and it seemed to cut into his soul with a powerful warning. "Boy, if you ever say that name again, I'll personally remove your wings from your back and mount them as a trophy on my wall. Do you understand me?"

Makarios dropped his head toward the ground. "Y-Yes sir."

"That's more like it. Now run along and do things that normal boys do, like killing rats or something." Thumacheo's men burst into a raucous laughter as they stepped away from Makarios.

For a moment, Makarios thought he sensed something. A warm breeze, perhaps, or a soft whisper on the wind. Then, in his mind, he heard it. A strange voice. He lifted his head, looked to the sky, and closed his eyes. He knew what he had seen, and it was more than simple fantasy. It was real. It was true.

"OURANOS HAS COME!" Makarios cried out.

Thumacheo and his men stopped suddenly and turned around. Thumacheo's face was not angry this time but sorrow filled and anguished. He closed his eyes, gave a nod of his head toward his men, and they quickly seized Makarios.

By now a large crowd had gathered, and the mood of the people had changed to cold and somber. Those who had hoped for a peaceful day of shopping the markets and enjoying the early morning blessings of the great city had now become the witnesses of a crime. A crime that was dealt with swiftly and with a devastating harshness to ensure its affect was lasting. The bloody punishment of one of their own was not something anyone wanted to be witness to, especially one so young. It had

36

been many years since someone had even thought to speak that name, and why the boy had picked such a time to bring this upon himself was as baffling as it was heartbreaking.

Thumacheo's men pushed Makarios to the ground as their commander drew his sword from its sheath and stepped over toward the boy. The crowd's anticipation was heightened all the more by a strong, hot breeze that mysteriously rose from the tops of the pines on each side of the great mountain city of Pterugas. Thumacheo's blade rose into the air over Makarios wings when, suddenly, a powerful screech echoed through the misty, cloud-filled skies. Everyone looked up to see if maybe the boy had been right, but Ouranos did not appear. Thumacheo readied himself and his blade again, but this time the screeching sound was followed by the entrance of a great gray owl, bomb-dropping through the clouds and onto the cobblestone road. For a moment everyone's eyes were captivated by the creature's awkwardly timed appearance. The gray owl slowly bobbled over toward Thumacheo and his men and cocked his head slightly to the right in curiosity.

"Be gone now!" Thumacheo kicked at the gray bird, but it remained unmovable.

Suddenly, bright flashes began speckling the insides of the clouds above them, and chirping like whispers turned heads left to right as the Petinon people gazed in wonder at the fascinating display of light. Then it happened. In an instant, through the misty streets of Pterugas, two red eyes appeared. A gasp from someone in the crowd and the voice of a small child calling out the forbidden name sent chills across everyone's wing tips.

"Ouranos, Momma," the child declared.

Thumacheo's sword slowly lowered to his side as if to hide a dirty deed. The flashing lights shot out from above the red eyes and down the center of the street. Then, the tiny creature, so fast one could hardly tell what it was, zipped and whizzed around them with its blinding light that forced many eyes to close. It was a small finch, and it circled around the boy blasting multiple flashes of light, and then it landed on his shoulder. It was a strange little bird with something stuck in its right eye, a piece of metal perhaps. Thumacheo and his warriors were so captivated by it, they hadn't realized that Makarios had stood up and stepped out of their circle of death. He snuck around behind them all, and before they knew it, he had run out into the center of the street for a closer look.

It was a wingless boy with glowing red eyes, and the heat coming from his body was so hot the people could feel its warmth traveling through the crowded street. None of the prophecies of Ouranos had ever spoken of his appearance. However, it was generally accepted among the wise men of the Convocation that the chosen one would be a full blooded Petinon. Therefore, wings were a foundational part of the prophetic teachings. As the boy slowly came into full view, the crowd was speechless, especially Makarios, who had seen him flying in the sky above the city. *What happened to his wings?* Makarios was embarrassed by Ouranos' appearance and began to worry that he truly was mistaken. He wanted to flee and hide, but curious anticipation took hold of him, so he waited for something—anything— to happen.

3

WITHOUT WINGS

*T*he misty mountain air rolled around his body as Elias stepped into view. His eyes were burning with flames from the fire berries he'd eaten at Epekneia's request, and though his vision was a bit distorted, he was still able to make out the greatness of the city. Massive pine trees as well as oak, cedar, maple and ash towered over white limestone buildings that lined the city streets. In the distance an enormous severed tree trunk sat atop the mountain, and a cobblestone path traveled into a large entrance at its base. Rising from the center of the broken tree trunk was an amazing, white limestone castle surrounded by bright red flowers. The Petinon kingdom was the greenest thing Elias had seen since his greenhouse home, and his heart leapt for joy at the sight of it all.

The street was filled with winged folk of all shapes and sizes. There were some with brown wings, black wings, red tipped, yellow tipped and even multicolored and speckled featured. Most of them wore no shoes on their clawed feet and no gloves to cover their clawed hands. Their tiny feather faces might have been odd to him, had Elias not grown so used to Epekneia 's face during the past three weeks, so that now they were commonplace for him. He could tell by their stunned, blank looks, that he was more of a shock to them than they were to him, and he figured it was best to capitalize on their emotions while he still had their attention.

"My name is Ouranos, and I seek an audience with King Arkhone, Lord Commander of the Convocation and ruler of the kingdom of Pterugas. Who among you will present... me to him?" Elias said with a small bit of confidence in his tone. The only response was Thumacheo's sword slipping from his hand and clattering to the stony road beneath his feet. No Petinon would dare speak the name of Ouranos, for fear of punishment, and now in a single morning a boy had not only spoken the name but cried it out loudly for all to hear. To complicate the day even more, another boy, possibly human, was standing before them claiming to be Ouranos, and they seemed to be struggling from the shock of it all.

The old Petinon who'd laughed at Makarios quickly spoke up. "He's got no wings. How can he be the chosen one without wings? The prophecy clearly said Ouranos would have wings." Suddenly, the people began to mutter, and Thumacheo picked up his sword.

"The old one is wrong. We were all taught the same books of prophecy, and none of them ever spoke of wings. They only said the one who hears the voice of the whispering prince is Ouranos," Makarios quickly corrected, but the people continued their confused muttering.

"Is there no one willing to present me to the king?" Red smoke poured from Elias' mouth as he asked with a frustrated tone, but deep down he began to wonder if this plan was the best idea. *Maybe we should have just landed in the center of the city and had Epekneia step out first?* He knew his crew was only seconds away, still hiding in the mist-filled pines below, and with the snap of a finger he could have their assistance if needed. He decided to wait.

The sound of clacking began to echo around the limestone walls of the city, and within moments a full company of Petinon warriors filled the street. At the center of the warriors stood a Petinon woman dressed in fine clothes and wearing a thin golden crown adorned with beautiful green stones. Her wings were solid white, as were the tiny feathers on her face, and she wore a fine green robe with beaded gold strands that shimmered even in the dullest of light. She spoke not a single word as the warriors moved aside for her to exit their protective wall. Then she approached Elias with the confidence of someone who held great authority. The mood of the people quickly changed, and every Petinon dropped to one knee, including Thumacheo and his men.

When she reached Elias she extended her arm toward his face and cupped his chin in her claws. "You look a little young to be Ouranos." She said with cold a gaze as she looked into his fiery red eyes for a time then placed her forehead to his with her eyes completely closed. She took a deep breath of the red smoke rolling out his mouth and then looked back at him. Her golden yellow eyes turned a solid red from inhaling his fire berry breath then she smiled at him and spoke, "I am Queen Elehos, and I will present you to the king. If you are who you claim to be then you have nothing to fear, but if you are not then you and your friends will pay with their lives."

Elias gave a nod, "I understand."

"Bring them out." The queen motioned with her claw, and in an instant, large Petinon warriors appeared through the misty streets, carrying the Whisper crew in their clutches.

"PUT ME DOWN!" Bogan yelled as one of the larger Petinon warriors dropped him to the ground. He picked himself up just as another warrior pushed Gideon onto him, knocking them both to the ground. Ava and Izzy were released more carefully, but Merlin and Jimmy were untouched as they strolled out hand in hand with Epekneia, who had apparently convinced the Petinon warriors it was best for everyone if they remained untouched.

"Sneaky lot, this bunch," Bogan quipped.

Izzy ran straight up to Elias and put herself between him and the queen. "Sorry, brother. They were so quiet. I've never seen anything like it. Even Jimmy didn't notice."

The queen's eyes grew large at Izzy's overprotective maneuver. "Siblings...interesting," she said with a twinkle in the corner of her eye.

As the rest of the crew gathered around Elias, the queen gave her personal assessment of them. "So these are the ones the great Ouranos travels with? A shamed Petinon child, a half breed sister, a great gray owl, and a crew full of mechanically modified humans. I don't believe this is what any of these people expected to see on the day of the Arrival."

"Don't forget Flit," Ava said with an exploding smile that instantly caught the queen's notice. The queen's gaze froze on Ava's face for a moment, then she closed her eyes and looked away.

"W-What? What was that look? Izzy...Bogan?" Ava quickly looked for some bit of reassurance, but no one responded to her.

"The king is away on a hunt. He will not return until night fall. If you like, I will give you a tour of the city while we await his return." Queen Elehos looked at Elias and gave a slight nod as if to prompt a guided response from him.

Elias looked at Izzy, who checked the faces of the Petinon people, then looked back at him. Izzy gave a nod of approval, and Elias answered the queen. "That sounds good to us. Lead the way."

"Good choice," The queen said, and with the wave of her claw the guards cleared a path in the streets for them to pass. Many Petinons with children were more than pleased to get out away from the humans with mods. Merlin and Jimmy were unlike anything they'd ever seen and from the looks of it they didn't care to ever see such things again.

"We'll make our way to the top of the mountain as we go. I'm certain your young Petinon companion can remember her way around some of these streets." The queen directed her gaze toward Epekneia, who was still down on her knee with her head bowed. "I remember you well. The burn mark on her face from the fire berry trials many years ago. You father's name... Mellontas, wasn't it?"

"Yes, my queen. I am Epekneia, his daughter, and I am a child of the failed trials." Epkeniea humbly bowed lower.

"Indeed, you are... I hope your father is well?" the queen sincerely asked in a hopeful tone.

"He is dead, my queen." Epekneia answered.

A powerful gasp shook the queen, but she tried to hide it. "Come now. There's a chill in the air." She turned around and began walking.

Elias could hear a gentle whimper in her voice, and in his mind he wanted say something, but now was not the right time. *She needs hope for now,* he thought to himself as he helped Epekneia to her feet.

"What did you say?" The queen instantly turned around and looked at Elias, who seemed baffled by her statement.

"N-Nothing. I didn't say anything." Elias shrugged and looked back at Izzy, and when the awkward moment passed, they continued on. The whole company of Petinon guards followed behind them, watching every move they made with great care.

The crew followed behind the queen, who seemed to be making a strong effort to regain her composure. Elias started to let go of Epekneia's hand, but she gripped it tight and refused to let go. He looked at her curiously, but she kept looking straight ahead, so he figured he'd just go with the flow and let it be. Izzy rolled her eyes at them and then checked her mod-arm to make certain her baton was still there. Bogan cracked his neck then adjusted his mod-leg for the elevation of the streets, while Ava was questioning Gideon about Charlie. Gideon did his level-best to calm Ava's nerves from the strange look the queen had given her, but he wasn't making much progress. Merlin followed close to Izzy, casting a sinister smile at Thumacheo, just for fun. Jimmy, for his part, seemed to do his best to annoy the royal guard by flying around them in circles and stopping directly in front of their faces, purposely screwing up their perfect marching rhythm.

Pterugas was a different kind of city for the Whisper crew. Gone were the fires and smoke stacks of coal production and steel mills, and in their place were fishing store houses and shops with hand-made trinkets and jewelry. There were also no Ever-Wheels or trains, no airships or dock–bots, and there certainly wasn't any black mist or creeping mold. No one had mods on their faces, although their faces were feathery and strange enough as it was. It was an odd culture shock, but not a single crew member complained about not having to wear their masks. The air was clean and fresh with the scent of the pines that towered over everything. With a few other exceptions, most everything seemed to operate in the same way an iron city would operate, but with a bit more color and flair. Bogan elbowed Merlin and said something about a city full of "Nancy boys," but he quickly backed off his snarky comment when Izzy gave him the old stink eye.

As the Whisper crew continued to follow Queen Elehos through the streets, she pointed out the magnificent architecture as well as the amazing art work. But the one thing they couldn't shake was the feeling of being watched by eyes that seemed to come from everywhere. It wasn't just the Petinon guard marching behind them or the citizens gazing in wonder, peering in secret or staring in judgment, but something else seemed to be watching them. Something with eyes, but could not see, ears but could not hear, mouths but could not speak, and wings but could not fly, and they were on every street corner of the great city.

"Are you guys seeing this?" Gideon whispered to Bogan and Izzy.

"How could we miss it?" Merlin added to the mix.

Even Epekneia hated to ruin her moment of pride in walking the streets hand in hand with Elias, but there were so many, they couldn't ignore it. "Why did they do this?" she asked in disappointment.

Epekneia set Elias' hand free as he quickly made his way up to one of the largest ones in the center of the city. Queen Elehos paused momentary then strolled up next to him. "There are hundreds of them, but this one is the largest of them all. He became something of a hero after his disappearance many years ago. The people just couldn't stop honoring him, and the king didn't have the heart to stop them. Sunago truly was the greatest Petinon to have ever lived."

A repulsed Elias turned around and looked directly at Izzy in astonishment.

4

CASSANDRA'S GIFT

*D*ark words of smoke filled the Chill Room as Cassandra worked her craft on Hans' beloved Emilia. For Hans' part, it was a terrifying thing to witness Cassandra work her evil magic on someone he loved so dearly. Tiny weeds growing in the dirty cracks of the floor, wilted at the sound of Cassandra's voice, and several windowpanes cracked as she thundered out her commands. Cold slivers of serpentine smoke wrapped around Emilia's body and traveled throughout the room. Several slid across his fingertips, and Hans jerked his boney hands back from their grasp, for fear he too would be entangled in her power. The Dream Slayer laughed wickedly as Cassandra and Forsythe worked together to bring his beloved back to him. Maybe not as he'd hoped, not as he'd dreamed, but at least back into his arms.

Suddenly, Cassandra's face turned an ashen gray color, then a solid cold black. Her eyes brightened to a strange, deep yellow until tiny droplets of blood leaked from her tear ducts. The lights in the room burst into fireballs of sparks that covered Emilia's body as she rose from the table. Forsythe, who seemed like he knew what he was doing for a time, now began to tremble and stepped away from his master.

Hans drew deep from his well of memories regarding Cassandra, but he could not recall a single story, event, or lie that served justice to her beauty, power, or mystery. The things he'd had been told regarding Cassandra quickly evaporated into the darkness of her smoke as it wrapped around Emilia like a cocoon. Hans knew now that whatever metamorphosis was taking place within that cocoon of black mist would forever change Emilia, but different is better than dead and he prepared his mind for it. As he watched Cassandra, he sensed a change within himself as well. The guilt of his past regrets and secret murders seemed more justified than ever. The beauty in her darkness had captivated him, and as his wonderful bride's body began to twitch and jerk about, Hans found himself laughing with the Dream Slayer as tears streamed down his metal cheeks.

Cassandra's voice suddenly grew deeper, and the Dream Slayer's laughter abruptly ended as if he'd never heard his master speak in this tone before. Forsythe crawled across the floor and slithered out the door in fear, while two of Hans' mind-controlled tunnel rats, standing behind him, began to shake. Their mod-hats sparked and popped as they short circuited, then all of a sudden one of the rat's heads exploded all over the room. Hans stood his ground. If this was what would bring his beloved back to him, then he wanted to witness it in all its maddening wonder. He gripped his dragon's head cane tighter as the Chill Room shook and glass shattered to the floor. Finally, Cassandra's power hit its peak level, and Hans felt parts of his own body begin to vibrate as if she were drawing energy from him or anything else nearby to accomplish her goal. It was at that point, just before the end, that Hans began to doubt his decision to save Emilia. *Who is this woman, and where did she acquire such power? There is nothing like her in all the land. Maybe she CAN save the world from the creeping mold?*

Cassandra dropped her arms back to her sides and stopped speaking. The dark clouds of serpentine smoke vanished into the air around them, and Emilia's body dropped back to the table with a hard thud. Steam rose from Cassandra's back and hands, and the darkness faded away from her face. She took several deep breaths then lumbered over to a table behind her. The table was lined with eight canisters of water and one canister filled with a bright green liquid. Inside the green-filled canister swirled black serpentine lines.

Water splashed from the sides of her mouth as she quickly proceeded to drink each canister, releasing them to the floor with a crash, as with one after the other she slaked her thirst. Finally, she came to the green canister and opened it carefully. As she sipped it slowly, Hans grew impatient with her and began to speak, but she raised her hand and halted him until she finished it.

"WHAT HAPPENED? Why did you stop? Did it work...is she going to be okay?" Hans begged her for answers.

Cassandra placed the empty canister back on the table and spoke, "We'll know in a few days. I've done all I can do now. In the meantime, you have work of your own to do. I'll stay with her until she comes to and make certain she is of sound mind. As I stated before, she will not be entirely the same as she was. She will no longer be able to eat normal food. She must consume the creeping mold every day and beyond that only raw meat and river water will do. Once a month you will need to bring her to me, and I will make sure she has the necessary things to sustain her." Cassandra paused for a moment and rested her hand on the table to steady herself. After a few deep breaths she spoke again. "I-In my bag on the floor is a set of blue prints... your mod-rats will need them to begin construction in the Valley of Bones. Once that has begun, meet me back at Grand Fortune City, and I will present Emilia to you just as we agreed."

Hans removed the blue prints from Cassandra's black bag and unrolled them. In his burned, grizzly-toned voice he gave his assessment of her demands. "This...this is a massive undertaking. There aren't enough healthy trees to building something like this...and...and why is it shaped this way? Such an odd shape for a castle."

"I never said it was a castle, Hans. Look, you're a brilliant scientist. I'm sure you'll figure something out. Besides, there are enough bones in that valley to build a keep twice that size... unless, of course, you've decided to back out of our agreement?" Cassandra drifted slowly over to Emilia then placed her hand on Emilia's body.

"NO! No, I'll make it work. I'll make it work." Hans rolled up the prints and stamped toward the door. The Dream Slayer looked him in the eyes and laughed mockingly at him as he exited the threshold.

BONES POPPED AND CRUNCHED UNDERNEATH HIS HEAVY BOOTS AS Hans trekked through the entrance to the Valley of Bones. A bright, full moon overhead fought desperately to shine its light through the waves of thick darkness from the ocean of Black Mist above. An army of mind-controlled tunnel rats followed close behind him and came to a stop instantly when he raised his dragon's head cane into the air. He stared out over the mass grave that was brought about in part by his own hand and in part by the anger of Owen Brock after Isabella was robbed of her arm for the mold cult's dark magic.

In his mind's eye, Hans remembered the very day he strapped Owen into the suit and set out into the Valley of Bones. The valley was filled with thousands and thousands of cultists standing amongst the fire berry flowers. Though Hans had remained a good distance away, he could still hear the screams of terror echoing out of the valley as Owen delivered their punishment in flames. There was no escape from the valley that day. Once Owen entered, he needed only to walk to the end and back again. What seemed an impossible task for anyone else was a mere stroll through the park for a fully armored, rage-filled Jackboot to accomplish.

Suddenly, Hans thought back to his decision to let the Jackboot live and as he gazed over the millions of bones strung out over the valley. His hand began to tremble, then he slumped down on a pile of bones and wept bitterly at his miscalculation.

"What have I done?" Hans said to himself. He sat there for a time until he realized two tunnel rats where pulling at his coat, trying to help him to his feet. *Get it together. You've chosen this path, now it's time to embrace it. Soon we will be complete again, my dear Emilia. I kept my promise.* Hans stood to his feet and turned around to face his army of builders. He plugged a cord into his lead rat's brain mod, and in an instant, he uploaded the blueprints for Cassandra's oddly shaped keep into the rat's mind. The rat's mod-lights turned green, then the lead rat looked out over the sea of rats filling the valley behind him. His mod-lights flashed in rapid succession, and in seconds the sea of red lights turned to green. Without hesitation they began their work, picking up bone after bone and drilling holes in them. The rats fitted each bone with bolts and iron plates, then one by one they began connecting them together to form a foundation in the center of the valley.

Within three days the foundation was complete, and from its base an oddly shaped tower began to rise up. Hans watched as his rats attached the sides of the tower to the sharp rocks pointing out over the valley for support, then he left his lead rat in charge and headed for Grand Fortune City to accept his gift.

Sᴜɴᴀɢᴏ ʟᴀʏ ᴡʀᴀᴘᴘᴇᴅ ɪɴ ᴀ ʙʟᴀɴᴋᴇᴛ ᴏғ ᴅᴀʀᴋɴᴇss ᴅᴇᴇᴘ ɪɴ ᴛʜᴇ heart of Karl's Labyrinth. The concrete walls of his room were more of a dungeon than a room for the sick, and the water dripping from the ceiling made his body feel cold and buried. The distinct smell of formaldehyde and rotting meat filled the air enough to make a tunnel rat vomit. To keep him safe, Cassandra had hidden him in one of her family's genetic modification labs that was difficult to find unless you knew the twisted history of the labyrinth people as she did. Sunago's body was broken and his heart damaged beyond repair from the strike of Elias' death blow. Defeated. Ruined. Shamed by a boy he'd tortured for years.

Tubes and wires flowed into his arms, legs and back, and another machine drained fluid from his chest. Beeping, hissing, and clicking sounds filled the air around him. A breathing mask covered his face while another machine pumped oxygen into his lungs. He stared helplessly at the ceiling while two women in white coats and masks attended to him. The Dream Slayer leaned, arms half-folded, against the doorway to his room, spinning a knife in his oversized hand. If he could have spoken, Sunago would have asked the Dream Slayer to slay him in his bed and end his misery, but he couldn't speak with a tube in his throat. He couldn't communicate with anything but his eyes, and Sunago's eyes were grieving with failure.

The words of his prince echoed in his mind. What did Enupnion mean when he said his people had built a statue in his honor? In his absence, had he gained fame? *What if I had never left? Would I now be someone great among my people? Maybe even High Elder of the Convocation. Or the right hand of the king. I would, at the very least, still have my glorious wings. My pride and selfish desire ruined me. My beautiful Cassandra was wrong, so very wrong, and I have made the gravest of errors to think that I could alter prophecy. YOU FOOL, SUNAGO! Such a fool. Your life is bankrupt.*

Worthless. Nothing but a slug laying here... waiting to be devoured by death.

Another woman in white peered into the room. She muttered something through her mask, and soon the other two left with her. After a time, the bored Dream Slayer began to whistle a cheap carnival tune as he twirled his blade. The sound raked at Sunago's nerves until he was able to let out a groan of disapproval. His groan caught the attention of the Dream Slayer, who instantly stopped his whistling and looked up toward Sunago.

"I-I'm sorry. Did you say something? Trying to speak, are you?" the Dream Slayer asked.

Sunago tried to groan again, but only an empty breath escaped through his breathing tube. Then the Dream Slayer approached and stood beside his bed, looking down into his eyes.

"Dude! You really screwed up; you know it? I can't believe you let the kid beat you." The Dream Slayer shook his head in disapproval then noticed Sunago staring at his blade. "Oh, you... you want this? Is that what you want?"

Sunago's eyes grew large. If only the Dream Slayer would end his misery. Set him free from his agony.

"Oh, ho, ho, boy! I know what you want." The Dream Slayer raised his blade to Sunago's throat. "With one tiny little cut, I could set you free from this place." He carefully slid the edge of his blade over the breathing tube and down toward Sunago's damaged heart. "Snip, snip and it's all over. Just that quick. I bet you'd like that, wouldn't you? But that would get me in some major—and boy do I mean big-time— CRUD if I did that." He snickered.

Suddenly, the door burst open and Cassandra entered. "Get away from him! If I ever catch you near him again, I'll make you believe you're starving and your arms are thick, juicy steaks."

"Y-YES MASTER! I-I WAS ONLY... Forgive me." The

Dream Slayer rushed back to his place by the door. Cowering, he slumped his shoulders downward as he leaned back on the wall, then placed his hooded cloak back over his head to hide himself from her gaze.

Cassandra removed her black hat and adjusted her long, black coat by the lapels with both hands to shake off the bugs and dirt. She handed her hat and umbrella to the Dream Slayer, then drifted over next to the bed. Gazing down at Sunago with sorrowful eyes, she leaned over and softly spoke. "Sunago, my love. Hans has begun construction on the keep. He has also been instructed to bring any fire berries directly to me if one of his workers finds even a single berry during their work." She wiped his brow with a warm cloth. "If only you would have told me how to find your people...I could have gone to them and... at least brought back berries to help heal you." She leaned in closer to his ear and whispered, "Your body is battered so terribly, my love. If circumstances don't change soon...you know what I'll be forced to do."

"Nuhhoo!" Sunago groaned out his strong disapproval of her statement. He knew what she wanted to do. She'd ask him once before, many years ago, after the Jackboot had taken his wings. He'd refused then, and there was nothing she could say to him now that would make him think differently. He would rather die than allow her to defile him in such a way.

"I know, I know, but I can't let you die. You're much too important to me. To our cause." She leaned in closer and kissed his forehead. "Besides, it might not be as bad as you think, and who knows what strength you could gain from it. I would do my best work, you know I would. You'd be beautiful beyond anything this land has ever seen." She pressed him all the more, but he managed to shake his head enough for her to understand.

Cassandra's voice pitched deeper and louder. "YOU WOULD THINK THERE WOULD BE AT LEAST ONE FLOWER, SOMEWHERE! Of all the wars the Jackboot fought, using those seeds to blow things up, and we can't find a single berry anywhere." She slammed her fist on the edge of his bed then marched over to the door. She paused for a moment beside the Dream Slayer, who shrunk back slightly at her presence. "I'm leaving for Grand Fortune City to present Hans' gift to him. Make sure Sunago has anything he desires...*except* your blade," she sneered.

"Certainly, your magnificence," the Dream Slayer said. Bowing his head, he offered her hat and umbrella to her. She jerked them from his hands then swooped out the door.

FIERCE RAIN BEAT AGAINST HANS' GLASS FACE COVER AS HE STOOD on the edge of the Grand Fortune City docks, waiting for Cassandra to bring his gift, a resurrected Emilia. The eerie, green glow from inside his mask complemented the mood of the night as the wind whipped hard against his body. Six large, heavily armed tunnel rats stood behind him, ready for whatever the night might bring. Betrayal, perhaps. A bright flash of lightning through thick storm clouds revealed the coming of his new business partner, and she was not alone. The lightning crashed around her, casting a glow across several hundred Umbrella Charmers floating through the tempest behind her, but one in the center stood out like no other. She was adorned in a bright green robe and top hat with her own umbrella to match.

Within two bright flashes, they were upon him, circling the sky above him. His rat guards let out a nasty hiss of disapproval as Cassandra and the woman in green slowly lowered themselves toward the dock. However, her army of Umbrella Charmers remained in the torrential skies above them. Floating. Hovering. Brooding over him. Cassandra approached him, but the other charmer waited. Inside himself, Hans began to burn with anger at her betrayal of him.

"WE HAD DEAL!" he cried out over the storm.

"YES, WE DID, AND I HAVE COME TO FULLFILL IT," Cassandra replied as she moved in closer toward him.

"Where is my wife? Where is Emilia?" he demanded.

Cassandra raised her gloved hand and motioned for the green-dressed charmer to approach. With a strange quickness, the charmer suddenly stood before them and spoke.

"Good evening, my dear husband," black mist rolled from Emilia's lips as she spoke.

Hans quickly looked at Cassandra. "I NEVER AGREED TO THIS!"

"Oh, my dear Hans, you most certainly did," Cassandra said. "In fact, I remember you specifically saying to me that I could do whatever it took to bring her back, and this is the price of that request." Cassandra smiled and raised Emilia's gloved hand to him. "Rejoice, Hans. She's alive and well. Take your bride's hand and start your new life together."

Emilia smiled at him. "You saved me, darling. You finally saved me from the darkness."

Hans stared into Emilia's strange, new golden eyes, then reached out and took her by the hand as Cassandra rose into the air.

"Don't forget the rest of our deal. You'll bring it back to me or I'll never tell you where to find the half-breed. I might even call Emilia back to me." Cassandra said as she disappeared into the storm with her charmers.

5

THE GUARDIAN AND THE SPARROW

*L*ush colors of green exploded all around the astonished Whisper Crew as a gentle breeze haunted its way through the pines towering over the city. Petinon citizens fluttered and dove from building to building as normally as the citizens of Grand Fortune City would recklessly drive Ever-Wheels through the streets. Feathers floated through the air all around them and covered the cobblestone road like a multicolored carpet that changed color as often as the mountain clouds changed shape. Soon the troubled crew forgot the disturbing images of Sunago that plagued the city, thanks in part to the Petinon children swooping playfully about over their heads. They seemed captivated by Flit's strange eye, and he seemed to be enjoying his job of flashing pictures for the Jackboot a little more than usual.

Oddly, the strangest thing of all was not the weird tongue-clicking dialect of the Petinons, or the off-putting odor of bird-people, but it was their own giant, great gray owl that caught the crew's attention. For whatever reason, Casper had decided that he would walk with the crew through the streets instead of fly. Maybe he'd figured there were enough birds in the air around them, or maybe he didn't want to steal the attention away from Flit, but there he was in all his goofiness, walking. Claw in front of claw, the giant owl stepped his way through the city streets as best he could, irritating Merlin along the way, and walking so close to Ava he nearly knocked her down. It had always bothered Merlin that Casper was nearly right level with his height. But now he was walking with his chest puffed up and looked to be about an inch taller than the miraculous brain boy.

"Casper! Stop it! You're embarrassing me," Merlin complained, but the giant gray owl persisted in his efforts to annoy his human companion. The entire Whisper crew quickly caught notice of Casper's mockery, and it brought them all some much need laughter, even a disheartened Ava. It was a joyous moment that was brought to an instantaneous stop with a fierce rumbling of the Petinon Mountain. Several rocks tumbled down the street, and the trees cast fresh leaves to the ground. The astonished crew stopped dead in their tracks and looked directly at Epekneia, who was still giggling from Casper's antics.

"What?" Epekneia inquisitively asked.

"WHAT THE BLAZES WAS THAT?" Bogan blurted out.

"What was what?" Epekneia asked again.

"The whole mountain shook. Didn't you feel it?" Gideon looked at her as if she'd forgotten the risks they had all taken in trusting her. The only one that seemed unfazed by the trembling mountain was Jimmy, who was still busy irritating the royal guards.

"Oh, that! I'm so sorry; I should have told you all about that. The mountain always rumbles. It's a normal thing for us Petinons. I guess I didn't realize it might be a bit traumatic for newcomers. A fair warning though, from here on out, that was a little rumble. Sometimes it shakes so hard it snaps trees in half. It's the fire berries heating up the mountain that cause the tremors, but it's also why the creeping mold can't grow here."

She peered into the growing circles of their eyes and tried to comfort them. "It's okay. Really, you'll get used to it." She smiled and ruffled the feathers on Casper's head then turned to follow the queen.

"This just keeps getting better and better, doesn't it?" Izzy shook her head at Elias, who responded with a tiny grin and a nervous chuckle.

THE FLUTTERING BUSTLE OF THE GREAT CITY SOON FELL SILENT behind them as they made their way up the cobbled road, toward the massive severed trunk atop the mountain. The entrance that looked so small from the city streets grew larger and larger with every step. Deep green vines crawled up the sides of the trunk, and fire berries speckled the road beside them. The warm air lifting off the fire berries smelled of a spicy cinnamon but was soon replaced by a fresh spring scent from two waterfalls rushing down each side of the trunk. The water sprinkled their faces with the clearest blue droplets the crew had ever seen, and it finally brought a smile to Bogan's grumpy demeanor. The falls continued into streams that slithered around rocks and lush vegetation all the way down to the city below. As they neared the opening arch at the base of the trunk, its awe-inspiring size brightened their faces with a joyous wonder of new adventure.

Around the entrance of the arch, two massive eagles were intricately carved out on each side of its opening, and they were complimented with detailed designs and strange words traveling to a peak at the very top of the arch. A massive crack traveled from the base of the arch, all the way to the top of the trunk, as if something terrible had tried to split the tree in half. A single, unarmed guardian was brooding by the forty-foot wooden doors. The guardian held a staff with an enormous claw, and his face was entirely hidden inside his dark green, hooded cloak. Around the sides of his hood was a golden rope design that followed down the center of the cloak and around its edges at the bottom. The queen stopped about twelve feet away from him and spoke in a strange language that clicked and clacked.

Epekneia translated her words for the crew. "Great guardian of the keep, it is I, Queen Elehos, and I request entrance to king's great hall." The old guardian said nothing to the queen but merely gave a subtle nod, then he approached an eight-foot door handle, lifted a bulbous lock arm, then slowly pulled the door open for them. The queen was first to enter, and the guards around her went next, followed by Epekneia, Izzy, Elias and Ava. Casper caught sight of a fish popping out of the waterfall to their left, and suddenly he dove down the mountainside.

Merlin let out a relief-filled sigh at Casper's departure then looked to Gideon and snickered as they entered, "You'd think she wouldn't have to ask permission to enter her own castle, now wouldn't you?" Gideon crinkled his nose and squinted a bit with his right eye, forcing a burst of steam from the mod on his face. In an instant the towering, old guardian dropped his staff across the path in front of them, preventing them from entering.

"Hey, what gives?" Merlin asked, capturing Elias' attention.

Elias spoke out toward the queen, who was a good distance ahead of them now. "WHAT ABOUT MY FRIENDS?"

The queen looked back at him and with an emotionless stare said, "He says no."

"But why? They aren't any different from us," Elias complained.

"You and your sister are one of us, as well as Epekneia," the queen said.

"What about Ava? She's not one of us, *is she?*" Elias' voice rose in wonder at the idea that maybe Ava was also a wingless Petinon.

Queen Elehos looked deeply into Ava's face. "No. No, she isn't."

"Then why does she get to go in, and they don't?" Elias was growing angry, and the burning flames in his eyes seemed to grow brighter.

"She's...known to us," the queen said and turned about to continue her walk.

"Well, if they don't go...then I don't go." Elias said in protest as Izzy folded her arms and stared at the queen.

Queen Elehos shook her head in frustration. "I would not recommend that course of action, but if that is your decision, you will have to live with it."

Elias looked back at Bogan, Merlin, Gideon and Jimmy. Bogan shrugged his shoulders and spoke, "It's a crummy tree, anyway. Go ahead, kid. We'll head down to the city and check out the sights."

But Elias was having none of it. He marched back to the entrance and spoke to the cloaked guardian. "Let them in." The guardian ignored him and refused to lift his staff out of the way. Elias raised his voice at the guard as Izzy released her baton from her arm and began to spin it. "LET THEM PASS!" he yelled out, sending red smoke from his nostrils. The queen's guard quickly assumed a protective posture, and the mood of the day began to sour.

The old guardian turned his gaze toward Elias as he held out his staff. Elias stepped up and placed his hand on the guardian's massive claw that gripped the long wooden staff. The mountain began to rumble as the two gazed intently at each other. Shaking and trembling, the mountain rolled under their feet while pebbles and dirt crumbled around them. Suddenly, from his hooded cloak came an enormous, full, yellow beak that opened up above Elias' head, and the clawed creature let out a terrible *SCREECH* of disapproval in his face. The mountain shook so badly, Izzy, Bogan and Ava were knocked to the ground. The guardian's hood fell off his head and onto the back of his neck to reveal before them the head of a great eagle. It was covered in white feathers from the top and down the neck, and his eyes were hauntingly fierce and golden in color.

This strong reaction caught the attention of Jimmy, who for the most part had been so captivated by the queen's guard that he hadn't been watching the events around him. His turbine instantly ramped up to a high-pitched whine, and fire shot out the back as he flew over in front of the great bird. Jimmy cocked his head left then right as he tried to figure out exactly was he was looking at. As the feathered beast and metal monster came face to face, everyone readied themselves for something terrible.

"I'm just like you. See..." Jimmy flew around in a circle through the air as his turbine rolled black smoke behind him. "I don't have wings, but I can still fly." Jimmy stopped directly in front of the great bird's bright yellow beak. The heat from his turbine warmed the old guardian's beak as they stared into each other's eyes. "We are the same, but different." Jimmy floated over top the guardian's staff, high above, to the peak of the great entrance. "See... it doesn't stop me. I can still go in."

The stunned group watched the two with great anticipation and hope that neither would start an unnecessary war then slowly but watchfully the old guardian raised his staff for the rest of the crew. Jimmy zipped behind him and lifted his hood back over his head. "There, that's better." Izzy snickered at Jimmy's odd act of kindness, and the crew of the Whisper cautiously passed through the great entrance to the king's palace.

ONCE THEY WERE IN THE CENTER OF THE LARGE TREE TRUNK, THE crew expected to see something wonderful and awe inspiring, but instead there was nothing. The whole of the inside was hollow and spiraling all the way to the top were rows of winged guards holding torches out over the top of them. Their gold helmets glistened in the soft orange light of their torches and complemented their deep red wings with silver tips. There was no elevator or any winding stairs to climb to the top since this was a Petinon castle, and Petinon's didn't need stairs or elevators to get to the tops of trees. That's what wings were for, and with a sudden, bursting jump into the sky, the queen took off, and her royal guards followed directly behind her. The crew stood there staring at each other for a moment, but before anyone could ask how they were going to get to the top, Epekneia grabbed Elias and leapt into the air. Then, one right after another, the crew was quickly lifted up by the Petinon guards behind them. One even grabbed Jimmy, who seemed to enjoy the free ride to the top. The sight of the guards on the walls was so intriguing that no one said a word as they traveled through the trunk towards a bright hole above them.

The Whisper crew surfaced into a large courtyard with magnificent shrubbery and nearly one hundred unique trees that wrapped around a white limestone wall. A gate at the entrance was manned by two black-winged guards that seemed fairly normal at first but upon closer inspection their faces looked similar to that of the guardian. They both held long poles with swords coming out of the tops, pointing upward to the sky. Despite their menacing weapons, the crew passed through unchallenged into the walled castle. Great pillars held the entrance to the castle, and four large towers rose into the sky over a center dome that's grandeur was much greater than what they'd viewed from the city below. They followed the queen through the entrance, and only two guards followed them inside.

The ceilings were made of limestone, and the arch at the top was nearly forty-feet high. The first great hall they entered was filled with paintings of the king and queen and even some of Prince Enupnion from youth to adulthood. Elias smiled at the boyhood paintings of his old friend, but the pale look on Bogan's face as he stared at the picture of Hunchy did not go unnoticed by the queen. Midway through the great hall, they came upon a very strange painting of Sunago and the king after a hunt. Beneath them lay a terrible beast that none of the crew had ever seen or heard described before. Also not lost on them was how handsome the young Sunago was, even more than any of them could have ever believed. The mountain rumbled and the castle walls trembled as Elias strolled up to Sunago's painting and looked at the eyes of his false father. It was difficult to process the events of his life up to that moment, but a gentle mod-hand took its place on his shoulder. "Come on, brother. Forget about him," Izzy said quietly, and so he followed her into the next section of the castle.

Rumbling from the mountain gave them all a familiar feeling as they entered the king's trophy room which was filled with all manner of freakish beasts mounted on the walls. There were single-horned creatures and bat winged serpents as well as massive red bears. Toward the end of the second great hall were four massive tunnel troll heads mounted on large mahogany plagues. Next to the heads was an enormous wild boar head with sixteen horns shooting up out of its snout, followed by rows and rows of giant black wolf heads of equal size mounted on the walls. As the mountain rumbled more and more, Elias tossed a smile back toward the wary Whisper crew to lighten their tension.

"I don't smell vanilla or hear any angry yelling yet. Do you guys?" he chuckled.

"That's not making me feel any better about this," Gideon

said as a nervous blast of steam popped from the relief valve on his head.

"What I'm worried about is what's in that next room," Bogan added while Jimmy zipped up to one of the wolf heads and stuck his finger up its nostril. Jimmy seemed disappointed that no door or wall opened up inside the great hall.

"Do you think Charlie might be here? You know, in the castle?" Ava asked Merlin.

"I'm not sure. When the time is right, we'll ask the queen. But, honestly, I'm starving here," Merlin said, rubbing his tummy and trying to divert Ava's thoughts away from what everyone already feared.

Izzy agreed, looking at Merlin's subtle nod toward a worried Ava. "Yeah...same here. Let's get some food, and soon."

As they entered the third and last great hall of the castle, their fears were somewhat eased as it was not nearly as terrifying as the third rail car on the Iron Weaver, at least not for humans, anyway. However, for the average Petinon, this great hall would have held significantly more shock and horror. On both sides of the hall were mounted the cleaved wings of those who had dishonored the king or the Convocation of Elders or, for whatever reason or another, would be deserving of such punishment. The queen seemed numb to the impact of the great hall, but for Epekneia it was a very disturbing sight to behold. She clung to Elias' arm as they made their way to the end of the hall. The crew stopped suddenly at the sight of a long sign carved into the limestone arch above the threshold of the king's throne room. The large cedar doors were closed, but the strange writing was enough capture Elias' curiosity.

"What does it say?" Elias asked Epekneia.

"It's the king's warning," she said then read it out loud for all the crew to hear. "It says, 'Death to all who dishonor the king. Death to all who dishonor the Convocation. Death to all who defile this great hall with lies, for darkness lies.'"

Elias and Izzy smiled at the words that had connected them to Prince Enupnion for so long, and a true sense belonging came over them both. In a place where most had cowered in fear for their lives, Queen Elehos looked on as Elias and Isabella embraced under the banner of their friend's words, for they knew now he was so much more than their friend. He was their prince, and his heart beat strong inside Elias' chest. Soon the rest of the crew embraced as they remembered that old hunchback who'd brought them all together. The impact of their embrace under the king's warning banner had a powerful effect on Queen Elehos, so much so that they all heard it in her voice as she spoke.

"C-Come with me," she said. "I-I want you all to dine with me at the king's table." She clapped her trembling claws together, and a small Petinon boy swooped into the hall. "Inform the king's chef that we have important guests for dinner and have him bring only the best to the king's table," she commanded.

"Yes, my queen!" the young Petinon said, and he spread both his wings to the ground in front of her then quickly jumped into the air and fluttered away.

"Come with me," she repeated.

THE WHISPER CREW FOLLOWED HER DOWN ANOTHER HALL AND into a large room with a long, wooden table. Forty high-backed chairs lined one side of the table, forty more complemented the opposing side, and one intricately carved chair towered over the others at the very end of the table. Each chair belonged to a specific member of the Convocation and was engraved with the name of the high elder at the top of the chair's arch. Queen Elehos motioned for the crew to sit anywhere they pleased, and she took her place in the large chair at the end of the table.

Painted on the ceiling of the great dining hall was a colorfully detailed painting of a great battle in the sky. Petinon against Petinon, and many were depicted as falling from the sky as they were struck down by other Petinon warriors. Bogan thought it was marvelous, but Gideon and Merlin were chilled to the bone at the faces of those being slain. Ava seemed captivated by the use of the colors, as if she never noticed the battle at all. Epekneia refused to look at it, but Izzy and Elias seemed worried it would trigger Jimmy again, so they kept a watchful eye on him. Flit stayed busy snapping pictures of everything he could until he finally tired and landed on the top edge of Epekneia's wing.

While the Whisper crew chose their places at the table, the queen wiped a tear from her eye as she struggled with the question she already feared she knew the answer to. She started to ask it, but instead her attention was drawn to Elias, choosing the chair farthest away from her and at the very end of the group.

"It's very interesting that you have chosen that chair," she said to Elias.

"Why?" he asked, slowly rising back out of the seat as if he had offended her.

"No, please sit. I was only intrigued by why you chose that specific place to sit."

"Uh, because it was empty," Elias said nervously, trying not to make any mistakes.

The queen smiled. "That is the seat of the high elder, Bebahyosis. His name means 'confirmation.' Maybe you truly are the chosen one. Of course, Bebahyosis is also known for murdering his mother and father."

Elias quickly sprung out of the seat in horror.

"No. Please sit. You've chosen the place meant for you. Besides, Bebahyosis killed his parents in self-defense. Otherwise, he wouldn't have a place at this table." She gave a nod for him to sit back down, and Elias slowly sat back on the very edge of the seat.

"Way to go, champ," Bogan snickered as he reached for a strange walnut-shaped treat in a bowl at the center of the table. He popped a few in his mouth and said, "These are crunchy... not bad."

"Ah, yes, dried rat brains are the king's favorite treat," the queen explained.

Bogan quickly spit them out of his mouth and into his hand. "WHAT!" He put the remains into his coat pocket then wiped his tongue several times with his hand.

"Me, on the other claw...or hand, as you say, I find them simply disgusting," the queen said with a grin, and the rest of the crew burst into laughter. The rumbling mountain shook a massive chandelier above them, silencing everyone for only a moment then sending them into laughter again as they slowly became accustomed to the mountain's temperamental personality.

Soon the room began filling with all manner of winged servants carrying tray after tray of fish, squid, fried eel dipped in thick, dark sauce and several strange smelling skewers of red meat. There was not a single tray of vegetables much to the crew's extreme pleasure. Queen Elehos watched with wonder at their laughter and joy for life as they devoured plate after plate. She especially enjoyed the flashing display of effects each different food had on Merlin's brain, but soon the flashing display of light on the war mural transported her mind back to days before that terrible war.

The young prince Enupnion had begged her to allow him to go to war with his father, but her refusal drove a wedge between them. So, the young prince spent his days in the libraries of prophecy until he was so caught up in them, he tried to force them into action. His failure brought so much shame to his father; the prince was banned from becoming a member of the

Convocation and thereby ended the king's chances for an heir to his throne. So, the king chose to spend the remainder of his rule hunting and killing and giving the people whatever they desired, so he would be remembered as the greatest king his people had ever known. She knew it was her husband's way of forever sealing his legacy among his people and that her decision, made out of concern for her young son, had cost her everything, including the honor of her people. She had defied the king openly, and too many times, and though the people still bowed to her out of respect for her title, she'd never felt more isolated in her own kingdom. Most of all, it had cost her the one thing that gives a mother purpose, her children.

Suddenly, her mind cleared of her thoughts as Izzy's mod-hand accidentally crushed one of the fine crystal glasses on the table. Four of the servants in the room screeched softly and bowed their wings in a submissive reaction, but Izzy and Ava laughed it off as a typical side effect of living with Izzy and the crushing personality of her mod-arm.

"Way to go, Iz!" Bogan muffled out as he chewed a dark skewered meat.

Izzy lifted her mod-hand into a fist and warned Bogan. "Hey! Don't make me warm your shoulder up in front of the queen, you lunk," she said with sly grin.

"OKAY! OKAY! I was just hackin on you. Take it easy, Iz," Bogan said with a hard swallow, but the looks on the servant's faces were hard for the queen to ignore.

Queen Elehos took a deep breath and looked to her servants. "It's okay. Go ahead and clean it up, and I'll take the blame."

"Did we do something wrong?" Elias asked the queen.

Izzy's mouth was full of food but she muttered, "HUH? Oh, no way. That's on me. I got no problem taking the blame. I'm good at."

"That would be an impossible thing for you to do, my dear," the queen explained.

Suddenly, the servant girls protested loudly until one of them said something terrible. "NO! Never, my queen! Let it be my wings!"

"WHAT? Are you saying you're going to have your wings cut off because we broke that glass?" Elias asked, horrified by the thought of it all.

"It is forbidden for anyone to drink from the cups of the High Elders of the Convocation or eat at the king's table or sit in the king's chair. Our laws demand that anyone who does these things have their wings cleaved and that they are to be... beheaded in front of the whole kingdom," Queen Elehos explained with subtle tremble to her voice.

Ava slammed her hand on the table in anger. "WHAT? Then why did you bring us here? Why did you do this to us? Are you saying we'll all be put to death because of this?" Ava jumped out of her chair. "A-A-AND...WHERE'S CHARLIE! WHAT DID YOU DO WITH HIM? IF YOU HURT HIM..." her tone dropped to a sinister pitch, "I'll have Jimmy wreck your whole city."

"But why?" a confused Jimmy asked.

"Ava...take your seat," Elias said gently. Ava looked into his eyes, the burning of the fire berries was nearly gone, but it was enough for her to remember who he was, so she slowly sat back in her seat.

"You will not be harmed. I promise, and this was not a trick to entrap you to have you killed. In fact, late at night, I've done this many times. One night, I even sat in every single chair just to know that I did it." She smiled and leaned in closer toward them. "Best night's sleep I ever had."

Izzy looked her deep in the eyes then flipped her knife into the air and caught it. She pointed it directly at the queen, shook the knife and said, "You know something? I think I like you."

The queen smiled then looked toward one of her servants. "Gemenon, bring me a sparrow, and quickly." In an instant, Gemenon dove out the castle window and returned within seconds with a tiny sparrow. She placed it in the queen's claw then stepped back to her place in the room. The queen rubbed her claw over the tiny bird's head and gave it a gentle kiss. "It is a dark sign for a sparrow to die in the castle." Her eyes softened as she took a deep breath and snapped the bird's neck with a *crack*. Deep within the mountain a low rumble caused the chandelier to clatter above them. "No one, not even the king's wise ones, will want to touch the broken cup now. Gemenon, take this little warrior and place him where the cup sits in the cabinet and pour the broken pieces around him... oh...and Gemenon, bring me one of his feathers, so I might remember his sacrifice."

The shaken crew sat silent at the table, afraid to touch even a single crumb on their plates. Finally, the queen spoke again. "This world is harsh, cold...unkind. It swallows up the tiny things that bring us simple joy and leaves us hollow inside. It steals the light from our hearts and leaves us in darkness. My son has been missing for several years now, but when I saw your embrace under the king's warning, I knew for certain you had known him. Now...tell me, what happened to my son," she said with a somber face.

6

THE CAPSTONE

ears streamed from every eye in the dining hall as Elias gave his explanation of Prince Enupnion's final days, and he finished by standing up to reveal the scar traveling down his chest. It seemed more irritated than ever as he spoke. "He was my friend, and he gave his life for me and that's why we brought him back to you. My father didn't mean to chain him. He feared Enupnion was like Sunago, and he is not a man that takes chances with his children. He sent us here in hopes we could bring our two people together for the good of everyone and save the land from the creeping mold and black mist. Well, he probably wouldn't mind if you helped him defeat the Umbrella Charmers as well."

The queen rose from the king's chair and quickly closed Elias' shirt. She motioned for her four servants to come close to her, and she spoke quietly to them. "You are sworn to secrecy," she said and suddenly the four Petinon girls cut the palms of their claws and rubbed the blood on her feet. "Do not tell the king that my son's heart beats in your chest. I have no idea what he will do if he finds out." She looked back at her servants, "The evening light is fading. The king will be returning soon. Clean this room and leave not a trace." Then, turning to the Whisper crew, she explained the rules of the king's court. "When the king returns, I will go before him and announce the arrival of guests. I am sure he is already aware that you are here and that I have brought you to the castle. He will be expecting me, but I still must follow the rules of his court or I will be punished."

Elias was confused by the Petinon's strange rules. "But, I don't understand. If you're the queen, why would the king treat you that way?"

"The king of the Trembling Mountain can get away with almost anything. Even murder. But the king will always be subject to the rules of the Convocation," Queen Elehos said. "Now, all of you come with me. I need to prepare you for the king's court and what protocols must be followed to keep you alive."

"This is CRACKED!" Bogan blasted out. "Why even go in there and speak to the old bird. I say we leave and forget this whole thing before we end up in a cage... or worse."

"There is no way out of this now. You must see it through, or the king will see it as a sign of weakness and probably have you all killed," The queen warned.

"I'd like to see him..." Izzy started to push her chair back, but Elias called her out.

"Isabella. We must listen to her," Elias said confidently and motioned for them to follow the queen, but only Epekneia followed him. Izzy stood her ground and didn't move, and the rest of the crew stood beside her until the queen spoke again.

"Isabella..." Queen Elehos said softly. "Please trust me. I don't want anything to happen to your friends and especially not you or your brother."

QUEEN ELEHOS TOOK THE CREW OF THE WHISPER TO A SMALL room with a connecting door into the king's great hall. There were no chairs and no pictures on the walls, but there was a large plaque with a list of more than six hundred laws about how to approach the king and the Convocation. Most of them ended with the phrase, *Or so shall you perish.* Several laws spoke of the king's ultimate authority as ruler of the Trembling Mountain and that he could basically get away with murder. Elias read a few but soon grew bored with the overbearing rules. After the queen left them, Merlin and Bogan complained about the impossibility of learning them all and that the crew should just cut their losses and get out before the king returned. Gideon seemed to like many of the rules and said he thought it might be beneficial for the Jackboot to adopt a few of them. Jimmy was angry about having to shut his generator off while in the tiny room, but Izzy kept him calm as best she could. Ava begged Elias to ask the king about Charlie as soon as he possibly could, but Elias feared the king's answer might be more than she could bear, considering the queen's face when she looked at Ava. Epekneia stayed busy keeping Flit comfortable as he snuggled under her wing for a short nap.

It wasn't long after the queen left that the slow rumble of the mountain began to intensify. Soon, everyone began to notice the look on Elias' face when the mountain shook. He turned pale white and his hands began to shake with the mountain. He scratched at the scar on his chest until he couldn't take it any longer. He lifted his shirt and checked the scar. It was bright red and looked like steam was rising from it. No one knew what to do. Izzy called for the queen, but no one came. The mountain rumbled and shook more and more violently than before and then stopped with a great boom.

"He's here," Epekneia said.

"Who's here?" Merlin asked.

"King Arkone, ruler of Pterugas," Epekneia said, bowing to one knee.

A voice thundered through the walls of the tiny room. It shook like the mountain and was strong like an angry beast before a feeding. Terror struck the hearts of the Whisper crew as they all looked to Elias and hoped beyond hope that he was who they had come to know him as, the chosen one of the Petinon people. The sounds of clacking and marching of strange feet filled the room beyond their wall and with a loud cry stomped, swished, thumped, and then everything went silent.

A powerful voice thundered, "DID YOU SEE THE LOOK ON THAT TROLL'S FACE WHEN I RAN HIM THROUGH?" The hall erupted into laughter and a loud beating of something on the floor. "AND THAT WILD BOAR? BEST MEAT I'VE HAD IN WEEKS." The hall roared with the sound of wings beating the wind like thunder, and the mountain rumbled and groaned. The cheering and thundering continued until the sound of a door opening and closing brought the roaring hall to a dead quiet.

A gentle voice spoke up, "Oh, great King Arkone, ruler of Pterugas, ruler of the ancient kingdom of Petinon's, Lord Commander of the Convocation and Slayer of Evil. It is I, Queen Elehos, your bride. If it pleases the king, I would request an audience with him on this joyous night of celebration."

Silence fell on their tiny room as the Whisper crew held their collective breath in wait for the king's response. Epekneia handed Elias twelve fire berries and told him to eat them, but both he and Izzy shook their heads at her. When she persisted, Elias finally agreed. One by one, he ate the berries slowly in hopes that he would be able to stave off any visions. Then a voice came from the great throne room of the king.

"Of course, my queen. What is it you wish to ask of the king at this late hour?" King Arkone said in a somewhat irritated tone.

"If it pleases the king, I would like to introduce to him guests from far away, important guests, your majesty," Queen Elehos explained. It was quiet again for a short time and then the king spoke.

"Oh, yes. What was it my messenger said?" he joked to someone in the hall.

Another voice spoke in a humble manner. "Ouranos...oh great king. Ouranos has come."

"OURANOS, IS IT?" the king thundered out and then broke into laughter and the rest of the hall followed. "WELL, IF IT'S OURANOS THEN, BY ALL MEANS, BRING HIM IN SO WE CAN SHARE ALE TOGETHER AND FEAST UPON MY GREAT KILL!" the king mocked as he motioned for someone to bring the queen's guests into the hall.

Bogan and Gideon looked at Izzy and Elias and shook their heads. Merlin agreed and said quietly, "Let's get out of here, NOW. I'll have Jimmy hold them off while we make it to the Whisper then we can send the Jackboot back to lay waste to them. No offense, Epekneia."

Ava looked at them all. "But...Charlie. We'll never know what happened to Charlie." A tear rushed down her cheek, but it was too late. The tiny door opened, and the queen looked directly at them all. They couldn't move. Their feet were frozen scared to the floor of the room. The queen looked at Elias, whose eyes were now burning with flames of fire unlike anything she had ever seen from a Petinon, and she looked terrified as she gazed into them.

"WELL, WHAT'S KEEPING THE GREAT OURANOS? DID YOU HAVE TO PUT HIM DOWN FOR A NAP?" The king laughed, and the warriors of the hall laughed with him. "OR MAYBE HE'S A GHOST. BY THE LOOK ON THE QUEEN'S FACE, I'D SAY SHE'S SEEN ONE!" The hall roared with laughter at the king's mockery of his queen. The queen stepped back from the door, turned and strutted away from the king in a confident posture. Gasps from the king's warriors filled the hall as the queen's offense was unheard of and a crime punishable by death. The king's face turned to a mask of anger as he sat on his royal throne boiling inside himself for his queen turning her back on him.

Reluctantly, Elias made his way to the threshold of the door, but his wonderfully glorious entrance into the king's throne room was horribly botched by the effects of the fire berries blurring his eyes. He clumsily tripped over Bogan's foot and fell across the threshold and out into the king's great hall. None of the king's men could see his eyes, but only a boy falling into the great hall, and a wingless boy at that. The king's warrior's instantly and fearfully looked back up at their king, waiting for him to call for a sentence of immediate death. The king drew back at the sight in shock then awkwardly broke into laughter, but not a single warrior follow in their laughter this time. King Arkone reached out his right arm, and his wing followed suit. "As king of this great hall, let me be the first to say to the Elders of the Convocation, warriors and battle hardened royal guard, I give you the great, OURANOS!" The hall burst into laughter, and even the Elders of the Convocation laughed. All but one.

The queen continued to back away from Elias until he finally got to his feet, turned, and faced the great hall. There were about two-hundred armed warriors standing in a row on one side and two-hundred armed royal guards on the opposite side of a one-hundred-foot path leading up to the king's massive, wooden throne. The warriors and guards carried long spears; many still dripping with blood from the hunt. The Elders of the Convocation were standing off to the right of the king's throne as the queen continued to back away from Elias in fear. As Elias journeyed down the path toward the king many of the guards broke royal protocol and began staring at his eyes.

Then the king caught a glimpse of Elias' eyes, and he stood to his feet. Every guard and Elder instantly dropped to their knees and flared their wings out in submission to the king. Elias knew what the queen had told him about respect and honor and what he must do to prevent a sentence of death on him and his crew, but he was so captivated by the king that he kept walking toward him, and the king marched toward Elias as well.

The mountain rumbled and shook as they both stopped about thirty feet from each other. King Arkone was a stout, powerful presence to behold, with oversized claws and deep-red wings speckled with silver throughout. His shoulders were broad, and his arms looked like fleshy iron that ended with claws the length of Elias' forearms. The blood of the hunt, still on his chest and talons, only solidified his intimidating presence all the more. However, the only weapon he carried was a knife, strapped to his side, and its golden hilt was sparkling clean. His legs were dark yellow, and he wore no boots on his clawed feet. One claw, on his left toe, was broken and jagged, but the jagged end looked worn as if it had been damaged many years ago. One might naturally assume this to have happened during the war he'd seen depicted on the ceiling of the great dining hall. King Arkone stared into Elias' fiery eyes while several guards peaked up from their positions to see what was taking place, a dangerous breach of protocol indeed.

The queen stood in the center of Elias and the king and finally dropped to her knees and flared out her wings, but she did this towards Elias and not the king. By now the Whisper crew had stepped out in to the hall and was staring down the long path. Jimmy had fired his turbine back up full force and was hovering a few feet from great doors. Izzy was holding her baton, but Epekneia had placed her hand on Izzy's mod-arm, preventing her from making a costly mistake.

There was complete silence for a few moments as the two stared at each other, then King Arkone spoke, "Arise, my great warriors and Elders of the Convocation." The warriors and elders stood up and faced the center of the hall, but the queen remained down. Then the king spotted the Whisper crew back by the door and roared out in anger, "OUTRAGE! DISGRACE! HOW DARE YOU BRING THIS WINGLESS FILTH INTO MY GREAT HALL!" The mountain roared and shook so violently that rubble began to fall from the ceiling of the limestone dome.

While King Arkone thundered away, the mountain responded in kind as the king's fury increased dramatically. In one swift move, he grabbed a spear from one of his warrior's claws and held it over the queen's back in preparation for removing her wings for the desecration of his great hall. "BY ORDER OF THE KING," he roared, and the mountain shook again, sending more rubble from the ceiling. There were so many bits of rubble this time that it caught Elias by surprise. He looked up at the large dome ceiling above the king and queen and noticed the rubble was falling from the edges of the capstone directly above them both. He tried to speak up and let the king know there might be a problem with the roof, but the king ignored him.

"I HEARBY SENTENCE YOU, QUEEN ELEHOS, TO..." The king stopped as rubble covered the floor around him, and he looked up to the capstone. It was weak, loose and starting to groan. Soon, everyone in the great hall looked up at the capstone in horror as it began to slip out of place. However, the stubborn king refused to move as he raised the large spear over his head to finish his sentence. Elias looked to his left at the warriors and to his right at the royal guard, and every eye in the room was on the capstone, not a single one was watching the king's punishment of his queen.

Elias raised his hand, quickly pointed up at the capstone, and cried out, "King Arkone! The stone!" It was at that moment Elias saw from the corner of his burning eyes, one of the guard's spears followed his hand up into the air. The spear shot

up into the crack of the capstone. *WHAT? Was that me?*
Suddenly, Elias' thoughts were transported back to his strike on
Sunago. *The spears are like the baton!* None of the warriors,
guards, or elders knew who had thrown the spear into the
crack and wedged it, but their eyes were quickly brought back
down to the king and queen at the center of the room. As the
king brought down the bladed spear toward the queen's back,
Elias reached for it, and suddenly it shot from the king's grip
and into Elias' hand. The entirety of the king's court looked
directly at Elias in shock. No one dared move or speak. All eyes
gazed into his until the mountain rumbled and the capstone
cracked the rest of the way above the king and queen. Screeches
of horror filled the hall, and in an instant Elias raised both arms
into the air, sending twelve spears soaring into the air and
driving them deep into the sides of the capstone. Then he sent
three more into the crack in the center, securely wedging the
stone in place.

Izzy had long-since broken free from Epekneia's hold and
had run straight down the center of the hall. She slid in front of
Elias with her baton in full spin then halted it and pointed at
every royal guard and warrior in the room. She reached down
and offered her hand to the queen, who gladly took hold of it
and stood to her feet. Merlin and Gideon were both holding
Jimmy by the legs while the machinal boy kept calling out to
"PROTECT!" Bogan had also soldiered up by pulling his hand
cannon out of from the back of his mod-leg.

King Arkone slowly began to clap his claws together and
motioned for the rest of his men to do the same. They quickly
and gladly followed the king's lead, and then he spoke, "Well…
well…well…now that's a first for me and everyone in this great
hall. Maybe you are truly Ouranos, but you have still violated
more laws than anyone in this room has ever heard of… you
and your defilers must be put to death."

"I'm afraid you can't do that, great King." Elias said,

"According to law number 467, no one shall put to death the one who saves the life of the king…not even the king himself."

A GASP FROM SEVERAL ELDERS OF THE CONVOCATION SEEMED TO catch the king's attention, and so he redirected his thoughts. Izzy watched as King Arkone paced the floor of his hall for a bit then spoke to Elias. "Maybe you truly are the chosen one many have spoken of in our books of prophecy, but you still must pass the three tests to prove you are who you claim to be. Tomorrow you will report to this great hall and prove yourself by a test of Great Strength, Great Wisdom, and of the Heart." The king approached Elias, but Izzy stopped him by stepping in between them. The king sneered at her and then finished his thought. "Keep in mind; no one has ever passed the first test." He smiled and had turned back toward his throne when one of the elders of the Convocation broke protocol and spoke up.

"Oh, great King, if I may. I believe this boy has completed all three tests in a single act. With one move of his hand he lifted twelve heavy spears and wedged the capstone into place, thereby saving the king and queen from certain death. A feat of Great Strength, Great Wisdom and of the Heart. Although, it seems he might have completed them all twice with the same maneuver, so it may take some time to fully process what has happened." The other elders of the Convocation quickly began to mutter, but then the king questioned the old one's one wisdom as if he was testing the old one.

"What do you mean he completed the Great Feats twice with one maneuver?" King Arkone asked.

"Oh, great King Arkone, he also spared Queen Elehos from a heartless punishment by the king's own hand, therefore saving the king's legacy with his wisdom, again while removing a spear from the hand of one of the strongest warriors our kingdom has ever known." Soon, the other elders began to nod in agreement at which point the king stormed out of his great hall alone in a huff. The warriors and elders seemed lost at what to do next as the king did not release them, and so after some period of waiting Queen Elehos sent them home. Then she presented the Whisper crew with bedrooms in one of the castle's towers that overlooked the back of the Trembling Mountain.

The troubled crew was at loss for words as they entered their rooms, but the queen assured them of their safety. Izzy, however, had already decided in her mind that the Petinon king was too hostile, and so the queen granted her demand to be placed in a room next to Elias. That night, after Ava cried herself to sleep, asking her pillow where Charlie was, Izzy opened the window and sent Flit out. He returned with two fire berry flowers containing six berries. She pocketed three, fed him the rest, and then sent him back to GFC.

7

THE FORGOTTEN

*I*n the place that light had forgotten, the Jackboot woke to the sounds of trickling water behind his head. A slimy stream of water wet the back of his neck, sending a shiver down his spine. It smelled of sour meat and rotten tunnel dirt mixed with something so pungent it burned the inside of his nostrils. The darkness was so thick he felt it crushing his eye as he tried to imagine where Hans and Cassandra might have dumped him. Some rustling and shuffling sounds came from his left and his right, and soon he knew he was not alone. He ignored it for the moment and sought to fulfill his basic desires to calm his thoughts of Hans' betrayal.

Reaching down, he checked for his iron boots. It was a nice comfort to know that Hans had, at the very least, left him with his boots on. He flicked a tiny toggle switch on the inside of his left boot, and a small square box popped open. He smiled in the dark as his hand felt the contents of the box, and he drew out a pouch and pipe. He gripped the bowl carefully as he filled its chamber then placed the stem in his mouth and put the pouch back into his boot. Fumbling with his match box, he clumsily

5

dropped it between his legs and scattered the matches all over the darkness of the floor.

"OF ALL THE BLASTED..." he shouted loudly of his own error but suddenly felt something furry reach between his legs then place a match in his open hand. In the murkiness of the cell, the only thing he could tell about his fellow cellmate was that he had enormous claws where fingers should have been. He held the match for a moment, wondering if he should light it or not. Whatever stood before him might simply be waiting to eat him, but he considered, if it could see him already, and he could not see it, then it would eaten him anyway. So he reached down and struck the match hard against his iron boot. It exploded into a whooshing blast of light that filled the room with a deep orange glow. He chose to light his pipe first before looking into the eyes of his cellmates, so he pursed on it for a bit, filling the air with a strong scent of vanilla.

"Ahhh! That's much better," he said, taking a moment to enjoy the smoke that soon began to irritate his cellmates.

One of them coughed and gagged and then spoke. "It's a disgusting habit."

The Jackboot used the remainder of his light from the match to spot the others that fell to the floor, and he quickly scooped them up into his hand, lit another, and then held it out into the center of the room. Staring back at him were two terrifyingly monstrous beasts. The light from his match pushed shadows across their faces like black clouds passing over mountaintops.

"I do believe his nose is broken, Hex," a massive tunnel troll said, leaning in close to his face. The Jackboot instantly jerked back and scooted into the corner of the room, dropping the match on the floor and instantly snuffing out its light.

"I believe you are correct, Grundorph," the other said.

The Jackboot quickly lit another match with the embers from his pipe and held it up again only to his left this time. There before him stood the biggest bird-man he'd ever seen, boasting six massive wings covered in tunnel grime. "Great! That's all I need right now, another bird-man," he said, moving the match back toward the giant kilt-wearing troll and then back toward the Petinon and figuring, since they hadn't killed him yet, they might not be the killing kind. So, he relaxed back against the wall and spoke. "Who are you two worthless slags, and what the devil is this place?" he asked with a puff of gray smoke rolling out his mouth.

"This is the place beneath hell, and we are the forgotten ones of our people," the large Petinon said.

"My friend Hex can be a bit dramatic, but I could imagine this a sort of hell myself, if it weren't for the fact that I grew up several levels above us," Grundorph said.

"Ah, so we're below the Labyrinth then," the Jackboot said, pursing hard on his pipe as he held the burning match until it reached his fingertips and suddenly faded out on his thumb nail. Silence filled the darkness for a moment followed by some tearing of cloth, then another whooshing blast of fire lit the small piece of cloth and filled darkness with hope again.

"Yes, this is the place where Mogdal the Magnificent keeps his bait for the games in the Arena of Heroes," Grundorph explained. His head was very large and had a square metal plate bolted into the top of it as if someone had made a poor effort to repair a crushed skull. If he'd wanted to, he could have swallowed the Jackboot in one single bite. Hex was not quite as big as the tunnel troll, but the thought had never entered the Jackboot's mind that a Petinon could grow so large or have six wings.

"So... how long have the both of you been down here?" the Jackboot asked sarcastically as he looked down the end of his pipe, studying their faces.

"Well, Hexpteroox... I call him Hex for short, but Hex has been down here," Grundorph looked over towards his cellmate for confirmation. "What would you say, Hex, maybe two?"

"Yes, at least two," Hex agreed.

"Yes, there it is, at least two years," Grundorph said.

The Jackboot's pipe nearly fell out of his mouth and into a slimy puddle between his legs, but he quickly caught it. "TWO YEARS!"

"Oh, that's a mere pittance compared to Grundorph. He's been here since the fall of Angus Grand," Hex explained. "That's just a tick over five years, wouldn't you say, Grundorph?"

"Indeed, at least five, but I prefer to count my days by the number of droplets hitting me in the face whilst I try to sleep and measure my successes one peaceful moment of darkness at a time. At least we do get to go topside once a week for a good beating." Dirt crumbed to the cell floor as Grundorph and Hex burst into a shared laughter at their own miserable circumstances, and the Jackboot got to his feet.

"You two have a sick sense of humor. I like you already." The Jackboot pointed at them with his pipe. "Now, how do we get out of here?"

"But for the dead, there is no way out," Hex answered.

"The only chance anyone would ever have in escaping here would be when they bring us topside for battle, but you would first have to defeat a Standing Hero. And then, after that, you would be forced to battle a Legendary Hero. No one has ever defeated a Legendary Hero...at least since we've been down here," Grundorph explained. "By the way, how good are you in a fight?"

"I can hold my own well enough. Tell me something, troll, just what did you do to get put in this place? Aren't you one of the labyrinth people?" the Jackboot asked. "You must have been a bad boy or done something really nasty to your own kind for them to drop you in this rat hole."

"It is true that I am a labyrinth troll, but when Mogdal became the ruler of the labyrinth, he set out to ruin, kill, or imprison any remaining member of Angus Grand's family."

Grundorph moved his head in closer toward the Jackboot's face. "Yes, I am one of the many sons of Ogg the Murderous, and half-brother to Angus Grand, and you're the madman they call the Jackboot, aren't you? You also have done many bad things and probably deserve to be down here more than the both of us."

The Jackboot backed away from the troll, whose hands were large enough to crush him with a single grasp, and stated, "I was betrayed by a friend." Removing his pipe, he blew the smoke into Grundorph's face. "I guess this means you'll be wanting revenge for what I did to your brother?"

The tunnel troll burst into a coughing laughter at the pipe smoke, and Hex followed after him. "Oh, dear me, certainly not. I never liked my half-breed brother. He was a liar and a cheat."

"That's certainly true," the Jackboot agreed and looked over to Hex. "What about you? How did you end up down here?" he asked.

"I left my people's mountain with several of my fellow Petinons and our great prince, on a wonderful quest for the future of our people, but I was...not worthy," he bowed his head then finished. "...not worthy of the task and was quickly captured by the labyrinth people and placed here for sport. If not for my good friend Grundorph, I would most certainly be dead by now," Hex explained.

Grundorph leaned in close to the Jackboot's ear and whispered. "Too gullible. Very nice person, but much too gullible for this hard world."

"Well, I guess you know who I am, then," the Jackboot said proudly.

To that, Hex responded, "No. Actually, I don't. I mean, I've heard of the man with the iron boots but not much more than what Grundorph has told me. What can you tell us of the outside world? Is the creeping mold still everywhere? Have you heard of the Whispering Prince? Is the world soaring with

Petinons?" Hex unloaded his flurry of questions with passionate excitement.

"He thinks his people are going to rule the world someday," Grundorph said, smiling at the Jackboot as he snugged down one of the bolts on his thick skull-plate.

"Hold up a bit, Hex. You just asked a mouthful, and honestly, I'm feeling a bit whipped here." The Jackboot adjusted his nose with a grimace and leaned back on the slimy wall of coal surrounding them. "I'm just going to catch a little bit of shut eye and then...and then maybe we can run through all those questions again...alright then, goodnight." The Jackboot's pipe drooped from the side of his mouth as he closed his eyes and folded his arms together. Ignoring the two monsters standing over him, he quickly fell asleep against the hard wall of black coal.

THE PEACEFUL QUIET OF DARKNESS WAS SUDDENLY BROKEN BY THE sounds of shrieking and howling from somewhere deep in the prison caves. The Jackboot quickly got to his feet and lit one of his matches. Hex and Grundorph were standing at the end of their cage, looking out into the darkness as if they were waiting for something important to happen. The Jackboot noticed Grundorph's hand was gripped into a fist as if he was preparing for a fight. The giant troll turned back and looked at him. "Better get on my back, little man. Things move quickly down here," Grundorph said.

"I'm not climbing on your gnarled, hairy back, you freak," the Jackboot snapped out.

"You're the smallest thing we've ever seen in here. You best take Grundorph's offer, or you might be trampled when the cell doors open," Hex warned.

"What do you mean, trampled?"

"When the doors open and the torches light up, everyone must run towards the ramp at the end of the hall, or they will be trampled to death by the beasts that come up after us." The troll looked back at him with a steely eyed gaze. "They are big enough to trample even me, Mr. Iron-boots," he sarcastically mocked.

The Jackboot took a moment and thought about it. "Alright, you talked me into it," he said, adjusting his eyepatch and straightening the lapels on his long coat. He stuffed his pipe and matches back into his boot and said. "These boots might hurt your back so bear with me." The Jackboot climbed on top of the massive troll's back and gripped his long neck hair tight around his hands.

"Ouch! Those boots do hurt. What are they made of?" Grundorph asked, wincing.

"It's a special metal. They make me strong," the Jackboot said with a nefarious grin.

Suddenly torch lights ignited into a burst of orange as if someone had opened a grave toward the sunlight. Light quickly filled the wide hallway in the center of a row of cells. The Jackboot instantly noticed Hex's claws were touching his boots when the torches brightened to a full glow. Hex started to speak, but the cell doors clacked and jerked open with great force. Before he knew what was happening, Hex and Grundorph had run out into the wide hallway, which quickly filled with all manner of strange beasts. Tunnel trolls with chains and irons on their necks as well as giant dogs and wild boars with twelve tusks running down both sides of their massive snouts. He held tight to Grundorph as the troll ran hard toward the ramp at the end of the hall. They were almost knocked over by another troll that was much bigger than Grundorph, but Hex caught Grundorph's arm and kept him steady as they ran.

Once they reached the top of the ramp, the light blinded the comfort of darkness away from their weary eyes, and even Hex had difficulty adjusting to the abrupt change. The massive Arena of Heroes was a quarter mile from one end to the other, and both man and beast poured out into it from seven other doors surrounding the room. The roar of the crowd was deafening, and the screams of horror from those inside the arena sent chills down the Jackboot's neck as he climbed higher up on Grundorph's hulking shoulders. The Jackboot watched the madness of the arena take full effect as he gazed out over the blood thirsty crowd. *Should be interesting.* He looked down at Hex, who was trying hard to find a good spot to position himself, and that's when he noticed the iron clasp around his leg. The clasp was hooked with a chain running over to an iron clasp that was hooked to Grundorph's leg. He wondered if their friendship was genuine or simply of mutual benefit and asked, "SO WHAT'S THE GOAL OF THIS GAME?"

"STAY ALIVE UNTIL THE LAST HORN BLOWS!" Grundorph yelled out.

Hex looked up at him with a sense of compassion in his eyes and affirmed Grundorph's thoughts more directly. "YES! STAY ALIVE!" Hex said, looking back down at his iron boots.

"HOW MANY HORNS ARE THERE?" the Jackboot asked.

"NINE! NINE BLASTS OF THE HORN!" Grundorph hollered out.

"OH, THAT SHOULDN'T BE TOO BAD," he said as several other poor souls stared resentfully up at him, perched safely atop his massive tunnel troll.

Soon the giant wild boars began running in a circle around the edges of the arena until the circle grew smaller and tighter. This was Mogdal's way of weeding out the small and weak creatures from last week's games. Most humans were instantly crushed and left as lumpy mounds on the arena floor until they were finally pounded into the dirt by giant troll feet. The uneven floor soon became a death trap of blood and bone. Hex was somewhat able to stay above the fray, to the extent the chain anchored to Grundorph's leg allowed him to, and he could get a much better view fluttering a few feet higher than Grundorph's head.

"WE'RE CLOSE NOW!" Hex cried out. "HE'S PICKED UP THE HORN! GET READY!"

The wild boars skewered everything in their path, including a tunnel troll on the far side of the arena. White foam rushed from the corners of the boar's mouths, and with grunting, snorting and squealing they squeezed the center in tighter. The sounds of bone crunching and snapping filled their ears as the three new companions worked hard to stay above the fray, above the madness; above the death. Soon the first horn blew from a great balcony overlooking the arena. The Jackboot looked up to see the biggest tunnel troll he'd ever seen standing there holding a giant horn. Everyone stopped. Even the wild boars stopped running in circles. All except one. It seemed to have someone stuck on one of its twelve horns, and it was trying to get them off. Mogdal was very disappointed in the beast and reached out an open hand to one of his attendants standing next to him. They placed a long spear in the palm of his hand, and he flung it deep into the boar's head, killing it instantly. The crowd erupted with cheers as Mogdal raised both his thick troll arms into the air as if he'd just won the games himself. However, Mogdal had no need to prove himself to anyone, because he was considered the greatest Legendary Hero the arena had ever produced.

Mogdal blew the horn again, and when the doors opened, giant black wolves rushed into the arena. One by one, they began picking off the weak and the broken as well as dragging off the dead. Mogdal blew the horn again, and the wolves rushed back out of the arena. Now, only a third of the original number remained, and moments later attendants started throwing weapons at the edges of the arena. Hex tried to grab one, but he couldn't get close enough and soon the three companions were the only ones left in the arena without weapons to defend themselves. Grundorph and Hex stayed back to back, circling around as best they could to keep their guard up and protect against the chaotic whirlwind of battle, they were now engulfed in.

"If we make it through this round alive, we'll get to go back to our cells," Hex explained quietly, not wanting to anger Mogdal.

"What? That's it?" the Jackboot complained.

Hex looked up at him in shock. "We don't want to win. We only need to survive. If we win, we have to stay out here longer, and we might be forced to fight a Standing Hero. No one ever beats those guys."

Mogdal blew his giant curved horn again, and suddenly the arena turned into a blood bath for survival. Monstrous beasts devoured one another as freakish, genetically altered men sliced and speared anything that moved, and soon even the wild boars began running for their lives. A tunnel troll cast a large stone into the air at Hex. He swooped down and for the most part it missed him, but it clipped the top of one of his wings, knocking him down onto the bloody floor of the arena. Grundorph tried to help him up, but their chain had become wrapped around two of his wings, and Hex fluttered desperately to regain his footing on the slippery, red, death-saturated ground.

Helplessly, Hex looked up at them both while beasts trampled all around him, and a giant wild boar worked its way to through the slaughter toward him. Suddenly, Hex reached up his claw toward the Jackboot and cried out, "SAVE ME!"

For the first time in many years, the Jackboot felt helplessly worthless. His mind rushed back to that night when Angus Grand took his feet from him and how death seemed emanate for him and his dear Isabella. In this room of death, where the only rule was to survive, he knew the only things that truly mattered now were his new companions. Why they'd chosen to show him pity and help him stay alive this long was a mystery to him, but whatever happened now, the Jackboot knew he couldn't let Hex die on that floor. Staring into the face of his fellow prisoner, he resolved himself to battle. The Jackboot climbed up on top of the metal plate on Grundorph's head, flicked the switch on his magnetic boots, and launched himself into the air.

The light glistened and sparkled off his boots as he shot up into the sky above the horror of the arena. It did not go unnoticed by Mogdal or the crowd, and as he reached his peak height the Jackboot spotted Mogdal's open hand reaching for a spear. By the time Mogdal had released his weapon at the Jackboot, it was too late. The Jackboot had begun his decent back toward the bloody slaughter below, back toward the wild beast heading for straight for Hex. Mogdal's spear missed him by several feet and soared to the other side of the arena where it struck a cheering spectator in the chest. The Jackboot came down hard on the wild beast's horned snout, snapping one of its thick tusks completely off and breaking the boar's snout with a loud crack. The beast fell face first into the bloody mess and on top of the Jackboot, burying him into the bloody ground. Pain rushed through his body as darkness closed around the Jackboot's eyes.

GRUNDORPH QUICKLY PULLED THE BROKEN JACKBOOT OUT FROM underneath the beast and slung his body over his left shoulder. Then he crushed the side of the boar's head with his meaty foot. He untangled Hex and picked up the broken boar tusk from the slop beneath his feet then, in a maddening fury of tunnel troll chaos, Grundorph commenced to punishing everything around him with it. He roared and growled at anything that came near them. With the slobbering fury of a rabid dog, the troll stabbed and struck beast, man and troll until the crowd moved away from him and his friends. Mogdal stood to his feet and held out his hand. Grundorph roared back at him in defiance, but instead of a spear, Mogdal's attendant placed the horn in his hand, and with a deep long blast from the horn, Mogdal ended the games early.

Not a single beast, man, troll or genetically altered freak followed Grundorph as he carried his two companions back to their cell in the ground beneath the arena. The fierce tunnel troll had awakened within himself, the terrible spirit of his father that day, and not a single being wanted to die as those he left on the floor of the arena. He knew what was coming next, and he tried to block it from his mind as best he could, but those words burned deep. The legacy his father had left him with was forever etched into his childhood. Echoing in his memory, Grundorph could hear his father, Ogg, say the words over and over again, *"Four-time Standing Hero, my son. One of only four Legendary Heroes."* He took a deep breath as he placed Hex on the floor of their cave-prison and then pulled the broken Jackboot from off his shoulder. He placed the Jackboot down as gently as a tunnel troll possibly can, and the man let out a horrible groan of pain. Grundorph studied the man for a moment and asked in wonder of the Jackboot, "Never before in my life have I ever heard of, nor seen with my eyes, a man do what you did today. So, tell me, what kind of man are you?"

"I-I don't knooow," the shattered man gargled out his answer in blood.

Hex sat up next to the Jackboot, shaken and battered, but for the most part unhurt. Grundorph watched as Hex used his claws to peal the matted clothes from the Jackboot's back. Once the Jackboot's shirt was off, Hex wiped away the blood with his wings then looked up at Grundorph. "He is no man. He is a Petinon."

8

HEART BREAKERS

*K*ing Arkone's temper took nearly three days to calm, but once he gained control of it, he called the queen back to the throne room. A grand apology was offered, and he lavished many gifts upon her as she stood statuesque before a full royal court that lined the path, left and right, all the way to the king's throne. She wore a solid black gown with no gold or silver, and upon her head she wore a crown of mourning, made from a pine branch and adorned with tiny cones. A dried, bristled rope tied around her waist was wrapped in fire berry flowers. Although she knew the whole of the court would accuse her of being overly dramatic in her efforts to entice the king, she had finally decided that now was the time for action. Now was the time for change.

Petinon's of the highest status were in attendance and many wore gold and silver crowns that looked like twisted rope on their heads. Their wings shone in the light of the sun, and their clothes, few that there were, were of the finest gray silk with strands of gold woven intricately into the fabric. Elehos' kept her composure and made no effort to accept the king's apology so he continued bringing gift after gift into the throne room until finally the bewildered king stepped down from his throne and approached her. Quietly, King Arkone leaned in to her ear, in an effort to hide his embarrassment, and asked what it would take for her to forgive him. Queen Elehos stilled her resolve then answered him openly and for all to hear. "I will accept nothing less than a royal burial...with full honors for my son— our son."

The king was taken aback by her request. "What do you mean?" he quietly asked. Though everyone in the hall had heard the queen's request, he still made an effort to speak softly.

Her eyes welled up with tears as she again explained loudly for all to hear. "The wingless boy and his friends...that's why they came to our mountain. They have brought to us the body of our son, Prince Enupnion."

King Arkone was devastated—visibly shaken—and caught himself with her arms to keep steady. Though his son had been a disappointment to him, Enupnion was still the little child he'd raised and loved. Before the prince had left, the king had stripped his son of all the rights to the throne or any royal benefits because of Enupnion's foolish efforts to force the prophecies of their people and the shame it had brought to his legacy. What the queen was now asking was not a simple request. It would be easier for him to give her all the gold in the kingdom than to reinstate their son's position and have his name written back into the chronicles of their people. The king began to tremble as he stared into her eyes. When the prince did not return, many people in the kingdom naturally assumed he was dead, including the king. But now, gazing into her eyes, the truth was evident. Somewhere, on this mountain, their son's body was waiting for burial. King Arkone stepped back from her and continued to tremble until he could stand no more. The king collapsed to his knees, and in front of the queen and a full royal court, his heart broke. The mountain trembled and shook and King Arkone sobbed uncontrollably.

"My son, the prince...is dead." There were only a few small gasps by those in the great hall and so she continued. "The wingless Petinon, Elias, whom some of you have called Ouranos, has returned his body to our great mountain, and with it, the story of his death." Still her news was met with dry emotion. "It is a story of how our great prince, my beloved son, fought the Great Alchemist and saved their city." Again, there was no stirring of their hearts or emotions for the young prince. He had been dead to them for years, and many were indifferent to it. Queen Elehos knew what Elias had told her about Sunago and her son's heart—that it now beat strong in Elias' chest—but she feared they would all turn on him and his crew if she told the truth. So she lied. Before the king, the Convocation of Elders, and a full royal court, she lied to them all, and she enjoyed every moment of it. "A story of how my wonderful son struck down the terrible Alchemist over top of Grand Fortune City," still no response from the people. "Prince of our people and heir to the king's throne. Prince Enupnion, slayer of the evil Alchemist. But you and I know this Great Alchemist by his true name...by his Petinon name." Now, they were listening. Now, she had the full attention of the royal court. "You and I know him as...Sunago the Great!"

Suddenly, the court was thrown into chaos. The king staggered to his feet in horror at her words. As the noise of the hall grew loud, the queen spoke louder. "YES! YES, IT'S TRUE. MY SON, PRINCE ENUPNION, HAS STRUCK DOWN THE WINGLESS SUNAGO THE GREAT!" And with that, the great hall fell silent. Dead silent. The wings of the royal court drooped down, and many faces became like stone as they gawked mindlessly at Queen Elehos, waiting for more devastating news.

99

"M-My…queen, did you say…wingless…Sunago?" the heart broken king asked as his countenance wilted even more.

"I did. According to Elias and his crew, Sunago had his wings removed and embraced the dark magic of the creeping mold. The dark magic our ancients fought so many years and gave so many lives to end has been revived. Elias and his crew also informed me that Sunago had taken a witch as his wife, and they ruled a cult of black mist speakers together." Queen Elehos stood strong as she explained, but many couldn't believe it.

"LIES!" one royal cried aloud. "WE ALL KNOW HOW SHE LIES."

"If I am lying, the king may strike me down now, because darkness lies. But if I speak the truth, and *truth matters*, then you will be the ones who have embraced the darkness," Queen Elehos warned them with a hardened look of confidence. But her wisdom was concrete, and no one dared to question her powerful words.

It was then that a wise old elder of the Convocation stepped forward and spoke. "May the king grant Queen Elehos' request for the burial of her son just as she has asked. In the meantime, oh great king, much has happened in the last few days, and much must be pondered. Let the Convocation grant the king and queen seven days of mourning, and during this time we will review all of the events that have taken place. At the end of the king's mourning, we shall give our report in full to the king, his queen and the entire royal court." The wise old elder stepped back into the row of elders and lowered his head.

The king stared at the floor of his throne room for several moments then replied with a trembling voice, "Agreed." King Arkone took the hand of the queen, and they walked out of the great hall together.

SILENCE FELL OVER THE KINGDOM OF PTERUGAS FOR SEVEN FULL days and on the seventh day Prince Enupnion was given a royal burial with the full honors of a Petinon prince, just as the queen had requested. With the exception of a few necessary functions, most of the great city remained quiet for several days after the funeral and even the mountain remained silent. For the crew of the Whisper, it felt as if they had lost their friend all over again, and Elias became so sick to his stomach he couldn't eat for three days. The day of the funeral he'd become so distraught over watching the prince being lowered into the ground that he lay in bed unable to move or speak. His mind was filled with morbid thoughts of his black heart, buried in the cold ground next to his friend. Finally, Epekneia had had enough of it and devised a plan with the crew to get him out of his depression. She hoped some food and the sights of the city would help him break free from the darkness in his mind and show him the joy and happiness Prince Enupnion would have wanted for him.

It was about dusk when the whole crew snuck into his room, and though rain was sprinkling the earth outside, it was warm and gentle enough to still be enjoyable. Bogan and Gideon grabbed him under the arms, lifted him out of bed, and then the whole crew quickly carried him through the great halls, running and giggling all the way. Once they were out of the castle, Merlin and Izzy grabbed his legs, and suddenly he was lying face up, toward the clouds, with the soft rain hitting his eyes. The warm, wet drizzle covered his bare chest and face as he looked up into the misty sky, and Elias got the impression they were trying to recreate the night they'd kidnapped him. A methodical pitter patter of rain dripping from the pines onto the cobble stone path was therapeutic for his broken heart, and he almost asked his friends to lay him down and leave him under the pines forever.

The moon fought its way through the gray vapor clouds that seemed to create a soft, teal hue about its surprised face, and soon the sounds of the city began to fill his ears. As they ran harder, the city closed in faster, and it became quite clear to Elias that the Petinons weren't letting the wet night hinder the joy of their evening. He could hear drums and flutes as well as singing as they came to a spot on the path that crested over top of the city lights. Elias could see torch lights roaring their bright orange flames in the distance. The smell of cooked fish and fresh meat filled the air, and the strange laughter of the Petinon people brought a smile to his face.

"Put me down. I'm okay. Please. Please, put me down," Elias asked his friends who were now soaking wet and laughing themselves silly with joy. They stood Elias to his feet, and Bogan spun him around in a dizzying circle until Epekneia stopped him with his face looking directly down at the city below. His eyes instantly caught sight of the wonder at the bottom of the path. The Whisper crew stood out over the city waiting for his response, and suddenly he started laughing. In wonder at his joy, they soon joined in until he took off running down the path. The stunned Whisper crew stared at each other momentarily, and then quickly ran after him. Elias picked up so much speed on the downhill that he lost his footing and fell headfirst, nearly smacking his face on the stone path, but Epekneia swooped in from behind and caught him. She spiraled into the sky over the city then landed at the bottom of the path. Moments later, the soaking wet crew finally caught up with them, and once they'd regained their breath, Epekneia spoke.

"So...you want to run, huh?" She smiled at him and took off through the damp streets of Pterugas like a playful child. Elias and the crew took out after her, all the while laughing away the rain and the heartbreak of their souls.

Epekneia knew the city streets well and weaved her way through the crowd so quickly Elias almost lost track of her. If not for the uniqueness of her bright red wings, he probably would have, but she was different than the other Petinons, in personality and appearance. Her burned face was a sign of shame to her people, but for Elias, she was beautifully and wonderfully unique. Now, more than ever before, as they ran through the misty streets, he felt connected to her. She belonged here, and he was beginning to feel as if he did too. Her wings folded and flipped as she darted around others, almost like she was leading him somewhere secret. Elias weaved through so many wings he thought he'd eaten a pound of feathers by the time he caught up and took hold of her.

"Hey! Would you slow down for just a second?" Elias begged.

"WHAT?" she asked, barely out of breath. "You said you wanted to run." her smile stole the last of his breath.

Elias smiled back. "True, but we've lost the others, and we can't leave them alone. They always manage to get into trouble without me." He smiled at his own lie, and she cocked her head slightly. "Okay, okay. Maybe it's the other way around, but we still can't leave them. Besides, I'm starving."

"You should be. You haven't eaten in days. Come on, I know just the place. The Whispers will love this place."

"The what?" he asked with a smirk.

"The Whispers. You know, the crew." She said it as if he was somehow privy to the nickname she had given them. "Sorry. That's what I call them. They're the Whisper crew, so I just call them the Whispers."

"Oh, okay. I guess that works for me." Elias grinned and took her by her clawed hand then turned back into the crowds. He could tell by the look on her face that she was filled with a strange pride as the crowded Petinon city gawked awkwardly at a wingless boy and shamed Petinon girl walking hand in claw through the streets. She was beaming and radiant, even in the rain, and her wings glistened from the torch lights of the city. Suddenly she took off running again, pulling him through the crowded streets, through wings, through rain; through heart-break and pain, until they came to a great circle in the center of the city. "There're Gideon and Izzy!" Elias yelled out and they switched roles as he pulled Epekneia through the crowd and over toward his friends.

The inner circle of the city was called the Old City. Its buildings were strangely shaped and made of cedar. The buildings weren't very tall, and they leaned to the left and then to the right in an awkwardly crooked fashion. Petinon people were gathered there, singing songs and dancing strange dances with a swirling and flapping of their wings. Others were eating and watching the dancing. Every now and again, a Petinon put down their food or drink and jumped right in with the others. It was also very common for a Petinon to suddenly drop in from the cloudy sky and land right next to them. One of them even knocked Gideon to the ground and never once apologized for his offense. He then had the nerve to lean down and poke Gideon's right mod-eye, but the blast of steam from his relief valve spooked the young Petinon away. It also happened that sometimes a Petinon might be standing at a street vendor purchasing food, and then suddenly, after the purchase was complete, it would leap into the air and with a powerful burst of their wings, disappearing into darkness of the night sky. Pterugas was a wonder to them all.

Izzy spoke over the sounds of music and dancing. "What happened to you two?"

"I guess we just got caught up in the joy of the city," Epekneia said with a twinkle in her eye.

"Well, can we eat some of this joy, or what?" Merlin asked, rubbing his tummy.

"YES!" Epekneia yelled out with a smile then leapt into the air. She landed next to a fish shack on the edge of the square then whispered something to the person at the counter in their strange tongue, and the Petinon gave a nod. "Take whatever you want, guests of the king."

Elias and the crew smiled and laughed as they grabbed all

sorts of fish from the counter. Fresh salmon, tuna and even roasted eel, and suddenly the crew was so happy they were ready to dance. Elias took his time and savored each bite carefully as he watched his friends run out into the pouring rain, dancing crazy like a Petinon. He and Epekneia laughed as many Petinons moved away from the weird humans with mods, but after a short time they became accustomed to their freakish nature and decided the night was to glorious to waste on bigotry.

As Elias stood next to Epekneia, watching their friends dancing on the misty mountain; his heart was filled with curiosity at the possibilities of their future. The burden of his past lifted, and his spirit soared like a bird in flight. Joy, happiness, and contentment were more possible to him now than ever before, and hope seemed real and plausible, not illusionary as he'd once believed. Epekneia handed him some kind of creamy, soft, red-colored treat, and with a single bite, his eyes suddenly lit up with flames.

"It has fire berry seeds in it." She smiled and grabbed him by the hand, pulling him through the crowd of dancers and next to his friends. The music was so infectious that even Ava released the burden of her thoughts of Charlie for the moment and let the rain and dancing wash her own heartache away.

Soon the rain began to pour heavier and stronger than before, and most of the Petinons sought cover in the shops and under trees, but Elias and his friends continued to dance in the downpour. The long scar on Elias' chest turned bright red from the fire berry treat Epekneia had given him, and it didn't take long before many of the Petinons took notice. His eyes were red hot, and the scar shown bright through the heavy rain. For a time, they ignored the looks and kept dancing without music until Merlin took Izzy by the arm and pointed at the crowd of onlookers. Everyone stopped dancing except Elias and Epekneia, who seemed to be in a world of their own as they laughed and danced away their troubles. Then Gideon stopped them both.

Rain rushed across the red-hot scar, lifting steam from it as Elias gazed into all the eyes staring at him, and from the looks in their eyes, they didn't seem very sure of his prophetic title any longer. In a powerful display of theatrics, a massive Petinon descended from the pouring sky and onto the city circle in front of him. His wings were enormous and strong and pushed the rain like buckets back into Elias' face. Once he landed, he lifted his wings over his head for a covering, and in an instant his eyes were free from the rain. The name on his helmet was Thumacheo, and he stared at Elias and the Whisper crew, unmovable and with great distain, then slowly beat his wings, rising back into the sky, into the rain, and toward the castle. The rain stung their faces with every drop as it rushed down hard on the crew of the Whisper for several minutes. Soon, the crowd of Petinons quietly disappeared into the darkness of the downpour, and the disheartened crew hung their heads. They had no plan for this or even a thought of how to explain it to the king, and all they could do now was hope with all hope that the queen would come through for them again. When the rain stopped, they slowly made their way back toward the castle, all the while expecting the king's guard to arrive and arrest them. But no one came. The guardian at the gate paused for a moment and took notice of Elias' red scar, then let them back in, each one to their room, unchallenged.

IZZY SAT ON AVA'S BED, HOLDING HER FRIEND AS SHE CRIED herself to sleep. She placed Ava's head gently back on her pillow and stepped over toward the window. Strange visions had struggled to enter her mind all night long, but she had resisted eating fire berries for the sole purpose of preventing confusion about who the chosen one truly was. Foolish prophecies had no place in her world of iron and smoke. She cared only for her brother's safety and that of her ship and crew. She stood at the window of her room, looking out over the misty mountain tops. She closed her eyes and tried to concentrate on what she felt, but nothing came to her. Reaching into her pocket, she pulled out the three fire berries Flit had brought to her, checked to make sure Ava was fast asleep, then placed them into her mouth and waited.

It had been awhile since she had eaten them, and for a moment she thought maybe they wouldn't work on her anymore, but after a short time she began to feel the heat in her blood. She turned around and sat down under the windowsill, took a deep breath, and readied herself for some kind of vision having to do with Elias. The vision was powerful and painful, and she began to shake as it took hold of her. Much to her surprise, her mind was transported back to Grand Fortune City. The city was overrun with tunnel rats, and her father was lying in a pool of blood under Isabella's Light. His boots were gone, and another man was wearing them. He stood in the shadows watching the tunnel rats devour her father's body, but every time she tried to see his face a cloud of black mist covered it from her sight. When the vision ended, she sat under the light of the cold, white moon trying to process what she had seen. The wind rushing into the room felt good on her warm skin, but when she noticed Ava was about to wake up from the cool air, she stood up to close the window, only to pause when she felt the mountain rumble.

Soon after, she noticed the large Petinon warrior, Thumacheo, flying away from the castle and back toward the city. Her thoughts traveled back to the throne room when the king spoke, and she remembered how the mountain rumbled every time he was angry. She considered her vision and the possibility something terrible was now taking place at GFC.

Even if it wasn't exactly like what she had seen, she'd had enough visions to know they were not completely literal in their interpretations. Either way, whatever was happening couldn't be good. She decided it was time to wake the crew and leave under the cover of darkness while they still had the chance. Isabella knew Ava would be the least likely to want to leave and might even put up a fight since she had no resolution to what had happened to Charlie, so Izzy pondered her options for moment. *Wake Merlin and Jimmy first... send them for the Whisper. Then wake Elias so he can get Epekneia, then I'll get Gideon and Bogan and we'll come back for Ava. We'll bind and gag her, if necessary, to keep her quiet.* Her eyes were burning hot with fire as she climbed out the castle window and across the edge to other rooms. She climbed into Merlin and Jimmy's room and found Merlin in the darkness.

"Hey," she whispered and shook Merlin. "Merlin, get up," but he didn't respond. She called his name several times and even tried his real name. He hated it, but she thought it would help. "Victor! Victor, get up!" she said louder.

Then a voice from behind her spoke. "Isabella! Over here."

She quickly turned around, and through the darkness she spotted Merlin and Jimmy hiding in the corner of the room. "What are you doing over there?" she asked as she approached them.

"We didn't trust the Petinons. We thought they might try to kill us in our sleep, so we've been sleeping in the corner every night. Isabella, y-your eyes, I thought..." But Izzy cut him off.

"I'll explain later. Good thinking on your decision to hide at night. I've barely slept in weeks myself."

"Merlin is the marvelous brain boy, Isabella." Jimmy offered his opinion from deep within his calculated memory banks.

"Yes, he is, Jimmy. He sure is." She smiled and helped Merlin to his feet, swallowing him up in a big hug. "Get the Whisper and park it outside Ava's window. I'm going to get Elias, Bogan and Gideon, but I'm afraid Ava might not want to go. She's been crying herself to sleep every night over Charlie. I don't think she will be able to handle leaving like this. At least not without the answers she wanted, but I'm afraid if we stay here any longer, we might end up dead."

"I agree! Me and Jimmy have been ready to leave since the first day we got here, but what about Elias? I'm not sure he'll want to go either. Did you see the look on his face tonight? He loves this place, and you know who else, too," Merlin said, referring to the obvious display of affection between Elias and Epekneia. Not that anyone was surprised by their growing relationship, but Merlin was more concerned with their situational awareness in a city with such a hostile view toward humans.

"Yes, I know it, but I think she knows how they are. I get the feeling she's ready to get out of here as much as we are. Stick to the plan and meet me in Ava's room."

"Okay, okay. Come on, Jimmy. Let's get the Whisper and get out of this place," Merlin said.

"I am ready, Merlin." Jimmy said with a blank stare. The brothers went to the window, and Jimmy went out first then dropped a looped cable from his metal back. Merlin reached out, took hold of it, placed his foot in the loop, and with a blast of smoke from Jimmy's turbine, the brothers disappeared into the night sky.

Isabella made her way out the window and climbed back over to the other side of her room where Elias was staying. The window to his room was open, just as she had expected it would be, but she wondered if Elias was sleeping or hiding like Merlin and Jimmy. She climbed in and right away noticed the light from the moon shining down on his scared chest. Though the strength of the fire berries was fading, the scar on his chest was still glowing softly in the darkness. She stood over his bed for a moment to consider her words and how she would explain her plan to him. *Best just get it over with and deal with his anger later. Maybe he won't be mad anyway.* She'd just reached down toward his shoulder to shake him when the door to his room slowly creaked open. She quickly dove back into the darkness of the room and placed her hands over her eyes to hide the fire glow. She couldn't tell who it was, but they had something in their hand, and they were walking over toward Elias.

KING ARKONE STOOD OUT ON THE BALCONY OF HIS BEDROOM AS the pouring rain drenched his royal wings. Though his days of mourning were over, the king had been unable to put the death of his son behind him. He wanted to punish himself for his treatment of Prince Enupnion during their final days together, but he could think of no equivalent pain harsh enough to bring about a satisfactory state of self-forgiveness. He sulked in the pouring rain until he spotted a Petinon in midflight, fighting the heavy rain as it drew closer and closer to his balcony. The king burned with anger at this Petinon's bold act of lawlessness, as it was forbidden for any Petinon to approach the king unannounced, or by one's own choosing, and especially not in the privacy of his own bedroom. Not even the queen was allowed to enter his bedroom without his express permission. The king stepped inside the room, pulled a spear from the wall, then stepped back out onto his balcony. He raised it and prepared to strike but held his hand when the Petinon fought the rain harder and harder. As the Petinon drew closer, the king lifted his spear and sent it directly at the lawbreaker. The Petinon dove and spiraled toward the ground then swooped back up toward the balcony with the spear in his hand, and within moments the Petinon dropped down onto the king's balcony. The king was furious as the Petinon stood in front of him holding the spear in his hand. The heavy rain hid the warrior's face momentarily but suddenly it let up and the king recognized him.

"THUMACHEO! WHAT IS THE MEANING OF THIS?" the king roared.

Thumacheo raised the spear and dropped to his knees in front of the king. He held it over his head and flared his wings, covering the floor and the king's feet, then he spoke. "Oh, great king, ruler of the greatest Petinon kingdom to have ever been and ever will be. Ruler of the great city of Pterugas and Lord Commander of the Convocation of Elders, if you must strike me dead for this offense then do as you please, but first let me speak to you of the imposter our people call Ouranos."

The king was intrigued by Thumacheo's willingness to die if only to get a message to him, and so he allowed his finest warrior to speak. "We will speak of your offense another day, great warrior, now, what is this message you have for me about the one called Ouranos?"

"He is not one of us, my lord. He is not Petinon," Thumacheo said with his face toward the floor.

"Stand up great warrior and tell me again so I can hear you more clearly," the king commanded, and Thumacheo rose to his feet and explained.

"My king, the boy is human. It is with great sadness and regret that I bring this message to you, my lord. But I believe the humans have murdered the king's son. I believe they have stolen the heart of our young prince and put it into the boy to trick us." He held his head down as he stood.

"How do you know this, Thumacheo?"

"I've seen the boy's chest for myself. A large scar traveling down the center, glowing bright red with a circular imprint around it much like the other boy that came to us years ago."

The king was enraged and felt the burning of the mountain deep inside his blood, but he calmed himself and spoke carefully. "Great warrior, you have done your king a most loyal service, and you shall not be punished for your act of approaching unannounced. Tell me, great warrior, what should we do with this usurper named Elias and his metal monsters?"

"My lord and king, I will do whatever you command, but it is a terrible offense for our great prince to be buried without his heart. Give the word now, my king, and I will go and remove it from his chest and return it to your son... for that is where it belongs." Thumacheo stood confident as he waited for the king to give the order.

"No! If this must be done, then let it be done by my own hand so that I might one day be able to forgive myself for my past offenses against my son," King Arkone protested. The two spoke for a short time, and then King Arkone sent Thumacheo away and made his way through the castle toward Elias' bedroom.

He passed several guards on the way and relieved them of their posts for the night. When he finally made his way to the door of the bedroom, he paused and waited for a moment when he thought for certain he'd heard a voice calling him. He looked down both ends of the hall and checked to see if anyone was there, but the hall was empty, so he drew his knife and carefully entered Elias' bedroom then closed the door behind him.

The light of the moon shone down on the boy's chest, and the bright burning scar in the center was proof that Thumacheo had told him the truth. The mountain rumbled softly as he lifted the blade, but the king held his anger to prevent the boy from waking. He started to place the blade on the boy's chest, but instead he carefully placed his claw down on top of the scar. The wonder of his son's heart beating beneath his claw filled his mind with so many thoughts and in the darkness of the room, he spoke to Elias' heart as if his son, Enupnion was still alive and laying before him.

"My boy, my—my wonderful boy. How I have longed to take you into my arms and beg your forgiveness for my cruel punishments I placed upon you. So many nights I have dreamed of our first hunt together and the glory of your first kill. I relive it in my heart every day, I truly do..." the king could barely stand, and his knife began to tremble in his hand. His legs shook and the mountain trembled, but he continued, "As I stand over you now, listening to your heart, beating again in my castle, I can't help but wonder if maybe my punishments were unjust. Forgiven me, my son, as I now fulfill my duty to the law of this kingdom and strike this usurper from our land." The king sobbed for several moments then raised his blade over top of Elias' heart and suddenly cried out, "IT DOESN'T BELONG IN YOUR CHEST!"

ISABELLA SAT IN THE DARKNESS OF ELIAS' ROOM, WATCHING THE madness of the king with great patience, in hopes that the shocking event taking place before her was nothing but a vision. She waited in the darkness with tears streaming down her face, unable to move her body forward. Her thoughts were filled with terrible sadness of what Prince Enupnion would think of her if she struck down his father, but her thoughts were also filled with what he would think of her if she didn't protect the heart that he had so freely given so Elias could live. She wanted to cry out and tell him to stop this madness, but she had seen too many old warriors like the king, and she knew he would only kill her as well. Her body was heavy, like iron, as she lifted herself off the floor and quietly crouched up behind King Arkone. As the king cried out, she drew her baton from her mod-arm and drove it straight through the king's back, through his wings, through his beating heart and out the front of his royal chest. And Izzy felt the mountain shake violently under her feet, the floor groaned and split with a loud crunching pop as King Arkone's breath escaped from his lungs.

Suddenly, the door to Elias' room burst open. The torch lights from the hall shone bright into the room, and Merlin stood in the doorway. "Isabella, what's taking so..." The shock on Merlin's face was unlike anything Isabella had ever seen from him. Isabella was now drenched in the king's blood from her chest all the way down to her feet, and her mod-arm was completely crimson.

Then Elias woke. He looked into her eyes of fire as if she were some sort of murdering monster. As if she somehow planned or wanted this. In the glistening light of a cold moon, King Arkone's blood dripped off the point of her baton now jutting out the front of his chest and it quickly covered Elias. The blood ran down her mod-arm and all over her as she stood, speechless, unable to explain herself to them. Then King Arkone slumped to his knees, and her baton slid out of his back as he fell over sideways on the floor. Elias was also speechless. He stared frozen with terror as the king's face turned from surprised to hollow pale, and Isabella knew there was only one option for her brother now.

"RUN, ELIAS, RUN! MERLIN, GET HIM OUT OF HERE. NOW! GET HIM TO FATHER!" Merlin grabbed a stunned Elias and pulled him to the window where the Whisper was hovering in whisper mode. Merlin passed Elias through to Jimmy, and within seconds they were gone. It didn't take long before the rest of the Whisper crew came running down the hallway to Elias' room. They stopped in horror as they saw her standing over the body of the king, her eyes burning with flames and her mod-arm and baton saturated in his blood. She reached down and picked up the king's knife and with red smoke rolling from her mouth she spoke.

"He was going to take it back. The heart. He was going to take it back, but I couldn't let him. I didn't let him," she said. But looking at their faces, she could tell they were more betrayed by the fact that she was like her brother in every way than they did by her murder of the king. As the king's guards quickly filled the halls, the castle was thrown into chaos, for their king—the Lord Commander of the Convocation, ruler of the Petinon people and ruler of the great city of Pterugas—King Arkone was dead.

9

INTO THE NIGHT

*T*he Whisper sailed into the night at full speed toward Grand Fortune City, away from its captain, away from death. Elias grabbed Merlin by his jacket and slammed him against the glass wall of windows on the ship's forward deck. Merlin's brain dome sparked and cracked one of the panes as it hit hard against the glass.

"WHY? WHY DID SHE DO THIS? WHY DID YOU TAKE ME AWAY FROM HER?" Elias screamed at his friend.

"HE WAS GOING TO KILL YOU!" Merlin answered as he held his hand at Jimmy in a stopping motion to prevent him from killing Elias. "IZZY SAVED YOU...AGAIN! She saved you again, Elias. It's all she's ever wanted to do. Do you understand that? All she ever wanted was to protect you. To have a family... a real family." Merlin held his ground and grabbed Elias by his shoulders.

Elias held Merlin tight in his grip, gazing fiercely into his eyes, until he realized Merlin was telling the truth. "I KNOW, I-I know." His grip loosened and his heart sank. "Why did it have to be this way? Why didn't the king just accept us for who we are? We only wanted to help. I don't even care if I'm their stupid prophecy or not. I-I-I just wanted to be with her." Elias slumped to his knees in front of Merlin.

"I know. I know, and that's all Izzy ever wanted as well," Merlin explained.

"What?" Elias asked.

"Yes, that's all Isabella ever wanted for you and her and your father. You know, to be a family."

"What?" Elias looked up at Merlin with confusion in his eyes and shook his head. "No, Merlin. Not Izzy. EPEKNEIA, MERLIN! EPEKNEIA! All I ever wanted was to be with Epekneia." Elias' eyes grew red hot as his anger boiled.

"Oh..." Merlin said, drawing back in confusion.

"I WANTED A FUTURE, MERLIN! I wanted something new. Something real." Elias beat his fist against the deck in anger, and his eyes suddenly lit up again, but Merlin was more hardened than Elias knew. Years of repairing battle-torn soldiers for the Jackboot and his father, Hans, had made him that way. The days had shaped the young Merlin into a man at an early age, and his response was powerfully effective on Elias.

"Well, yes, of course. I didn't mean to say that you didn't care about Epekneia. I was just saying how Izzy cared enough about you to risk everything for your life again. You know, like she did when she tricked us into kidnapping you to save you from Sunago, and how she killed a king to stop him from cutting out your heart that was given to you by Hunchy." Merlin's head lit with blue bolts of lightning as he hardened his gaze at Elias. "Remember him, Elias? Remember our friend? The one who died so you could live... But don't worry about Izzy and the rest of our friends. I'm sure they're fine. Maybe the Petinons will only cut off half their heads and put them on a pikes, or maybe they will just burn them alive like Angus Grand did to Isabella! But don't worry about them and their lives; I'm sure they don't mind dying for you, you selfish little punk!"

"What?" Elias asked, beginning to feel like a parrot that had only learned one word, but at the moment he simply could think of any other way to respond.

"Oh, don't pretend you didn't hear me. I said, 'You selfish little punk!'" Merlin scoffed.

"No...I...you said Angus Grand burned Isabella alive, but she's alive. I don't understand."

Merlin sneered at Elias. "Yeah, that's right. There's a lot you don't understand, Elias. You've been livin' in a bubble, man. Your perfect little bubble on that green mountain with your mold-eating mother and that freak, Sunago." Merlin pointed toward Jimmy, who was obediently flying the Whisper out of Petinon territory. "This is the world you live in now, Elias. THIS!" He shook his finger at his brother's body. "This is the real world, man. This is the darkness you never saw in your perfect little princess tower. THIS! My brother, me, Isabella," Merlin yelled and slumped down against the windows.

Elias crawled over and sat next to him. Both of them sat there for several minutes, and neither said a word as the wind whistled past the Whisper while it sailed into darkness. Finally, Elias put his arm around Merlin's shoulder and spoke. "Did you say, 'Perfect little princess tower'?"

Merlin looked over at him and grinned. "Yeah. Yeah. I guess I did." Suddenly, the two let out a laugh together, and the thick cloud of tension evaporated around them.

"I'm sorry. Okay? I'm sorry. I just...I wanted something new. Something better," Elias said.

"And you think I don't?" Merlin raised his hands to his glass globe. "Look at me! I'm a freak with this crazy brain cap." And suddenly Merlin spoke words he had never spoken to anyone before. Not even Jimmy, and certainly not Isabella. "Do you really think she is ever going to love a freak like me?" he asked.

Elias was confused. "Who?"

Merlin dropped his head and spoke softly as he seemed to

realize his secret had somehow slipped out through his emotions. "Isabella. She's never going to love a freak like me."

Elias' eyes grew big, and he sat back hard on the glass. "Okay. Okay...um...well. I didn't see that coming tonight, but... yeah...sure, why not?"

Merlin looked over at Elias, who was looking out into the night sky. "Sorry. I didn't ever want anyone to know that unless I knew she truly felt the same about me."

Elias looked back at Merlin and started laughing uncontrollably, and suddenly the two ship mates began to laugh at their messed-up love lives. Gazing into the darkness of the sky, Elias said, "We should have talked about this stuff sooner."

"Yeah, we should have," Merlin said with a tear-filled grin. "Look...Elias, there's a lot I need to tell you about Isabella and your father. I'm guessing we have a lot of time until we get back to GFC, so we need to go over as much as possible before we get there."

"Why don't we just fill the boiler with fire berries and cut our time in half?" Elias asked.

Merlin thought for a second. "Now why didn't I think of that on the way here? You're as CRACKED as your sister, you know it!" Merlin's face went blank with emotion as he stared into Elias' burning eyes.

"So it's a bad idea, then?"

"NO! No way! It's brilliant...well as long as we don't blow the boiler out the back of the Whisper. Isabella would never forgive me for that. We'll start with just one and see if that works first." Merlin grinned.

Elias smiled back, pulled out a hand full of fire berries, and with a nefarious grin he said, "Let's go get our dads!" The two got back on their feet and headed to the boiler room, and soon the sky was cut sharp through the center with a bright red streak as the Whisper rocketed toward GFC.

BLOOD DRIPPED FROM ISABELLA'S BATON AS THE JUDGMENTAL EYES of her friends pierced through her soul. The heavy sounds of soldiers marching clacked through the hallways of King Arkone's castle, and every crew member knew there was no escape. Not here. Not this time. Epekneia rushed through the halls ahead of the soldiers and stopped in horror at what her eyes beheld. Isabella wanted to explain again to her, but the look in Epekneia's eyes stole away her excuses. Even the king's guard stopped dead in their tracks at the terrible sight of a bloodied Isabella with eyes of fire. No one knew what to do. Not even the king's guard. There was no king to give them an order, and the one standing before them looked a lot like the child of prophecy. However, Isabella wasn't taking any chances with the hardened warriors and pointed her bloody weapon directly at them. For a brief moment, all anyone could do was to stand gobsmacked, horrified by what had happened to King Arkone, until the queen arrived. She carefully and slowly moved her way in between the crew of the Whisper and the royal guard then reached out her claw toward Isabella.

"Child, give me the weapon," Queen Elehos said gently, but Isabella did not respond. Two of the king's royal guard suddenly swooped in through the open window behind her, and Isabella turned and spun her weapon with blurring speed behind her back then around her front as she blocked their attack. She pointed it back at the queen's neck and spoke.

"He tried to kill him. He tried to kill Elias. H-He was going to take it back," she said with burning eyes and red smoke pouring from her mouth. "But, but, but I-I stopped him, a-and I'll stop all of you."

"Please, child. Please, give me the weapon," Queen Elehos said with a soft compassionate voice. "It's okay. You don't need to explain right now, but if you don't lay down your weapon, they will kill you and your friends." She reached her claw out slowly toward Isabella. All of a sudden, one of the guards behind Isabella moved in to strike her with his blade. Queen Elehos screamed and leapt in front of the warrior with a strange quickness of speed that startled everyone, then her voice roared against the warrior so loud the mountain shook. "HOW DARE YOU DEFY ME!" She shouted with authority. "HOW DARE YOU STRIKE AT HER WITHOUT MY APPROVAL," In an instant, every warrior in her presence dropped to their knees in fear, for the Trembling Mountain of Pterugas now trembled at the sound of her voice. Queen Elehos turned back toward Isabella and said, "By our laws, you and your friends must now be arrested and tried for the murder of King Arkone." She paused for a moment and stared into Isabella's burning eyes then spoke to the royal guard. "Put them in prison and send word to the Convocation of Elders," she said and then marched back down the hall toward the royal throne room.

Isabella's weapon slipped from her hand, bounced off the king's body and rattled to a stop on the bloody floor beneath her feet. The guards grabbed her by the arms with such force, for the first time in her life the fire berries were of no help to her. Their claws were terribly sharp and scratched her fleshy arm as they grabbed her. The queen's warriors then grabbed Gideon, Bogan, and Ava, but Izzy was disturbed when they grabbed Epekneia as well. One of them grabbed her wings, while two others locked a bar with metal clamps attached to each side around the tops of each wing. Epekneia cried out in pain as the clamps locked in place, and the crushing weight of Isabella's actions suddenly pressed down upon her.

With Queen Elehos gone, the guards' cautious, gentle nature was transformed into angry words and harsh treatment. One tripped Bogan while several others kicked him down the hallway. Another punched Gideon in his head so hard his mod began malfunctioning and sent him into horrible screams of pain. Ava tried to help him, but she was pushed to the ground and threatened with her life if she tried to help again. Epekneia simply held her head down and followed quietly with the guard, keeping her gaze away from Izzy, who was busy struggling to break free. By the time they reached the guardian at the gate, the king's guards had become so cruel, Izzy thought her crew would all be dead by morning.

While exiting the massive tree trunk entrance; Ava tripped over the threshold and fell directly in front of the guardian. One of the guards raised his weapon to strike her for her clumsiness, but as his sword came down toward her back, the guardian caught it in his enormous claw. The entire king's guard stopped and backed away from their fellow brother in arms, as if to indicate they wanted no part of his deed, or at the very least, no part of the guardian's wrath. In a horrible display of pain and gore, the guardian cast the warrior to the ground face first and placed his clawed foot into the warrior's back. Swiftly and gruesomely, the guardian grabbed the warrior's right wing and tore it from his back and then the left. The warrior cried out for a moment, and soon after, death took him. The guardian stepped back to his place next to the threshold, and with a heavy sigh of grief, he resumed his duty as guardian of the great tree.

The crew of the Whisper didn't know if the guardian did what he did to save Ava, or if he was simply doing his duty as guardian. Either way, the king's guard quickly changed their attitude toward the crew and even picked up Bogan and Gideon to help them down the long path, but none of them touched the dead warrior. The guards didn't fight as Izzy pulled away from them and instinctively helped Ava back to her feet. It was simply a natural reaction for her to help her friend. At first Izzy didn't realize what had happened, but her clothes were still covered in the king's wet blood and when she helped Ava back to her feet, she accidentally covered her friend's clothes with it. Ava suddenly jerked away from her and looked down at her shirt, now ruined by the crimson stain, then Ava looked back at Izzy, shook her head in disapproval and stepped away from her.

For many years the two girls had been close friends and even closer since Charlie had to go, but a trust had been broken, and it was now clear to everyone just how dangerous Isabella was. Izzy wanted to explain, but the look in Ava's eyes stole her words away. As Ava turned away and followed the guards, Izzy looked down at her blood-covered mod-arm and the rest of her saturated clothes. Large drops were still leaking from her metal fingertips to the ground, and she realized her hair was matted to the side of her face with blood. She didn't want to think about how horrifying she must have looked to her friends, but as the guards grabbed her again and pulled her down the cobblestone path, she could think of only one thing. *Truth matters.*

JIMMY WAS SOON OVERCOME WITH EXHAUSTION AFTER FLYING THE Whisper at breakneck speeds thanks to Elias' idea of using fire berries for fuel. Although, Jimmy's exhaustion was mostly due to his poor sleeping patterns over the last many nights since Merlin feared the king would try to execute them all in their sleep. During the course of their journey to the Petinons, Elias had taken several opportunities to pilot the Whisper and thought it would be best if the brothers got some much needed rest and let him take over. Merlin didn't like the idea at first, but when Elias took him to the window and showed him his own reflection and Jimmy struggling to hold the ship steady, Merlin relented. Elias stepped into the round, glass cockpit and took the controls while Merlin and Jimmy went to their quarters. He waited until he felt comfortable that they were well enough asleep, then he reached into his pocket and took out several fire berries and ate them. He didn't need them to hear a voice or see a vision or anything of the sort, even though he knew it was a possibility, but the berries seemed to be the only thing that stopped the terrible irritation of his scar. Maybe the berries were healing him, or maybe the Petinon heart just needed him to eat the berries. He wasn't sure, but either way they helped.

Elias flicked several buttons, and pulled the levers, and the doors to the sphere closed. A hole opened above him, and hot air rushed down through the hole momentarily as the flexible pole quickly pulled the glass globe up inside the ship's envelope and into the clear glass dome at the top of the ship. The dome at the top allowed him to see in every direction even down on the forward deck below, but Elias was more interested in the clear night sky that lay before him. He pushed the Whisper's throttle all the way forward and sent the ship blasting toward the west.

Sitting inside the glass dome on top of the Whisper was his favorite place in the whole ship, and he loved it even more during the night. He could hear the wind whistling through the cracks of the glass dome, stronger than he'd ever heard it before, and it brought a smile to his face. As Elias rocketed through the sky like a flaming bullet toward Grand Fortune City, no vision or whispering voice came to him. However, after a short time, he began to feel a pain in his back and ribs. At first it came on slow, and Elias thought maybe his scar was irritating him or that maybe he'd eaten some bad fire berries. But the pain nagged and nagged at him until suddenly it hit him so hard, he let go of the controls. He slammed both hands against the glass dome and let out a horrified scream that filled the sphere with red smoke. His arms shook. His face dripped with sweat, and that old darkness closed in around his eyes. As the Whisper shot through the darkness of the sky, Elias' screams of agony went unheard by his exhausted crew mates below. He stared at the cold moon shining in the western sky and tried to focus in on it. If he blacked out inside the upper dome, the Whisper would crash to the earth, and Merlin and Jimmy would die in their sleep. Elias looked at his hands appalled to see they had become so hot, with a bright red glow, he thought for sure he was going to melt the glass. He tried with all his strength to pull back, but the pain was too great. All he could do was push against the glass and scream out his pain into the night.

When the pain became too much, Elias remembered the words of his old hunchback friend and wondered if maybe the prince had been wrong about him being a Petinon. Maybe he was about to die in a horrible bone-melting explosion on top of the Whisper, on top of the world, and no one would ever know what happened to him. His mind filled with doubt as darkness closed in around his eyes. He could see his own reflection in the glass as he hurled through the sky, and it was the first time he'd ever seen his face during one of his fire berry events. He was horrified by it all. *Is this what everyone sees when I eat these things?* Flames lit inside of his eyes and flickered back at him a bright-red face of agony, and his screaming breath melted a circular hole in the glass dome. Cool air rushed in, and for a brief moment it cooled his face, but it was not enough. Then a vision hit him hard, and in a violent, shaking fit of madness, Elias blacked out and slumped over the controls of the Whisper.

AVA RUBBED HER BRUISED SHOULDER FROM HER FALL BACK AT THE threshold and kept her eyes forward as she followed the guards down the path toward the prison. She had no idea where the prison was or what it would look like, but she couldn't bear to look her friend in the face, especially with those flaming eyes of hers. *First, she doesn't need a mask, and now she's exactly like Elias. And no one here cares anything about Charlie. I don't get it. Why hide something like this from me? Since Charlie, we've been best friends. We've shared everything, or at least I thought we did. How many more things has she lied about? What if she's like her mother?* Ava glanced back at Izzy. *What if she's witch? And where're Merlin, Jimmy and*

Elias? I hope they don't put me in a cell with her. I'm so sick of her lies. I'm so sick of her privileged attitude.

Ava continued her angry argument with herself as they made their way into the city entrance. By now, many Petinons had returned to the city after they heard the news of the king's murder by the half-breed, wingless girl. Some of them screeched strange sounds at Izzy, while others cast stones or food at her, and even Ava considered picking up an old piece of fruit and hitting her in the face, but her better angels won out. Instead, she decided to sneer at her friend to prove to the Petinon people that she didn't approve of what Izzy had done. Ava made sure a good number of Petinon people were watching, and when she sensed the timing was right, she turned her head back toward Izzy and gave the ugliest sneer of disapproval she could give. It was her best mean look, and she knew by the heartbreak on her friend's face that it'd worked.

It must have been even better than Ava thought, because Izzy stopped for a moment and stared at the ground. Several Petinons hit her with rocks, and at first Ava thought one of the rocks made contact too hard because Izzy let out a horrible scream unlike anything Ava had ever heard. It sounded much like the Petinon people's cries of anger, but even some of them drew back at her scream. Suddenly, Izzy began to shake uncontrollably, but Ava was having none of it.

"Don't believe her!" Ava spoke out to the Petinons. "She's a liar and a fake. She's probably just trying to pull some stunt to attack you." Ava's words fell flat as many Petinon's seemed to believe the cries of pain coming from Izzy were real.

About that time Bogan was coming to and noticed Izzy's pain. "ISABELLA! WHAT'S WRONG WITH HER? AVA, HELP HER!" he cried out, but Ava was unsure what to do. If Bogan believed it then maybe Izzy wasn't lying. Maybe it wasn't a trick.

Then a powerful shockwave of pain must have hit Izzy,

because she screamed in horror so loud that many Petinon children in the crowd began to cry, and even one of the warriors next her asked if she was okay. Izzy's eyes lit up with bright red flames, and her face grew hot as she fell to her knees on the cobblestone road. The stones cracked as she hit the ground with trembling hands, and the great mountain shook with such force that it frightened all the Petinons standing around them. Izzy looked up at Ava with sorrow-filled eyes and called out to her.

"A-AVA! AVA, HELP ME! IT...HURTS...SO BAD!" Izzy screeched out with red smoke filling the air around her. Many Petinons quickly left, and others cried out that she was Ouranos and bowed down to her in confusion. But Izzy's pain had now turned into something nightmarish. When one of the guards reached down and grabbed her arm to help her back up, he burned his claw on her arm. The guard let out a groan and stepped away from her.

"P-Please, Ava. Don't h-hate m-me." Izzy fell over and shook so violently that she blacked out on the road. At that moment, the truth hit Ava like the mountain when it trembled.

"Izzy?" Ava asked softly as her eyes welled up with tears. She ran over to her friend and touched her mod-arm. It was cool unlike the rest of her body. Ava ran over to a small fountain by the street, grabbed some water with her hands, and began pouring it on Izzy. Steam rose from Izzy until finally she began to cool down, and Ava proved to the guards that she was okay to carry, but when they refused, Ava asked them to let Bogan help her. The guards finally agreed since they didn't want to move her themselves for fear of being burned.

Ava and Bogan carried Isabella through the empty streets and onto a dirt path leading into the woods. The guards brought them to a large, wooden door in the side of the mountain and dropped Gideon on the ground in front of it. One of them beat on the gate and waited for a short time, then the gate opened and another guardian, much like the one at the threshold of the great tree trunk, stepped out and motioned for them to enter. The guards dragged Gideon by the leg into the dark tunnel as the others followed behind.

When they finally reached the cell they were to be placed in, the guardian unlocked it and the iron bars opened with a pitiful groan. The cloaked guardian said nothing, but with a subtle nod of his hood they understood what he meant. After they placed Izzy down on the floor, they grabbed Gideon and laid him down carefully. Bogan checked him out to make sure he was still alive, but when Ava checked back to see where Epekneia was, the cell door slammed in her face. The iron door echoed with the coldest sound Ava had ever heard in her life, and her heart jumped in fear at how final it felt. She cried out and demanded that the guardian return Epekneia, but the cloaked figure paid no attention to her pleas as he took Epekneia deeper into the mountain.

"You want to tell me what was going on out there?" Bogan asked Ava as she dashed over to help him with Izzy.

Ava knew exactly what Bogan meant, but she tried to play it off. "What are you talking about?"

"Why didn't you want to help her? Why didn't you help Izzy? Why were you acting all strange?"

"I don't want to talk about it right now, so just drop it, okay! Just drop it!" Ava said with a tear slipping out of her eye.

"Fine, but you're going tell me. I kid you not, Ava, you're gonna tell me."

"I'll think about it," Ava said as she wiped the blood-matted hair from Izzy's face. "She's still breathing, but she needs help. I don't have anything with me to help either of them, and I don't know if Gideon going to make it. He looks awful." Exhausted, Ava leaned up against the cell bars of the opposing cell to rest, and Bogan joined her.

"What happened to Merlin, Jimmy, and Elias? I mean, are they even still here?" Bogan asked.

"I don't know. Izzy didn't say." Ava looked around at the ceiling and the iron bars in wonder. "How are we going to get out of here?" she asked, but instead of Bogan answering, a voice came from the cell behind them.

"There is no way out," the pained voice said.

Bogan and Ava sprang up and turned around to see who spoke, but all they could see was a dark figure sitting in the corner of the other cell. It was too dark to see his face, but the putrid smell of rotting flesh coming from the corner was evidence they might not want to associate with their neighboring prisoner.

"Why do you say that?" Bogan asked.

"The reason I would say that is because…" The prisoner slowly rose to their feet by placing one hand on the wall and groaning painfully as they struggled to gain their footing. It almost seemed as though pieces of their body were falling off as they stood up, and the obviously frail physique was that of an old, diseased Petinon. The prisoner fell over on the wall for a moment and then staggered their way into the soft glow of light coming from the far hallway entrance. His face was horribly disfigured, and Bogan stepped in front of Ava as the prisoner wrapped a deformed claw around the cell bars.

"It's good to see you again, little brother. Don't you recognize me? I'm Charlie, or what's left of him."

10

BOND OF FIRE

*E*lias and Isabella's father lay face down in the grime of a rotten labyrinth cell as Grundorph the troll and Hex the Petinon stood over him discussing his fate. Their voices fazed in and out to the rhythm of his consciousness. Every time he came to, he tried desperately to speak something, anything, but the only things that came out of his mouth were empty breaths. His only eye stared at the feet of the two strange beasts, one of whom he never would have considered saving and the other of whom he never thought would save him. His body was racked with pain from his injuries, but the only thing he could think of at the moment was to stay alive for his children. He hoped they were okay, that they would be okay if he didn't make it and that he might live long enough to tell them how much he wanted to be a family again.

"I think he's dead, Hex," Grundorph said, scratching the edge of the iron plate bolted to his head.

"No. He's alive, but he won't be for long if we don't get him some help," Hex replied.

"What kind of madness would make him do something like that? Did he really think he was going to survive a battle with a giant boar? Insanity! That's what it was, or foolishness, I suppose. That look in his eye when he landed on that thing...he had no fear. That's a rare breed, Hex. WAIT! You don't think he took our words to heart, do you?" Grundorph questioned, trying to understand the man's actions.

"What words?" Hex asked.

"About the dead. You know, only the dead getting out of here. Maybe he figured he would just end it all. Maybe he figured it was his only way out," Grundorph reasoned.

Hex didn't seem offended by Grundorph's misunderstanding of his people in the least bit and kept the tone of his voice like that of a patient teacher. "Impossible, my friend. Petinons are lovers of life. We might sacrifice ourselves for someone else, but we would never kill ourselves."

Grundorph stroked his mighty chin as if to be in deep contemplation. "I understand, but how can you be so sure this man is a Petinon? He doesn't look anything like you and... well...he clearly doesn't have wings. As much as I want to believe you, I'm struggling to buy into your fantasy here, my friend."

"Well, I'm not entirely sure. However, the two nodules on his back are a very familiar trait of wingless Petinon, and his boots are made from the sacred metal of our people. Of that, I have no doubt. Is it possible for humans to wear things made from our sacred metal? Yes, it is, but not many can, and most have terrible reactions to it. There is one way to find out if he is, but if I am wrong then he will die a terrible death," Hex explained.

"You've most certainly tickled the curiosity of my inner tunnel troll. Please explain."

"Remember when we first met? When they cast me into your cell?" Hex asked.

"Ah yes. How could I forget," Grundorph said with a grin as he touched a terrible scar running down his left arm and all the way to his leg. "A bond sealed in blood, old friend." He rubbed the scars as if they were something precious to him now.

Hex nodded in approval at Grundorph's nostalgia. "Good. After our battle I made a paste and covered my wounds with it to help me heal, but when we tried it on you, it almost killed you."

"Ah yes, the red paste from the seeds. Of that I will say... NOT a fan." Grundorph grunted and shook his head.

"I could do the same for him, or we could wait and see if he recovers. Either way, it's a risk."

Grundorph studied the broken Jackboot for a moment and gave his body a small push with his large index finger. The Jackboot let out a fainted breath as the pain of being moved took hold of him. "This fellow has nothing to lose, Hex. You might as well get on with it."

Hex knelt down close to the Jackboot's face and spoke. "I'm going to try and help you, but know this; if I fail, you will die a terrible death. Do you understand what I'm saying?"

Through the agony of pain and blurred confusion, the Jackboot nodded his head yes, and a sound that closely resembled the word yes breathed out from his mouth.

"Alright then, I'll make a paste and apply it to your wounds. I apologize in advance if this doesn't work and you die," Hex said. Standing back to his feet, he looked to Grundorph. "My friend, there is also another matter of great concern in regards to your win in the arena."

"Yes. Yes, I know." Grundorph breathed a heavy sigh.

"And did you see the workers...welding on those beams above the arena?"

"Mogdal always talked about opening the arena to the ground above. Maybe he finally convinced the labyrinth leaders to let him do it. Or...maybe he just had them killed." Grundorph rubbed the back of his head. "One problem at a time, old Hex. One problem at a time," He smiled.

"Agreed," Hex said, and he removed a small pouch from under one of his wings then poured some seeds into a food bowl and began grinding them into a paste with a stone from the cell floor.

SUNAGO LAY MOTIONLESS AS HE STARED UP AT THE CEILING OF HIS cold labyrinth hospital bed. A white light with a dirty lens hung over top his head, and a strange purple liquid he'd never seen before was pumping into his body from a glass ball to his left. Bugs crawled across the lights and down the walls as the Dream Slayer leaned against the doorway, picking his fingernails free of a juicy bug he'd just squashed. Unable to move or speak, the once great Alchemist and Petinon hero began to sulk in his failures again. It was something he had become quiet fond of doing, and it helped past the time. *If I could only see the Trembling Mountain once again before I die, that would be enough. Why won't she just let me die? I hate this place. I hate this life! I want to see the sunrise again and breathe the fresh mountain air of Pterugas. Why did I leave? WHY!* He screamed in his mind, the anger of his poor choices. *Maybe I could convince the boy to take me from here. To take me to the mountain. I could offer him a reward from the king if he would only help me.* Sunago grunted several times until he got the Dream Slayer's attention. The Dream Slayer made his way to the bedside and looked down on him with the awkward smugness of a conqueror.

"Just look at you. I used to think you were something great. His magnificence, The Great Alchemist—HA! I'm sure not seeing it. I mean, what is it that you did that was so great, anyway? All you ever tried to do was kill the boy, and how did that work out for you?" The Dream Slayer mockingly laughed out loud at him.

Sunago gasped for breath as he tried to explain himself, but the breathing tube down his throat prevented him from speaking. He grunted and groaned fiercely until the Dream Slayer finally understood what he was wanting.

"You want to talk, right? Okay, but only for a few seconds. She'll kill me if anything happened to you." The Dream Slayer slowly removed the tube, and Sunago fought to catch his breath.

"L-Listen c-carefully, t-t-take me...n-no...get me out of here. To my peop...my people's mountain. P-Pay much gold for my arrival. P-Please, don't l-let her..." Sunago fought within himself to maintain his breath, but he could no longer speak and began to blackout. The Dream Slayer quickly shoved the tube back down his throat like an amateur nurse, scraping his esophagus in the process. It was agonizingly painful, but he was helpless to react to it.

"See there? You see, that's why I don't do this kind of stuff. That's why she doesn't want me messing with you. I bet that hurt, didn't it?" He grinned a little at the pain he'd caused Sunago and reached up to the overhead light and pulled it in close so he could get a better look at him. "So, let me get this straight. You want me to break you out of here and take you to your people, and they will pay me a bunch of gold for your return. Is that right?" he asked.

Sunago nodded with a grunt as his eyes grew large.

"And what do you think she will do to me when she finds out I betrayed her? Huh? All the gold in the world won't save me from her. HA! You know, I used to fear you, but let me tell you something—your Great Magnificence—I think she's more powerful than you've ever been, and you know it. Yes, yes, it's true. I can see the terror in your eyes even now." The Dream Slayer stepped back over to his place by the door and finished his thought. "I think you're here to stay, mister. At least until she's done with you." He laughed with a haughty smile as he went back to picking his fingernails and whistling his cheap carnival tunes.

THOUGH NIGHT HAD LONG SETTLED ABOVE THE LABYRINTH, IT WAS always dark in Karl's Labyrinth, and so the city was perpetually lit with gas lamps for miles and miles. Every sidewalk, street, storefront and alley was illuminated with an eerie orange glow from the gas-lit streetlamps that beat the darkness back into the tunnels. The main road running through the labyrinth was about two hundred feet across and paved with concrete. In the center it had two railway tracks running through it, and on each side were massive sidewalks large enough for Ever-Wheels to travel in either direction. Only a few labyrinth folk were out this night, with the exception of the normal burly men guarding the city and a dark figure floating effortlessly above the sidewalk. There were no sounds of the clacking and clopping of high-heeled boots echoing through the city as the shadowy figure moved like an apparition about two inches above the sidewalk. The gas flames flickered as the woman passed by each one in her long dress coat. She carried her umbrella in her left hand and a perfectly square black case in her right hand, and tiny puffs of smoke rolled out from her umbrella as she moved along with ease.

The city was much cleaner than the days of her youth, thanks to Mogdal, who forced peace between the burly tunnel people and the genetically altered folk. It was almost nice enough for her to call home again, but living underground was never quite to her taste. Floating in the clouds was where she belonged, and soon she would be able to leave here. Soon she would be able to rebuild her army of Charmers. Soon she would be able to save her beloved Sunago and take back the life that was stolen from her. She turned down a dark tunnel with no light and, with a sudden, single word a bright green ball rose out of her long black coat and lit the tunnel ahead of her. Deeper and deeper into the tunnels she went until she came to an iron door with warnings and chemical signs all over it. In the center of the door was a symbol of two crossed hammers and a sparkling wand. She tapped on it with the end of her umbrella, and soon it open up. She floated down several hallways and labs until she came to a door that opened without a knock. Inside the room was her lover, Sunago, who watched her move as she floated over to his bed. His eyes fixating on the large, square box she carried.

"I've found the perfect one, my love. He was the biggest of all my servants, and he gave it willingly. It doesn't have to be permanent, though. I promise, we'll only leave it in long enough to get you well and find the right fit from among your own people. As soon as you've healed, we'll leave for the Petinon kingdom." She brushed the back of her hand across the side of his cheek gently. Though her words were soft and lovely, Sunago's response was far from joyful. He groaned and yelled his disapproval with his throat as loud as he could, but she was not fazed or concerned by his anger.

"Please, my love. You must trust me. This is for the best. And besides, did I tell you how beautiful you will be when it's done?" She folded her umbrella and handed it to the Dream Slayer then drifted over to a bookshelf on the far wall and pulled a large book from the top shelf. It had iron clasps that bound the spine and a single locked clasp on the fore-edge. On the front of the book was a large winged creature, but the title across the face of it was worn. She spoke several words of smoke into a warped key shape and sent it into the keyhole. With a clack the lock popped, and she opened the book to the beginning, ran her finger over the words, turned several pages, then smiled. "You're going to be beautiful, my love. Simply beautiful."

Sunago gave no response, but his eyes were screaming in horror.

When Hex had finished mashing the seeds into his healing paste, he took a breath and knelt beside the Jackboot. "Are you sure you want me to do this?" he asked, as if he was uncertain himself.

The Jackboot mustered every last bit of strength he had in his bones and said, "I want to liiive."

"Alright, then. Let's begin," Hex said as he began applying the paste. The Jackboot winced a few times but nothing that would indicate a problem. Once Hex had completely covered the Jackboot's wounds in the red goop, he looked back up at Grundorph with a smile. "This is a good sign. A good sign. There's no reaction."

"So what do we do now?" Grundorph asked.

"Now we wait. He needs to heal, and that could take some time."

The two companions took a seat on the floor across from the injured man and leaned against the grungy cave wall to rest their bodies from the exhaustion of the arena. The question of the other matter soon began nagging at Hex, and so in the darkness of their cave cell, he voiced his concerns to his friend. "Will you fight?"

"I have no choice but to do so. If I don't then you will die. Unless you have some way to break these chains," Grundorph said as he jingled the chains about their legs. "Maybe just this once you should consider breaking your vow to not kill another creature. It might come in handy out there...you know...share the load, so to speak."

"I cannot break my oath to my prince. He alone can release me from my sacred vow," Hex explained.

"It sure will make for an interesting battle against a Standing Hero—having your wings flopping about all over the place like a chicken with its head cut off," Grundorph said with a slight chuckle.

"Of that I have no doubt my frien..." Hex paused his words

and sniffed the air of their cave.

"Something caught that sensitive beak of yours?" Grundorph snickered.

Hex pointed over toward the Jackboot's body. "Does it look like he is starting to glow to you? Maybe it's just the darkness of the cave, but I…oh no…Grundorph, we might be in grave danger here. I think this fellow is not going to make it."

"He looks fine to me, Hex. I think you're being overly cautious." Grundorph paused, "Um…okay, okay, maybe he is glowing a little bit, but…um…okay, maybe more than before." Soon, the red paste covering the man's body was bright enough to light their entire cell. He began groaning and rolling around on the ground, and then suddenly he started to crawl toward them on his hands and knees. The two creatures sat against the wall, unsure of what to do and unsure of what was about to happen. They both called out to the Jackboot, but he gave no indication he could hear them, and he seemed to be in a great deal of pain as he raised his face toward theirs.

"W-What's happening to me?" the Jackboot asked.

SEVERAL ATTENDANTS WHEELED SUNAGO'S BED INTO A LARGE operating room filled with abnormally shaped tubes and beakers as well as jars of floating body parts. To his own shock, there were even Petinon heads in several containers and a few large claws floating in yellowish goo filling other jars. White operating lights exploded on and washed the room with so much light he could hardly see, but at this point it was for the best. The room was filled with many people dressed in white clothing and wearing masks. All but one, his beloved Cassandra. She was still wearing her black coat, but she soon removed it, along with her short top hat, and placed it in someone's hand. Then she shook out her long, dark hair, clapped her hands together and in a powerful voice said, "LET'S BEGIN!"

The white coats placed him on another table and began hooking him up to all sorts of tubes and wires. Then suddenly someone drove a long, sharp needle into his spine, and his vision exploded with blinding light that seemed to come from everywhere. As the powerful injection began to take hold of him, Sunago felt as though he was losing himself—as if his mind was being invaded by something else, someone else. His cries turned to begging and sobbing, as a child would cry for their mother in the darkness, but his beloved Cassandra did not acknowledge him. He could hear himself screaming, and he wanted to believe he was somewhere else. That the screams were someone else's, and that he was back on his Trembling Mountain, perhaps, or soaring over the treetops of the great city. That he was enjoying the company of the king and the Elders of the Convocation, or even walking the cobblestone streets of Pterugas. But no, he was where darkness gave birth to monsters. He was in the Labyrinth now.

THE JACKBOOT'S EYE LIT WITH FIRE, AND THE RED PASTE ON HIS body began to burn as he crawled toward Hex and Grundorph. Though the pain was excruciating, he could feel something deep inside him changing— healing—and suddenly he stood to his feet in front of them. He knew his prison companions were in the same room with him because he could still see them, but he felt as if he was in another place—a place he'd never been or seen before, but familiar to his soul. He paced around the cell as if he was in the strange place and held his hands out in front of him to try and touch the walls. It seemed real, but not completely, and soon he remembered all the visions he'd watched Isabella have when she'd eaten the fire berries. How she walked with her hands out in front of her as if she were in another place, and now he knew what was happening to him. All of a sudden a voice came from behind him, but it spoke no words he knew or could understand. When he turned around, he realized he was standing in the center of a burning mountain. Running through its center was a river of hot magma and in its center, an empty throne. The river of lava flowed beneath his feet, but he didn't burn or sink into the flowing death. His mind played tricks on him, and he stepped forward to get away from the heat behind him, but the ring of fire closed in around him. Finally, he was standing next to the throne as if he had been pushed there by the fire. It was cool and relieved the terrible heat surrounding him, and so he sat down on the throne to rest from his pain. Within moments a shadowy figure passed through the fire and into the mountain with him. It was her. It was Isabella.

"ISABELLA!" he cried out to her as she approached. She was a child again, and her right arm was fully restored. She approached him and stopped directly in front of the throne. He wanted to touch her, but the throne had somehow locked his arms and legs in place. Isabella's eyes were burning bright with flames, and she was whispering something. He leaned his head in as far as the throne would allow him so he might hear her better, and suddenly she reached from behind her back and drew out a flaming crown of iron. She slammed the crown down upon his head so hard he thought his skull cracked, and in an instant she disappeared into the flames. The crown burned into his head so hot, he began to scream as it melted into his skull. The pain was worse than anything he'd ever experienced, even at the hands of Angus Grand, and at that moment he could feel himself dying inside.

GRUNDORPH AND HEX WATCHED AS THE JACKBOOT SCREAMED THE most terrible, maddening cries of pain they had ever witnessed in all their days of battle in the arena. Torch lights burst into flames, brighter and brighter, filling the halls of the cave with so much light they could see the creatures across the hall staring at them in horror. The sight of the Jackboot covered in flames and his body not burning was enough to strike terror in the hearts of the most monstrous of beasts in the prison. Grundorph and Hex leaned as far away from him as they could, in fear that they too might catch fire and burn alive. Suddenly, the burning man collapsed to the ground by their feet, and the flames quickly died out. His skin was unburned, and his wounds were fading away.

"WHAT HAPPENED?" Grundorph asked in shock.

"I have no idea," Hex replied.

Grundorph looked over at Hex in disbelief. "What do you mean, you have no idea? I thought you knew all about this stuff."

"I-I do, but I've never seen anything like this before. I thought he was dying, but, but...look at him! He's nearly healed." Hex was gobsmacked.

"Well, is he?" Grundorph asked in wonder.

A disheveled Hex looked over at his friend. "Is he what?"

"Is he like you? You know, one of your people, a Petinon?"

"I'm not sure I know what he is, but I think I know who he might be," Hex replied.

"So out with! Who is he, then?" Grundorph demanded.

"I think he might be the chosen one my people have waited so long for. He is going to bring peace and harmony to the world and lead us into a wonderful new life. This is truly a grand day, my friend, a grand day!" Hex's voice was filled with a joyful tone, but his face was frozen and immovable like stone.

Grundorph gave the Jackboot's body a nudge with his massive index finger and said, "Hex, I think your chosen one might be dead."

11

ALIVE

*C*harlie gripped the cell bars tightly with his claws. His left hand had completely changed into a fully formed Petinon claw, but his right still had three human fingers, and only his index finger and thumb had changed. He leaned his partially feathered face against the bars and stared toward them in the darkness. "I have thought about your face every moment of every day. The smell of your hair and the sound of your voice have filled my thoughts and lifted my spirit more times than you could imagine...Ava."

Ava's hands trembled nervously at the sight of the monster's cold, black eyes glaring back at her through the bars. The voice resembled Charlie's voice in some ways, but this person looked nothing like Charlie. Maybe it was the darkness of their cell that confused her. Maybe a closer look would help clear things up. Bogan started to hold her back when she snuck out from behind him, but he stopped when she paused and pushed his hand away. She approached the cell bars and placed her face only a few inches from the creature's face. Before she realized it, her own trembling hand was touching the soft, tiny, white feathers covering his face. She leaned in closer and gazed into the creature's cold, black eyes. "Charlie?" she asked carefully, still unsure if it was him.

"Yes, Ava… it is," he said with subtle hopefulness to his voice.

Ava placed her other hand on his face and leaned her forehead to his. "I-I don't care what they did to you." She spoke with her eyes closed as if she hoped to open them and Charlie would be normal again. "I-I knew it all along, Charlie. I knew it in my heart. I did. I just knew it." Ava turned her head and pressed her cheek through the bars and against his feathered face. "For so long now I've always had this sense that you were alive, watching me somehow, and now more than ever I believe it with all my heart. We were meant to be together."

Charlie raised his partially formed hand to her face and touched her cheek with his three human fingers. "I have been watching you, Ava. I've been watching you all for some time now." Charlie's words were incomprehensible at first, and Bogan blurted out a laugh at the creature in disbelief.

"So, how have you been doing that, brother?" Bogan scoffed sarcastically at the monster. "And what proof do we have that y-you're really Charlie? You know our names and that's all. We've been here long enough that someone could have told you about us. You say you're Charlie…then prove it," Bogan demanded as he scratched at his mod-leg.

"To start with, your mod-leg was installed by Hans Kloppenheimer with the help of Merlin and Ava after you stepped on a land mine during the war for GFC. That girl waking up over there," he raised his nose and sniffed the air. "…with the bloody mod-arm, is Isabella Brock, and the unconscious guy was once my first mate, Gideon." Charlie smiled, though his black eyes seemed blank as if they were still staring at nothing.

As Ava stepped back to check on Izzy, Bogan stepped up closer to his brother and grimaced. "Charlie? Is it really you? Are you really…alive?" Bogan asked, still struggling with Charlie's strange features.

"It really is, brother. I am alive. If you want to call this living," Charlie said as his knees suddenly gave way, and he collapsed to the floor of his cell.

Bogan knelt down and took hold of his arm. "Brother, what did they do to you? What happened? How...how can it be? I don't understand. They...they turned you into a Petinon? But why?"

"I'll explain when Isabella gets her bearings. She needs to hear this." He breathed out his words with an exhausted voice.

Ava brushed Izzy's blood-dried hair from her face. "Bogan! Do you have any water? She needs some water."

"Over by your cell door is a bowl of water," Charlie pointed out.

Bogan handed it to Ava, and she helped Izzy drink it slowly. Once Izzy had finished, she looked up at Ava and asked, "What happened?"

"You passed out from the pain," Ava explained with a gentle smile.

"W-What pain?" Izzy asked scratching vigorously at her back.

"You don't remember?" Bogan seemed surprised that she couldn't remember something so terribly painful that it had caused her to lose consciousness.

"No. I guess it wasn't as painful as you thought." Izzy grinned, looking up at Bogan. "Ugh! What's that terrible smell? It smells like rotting flesh and bird droppings." But no one responded to her question as they didn't seem to want to offend Charlie.

Ava wet her fingers with the tiny drops of water left in the bowl and wiped the dried blood from Izzy's cheeks. Her smile grew brighter as she slowly pulled another strand of blood-matted hair from Izzy's forehead. Her dear friend couldn't remember her betrayal, and in the darkness of their cold cell,

Ava felt a small sense of hope that she hadn't ruined their friendship.

Suddenly, Izzy seemed to notice the half-Petinon, human monster in the cell next to them and jumped back against the grimy cell wall behind her. "WHAT IS THAT?" Izzy cried out, reaching for her baton. "WHAT? Where's my baton? Who took my baton?"

Ava and Bogan looked at each other, hoping her memory hadn't completely gone, but when Izzy looked closer at the dried blood on her mod-arm, everything came rushing back to her. "Oh, yeah...that's right," she said with a somber voice then looked at Ava with cold glare.

"Izzy...we found someone. We've found Charlie." Ava pointed to the creature in the other cell.

"WHAT!" Izzy got to her feet and dashed over next to Bogan then knelt down beside him. "Charlie? Is it really you?" she asked, placing her hand on the creature's claw.

"Bear with me as it is difficult for me to speak sometimes, but...yes. I am Charlie," he said, taking a deep breath.

Ava briefly checked on Gideon and then joined her friends. She could tell Charlie was weak, and whatever they had done to him had both saved him and possibly destroyed him. She rallied her strength then decided to take a more positive view of things. *I've found him. He's alive and I always knew it.* Her heart soared as Charlie began to explain how he'd become close friends with a Petinon warrior who was injured during one of the king's hunting adventures. Because the warrior was one of the king's mightiest, the king openly granted him a last request without condition or restriction. When the warrior asked that his heart be given to Charlie in hopes of saving Charlie's life, the king was enraged but soon relented when the Elders explained that Charlie would not survive anyway. The Elders also warned the king about how loved Charlie had become with some of the Petinon people and that it would be beneficial for his legacy.

The king granted the warrior's request, and when the warrior passed, the Petinon kingdom did something it had never done before and gave a human, named Charlie, a Petinon heart. Several days passed and when Charlie didn't die the king became worried. He summoned the Convocation of Elders and demanded someone explain how Charlie was still alive. The Elders convinced the king to give it more time, but Charlie got better and better and soon was walking the cobblestone streets of Pterugas again. This infuriated the king because he felt he'd defiled the heart of one of his best warriors, but the Petinon people liked Charlie all the more for it. Soon, Charlie and the king's son, Prince Enupnion, became friends, and it became more and more difficult for the king to accept him.

"The best I can figure, King Arkone and the Elders must have decided that if they were going to let me live, I would have to become one of them. At least, that's the only explanation I've been able to come up with. One night while I was sleeping, someone snuck into my room and injected my new heart with something. I have no idea what it was, but I believe it had something to do with Casper. Soon, I began to change into a Petinon, but I don't think it worked out the way the king wanted, and I never completely changed. King Arkone had me cast into prison when I became too hideous even for the Petinons who liked me. Although, I think maybe it's a slower process than what the king had originally thought. Either way, this is who I am now, half Charlie and half Petinon." Charlie finished and rested for a moment as everyone took in everything he'd told them.

"What do you mean it had something to do with Casper?" Izzy asked.

Charlie looked toward Ava. "Remember when I told you that I've been watching you?" Ava's eyes grew large with wonder. "I believe that whatever they did to me had something to do with Casper, or maybe they even used Casper or something from him. Not long after the king's guard injected something into my heart, I started to have strange visions of flying and eating fire berries and killing things. With the help of Prince Enupnion, we were able to figure out that I was seeing what Casper was seeing after he ate the fire berries. I was overjoyed by it and begged the prince to send Casper to look after you all. Well, maybe for my own selfish reasons as well, so that I might be with you in some small way through Casper's eyes. The prince was reluctant to do so, but when I promised him I would help devise a plan to replant, with the help of the Jackboot, the prince quickly agreed." Charlie dropped his head. "I feel as if I've been with you all these many days while locked away in this mountain prison. This is how I know my friend, the prince, gave his life for your brother, Isabella. However, the price I've paid for this gift has been another kind of prison. You see…" Charlie leaned in closer to the torch light. "…but for Casper's sight, I am blind."

In an instant, Ava's breath left her, and she passed out in Izzy's arms.

ELIAS OPENED HIS EYES TO THE SIGHT OF HIS GREAT GRAY FRIEND brooding back at him from the cage, and Casper seemed not the least bit pleased by it. Jimmy was strapped into the bed next to Elias, and Merlin was fixing something on Jimmy's arm with the welder. When Merlin finished, he removed his welding helmet and turned around to check on Elias.

"Oh good, you're awake," Merlin said in a cold, matter-of-fact tone. He strolled over to Elias' bedside and asked, "What happened up there? Were we attacked?"

Elias thought for a moment and got his bearings as he remembered the terrible pain from his vision. "No…I-I think it was me."

"WHAT?" Merlin said in shock. "The dome on top of the Whisper was melted like we were hit by something hot. The ship went spiraling out of control. I thought we were going to die, but Jimmy saved us."

"How?" Elias asked in bewilderment.

"I'm not really sure how he did it, because I was busy getting bashed around inside the Whisper while it was falling. I do know after he left I heard something hit the forward deck. I'm guessing that's how you got that bump on your head." Merlin grinned. "When Jimmy got the ship stable, I found you strapped to the railing with the cords. I'm not sure how that happened either, but at least we're all still alive. Anyway, we're losing time because we've been stuck in Whisper Mode while I repaired Jimmy's arm."

"I'm sorry. I had a terrible vision. I think Isabella and my father had one at the same time. I could hear them screaming inside my head. It was very strange. Something happened, and I think it happened to all of us." Elias tried to make sense of it in his head and remember the vision as best he could. "Quick! Get some paper and write this down. I don't want to forget it in case it means something." Merlin grabbed some paper and a pen and began writing furiously as Elias explained his vision.

"I was flying but not me. I was riding on the back of something, and it took me over Grand Fortune City and Gabriel's Harbor and some places I'd never seen before. Then I saw my father—I mean the Jackboot— and Isabella. They were lost inside a great, burning mountain, and suddenly an army of Petinons surrounded them and drew their swords at my father, but Izzy did nothing to help him as they brought their swords down on him." Elias stared at Merlin for a moment. "What do you think it means?"

"I got no idea, kid. All this prophecy stuff is for the birds, if you ask me. Well...I didn't mean it that way, but...look, I didn't understand half of what Hunchy—I mean Prince Enupnion— talked about anyway. Science is my thing. Here, you can keep the notes. I have to get Jimmy back to the pilot seat so we can make up for lost time. Are you feeling better? Any other problems besides your head?"

"I don't think so...well, my back itches a little bit, but mostly my head is sore. I'm sorry you both didn't get much sleep." Elias grimaced.

"Oh, that's fine. I'm sure we got a solid two hours. Should be good enough for another week now," Merlin smiled as he unstrapped an angry Jimmy from the bed. Jimmy instantly powered up and rose about two feet off the floor, stretched his arms, and let out a blast of steam from his exhaust port. Jimmy shot over toward Elias' bedside, looked at him carefully, and said, "You were burning alive." Jimmy placed his hand on Elias' forehead for moment then abruptly left the room. Merlin was about to follow him when Elias spoke up.

"Hey, I didn't realize we had Casper with us."

"Yeah, I wasn't about to leave him on the mountain even if he did like it better. I tricked him with some fish so he wouldn't scratch my arms off this time. He's a sucker for a deck flopper, huh?" Merlin laughed as he headed out toward the bridge.

"I guess so." Elias smiled at the owl as he climbed out of the lab bed then strolled over toward his feathered friend. "I guess we can let you out now, especially since we're far enough away from Pterugas." Elias opened the cage door, and the giant gray hopped out onto the bed where Merlin had been working on Jimmy. His eyes were fixated on something out the far window across the hallway. "Hey, old friend, something catch your eye?" Elias asked as he pulled out a fire berry to entice the bird's friendly nature. Casper instantly gobbled it down but returned his gaze to the window, ignoring Elias' kind gesture. The owl's piecing gaze was rock solid as if he was waiting for something. Elias looked out the window and then back at the bird. "What is it?" Elias asked again. Suddenly, Casper freed his sight from the window and with fiery eyes looked straight up at Elias and let out a fierce *screech* right into Elias' face. It jolted Elias' memory of Casper's war cry, and he lit out of the room and down the hall toward the bridge.

Izzy helped Ava as she came to and then quickly pawned her off on Bogan. She needed answers from Charlie and didn't have time to deal with Ava's sensitive nature at the moment. Izzy did harbor a bit of resentment towards Ava for the slight betrayal, but it was less than Ava probably felt at the moment. "Charlie, are you saying it's the Petinon heart that's making you change or the stuff they injected into the heart?" Izzy asked firmly.

"I'm not entirely sure. Maybe a bit of both, but I didn't start to change until they injected the heart with something." Charlie reached out and gripped Izzy's hand with his claw. "Be careful of the queen. She's not to be trusted. I'm certain she was here the night they injected me. I-I could smell her perfume in the air."

"THE QUEEN!" Izzy blurted out. "She's been nothing but good to us. It was the king that tried to hurt Elias. That's why I killed him."

"YOU WHAT?" Charlie asked, in astonishment.

"Oh...yeah. I forgot about that little detail, I guess, but..." Izzy's tone and anger increased. "HE TRIED TO TAKE ELIAS' HEART BACK! What was I supposed to do?"

"He's really dead?" Charlie asked in disbelief.

Bogan looked up at his brother. "Yeah. She really killed him."

Charlie breathed out a deep sigh. "Good," he said, much to the surprise of everyone.

Ava's face was filled with confusion and grief at Charlie's joyful tone. "Are you saying you're happy that Izzy killed the king?"

"Well, I'm certainly not going to lose any sleep over it. King

Arkone was cruel to me and Prince Enupnion. He tried to kill me several times. I always wondered if he'd been driven mad by something, but I soon realized it was just his nature. When I learned that he and Sunago were responsible for the creeping mold covering the earth, I wanted to kill him for sure." Charlie's words astounded the crew, and for a while they sat shell shocked.

"Brother, is it really true?" Bogan asked.

"It is," Charlie answered with a somber tone. "Sunago was King Arkone's best friend when they were only boys. They hated humans and were tired of their responsibilities of planting the seeds to keep the mold under control. It was Sunago's plan, but the young Prince Arkone loved it, and when his father passed, the new King Arkone put the plan into motion. He let the world fall to the creeping mold so the Petinons could rule over everything. When the king and Sunago had a falling out, Sunago left. I don't know everything that happened, but I was able to see a lot through Casper's eyes. I would love it if you could fill in the details…" Charlie stopped speaking for a moment. "Someone is coming."

"Wait!" Izzy said. "Elias isn't going to turn into some kind of bird freak like…like you, is he?"

Bogan yelled out his displeasure at her lack of concern for Charlie. "IZZY!"

"I don't mean to be rude, but we put the prince's heart inside him. That's how we saved him. I don't want him turning into some kind of bird freak or going blind," Izzy tried to explain, but it all came out the wrong way.

"Izzy, I can't believe you. This is Charlie! Our Charlie. And all you can think about is Elias. Nothing is even wrong with Elias. He's perfectly healthy," Ava scoffed.

"No. Please. I'm not offended," Charlie said. "She has every right to be concerned. I don't know if Elias will start to turn like me or not, but what I don't understand is why you're even concerned." Charlie cocked his head slightly to the right as torch lights began filling the hallway.

"What do you mean? Why shouldn't I be concerned?" Izzy scoffed back.

"Because they're your people. The Petinons, you're one of them, aren't you, Isabella?" Charlie asked, dropping the cold harsh reality that Izzy continued to deny in her own mind. "So many things make sense to me now. Your father, the Jackboot, and your brother, Elias. You're all Petinons, aren't you? No wings, of course, but you're one of them, of that I am certain. "

Izzy said nothing in reply as the guards arrived at their cell door. "The queen wishes to speak to the girl with the metal arm. She demands you come immediately."

"Don't do it, Iz. You don't know what she's going to do to you," Bogan snapped out.

Charlie suddenly interrupted and much to Bogan disappointment, Charlie disagreed. "Isabella, go with them. Do as the queen says. See if you can win her over and save us."

"But, I thought you said she was bad?" Izzy cast a confused glare back at Charlie.

"I said I don't trust her, but if the king is dead then she is the new ruler. Maybe she will set us free." Charlie explained with a hopeful voice, but his claws gripped the cell bars as if he were in terrible pain. "Go," he grunted out.

"Okay, okay. I'll see what I can do," Izzy said. Then the guards took her by the arms, and soon she disappeared into the darkness of their tunnel prison.

As soon as Izzy was out of sight, Charlie spoke. "The Whisper is in danger. Even now, I can see it through Casper's eyes."

153

ELIAS RAN DOWN THE HALLWAY CALLING OUT FOR MERLIN, BUT AS soon as he stepped onto the bridge, he quickly bounced back into the hallway. What he'd seen on the deck of the Whisper was unbelievable, and he gave a second peak to make sure his eyes weren't playing tricks on him. The bridge of the Whisper was filled with bat-winged serpents, and one was wrapped around Merlin's legs and another around his chest as he tried to fight them off. Both of Jimmy's arms were being pulled in either direction, and he'd lost complete control of the ship. Seven, maybe eight more, serpents were on the bridge, and several more were coming in through the open door. The forward deck was covered with them as the light of morning began to dawn on the troubled airship.

Something brushed Elias' legs from behind him, and it startled him so badly he nearly fell out onto the bridge. It was Casper, and his eyes were burning red from the fire berry. Casper looked up at Elias as if he were confused as to why Elias hadn't joined in the battle yet. Casper pecked at Elias' pocket filled with fire berries then suddenly swooped out into the mess of winged snakes attacking Merlin. Elias pulled the berries out of his pocket and stared at the red fruit resting in his hand. He'd always considered the berries a means of fuel to power his generator or to reveal some vision, but standing here now, he finally realized they were so much more than that. The berries had not only powered his heart generator and the ship, but they'd saved his life many times over in battle. His mind went back to the night Casper had saved him on the forward deck, and he realized it wasn't just a treat Casper liked, but a tool he used for hunting those bat-winged freaks that were killing his friends at this very moment. Elias shoved some berries into his mouth then ran out onto the deck to join the battle about the time Casper snapped the head off the one that had been trying to strangle Merlin and set him free.

"WHERE YOU BEEN, KID? WE'RE GETTING KILLED

OUT HERE!" Merlin yelled.

"I WAS LEARNING!" Elias blurted out as he tried to pull one of them off Jimmy.

"WELL," Merlin grunted, "SCHOOL'S OUT! IT'S DO OR DIE NOW!"

Elias pulled as hard as he could on the serpent wrapped around Jimmy's arms until, suddenly, both of Jimmy's hands popped off onto the floor. "WHAT?" Elias looked at Merlin in shock.

"DON'T WORRY," Merlin said tossing a serpent into Casper's claws. "THEY COME OFF LIKE THAT."

Elias was so flabbergasted by his accidental removal of Jimmy's hands that he'd forgotten about the serpent, and it quickly coiled around his neck. He looked for help from Casper, but Casper had his claws full at the moment and couldn't come to his rescue this time. Merlin was also busy shocking a couple with lightning bolts from his marvelous brain as he tried to remove another one from his legs. Jimmy was currently burning one alive with his chest turbine, while trying to pilot the ship with a cable that shot out of his arm after Elias popped his hands off. No help was coming for Elias this time.

Elias' eyes lit with flames as he reached out toward Casper gasping for air. Suddenly, one of Jimmy's hands rose into the air and shot right into Elias' hand. *WHAT? Jimmy is made with Petinon metal!* Elias reached for the other hand, but it simply rose into the air and floated in front of his face. He tried to grab it with his other hand, but when he let go of the serpent, it squeezed tighter around his neck, stealing away his breath. Elias gripped his hand into a fist and began punching at it when, out of the blue, Jimmy's floating hand formed into a fist and began punching at the serpent as well. Elias was utterly flabbergasted but decided it was time to fight back and so he did. He made a fist with both of his hands, closed his eyes and began to punch at the air. He couldn't see it, but he could feel Jimmy's hands beating the snot out of the winged beast. It hissed and squealed until it finally fell to the floor.

"WHAT IN THE WORLD ARE YOU?" Merlin shouted in shock but was too busy at the moment to run a scientific analysis on Jimmy's missing hands.

"I-I d-don't k-know!" an exhausted Elias breathed out.

Jimmy didn't seem too pleased with Elias' theft of his metal appendages and felt he should register a full complaint. "MERLIN, ELIAS HAS STOLEN MY HANDS!"

"FLY THE SHIP, JIMMY! JUST FLY THE SHIP!" Merlin yelled as he grabbed a nasty serpent by the tail and beat it against the back wall of the bridge.

Once Elias regained his breath, he looked at the onslaught of winged beasts filling his favorite ship, formed his hands into two fists, and watched Jimmy's floating hands follow suit. He grinned a nefarious red grin at Merlin, who cast a wonky eyed look back at him.

"WELL...DON'T JUST STAND THERE! HIT SOME-THING!" Merlin cried out.

"OH...RIGHT!" Elias said, wiping the smile from his face. He wasn't very good at punching and managed to put a few holes in the back wall of the bridge and even smash one of the large pieces of glass on the forward deck, but he got the hang of it. Soon, Elias was pummeling serpents left and right, and he almost felt like he was making progress until he looked out on the forward deck. The serpents were so numerous they looked like an invasion of oversized gnats in the distance. Elias smashed one's head between Jimmy's two fists by pulling his own knuckled fists together with a crack. Then he stabbed one that was headed for Casper and another wrapping around Jimmy's head again. He held his ground and smashed two of their heads together then broke off a couple of fangs from a rather large one and began stabbing as many as possible. Elias quickly laid waste to the nasty creatures with Jimmy's floating hands as the baffled serpents had no idea how to attack the invisible fourth man with only two hands.

Merlin finally got free and managed to close the door to the bridge as Casper finished off the last one he had. Elias killed the one trying to hopelessly to bite through Jimmy's metal head, and they all took a breather for a moment as they stared at the winged death outside the Whisper. Hundreds of golden serpent eyes glared back at them through the windows of the bridge as their rotten venom oozed off pearly, white fangs onto the Whisper's forward deck. Their pungent poison was so powerful, it burned the cedar boards, sending tiny puffs of smoke into the air all around them, and they danced a wicked waltz to the dawning of the morning sun.

"Elias," an exhausted Merlin said, "give Jimmy his hands back and take the controls. I want you to fly the Whisper."

"But shouldn't I try and fight these things? How are we going to make it back to GFC with these things all over us?" Elias complained.

"Just give Jimmy his hands back and take the controls, please," Merlin said, resting his hands on his knees. He looked pale, and Elias could tell he must have been bitten by one of the beasts. Blood was dripping to the floor off the edge of his left hand. "Just do it, okay?"

"Okay. Yeah, sure." Elias put one of Jimmy's hands back in his wrist socket and handed Jimmy his other hand. Jimmy quickly put the hand back in and locked each of them in place with a blast of steam.

"Jimmy," Merlin said.

"Yes, Merlin?" Jimmy replied as if it were a normal morning rising in the sky and there were never any bat-winged freaks trying to kill them just moments before.

"Kill them all, Jimmy! Kill them all!" Merlin said, and Jimmy instantly rose out of the pilot's chair. Elias hopped in while Merlin opened the door to the forward deck, and Jimmy fearlessly floated out into war with the winged beasts. Merlin looked to Elias and said, "Keep an eye on him, would you? I have to take care of something."

"Uh...okay. Hey, Merlin...are you okay?" Elias asked.

"Yeah, I'll be fine," Merlin said, walking toward the back.

Elias watched in awe as winged beasts surrounded Jimmy in the sky a good distance in front of the Whisper. There were so many, Jimmy soon disappeared into their sea of black wings until, suddenly, lightning brightened the morning sky with fierce blue bolts from the center of the serpent's circle. Wingless serpents fell from the sky all around their tiny ship, and lonely wings without masters floated down onto the forward deck. It was the first time Elias had ever witnessed Jimmy in battle, and Jimmy's cold bravery sent chills through Elias' heart as he watch the mechanical boy single-handedly lay waste to an army of bat-winged serpents.

THE QUEEN'S GUARDS MARCHED IZZY BACK THROUGH THE TUNNEL and then exited the entrance where the other guardian was standing. The guardian made no effort to stop them so they continued through the forest and back onto the cobblestone path leading into the city. The morning had long dawned, and the sounds of songbirds filled the trees around them as they journeyed. The smelled of fresh-cut pine lingered heavy the air as dew slipped from all the leaves onto the path in front of Izzy with a soft pitter patter as it splashed. While the guards pulled her along, she tipped her head back and caught some of the dew in her parched mouth. She played it off as if she were just a child having a good time, but she knew if they were about to execute her, she was going to have to be hydrated enough for battle. At the entrance to the city was a small stone fountain and standing next to it was Queen Elehos. The guards stopped and bowed down and forced a bow from Izzy by pushing her to her knees in front of the queen.

"Thank you. You may leave now," the queen commanded the reluctant guards. "I said, *LEAVE*. I wish to be alone with her." The guards looked at each other as if the queen had lost her mind.

"My queen, she's the murderer of your husband and you..." one guard protested.

"Leave now or I will have you both punished," Queen Elehos demanded.

"Yes, my queen," the guards replied and with a rush of wings, quickly left them alone.

"Are you thirsty, child?" the queen asked.

"Uh, no. I don't guess so," Izzy said with a sneer and a sigh.

"Are you certain? This tiny fountain has some of the best water on the mountain. Here, give it a try." The queen stepped aside and pointed to the water. When Izzy didn't move, the queen reached down toward the pouring water and took a sip. "Try it."

Izzy smirked but stepped up and took a few drinks, then several more after she got a taste for the crispness of the water. "Thank you," Izzy said with a smile and she soon felt more at ease.

The queen gave a nod of recognition then said, "Walk with me." And she turned down the cobblestone path leading behind the city. Izzy looked back down the path to where her friends were imprisoned, and thoughts of escape quickly filled her mind. She looked back at the queen who was patiently waiting for her to obey. The queen's voice changed from formal and distant to relaxed and gentle. "Please, child, walk with me."

"You know, when my dad gets here, he is going to be very angry with you if anything happens to me," Izzy threatened, hoping to fill the queen with dread. But she was taken aback by the queen's response.

"I've no doubt any father worth his salt would want to protect his daughter. Why don't you tell me about your father and mother?" Queen Elehos suggested, motioning with her snowy white wing for Izzy to follow her down the path.

The queen's compassionate demeanor was difficult to resist. "HA! My mother? Let's not go there, okay? My father, on the other hand, is extremely over-protective and a bit odd. Sometimes he's crazy and even a little mad. He's not what I would consider "normal," if you know what I mean?" Izzy suddenly found herself explaining every detail about her father as if the queen had commanded her to do so. Queen Elehos listened carefully as the two trekked the cobblestone path around the back of the city all the way to the place where they had buried Prince Enupnion. The grave of Prince Enupnion was under a massive ash tree that seemed to tower up into the clouds. The tree itself was adorned with multicolored flowers from some vines and even fire berry flowers growing out of the cracks. The tree was located at the very edge of the mountain and its roots crawled down the side and into a stream that flowed all the way down from the castle waterfalls. The place was not entirely secluded from the city, and the sounds of bustling activity soon filled the background of a gentle breeze.

"Why did you bring me here?" Izzy asked, somewhat upset by the queen forcing her to remember the loss of her friend all over again. Also not lost in Izzy's thoughts was why the queen was not asking about the night with the king or any details about why she'd killed him.

"This is the grave of my beloved son. He gave his life for your brother, so we will be forever connected to his life and his death." The queen looked out over the edge of the mountain into the passing clouds. "My husband, the king, was not a very loving father like your father has been to you. At times he was cruel to my son...but...he was always cruel to me."

Izzy's eyes grew large at the queen's honesty.

"I'm going to tell you a story that very few Petinons know of, although, some older ones do, but they were forced to swear an oath on their life so as not to shame their king." The queen took a deep breath. She trembled. She placed her right claw on Enupnion's tree to steady herself then smiled when Izzy's metal hand reached out and grabbed her arm to help her.

"When I planted this tree, it was never meant for my son, Enupnion, but life has a strange way of coming full circle." She trembled some more and caught her breath.

"I-It's okay. Take your time," Izzy said, staring into the queen's teary eyes. She tightened her grip on the queen's arm with her mod-arm as she didn't want the queen to fall over the edge of the mountain and die. True, she had wings, but Izzy wasn't taking any chances on killing another royal in the same week.

"I know it's not possible to see now, but on the other side of this tree lies another grave. It is the grave of my first child. A wingless Petinon like you. On the night the child was born, King Arkone burst into the room, filled with excitement for the birth of our first born. His pride was instantly crushed when he saw the child was born an outcast among our people." Her claw scraped down the side of the ash tree as she held her composure.

"My husband—the king...father of our first born—immediately tried to kill the child, but I hid it for as long as I could. When he found the baby, he brought down the full weight of his army on me and those hiding the child. Many people died that day."

Izzy was filled with grief for the queen and wanted to give her a hug, but hugging with wings seemed strange so she gave the queen a pat on the wing. "I'm so sorry. So this tree was for your first child, then?"

"Yes. This great tree was the monument for my first child. I planted it in secret when the king refused to let me plant one in honor of my loss. Beneath our feet is the grave of my first-born child—Ouranos."

"WHAT! Are you saying this whole prophecy thing is BUNK?" Izzy blurted out. "I mean, I'm sorry, I didn't mean to be disrespectful, but I thought Elias was Ouranos." Izzy was gobsmacked.

"I named the child Ouranos to anger the king and ruin their perfect prophecies, but when he learned of it…well, let's just say he was never the same. He had the name Ouranos outlawed from the lips of our people, and no one was allowed to study the prophecies ever again. My husband drew deeper into the darkness and became a cruel ruler, driven only by the old code of honor, without compassion." The queen stilled her trembling for a moment and breathed more in anger than grief.

"So, if Ouranos is dead, then what is Elias?" Izzy asked.

Queen Elehos, ignoring her question entirely, turned and took Izzy by both shoulders and stared intently into her eyes. Her own eyes streamed with tears, and a joyful smile crept upon her face. "Listen carefully, my child. Beneath our feet lies the grave of Ouranos, and that much is true in my mind and my heart, and it always has been until now."

A wonky-eyed look filled Izzy's gaze. "I'm sorry, I don't understand."

"Isabella, this grave is empty." Queen Elehos pulled Izzy into her arms and held her tight. Izzy's eyes grew big as the queen squeezed her harder then suddenly let go and dropped to her knees in front of her. Her massive white wings flared out to both sides as she knelt.

"So, where is Ouranos?" Izzy asked.

"I don't know, but I'm staring into the eyes of his daughter and my granddaughter right now, and I am so, so happy for it," she said, wrapping her wings around Izzy in a full embrace. "I'm so happy for it!"

12

A DEAL WITH DARKNESS

*N*ight fell hard on the tiny airship as they approached Grand Fortune City through a sinister fog that wrapped around its tower like a serpent. However, it wasn't the ghostly vapor that concerned the skeleton crew of the Whisper. It was more the rattle and shaking coming from the boiler room. The strain of the fire berry fuel had taken its toll, and by the time Elias found an empty space in the docks, he thought the boiler was going to fall out the back end of the ship. Elias glanced at Merlin, who had a disappointed look on his face, but he knew they'd made good time.

Jimmy was resting on the floor, completely exhausted. Twice during their speedy journey, Jimmy had gone outside and pushed the Whisper from behind to help make up for lost time. He pushed until his turbine would overheat and then he would return to Merlin's lab to cool it down, but the results were staggering. They'd made the trip back from Pterugas in just two days and nights. But something seemed off...different about Grand Fortune City. It was deathly quiet throughout the entire dock area, an unusual thing for the city even during a major fog event. Elias felt like he should say something about the damage to the Whisper's boiler since it was his brilliant idea to load fire berries into it, but the look on Merlin's face was holding him back. *Best keep my mouth shut. He looks really angry right now.* But, the silence was too much for him.

"Do you think we can fix it?" Elias asked, gritting his teeth. Merlin said nothing but simply stared out into the foggy streets of GFC with a gnarled scowl on his face.

Elias figured a more positive tone would help settle the tension. "Hey, at least we made it back, right? Let's get our dads and get back to Pterugas before anything happens to the crew. Besides, I'm sure Izzy can fix it. She can fix anything with that boiler, she even..." Elias paused as the boiler shook violently for about fifteen seconds, let out a bang, and the Whisper dropped on the dock plate with a loud thud. Merlin looked back at him with thousands of bright blue bolts striking the inside of his globe like a plasma ball gone mad. Elias started to speak again, but Merlin cut him off when something caught his eye.

"Kill the lights. Shut everything down," Merlin snapped.

"Why?" Elias asked foolishly.

"Something's not right." Merlin ran over, reached into the glass cockpit in front of Elias, and killed power to the whole ship.

"Hey, what gives? You didn't even give me a chance."

"Something is out there. I don't know what, but something's not right," Merlin whispered then turned toward his brother. "Jimmy, are you good yet?"

"I'm tired, Merlin," Jimmy replied with his head slightly tilted left and a frozen gaze toward the floor.

Merlin groaned out his frustration at their situation but shook it off and snuck over to the forward windows for a closer look. After some time passed, Merlin gave up on his notion of something sinister with GFC and spoke up. "Ah, maybe it's nothing. Go find us a four-wheeled dock cart so we can take Jimmy with us, and I'll get some flashlights."

"Okay," Elias said and clumsily climbed out of the cockpit and fell onto the floor with a heavy thud. He laughed it off, but when he looked up at Merlin it was clear the marvelous brain boy didn't think it was very funny. "What? I thought you said there was nothing out there," Elias grunted.

"Yeah, but can you at least keep it...be more careful, just in case there is, okay?" Merlin said, shaping his hands into an imaginary strangling of Elias' neck.

"Okay, okay. Geez...I'll get a cart." Elias said. Then, begrudgingly, he stepped out of the bridge and onto the deck of the Whisper.

The air smelled foul, with a rank moistness of a wet sock, and the fog taste was no different. Elias nearly gagged as he fumbled his way around the dock looking for a cart. The city was the quietest he'd ever heard it, and soon Merlin's words of concern began to eat away at his thoughts. The thick fog filled the streets with silence, and dark brooding shadows washed their way across the gray clouds of fog like lost ghosts mysteriously searching for something. Even the dead headlights on parked Ever-Wheels seemed to cast watchful eyes on every move he made. Elias shivered and kept walking. Maybe there was something wrong in GFC, but he didn't have the foggiest of ideas what it could be. He tried to wrap his mind around it but soon shook off his uneasy feelings when he spotted a cart by the edge of some storage crates. He grabbed the handle on the cart and gave it a pull. His eyes were instantly drawn to a long coarse rope with a pointy end slithering around the side of a large stack of wooden crates. He peered behind it, but when he couldn't find anything he headed back toward the Whisper. A grimaced look rose up on his face as the wheel on the cart began to squeak. He pulled up beside the Whisper, and Merlin carried Jimmy out and placed him in the cart. Jimmy curled into a ball and stared out at Casper as the owl disappeared into the darkness of the ghoulish vapor.

"Jimmy needs help. We need to find my father before he gets any worse," Merlin said with grave concern in his voice.

Elias was surprised at how someone with so much power and ability could be brought low so quickly. It was a good reminder that Jimmy wasn't just a machine, and he quickly remembered some of the things Izzy had told him to look for in case Jimmy needed help.

As Merlin pushed the squeaky cart down the docks, he looked back at Elias with a long face. "Did you have to get the cart with the squeaky wheel?" he whispered.

"It was the only one I could find. I mean, there was nothing. Trust me, I looked." Elias frowned at Merlin and was beginning to feel as if he couldn't do anything right on this trip. The fog swirled around them and soon engulfed their bodies as they entered Station Street. The sound of their boots clopping, and the squeaky wheel was all they could hear throughout the entire city, and the feeling of dread quickly fell on them.

"This is not right at all," Merlin said.

"Tell me about it," Elias heartily agreed. "What's going on?"

"I don't know, but we have a long walk to get to the Iron Weaver's station, and I'm worried we aren't going to make it there." Merlin glanced back at Elias as a long wisp of serpentine fog slithered between them. They watched it pass through as if it were carrying an evil warning with it: "Turn back! Leave this place! You've been warned!" Merlin stopped the cart and checked the side streets, but when he didn't see anything he continued. Soon they both began to hear hissing sounds echoing through the street until suddenly a scruffy boy with worn shoes jumped out in front of them.

"Quick! Come with me if you want to live," he said. "It's okay. My name's Henry, and I'm one of the Jackboot's rascals. Hurry! There's not much time and they'll be back around. Hurry!" Henry warned.

Merlin started to push the cart, but when Henry heard it, he stopped him. "Leave the cart. Pick him up. Carry him."

"He's too heavy," Elias said.

Henry grimaced and suddenly ran back into the alley alone. The sounds of rummaging echoed from the alleyway, and a few seconds later he returned with a rotten piece of meat. He rubbed the greasy chunk all over the squeaky wheel then repeated. "Hurry, we don't have much time."

Merlin pushed the cart into the alley, and after a few short turns, the squeaky wheel went silent. Merlin grinned, "I like this kid," he said to Elias, who also nodded his approval. Henry took them all the way down the alley so fast they had a difficult time keeping up with him. Soon he stopped and crouched down behind a dumpster. They followed suit and waited for whatever Henry was trying to hide them from. After a short check into the streets, Henry reached into the dumpster and grabbed a bunch of rotten food and instantly started rubbing it all over Elias, Merlin, and Jimmy.

"Hey! What are doing?" Merlin barked out at the kid.

"They're not allowed to eat trash unless they're told," Henry said. Merlin cocked his head to Elias then closed his eyes as if he knew something. Soon, Henry pointed out into the streets, and four large tunnel rats passed by. One of them stopped and sniffed the air for a second, but when a red light flashed on its brain mod, the rat continued on with his pack.

"Look, kid. I know you're worried about those guys, but those are my dad's rats. Trust me, we'll be fine." Merlin said standing to his feet.

"No! No, you won't. They killed the Jackboot's men and took him away," Henry blurted out.

"WHAT!" Elias accidentally yelled out.

"I don't believe it," Merlin quietly scoffed. "Come on, Elias, we'll be fine." he started to wheel Jimmy out into the street then

Elias got up from behind the dumpster and started to follow the brothers, but Henry tackled him to the ground.

"Hey! What you are doing?"

"Don't do it!" Henry warned. "They might be safe, but you won't." Henry held on tight until suddenly Elias heard the sounds of rats scurrying everywhere. Then he heard Merlin's voice through the fog.

"What are guys doing? Where's my father?" Merlin demanded. The sounds of weapons ratcheting echoed through the dense fog into the alleyway. "Fine! Have it your way, but I'm going to have my father turn you all into rat stew when we get to him."

Elias' eyes grew large as Henry quietly pulled him back up to his feet. The boy was small, wiry, and much stronger than he looked. "What's going on?" Elias asked.

"Come with me. I'll show you," Henry said, pulling Elias the opposite direction the rats were taking Merlin and Jimmy.

THROUGH THE MISTY FOG OF GRAND FORTUNE CITY, ELIAS RAN after Henry. He was shocked at how easily the young boy was able to stay ahead of him and nearly lost him until something reached from behind a parked carriage and pulled Elias back. It was Henry. He gripped Elias by the front of his shirt and quickly held his other hand over Elias' mouth then pointed back out into the street with a roll of his eyes. Six Umbrella Charmers were floating down the center of the foggy city street. They were dressed all in black, and their faces were completely covered with the umbrellas, making it seem as if they were headless apparitions floating through this life and into the next. Henry's eyes were filled with terror, and Elias could feel the boy's hand trembling on his face. He sympathized with the boy's anxiety and remembered what it was like when he feared death, but those days were long gone. He'd died enough and lived enough now that he didn't fear living or dying. However, he hated death with a deep-seeded anger that Henry would never understand. Elias stood there calmly as he looked into the boy's eyes and hoped maybe his calm demeanor would help Henry gain control of his fear. Once the Umbrella Charmers had passed, Henry made an attempt at explaining what they were and who they were. A poor attempt, but Elias decided it was best not to correct the boy as it was clear Henry's healthy dose of fear had kept him alive this long.

"Come on. I want to show you something." And suddenly Henry darted back down the cloudy streets. Elias rolled his eyes and took out after him. They ran for what seemed like an hour, but in reality was only about fifteen minutes. Henry stopped just outside the gates to the iron yard and hid behind an old rail car. He pointed over to the Iron Weaver out in the center of the yard. It was covered in tunnel rats, and they were welding and hooking up all sorts of equipment to the black iron beast. One of the rats let out a loud squeak, and the other rats instantly stepped back from the train. The rat pushed a button on something in his hand then something under the train lit up with a bright green glow. Suddenly, the Iron Weaver rumbled and shook then rose from its tracks and into the air about fifty feet above the rats. It shook violently for a minute and then slowly rumbled back to the ground. The lead rat let out an angry squeal, and the other rats quickly went back to work for their master.

Henry looked over at Elias and said, "They made it fly. They made the Iron Weaver fly through the sky. I've seen it travel all the way around the city and into the sky twice now. It's the Jackboot's train. Can you believe it? Tunnel rats made the train fly. That's crazy insane, don't you think?"

Elias was dumbstruck and couldn't speak. Henry waved his hand in front of Elias' face and asked, "You're him, aren't you?"

"Huh?" Elias grunted.

"You're Elias. The Jackboot's son!" Henry smiled.

"Oh yeah, uh…yes, that's me," Elias answered, but in his mind he wasn't sure of much. *I haven't a clue who I am anymore. Ouranos, Elias, the Jackboot's son, Whisper crew member, or whatever,* Elias thought to himself as a subtle feeling of embarrassment washed over his shoulders.

"Hi! I'm Henry. Sometimes I say the wrong things, but Billy still remembered my name." Henry smiled joyfully and held out his hand.

"Oh…okay. It's nice to meet you, Henry. Thanks for helping us out." Elias said returning the handshake.

"I know where they took him! Your father."

"Great! Let's go get him."

"Okay, but I have to show you one more thing. Come on!" Henry sprang up from their hiding place and darted back into the foggy streets.

Elias whisper yelled at the mad runner to hold up, but Henry was too fast on his feet. Elias grimaced and took out after the rascal. Back into the dense fog they ran, and soon Elias noticed two fiery eyes soaring above him. He grinned at the thought of his old gray protector following him, and it gave him a sense a hope that maybe this was all a big misunderstanding. Henry stopped just outside the Jackboot's library train station where he'd first met his father on the train. Elias put his hands on his knees to catch his breath, but Henry was adamant that Elias come over to the window and look inside the building. He made his way over to Henry and scolded the boy for a moment. "Can you please stop running? I've only had this heart for a few months, and you're going to kill it before I can enjoy it." Elias struggled to catch his breath.

"Sorry. Sorry. I just didn't want you to miss out on this. You have to know so you can tell everyone what happened," Henry said, pointing up to the window. "Look inside, but don't let them see you."

Elias peered into the station house not knowing what to expect. Did Bosarus finally betray the Jackboot or someone else? His mind rushed with every possibility of what might have happened, but nothing could have prepared him for what his eyes saw. Hans Kloppenheimer, the Puppet Master himself, was standing inside the warehouse with an army of tunnel rats behind him, and in front of him was none other than Cassandra, Elias' mother. She was dressed in her traditional black leather trench coat and floating about four feet above the Iron Weaver's rail tracks with her umbrella perfectly poised and her heels together. Floating behind her were about thirty Umbrella Charmers and one dressed all in green. At first Elias thought Izzy's step mother Vanessa had survived being run over by the Iron Weaver, but upon closer investigation he could tell this woman was much prettier than what he remembered of Vanessa. It was difficult to understand what was being said, but as the tensions rose, it became clear to Elisa that Merlin and Jimmy's father had made a dirty deal with the Queen of Darkness herself.

"Master of Puppets, you already agreed to this in blood. Besides, this is the last part of our agreement. Once you have completed this task, you have my word that Emilia will be yours forever." Cassandra's shadow seemed to stretch further over top of Hans as she spoke, but he did not seem concerned by her intimidations of darkness.

"This was never mentioned in our agreement, nor did I agree to any such deal. Emilia was to stay with me from the moment you brought her back. I demand that you release her from your grip at once." Hans lectured in his coarse-toned voice, and it sounded to Elias like death was scolding darkness.

"My dearest Hans, I only need Emilia for a short time. She will travel to Sullivan's Coast to solve a problem for my people there, and then she will be returned to you in full by the time you have returned to me." As Cassandra spoke, Elias noticed the green-dressed woman was holding a cage in her left hand. Inside the cage was Flit, and he did not seem pleased in the least bit to be caged by her. His quirky eye was flashing like mad, and his tiny beak gnawed at the bars of the cage.

"I have never been to this kingdom before. How will I ever find it?" Hans asked.

"Emilia, bring the finch." Cassandra motioned and the green cloaked woman floated over toward her with Flit. "This bird has been there and back. We caught him on his return trip to inform them of our removal of the Jackboot. He only knows what his master, the Jackboot, has commanded him to do, and his last command was to...um, no offense to present company, but, to rat us out. You only need to set him free with one of your tracking clips, and he will take you there."

"I don't have time to follow a bird over mountains and valleys. I need something concrete. I need a map, and I will have your precious black heart back to you in days." Hans' words struck Elias deep in the chest. Why did his mother want his damaged heart? What purpose would it serve her now? Sunago was dead, or was he? Either way, the heart was dead, what could his mother want with a ruined heart?

"I'm afraid this little creature is all we have to go on. Sunago is too weak to speak at the moment," Cassandra replied.

Sunago's alive! How? Cassandra's words struck Elias in his heart.

"Well, if you can find a way to access this little fellow's camera roll, I'm sure the great Puppet Master will be able to construct enough information to piece together some faster directions. Emilia, give your husband his informant, please." Cassandra giggled and black smoke poured from her nose as she laughed.

"When I return, I expect you to fulfill your end of our bargain, or I promise you...I will come for you," Hans warned.

"Once you have delivered my son's black heart to me, I will tell you where to find the monster you seek, but don't threaten me with your rats. They are no match for my Umbrella Charmers," Cassandra scoffed.

Hans raised his black top hat slightly and looked into her eyes. His face was very clear and terrifying to Elias now. The once fleshy Puppet Master was now much like Jimmy with fire berry metal covering his face, and his eyes were modified much like that of Gideon's eyes. The Puppet Master spoke, but with a scorched metal tone that sent chills down Elias' neck. "If you think rats are the only things I have slapped my brain mods on over these past many years, then you've no idea who you're dealing with, *WITCH*. My army is as vast as the stars in the sky. If you cross me, I will rain havoc on you, the likes of which the world has never seen."

Cassandra's shoulders moved back just slightly at his words, but it was enough for Elias to know the Puppet Master had alarmed his mother's wicked heart.

"There will be no need for violence, Master of Puppets. You have my word. Bring back the black heart and I will give you the information you seek. Now, I will give you some time alone with your beloved Emilia before she leaves for the coast. Forsythe is waiting for her, and I promise you, he will take good care of her. Not that she needs it." Cassandra glared at him with a nefarious grin then waved her hand at her Umbrella Charmers. In moments they swept themselves through the large open door of the Iron Weaver's warehouse and off into the gloomy darkness of the city.

Elias slumped down next to Henry with his back against the outside wall. He brushed both hands over his head then down across his face. Deep down inside himself, he wished his old hunchback friend was still alive, whether as the prince or

Hunchy, he didn't care. He just wanted someone to give him some direction. The sound of a squeaky cart soon filled Elias and Henry's ears, and they both peered back up through the window. The tunnel rats had finally arrived with Merlin and Jimmy while their father was still speaking to an umbrella floating Emilia dressed in her green trench coat and top hat.

"DAD!" Merlin cried out. "What's going on?" Suddenly, the green dressed Umbrella Charmer turned around, and Merlin dropped to his knees in shock.

A weak Jimmy instantly regained some of his mental faculties and fired up his generator. He rose into the air and circled the woman, cocking his head left to right. "Mother?" he asked, as his turbine sputtered black smoke through the air.

"Yes, my boys. She is your mother. I've finally saved her," Hans said proudly.

"SAVED HER?" Merlin yelled in anger. "NO, DAD! You've destroyed her. How did you even do this? *Who* did this?" Merlin demanded in defiance of his father's dark deed. His blue brain bolts spiraled around in his head as Jimmy continued circling their mother in confusion.

"KILL! No wait—be gentle...Protect! Father, I don't understand." Jimmy was utterly baffled.

The golden-eyed Emilia interjected herself into the boy's question. "Yes, my dear, sweet James. I am your mother. I know I am a little different than you remember, but I'm alive and that's all that really matters, now isn't it?"

Suddenly, Henry pulled on Elias' arm. "We need to get out of here."

"No! We need to help them," Elias snapped back.

"It's they're sons. They're not going to harm them, but if they catch you...well, who knows what they will do to you. The Puppet Master betrayed your father and sent him to the labyrinth prisons then he took over GFC. Not only GFC, but I ran into a miner and he said the Puppet Master was using Bryn-wolves to raid all the mines."

"WHAT!" Elias whispered forcefully at Henry.

"I'm telling the truth. If you want to help them, then let's get the Jackboot out of there before something bad happens to him."

Elias gritted his teeth and nodded in agreement. "Okay. You're right, but as soon as we break him out, we come back for Merlin and Jimmy."

"Of course," Henry agreed, and the two boys slipped back out into the darkness of the city.

"Boys, just look around, we're a family again. Everything we've suffered through has finally paid off. We're together after all these years. We survived the "Sky Falling" and burning alive. We've survived the wars and rise and fall of cities. Nothing will stop us now. Once I've completed my final task for the witch, I'll bring her into submission under my armies, and we'll rule the western mountain kingdoms and every tower city on the coast."

Merlin sneered. "So you made a deal with Cassandra, Elias' mother? What does she want?"

"Victor, I know you and James can't understand the full weight of everything I've had to suffer these many years, but none of this will matter when I am ready to strike." Hans looked over at Emilia as Jimmy continued to circle around her.

"What does she want, Dad?" Merlin pressed.

"She wants the black heart of her son Elias. For what reason, I cannot begin to understand, but she is a witch and she does what witches do. Who am I to question why a mother would want the heart of her son?" Hans explained as he twisted his dragon's head cane in his hand. The eyes of the cane glared at

Merlin, as if to warn him of his father's unstable mind, but Merlin stepped closer to his father and continued his complaint.

"Why she wants Elias' bad heart is no concern of ours? Really? Are you listening to yourself, Father? She wants it for dark magic. She's going to use if for something terrible, and you think our rats, moles, giant wolves and war bots are going to stop her? Do you remember what she did to Grand Fortune City? She nearly brought the tower down with smoke hammers, and she would have if not for Elias. She's powerful, unlike anything anyone has ever seen, and she has more Charmers now. How did she recover her forces so quickly? How long has she been working and building her army? We don't know any of these things. You never should have cut a deal with her." Merlin looked over at Jimmy, who was still circling. "Just look at him, Dad...he's still trying to figure out if she's Mom or not. He doesn't need this right now."

Emilia glanced over at Merlin and softened her golden charmer eyes at him, but it was the smell of creeping mold on her breath that Merlin was struggling with the most. "Victor, it truly is me. I remember everything, even the night our airship crashed into the mine on the very first "Sky Falling" of Angus Grand. I didn't ask for Cassandra to turn me into this, but she did, and because of it, I can now see my sons again, and soon we'll finally be able live as a family again." She floated close toward Merlin but stopped when he stepped back away from her. "In time, you and James will learn to accept me as I am and for whom I was many years ago, your loving mother."

Merlin said nothing in response but looked over at his father instead. "You betrayed your best friend. Maybe even the only true friend you ever had, and for what?"

"For love, my son, I did it for love," Hans replied.

13

RAT TRAP

*E*lias and Henry ran through the murky streets of GFC, avoiding every streetlamp possible so as not to be seen by the Puppet Master's rodent minions. The dense fog wet their shirts and hair like a light rain as their bodies cut through it. Elias' mind was filled with thoughts of dread and concern for his father and his sister. As he followed Henry through the fog, his mind raced back to the painful events on top of the Whisper. He soon began to wonder if something might have happened to them but was quickly pulled back into the reality of his situation when Henry grabbed his shirt and yanked him back, into a dark alleyway.

"Why did you do that?" Elias asked. Henry didn't speak but simply pointed to several rats moving down the cross street. Henry pulled him down the back alley, and soon they were running from alleyway to cross street, stopping for a moment and then into the next alleyway. They darted through the gray clouds of fog as fast as possible and back into dark alleys, weaving their way around dumpsters and across drainage grates until Henry spotted something in the next cross street. It was the Jackboot's Ever-Wheel, and it was lying on its side as if it had crashed. Henry pointed to it but said nothing.

"I can't drive that thing. I've only ridden on one of them one time," Elias said. "I wouldn't even know how to start it and look how big it is! You and I could never get it upright, anyway."

Henry whispered into his right ear, "Just push the start button and it will right itself."

"What?"

"Yeah, it's self-balancing."

"Seriously? Is it self-driving? Because there's no way I can drive that thing, Henry."

"Well, we can't walk to the labyrinth, and we can't take the train. There's no other way. I can't reach the handle bars, so it has to be you." Henry's frustration with Elias was evident by the scowl on his face and his right eye twitching like it was about to pop out of his skull, but Elias felt like maybe there was more than Henry's size that was the problem.

Elias stared into the boy's eyes. *This kid is insane! I'll just scare him a little, and he'll think of another way.* "Okay, but we're probably going to die, so if you're good with that, I'll give it a try," Elias said sarcastically, hoping Henry would back down.

"Sounds good to me! I've been running for weeks now, and my shoes are blown out. Besides, it's better than being eaten by tunnel rats," Henry quickly replied then ran out into the street to the Ever-wheel, flicked on the power and the self-balancing switch.

Elias rolled his eyes and took a deep breath then ran out into the street after him. The Jackboot's Ever-Wheel instantly rumbled to a start and popped upright, then Henry removed a severed tunnel rat leg from the back seat and climbed onboard. The Jackboot's Ever-Wheel was nothing like the one Elias had ridden on with Thomas Rand that night at Gabriel's Harbor. This one was a beast of iron, and the control center on the front was filled with all kinds of buttons and switches that had no labels to identify their purpose. The center wheel was split into two separate wheels and you could see between them. There were also large mirrors on each side and a light brown leather seat for the driver. The tires were thick, airless rubber and looked as if they could run through deep mud. Elias glared at the monstrous beast of iron with an overwhelming dread of the unknown and wished his father was there to show him what to do.

"HURRY UP! THEY'RE COMING!" Henry pointed down the gloomy street at four heavily-armed tunnel rats standing under a street lamp. Their green, glowing eyes reminded Elias of Merlin's eyes on the night they stuck the heart mod into his chest. Before Elias could get his mind around climbing onto the Ever-Wheel, the rats took aim and let loose their fury.

"WHAT ARE YOU DOING? GET IN!" Henry screamed.

Elias quickly jumped in, and with the twist of the throttle the iron beast filled the foggy street with thick black smoke. A glance behind him in the review mirror showed the rats were fading into the fog, but the last thing he saw was two fiery red eyes headed straight for the rats. *Casper!* Their gun fire stopped as he rounded the first corner, and the sound of Henry yelling directions soon filled his ears. Elias' view changed quickly when Henry pushed a pair of goggles onto his head, then Henry yelled out something about a big white switch on the control panel and Elias gave it a flip. Bright fog lights instantly cut through the night, and they were soon plowing their way through the city.

The city streets were stilled and vacant as the cold fog wisped by his cheeks, and Elias wondered if those were the only tunnel rats, they would encounter that night. His father's Ever-Wheel roared and belched smoke like an angry beast of iron, scouring the darkness for prey, and a smile rose up on his face as he soon got the hang of it. For the most part, the Ever-Wheel required no skill to balance or steady, but Elias learned quickly to simply gauge the distance between turns and brake at the right times. When he missed the turns by more than what was needed, he just rode up on to the empty sidewalks then back out into the streets with a tiny laugh at his mistake. All was going quite well until three tunnel rats sprang up in front of his iron horse. He ran the middle one over with a crunch, but the other two latched onto the sides and tried to pull him off. In a shocking display of fury and gore, Henry blasted each of them off the Ever-Wheel with a sawed-off shotgun. Elias was instantly covered in tunnel rat slime and guts but let out a laugh when Henry gave him a pat on the shoulder.

"KEEP DRIVING AND DON'T LOOK BACK! I'LL TAKE CARE OF THE RATS!" Henry hollered out.

Elias gave a looksee in his rearview mirrors and instantly wished he'd never looked back. Rats were clawing, climbing, and scratching their way down buildings and lamp posts from everywhere. He couldn't tell how many there were, but when Henry took the Gatlin gun controls many of them disappeared from view with squeals and squeaks of agony.

When Elias finally got to the tunnel entrance at the train yards, Henry yelled out his directions, "GO LEFT! GO LEFT!" But there were two entrances to the left and two to the right. Elias picked left just as Henry had said to do, but Henry should have said "far left," because their ride down the tower took a horrendous turn for the worse.

"W-W-W-WHY D-D-D-DID Y-Y-Y-YOU D-D-D-DO T-T-T-THAT?!" Henry complained.

"Y-Y-Y-YOU S-S-S-SAID L-L-L-LEFT!" Elias stuttered out.

"I...M-M-MEANT F-F-F-FAR L-L-L-LEFT!" Henry chattered out.

Elias had accidentally taken the train track entrance down the tower and their nice smooth ride to the bottom suddenly became a terrible teeth chattering descent. The tunnel rats didn't seem to mind this route at all, and within moments the

whole inside of the tower began filling with the mangy creatures. Henry did his level best to keep the rats off their Ever-
Wheel, but now more than ever, Elias wished the Puppet
Master's sons were with him. The tracks in front and behind
them quickly piled up with tunnel rats, glaring their angry
green eyes at them, and the dry clicking sound from Henry's
gun was not a good sign.

"I-I'M O-OUT!" Henry's yelled.

A large tunnel rat with a strange gun shot a cable at them,
and it wrapped around the Ever-Wheel, jerking it off the tracks
and out into the center of the tower. The rat hooked the cable to
one of the tower support struts that weaved together in the
center of the tower like a giant spider web made of cables, and
suddenly they were left dangling several hundred feet out in the
center of the tower. One by one the rats crawled out on the
tower support struts toward them as they hung helplessly in
their rumbling Ever-Wheel.

"DO SOMETHING!" Henry yelled at Elias.

"LIKE WHAT?" Elias yelled back as he flicked switch after
switch, hoping for something to help get them out of their rat
trap. Tunnel rats crawled from every tower support above,
below, and in front of them. Their sharp, nasty claws latched to
the support struts like skilled acrobats without a balance pole.
Some even climbed underneath others on the same struts with
methodically accurate movements as if they somehow knew
what the other rats were thinking. Elias finally hit a switch that
popped two mini-guns out the front of the Ever-Wheel, and he
blasted the row of tunnel rats in front of him off their strut, but
the rats behind them gripped their claws around the cables
faster and faster until they were almost on them.

"Henry, we need to spin the Ever-Wheel. Can you push off
the cable beside you?" Elias pointed to a support strut next to
Henry's head. Henry gave it a slight push and the Ever-Wheel
turned a little, but it wasn't enough. Their Ever-Wheel momen-

tarily moved away from the strut and then back towards it again. "NOW! PUSH IT HARDER THIS TIME!" Elias yelled out, hopefully gritting his teeth.

Henry reached out his foot and kicked the tower support strut, sending their Ever-Wheel into a spinning fury of madness, and Elias let loose on the mini-guns. Rats fell all around them as flames erupted from the hot, stinging rounds of death that pierced the filthy rats. The Jackboot's Ever-Wheel looked like an angry ornament, spitting fire at anything that sought to touch it. It was dizzying insanity, and Elias enjoyed it far more than Henry, who must have emptied the contents of his stomach twice during the joy ride. However, the tunnel rats were far more intelligent than the boys realized, and they soon changed their strategy to a more top-down approach, and suddenly the rats were reaching for them from above.

"I-I'm sorry, Henry," Elias said in a regretful tone as the rats closed in and grabbed them by the arms. Henry said nothing in response as terror had finally gripped the young boy's mind. Then, in the blink of an eye the tunnel rat's mod-lights switched from green to red, and they stopped their attack. The lights on their heads flashed several times, and then the rats quickly began to scurry their way back to the top of the tower.

"WHAT! What just happened?" Elias asked the terrified rascal.

"I-I don't know. They must have been called back for something. They never stop an attack unless something or someone calls them back," Henry explained. The boys breathed a sigh of relief as the rats disappeared into the darkness of the tower but soon realized they were stuck, hanging out in the middle with no way down.

"Okay, so what's the plan for getting this thing back onto the tracks?" Henry asked, looking around in wonder.

Elias took a short assessment of their predicament and gave his answer. "Well...I don't think this thing's going anywhere.

We're going to have to climb across the struts and walk the tracks the rest of the way." Henry seemed a bit reluctant at first but followed Elias' lead, and the boys began their slow climb down to the bottom of Grand Fortune City's tower. It took them nearly a full hour to make it to the bottom because of the slimy conditions the tunnel rats had created on the cables and rails. When they finally stepped off the last rail, Henry spotted something with glowing red eyes land on top of the Jackboot's Ever-Wheel. He pointed it out to Elias, who was over joyed.

"CASPER!" Elias raised his hands in the air and motioned for the giant owl to join them, but instead the bird began pecking away at the cables wrapped about the Jackboot's ride. All of a sudden, the cables snapped, sending the massive single-wheeled vehicle crashing toward the ground. The boys dove out of the way, expecting the worst, but the Ever-Wheel slowed to a stop about four feet above their heads. A baffled Elias was completely gobsmacked by the trick, but Henry smacked his hand to his forehead.

"AH! THAT'S RIGHT, I FORGOT. Hans installed the hover safety on the Jackboot's Ever-Wheel," Henry yelled out in disappointment with himself. At first Elias wanted to strangle him but quickly realized they had their ride back and could get to the labyrinth sooner than walking. Elias decided to keep quiet and not scold the boy, who seemed to be punishing himself enough at the moment. And so, the boys climbed back on their ride as Casper dropped down next to them. Elias wanted to kiss the big bird, but smiled and stoked the engine for fun.

"Well, come on, Casper. Let's get moving!" Elias gave a nod and they shot out of the tunnel together.

14

IDENTITY

Queen Elehos had long given up on the possibility of grandchildren when her beloved son, Enupnion, fled the safety and security of their mountain fortress. But now, standing before her, was one of three impossible dreams of hope fleshed out before her eyes. Her son, Ouranos, was alive, and she was now twice a grandmother. Her heart soared and her mind raced with so many thoughts and not the least among them was the fact the child had just slain her own grandfather. Isabella's brother now carried in his chest the heart of his uncle, Prince Enupnion, and Charlie, her granddaughter's close friend, was now changing into something no one had imagined possible. In Queen Elehos' mind, these things were small problems to overcome in comparison to the fact that Petinon law now required her to behead her granddaughter in front of the Convocation of Elders. It was, of course, something she simply would not allow to happen, but at the moment she could think of no way around the punishment for the murder of her husband, King Arkone. For now, she would focus on the child's needs and hope the weight of her information was not more than the child could bear.

Izzy pushed herself out of the queen's embrace. "Wait, are you saying my father is your son?"

"There is no other explanation for your and your brother's strange abilities. Although, I've searched the books of prophecy and I haven't found anything about your brother. I have someone close to me searching for those answers at this very moment, but I truly believe your father is my son, Ouranos."

Izzy shook her head in disbelief. "But I don't understand!"

Queen Elehos rose up and looked back at the great tree towering over Prince Enupnion's grave. "From the moment the king knew of his wingless child, he sought him out so he could put to death the wingless abomination. Among the Petinon people, a wingless child has always been considered a disgrace. Most Petinon families would discard them quietly so as not to be tied to such a dishonorable curse, but when I looked into the eyes of my wingless son, our Petinon ways seemed too heartless. So I fled our mountain in search of a human mother who could show him the love that I wanted him to have but couldn't give because of our laws."

"So...my Grandma Cyndelia's stories, they weren't just stories." Izzy looked at her white wings. "She always told me a great white bird had brought my father to her one night. I thought she was just dramatizing the events to make me feel special, but it was you. You were the great white bird that brought him."

"Yes, that name, Cyndelia, it sounds familiar to me." The queen smiled.

"And the terrible creatures that came during the great storm to kill my father must have been the king's royal guard?" Izzy asked rhetorically.

"Yes, and I thought they had succeeded. When the king set out to find my child and have him put to death, he locked me away in the castle under heavy guard for several months. When he returned, a ceremony was held and a child was put to death, or at least, that's what I was told. After a few more months of being locked away, the king finally let me out. Almost immediately I noticed the royal guard acting strange, but no one would tell me what happened. They had been sworn to secrecy by the king. It wasn't until the Festival of Fire that I noticed two of the king's closest guards were missing and several others had wounds they were still healing from, and I knew that the woman had fought for the child." The queen smiled nefariously at Izzy and said, "It pleased me to see their wounds and that the king had also suffered a great loss. He never spoke to me of it, but I knew he'd been beaten badly by the woman...well, I mean, your grandmother or someone." She lowered her head as she forfeited her title to another woman out of respect for her granddaughter's childhood.

Izzy smiled at her for the kind gesture toward Grandma Cyndelia and scratched at her back that still seemed to be healing from the strange event in the city streets.

Queen Elehos' heart beat hard in her chest as she released her long-held emotions. "I never wanted to give my son away. I would have died for him, but it was the only way I could save him. It is only now that I realize in my anger toward my husband that I alone was the catalyst of the prophecies when I named our son Ouranos. What wisdom can explain to me why I have lost my beloved son and in the process I have found my lost child of prophecy? I am broken inside... and at the same time I am filled with such tremendous joy to see my grandchild standing before me. I wish to show you something. Would you walk with me some more?" she asked.

"Sure. I mean, it's not like I have much of a choice, do I?" Izzy said in a snarky-toned voice.

Queen Elehos was a little taken aback by the child's brash statement. "If you do not want to continue with me then you may return to be with your friends if you like."

"No, no. That's fine. More walking is good," Izzy agreed with a smile.

"Good. Now that we have a bit of a walk ahead of us, would you do something for me?" She wrapped her right wing around her granddaughter as they strolled back onto the dirt path toward the city.

"Sure. I-I guess so. What is it you need me to do? I'm really good at spy work and stealing things for the Jackboot. Do you need me to get something for you? My crew is the best at odd jobs for spying or stealing or bot repair," Izzy eagerly offered.

"Would you tell me of your father and my son, Ouranos, and what has become of him? And of yourself? I truly want to know who you are, who the real Isabella is?" she asked sincerely.

"Oh…um…are you sure? I-I mean, do you want the whole truth, or should I embellish it a little to lessen the blow?" Izzy asked with a raised eyebrow and a sly grin.

"The truth will do fine, child. Oh, and I want to know of your mother. She must be an amazing woman to have raised such a brave daughter." The queen pulled Izzy in closer with her wing, lovingly, as if she was her own child.

"Um…let's just start with my dad. Okay?" Izzy winced.

The queen was surprised at the child's reaction and wondered if maybe there had been some family issues she felt uncomfortable discussing so early. "Oh, okay. That's quite alright then. One at a time it is."

"Well, Grandma Cyndelia named him Owen, but everyone calls him the Jackboot because of his iron boots he had fixed to his legs after Angus Grand cut off his feet," Izzy bluntly spat out.

The queen giggled for a moment. "Isabella dear, I said there was no need for embellishment. The truth will do just fine."

Izzy looked back up at the queen with a stone-faced gaze and said, "Okay then, what I was going to say was that we live in a nice blue house on a quiet mountain overlooking the sea shores of Sullivan's Coast. It has a white fence around it and the greenest grass you could ever imagine. The sky is always baby blue with puffy clouds shaped like animals, and we're never hungry or tired. My mother always has a meal for my father by the time he gets home from work, and it's the most wonderfulistic place in the whole wide world. *But no*, you asked for the truth so I gave it to you. Now, would you like me to continue with my lies or go back to the truth?" Izzy pursed her lips together in frustration at the queen's perfect idea of the world outside her mountain paradise.

"Oh child, I-I didn't know." A cool breeze suddenly chilled the air around her as if some ghostly apparition had slithered through the leaves of Enupnion's burial tree and down the back of her neck. Queen Elehos glanced down at Isabella's metal arm, and the cold, hard truth of the world of iron and smoke took hold of her thoughts. Her wings drooped down to her sides and dread gripped her thoughts. Had she doomed her baby to be some kind of mechanical monster of iron?

"Oh yeah, and that's another thing. You can stop calling me child," Izzy said, staring down her grandmother. "I'm seventeen and I've seen more war that any child should ever have to see. Who am I? To start with, Eddie Grand cut off my arm when I was like four, or something, and I fought Brom the Bull to relight the torch on the Night of Darkness. I've killed things that would terrify every child on your precious mountain and give your warriors nightmares for years to come. Oh…let's not forget Angus Grand and Sunago, who tried to burn me alive, but something like wings of fire saved me. I also just killed the king, who, I just learned, is really my grandfather, and he's not even the first family member I've killed. I killed my evil stepmother during the battle of Iron and Smoke where I watched Prince Enupnion die in my brother's arms. Prince Enupnion, who we called Hunchy, because he was the dirty hunchback my father kept chained as a prisoner in his coal mine, since my father thought he was like Sunago and worried he would try to kill us, but come to find out, the prince was really my long lost uncle all this time. I hope you're following me here because that's not even the half of it! My newly discovered grandmother is a powerful queen who imprisoned me in a dungeon in the ground with my best friends while my little brother fled for his life because his grandfather, the king, tried to cut out his heart—again—just like his mother, the witch that fell in love with Sunago." Izzy took a breath from her anger-filled tirade. "So…if you don't mind, I'm not trying to make little of everything you've been through, but can you please—*Grandmother*—let my friends out so I can find my little brother, because I'm scared to death my witch-mother will find him again, and I have no idea what she will do to him if she does."

Queen Elehos stood silent as her granddaughter let loose her anger. She didn't blame the child for it at all. Her people were an emotionally calloused people, and their laws were cruel and heartless. She looked into the sky and made a clicking sound with her tongue. Suddenly, two Petinon warriors dropped in from the sky above them and landed on either side of Izzy. "Return her to her friends," she said in a formal voice and gave a nod to her warriors. They took the child by her arms, and she let out a groan of disapproval at her grandmother's decision.

"WHAT? That's it?" Izzy complained with a scowl and a scoff.

"I'll see what I can do, but I am restricted by our laws." The queen looked back toward Enupnion's burial tree as the warriors carried Izzy away to the forest. She knew the world she'd sent her child to was a harsh and unforgiving place, but she hadn't been prepared for the words Isabella delivered to her. She needed time to think. She needed time to consult with one of the elders she trusted. The only one she trusted.

CHARLIE GRIPPED AVA'S TINY HAND INSIDE HIS FULLY FORMED claw. He could sense the fear and uncertainty in her voice as she tried to reassure him of her undying love, but all he could think of was how terrible the smell coming from his body must be for her. Gideon had awoken from his injuries several moments before, and Bogan pulled him aside for a situational report. He wasn't taking it as well as the rest of the crew, and Charlie worried for his first mate's state of mind for a moment. His thoughts were quickly redirected back to Ava when she spoke.

"Charlie, I-I have a whole notebook back in our room at the king's castle. I documented everything, even with as many pictures as I could. Of course, I guess you don't need that now that I know you were able to see most everything through Casper's eyes." Ava seemed disappointed with Charlie's strange gift.

"Oh no, I would love to see them. Maybe we can have one of the guards bring your notes when Izzy returns."

"What do you mean when she returns? Charlie, we can't stay here forever. We need to get out of this...this prison. We need to get you some help," Ava said, gripping his claw.

Charlie smiled, although he wasn't sure if she could tell. Her positive outlook was a welcome light in the darkness of their dungeon, but Charlie feared what the daylight might reveal to her and his friends. He'd lived among the roots and worms for more than a year, and he was much different from what he was when he'd first been locked away. Both physically and mentally a change was still taking place inside him. Even now, crouching in front of Ava, he knew he was much larger than she could tell in the darkness. If they were to force him outside, they would see him as he truly was, and he worried what it might do to them, to her, his lovely Ava. At least, here in the darkness, she was blind to most of his features, and here in the darkness she could cling to hope, but in the light, everything would be revealed to her. Every gruesome feature would stand out, and she would see him as he was, a repulsive monster. The pain and suffering he'd gone through was not something he wanted his friends to witness. There were moments of peace when nothing was happening to him, but there were also moments of ghastly terror and hideous agony that he hoped they would never see. Much to his surprise, he'd not had a single moment of suffering since his old crew had arrived in the dirt-dungeon of prison cell next him, and he hoped it would remain that way until they were gone.

"Ava...I can't go with you when you leave." Charlie bowed his head and stared at his partially formed claw.

"WHAT DO YOU MEAN? OF COURSE YOU CAN, AND YOU WILL!" Ava demanded, squeezing his claw forcefully in anger at his words. She caught the attention of Bogan and Gideon, and the two stepped over to see what the commotion was about.

"You don't understand, Ava. I can't leave here. They didn't put me here just because the king was angry. They put me here out of fear of what is happening to me," Charlie explained, but his friends simply couldn't comprehend the unknown horror that stood before them now.

"Brother, we will find a way to fix you; a cure or something. The Jackboot will have a plan, I guarantee it," Bogan boasted in a valiant effort to reassure him.

"Charlie, I don't know or even pretend to know what you've been through, but Bogan is right. We will find a way to help you," Gideon said, rubbing his head where his mod attached. It looked badly bruised and painful, but Charlie offered no words for his friend's pain. He knew they had all suffered in this life, and Gideon may have suffered more than the rest, but none of them knew suffering like Charlie did.

"I appreciate your kind words, but there is nothing that can be done for me now. This is my fate. I am bound to it until the end of it all." Charlie stepped back from the bars. *No! Not now!*

Not here! He screamed in his mind as he felt it coming. Shocks of pain crawled through his body while he made his way back, deeper into the darkness.

"Brother, I-I didn't mean to offend you. I just want help you somehow." Bogan's voice was filled with concern, and he motioned for Charlie to come back toward the bars.

"NO! NO! LOOK AWAY! TAKE HER AWAY, BOGAN! OH, PLEASE, NOT HERE, NOT NOW! NOT NOW!" Charlie cried out as he backed away into the dark corner of his muddy cell. He looped his arms through the roots as he'd done so many times before to help guide him through the pain. Thankfully, it was pitch dark and the torch lights had nearly gone out, so they wouldn't be able to see him. So, *she* wouldn't be able to see him. When the waves of pain finally reached their pentacle, Charlie could hear nothing of his friend's voices, only the sound of his own violent cries of agony. For Charlie's part, it truly was poor timing as the guards returned Izzy to her cell with full torchlights blazing bright. They slammed the door on her, then both guards fled in terror at Charlie's screams. In their hasty retreat, one of the guards dropped his torch. Izzy picked it up and raised it toward Charlie's cell so everyone could see what was happening. Half bird and half human, Charlie was caught between both worlds and in the midst of some kind of metamorphosis the likes of which even the labyrinth would envy. His partially formed hand rose to cover his face from the light and from his friends' view, but it was a hopeless attempt at a coverup. The Whisper crew watched as talons tore through his last remaining fingers, and Charlie's only good hand was now a fully formed claw. For a time, the darkness worked like a comforting veil to cover his grotesque features, but now Charlie's horrible metamorphoses was laid bare before them.

"WHAT IS THAT?" Izzy screamed out. "CHARLIE'S IN THERE! WE HAVE TO GET CHARLIE OUT OF THERE!" she yelled again, and Bogan quickly made his way over to her and grabbed the torch.

"Give it to me. Isabella, give me the torch." Bogan had never called her Isabella in all the days she'd known him, and it stunned her as much as Charlie.

"But Bogan, Charlie's in there with that…that thing."

Bogan placed his hand on her mod-arm. "Izzy…that thing is Charlie."

Izzy slumped down on the dirt floor of their prison cave, speechless. All they could do now was wait out the screams until Charlie's pain was complete. The crew pulled their jackets over their heads and did their best to block out his terrible sounds. When it became too much to bare, they finally ended up cowering in the corner of their cell together in an attempt to completely block him from their view.

IN THE DEEP DARKNESS OF THE LABYRINTH LAIR, SUNAGO AWOKE. He felt different but not in a way he could describe to himself or completely understand. The world seemed as strange as the woman standing over him, smiling and calling out a name as if he should recognize it. She was beautiful in so many ways, but her face looked distorted and awkwardly shaped. He wondered if it was the slime covering his eyes that distorted his view of her. She seemed small and weak in his presence, but he felt connected to her as a child is connected to its mother by an inseverable umbilical cord. His heart felt strong, powerful, as if it were new, and he listened as the woman called the name loudly.

"SUNAGO! SUNAGO! CAN YOU HEAR ME, MY LOVE?" she cried out then suddenly laughed a frightening laugh as he lifted his head. Her voice startled him, and he drew back from it until she gently pulled him close again. The room was filled with lights, and he struggled to see behind her, but that name she kept calling, it felt right to him. Familiar. Yes. Yes. He knew that name, but he didn't feel as though it belonged to him.

The woman was dressed in a long black coat, and she continued to wipe away the slime from his eyes, away from his body, as she spoke. "Only two more times and we'll be finished...I promise! I know it's hard right now, but you're going to be amazing, darling, simply amazing. We can't do the other ones here." She smiled. "You'll be far too big the next time around. We're taking you to a very special place where you'll have plenty of room to grow. I had it built just for you, my love. Just for you."

She continued wiping away the slippery substance from his body and removed what seemed to be a hard shell surrounding him. Several others discarded the pieces into a dumpster next to him as the woman continued her loving kindness toward him. "You're going to be so beautiful when you've finally finished your transformation. It's so exciting! Isn't it exciting?" She squealed with glee and kissed him on his wet nose.

"Come with me," the woman said, pulling on him. She led him out of the brightness of the lights, and the room became clearer to him. It was an enormous airship garage with a large iron dome above them. The dome was adorned with two crossed hammers and a sparkling wand in the center. She helped him up a ramp into a large cargo ship then helped him get settled in while the ship powered up. The inside of the ship was cold and hard, and he felt as if he might injure himself on its metal walls. The iron dome groaned as it slowly opened to the outside world above them, and it startled him. In his momentary fright he noticed that the workers on the ship seemed more terrified of him during his frightful moment, and he wondered if they were scared of the ship as well. Suddenly, he felt a sharp stick in him and the world became blurry and distorted.

Sometime later he awoke into another blurry eyed daze that felt more synthetically induced than a normal sleep. The drug wore off quickly, and he realized he was alone in a cargo hold of the ship. Clouds rushed by the windows as morning had dawned bright and new, and he felt new as well—stronger than he'd ever felt before. His skin also felt different. It was soft and peachy, but beneath it, something was growing. Something hard, like scales. He tried desperately to clear the fog from his mind and remember who he was. Like the shadows from the passing clouds, his memory seemed to elude his grasp. Small pictures of a sick, young boy and a room filled with plants passed in and out of his mind. Memories, like lightning, flashed through his brain, striking thoughts of a royal palace with a king laughing joyfully, towering, green oak trees, waterfalls and bright red flowers electrified his mind. He felt as if he was someone else trapped inside of something that didn't really belong to him. Not yet, anyway, but soon, soon.

The airship slowed as it reached its destination over top a massive tower structure in the center of a forsaken valley. There were no tall oaks or ash trees growing here nor was there any green grass to brush across his feet. Only mud and bone, fire and ash filled this valley. This was a place haunted by death, and he felt its grip closing in on his identity as he tried to remember who he used to be. Hundreds of rats were crawling all over the egg-shaped structure that was brooding over the sharp rocks of the valley. However, the rodents were not infesting the structure but seemed to be crafting parts of it together. There was a large opening in the top of the structure, and soon the airship made its way down through it. The ship slowly and carefully entered the opening. Inside was another egg-shaped structure, only it was about half the size of the one they had just entered. It was filled with a strange green liquid that seemed to glow and crackle with lightning. The woman dressed in black found him gazing out over the center egg as she entered the room.

"Time for round two, my beloved. This one will be difficult but...also the most rewarding." She gently brushed her hand across his face, and suddenly he felt another sharp stick in his side. "Sleep, my darling, sleep and fear not, I'm the only thing you will remember when it's over, but I promise you it will be worth it in the end."

The woman dressed in black hooked a large cable to a belt around his waist. He hadn't even noticed it before, but now as she hooked it up, he realized it had been there the whole time. She flicked a switch on a hanging cable, and with a loud bang a large door began opening in the floor of the airship. As his vision began to blur again, he watched her towering over him from above, but this time there was no smile on her face or joyous laughter. Her face was cold now like the macabre gaze of an undertaker waiting by his bed, waiting for him to finally die.

Suddenly he remembered. *THAT'S IT! CASSANDRA! WAIT! NO, PLEASE! YOU DON'T HAVE TO DO THIS...I-I'M BETTER NOW!* He tried to cry out to her, but nothing came from his mouth. Only now as she lowered him into his slimy cage did he realize his mouth would not open due to its strange new shape. His consciousness began to leave him as his body slumped into the warm slime of the skeletal egg. Its warmth was comforting to him during this shocking moment of realization. Like a mother's womb, he welcomed the relief it brought to his sensitive skin, and as lightning flashes of memories forever faded from his thoughts, Sunago accepted his strange new fate.

IN THE PRIVACY OF KING ARKONE'S CASTLE, QUEEN ELEHOS SAT across from her most trusted elder in the entire kingdom, Bebahyosis. She could tell he was more than a little shaken by her information about her grandchild as he paced the floor quietly thinking through her words. His bright silver robe skimmed the floor as he paced, and the strands of gold running down every edge glistened in the morning light of the open window. However, the joyous light of this morning was robbed by the weight of her words she had cast upon his shoulders. She needed to save her grandchild from death, but there was no law she could use to do so. Bebahyosis brushed his claw over the back of his white feathered head and down his neck. His piercing eyes seemed even smaller as he grimaced in thought then almost spoke an answer to her.

"Maybe... no... no." he said then continued pacing. The books of their laws were laid out all over the room in a frantic effort to find an answer, but he'd given up on those for the moment.

"PLEASE, Bebahyosis. There must be a way," she begged.

"I AM TRYING TO THINK THIS THROUGH! PLEASE, your majesty... give me a moment to think." Bebahyosis calmed himself before he crossed the line and brought her wrath upon his own head.

She said nothing in return to his outburst. She knew if anyone could find the answers she needed, it was him. Bebahyosis had found a way around the law to save himself after he'd killed his parents in self-defense. The king was about to put the young Bebahyosis to death, but the elder in training had studied their laws enough to find the only law that could prevent his own death. So, she waited hopefully, with bated breath, for him to come up with the right solution.

After a short time, the high elder stopped his pacing and stepped over to her side. "Your majesty," he said with a bow. "I'm afraid there is no way around this. Only the ruler of the Trembling Mountain is above the law. If the child was queen, then she would not be subject to the laws, and no one could put her to death."

"So, I would have to step down for her to live?" she asked.

He winced at her statement. "I'm afraid it's not that simple."

"It is for me!" she snapped back at him.

"Your majesty, how certain are you that she is even your grandchild? Have you forgotten the warriors long ago who tried to take the crown by force? They died terrible deaths because the mountain rejected them, and you want to place the crown upon a half-breed child in hopes of saving her from a quick death? In the process, you may bring upon the child one of the most horrible deaths anyone could ever know." He paused for moment as if to gage her emotional state. "You said yourself that her mother was a witch. Do you honestly believe the Trembling Mountain would accept a child from such a person?"

Queen Elehos stepped over to the window and looked out into the puffy, white clouds slowly rolling by. She took a deep breath of the air as she placed her claws on the window sill and began to weep. "I-I have waited and h-hoped for so long now that he'd survived...my, my boy, Ouranos...THE CHOSEN ONE OF OUR PEOPLE!" She beat her fisted claw on the window's ledge. "AND YOU STAND HERE, AND TELL ME YOU HAVE NO ANSWER, NO WAY TO SAVE MY GRAND-DAUGHTER FROM YOUR CRUEL LAWS!" The great mountain shook from her anger, sending birds fleeing in every direction as if the treetops were frightened. "I AM THE RULER OF THIS MOUNTAIN, AND I WILL DECIDE WHO LIVES AND WHO DIES! Do you understand me?" Her breath seethed with her anger. She released her clawed fist, now filled with blood from her own talons, and placed her shaking palms carefully on the ledge.

Bebahyosis knew his role, and his response was carefully measured. "Oh, great Queen Elehos, compassionate ruler of Pterugas, ruler of the ancient kingdom of Petinon's and the city of Pterugas, Commander of the Convocation and ruler of the Trembling Mountain. If you do this, they will kill you, and our kingdom will be cast into chaos for years to come. There will be no season of planting or chance to save this world from the encroaching darkness at our doorstep, and your grandchild will die alongside you in their anger." He stepped back to the doorway. "I will take my leave, your majesty," he said with a bow and left.

Queen Elehos stood by the window for some time and then called out to her attendant. "Gemenon!"

"Yes, my queen," a servant replied entering from the adjacent room as if she'd been eavesdropping on the queen's conversation. However, she carried herself confidently into the room as if she'd been listening more out of obedience than of malicious intent. Her deep, green-colored wings shimmered in the sunlight, and her hair draped down the sides of her head like red iron strands. Her shoulders were strong, and she strutted with the gate of a warrior. Queen Elehos turned away from the window and met the girl next to a large table. The table was covered with the books of prophecy and the books of their laws, and the queen quickly shuffled through them until she pulled a large map out from underneath the pile. She ran her talon across the map until it stopped on the place she was looking for.

"Do you know this place, Gemenon?" she asked the girl.

"It's the wooded area behind the prison, is it not?"

"That is correct, and over here," Queen Elehos pointed to a tiny spot on the map. "This is a secret entrance to the cave. I want to you sneak in and free the Petinon girl with the red mark on her face. Tell her to find my grandson and bring him back to me. I believe he is in grave danger."

"Yes, my queen. Right away!"

The queen smiled and placed her clawed hand on her servant's wing. "Do not return to me Gemenon. I want you to protect her and my grandson once you've found him. Epekneia will know where he's gone. She will know how to find him." Queen Elehos handed her a set of keys. "Take these keys for Epekneia's wing clamps and the cell door. You will need a weapon as well." The queen stepped out of the room and moments later returned with a sword. "This is King Arkone's sword. It has slain many beasts and even some of our own kind. If anything will empower you to protect my grandson, it is surely this instrument of death."

Gemenon dropped to her knees. "My queen, I-I am not worthy to carry this weapon."

"You *WILL* take it with you, Gemenon. That is an order from your queen. Your renown as a warrior and faithfulness to me is why I have always kept you close in my confidence. At this moment in time, there is no one in this kingdom more worthy to carry this sword than you are."

Gemenon humbly stood to her feet. "I won't fail you, my queen. I promise." Gemenon said with a proud gaze and confident voice.

Queen Elehos embraced her and kissed her forehead. "I know, Gemenon. Now go and may the wind be in your favor this day." Queen Elehos smiled as Gemenon dove out the window and swiftly disappeared into the forest trees toward the mountain prison. *If my wisest of elders can't provide me with solutions then I'll craft my own plan.*

15

PRISONERS OF DESTINY

*H*aunting shadows crawled up the walls of the labyrinth tunnels, and crooked vines reached out like boney fingers grasping for fresh victims in the darkness. Giant centipedes, slithering snakes with green, glowing eyes, and crunchy bugs enjoyed their search for something rotten or dead to devour, so they might fill their stomachs with joy. Bats and bat-winged serpents fluttered about snatching bugs and mice from the labyrinth walls in their quiet world of creeping things until something gave them pause. Their world stopped, and they suddenly scurried into their holes and caverns, fleeing in fear from the sound of an iron beast roaring through their pleasant world of dirt. Black clouds of smoke and fierce rumblings echoed loudly and shook them back where they belong, back into hiding, back beneath the cold, hard ground.

Elias and Henry blasted through dark tunnel after dark tunnel, and Elias was certain he'd eaten several bugs in the process. He looked back at Henry, who seemed to be enjoying the ride much more than he was, and Henry's white teeth sparkled in the light of the Ever-Wheel's high-beams. A goodly sized bug was stuck directly in the center of Henry's two front teeth. Elias wanted to laugh, but he didn't want to join Henry for another crunchy creature meal, so he bit his lip and plowed through another mess of dirt and vines.

After a few more tunnels, Henry yelled out, "WE'RE GETTING CLOSE, NOW!"

"HOW DO YOU KNOW?" Elias asked.

"IT'S GETTING COLDER, AND THE AIR IS WET AND SLIMY!" Henry replied.

"IT'S BEEN COLD, WET, AND SLIMY SINCE WE ENTERED THE TUNNELS!" Elias yelled back.

"OKAY, EVEN MORE SO THAN BEFORE!"

Henry's words were not very comforting, but Elias had come this far through dirt and grime and figured colder and wetter air wasn't going to hurt anything. He knew they had lost Casper somewhere in the madness of their ride but figured the great gray would find his way to them soon enough. It was a good comfort that Casper always had a way of finding him. Henry hollered for him to stop as they reached a strange crack in the tunnel wall. It was shaped like a jagged "S" as if someone had tried to hack their way through it with a stone. Elias left the Ever-Wheel's engine running and hopped off for a quick look at his way inside the labyrinth prison. When he determined he would be an easy fit for the hole, he dashed back to Henry, who was still climbing off. Elias checked the seat, and underneath it he found an adjustment lever. He pulled it, and the seat popped forward. In his most convincing tone of voice, Elias rested his hand on Henry's shoulder and spoke. "Henry, I know you are worried about riding this, or maybe even crashing it and getting in trouble with the Jackboot, but I need you to go back to GFC and tell Merlin where I'm at. Tell him not to come and get me but to go and save Isabella and Epekneia and the whole Whisper crew. There's no time to delay. I only just realized this as we were traveling through the tunnels, but I believe their father is going to attack the Petinons to retrieve my black heart for my mother. You have to do this, Henry! You have to get this message to Merlin. Their father has Flit. Merlin has to get to the Petinons before his father, or something terrible might happen. And Henry, whatever you do, don't get caught."

Henry looked at the large seat on the Ever-Wheel and swallowed hard enough that it echoed through the tunnel. "Okay, but... if something happens I don't..."

Elias stopped him. "Nothing is going to happen to it, and I know you can do it. I've never met anyone so young and brave as you, Henry. Or as fast, for that matter. This is your message that I'm giving you as the son of the Jackboot. Get this to Merlin as fast as you can, and Henry," Elias paused.

"Yes?"

"Don't look back, just go." Elias had no inkling of Henry's personal motto when he told the boy, but it felt natural at the time, and it worked like magic for the boy's confidence. Henry raised his head and smiled at Elias then climbed onto the Ever-Wheel, and in a flash, the boy was gone.

DARKNESS SURROUNDED ELIAS AS HE FELT HIS WAY THROUGH THE jagged opening in the wall about the time two red, glowing eyes appeared in the tunnel. Elias peeked his head back out and directed Casper toward him but slipped and fell backward into the hole, tumbling through the wall and landing at the feet of someone large.

"Well, what have we here?" the voice asked.

Elias looked up at the beastly man brooding under the light of a small torch. His clothes were ragged, and his arms were folded and relaxed. His hands were severely marred, and he seemed to be picking at a terrible scab on his right thumb with the fingernail of his index finger. The wound looked somewhat fresh, and Elias wondered if he'd injured it trying to escape the labyrinth prison. The torch above him sprinkled hot sparks down on top of his bald head, but the man didn't seem bothered in the least bit by the pain. What was gnawing, scratching, clawing away at Elias, though, was the fact that Henry didn't tell him the "S" entrance to the labyrinth would lead him directly into a prison cell with a monster.

"Look, mister. If you're going to kill me and eat me or something, just know that I don't really have much meat on my bones as it is, so I won't make much of a meal," Elias said hoping to redirect the man's thoughts ahead of time.

"Why in the world would I want to eat you, boy?" the man asked in his graveled voice.

"Well... I just thought... alright then, never mind." Elias got to his feet and dusted himself off. He wanted to be nice and offer his hand for a formal introduction, but the man's hands were so large, Elias was afraid his fingers would be crushed in a single grip. He was relieved when the man reached out his massive index finger for Elias to grip for a shake.

"Pleased to meet you, kid. The name's Mr. Black," the man said with a gnarled grin. Elias shook the man's index finger and quickly wished he hadn't when he noticed blood all over it from the man's scab picking. The man could see Elias was a bit disturbed by it and added his view of the new circumstances.

"I would apologize for the bloody hands, but you better get used to it down here, boy." Mr. Black tossed him a small cloth to wipe his hand, and Elias nervously cleaned it off.

"Thank you, Mr. Black," Elias said reaching to hand the rag back to the man. "So, um, Mr. Black... that's an interesting name," Elias said in an effort at small talk as he still feared the man would crush him to death.

"It is, isn't it, now?" Mr. Black snidely replied. "They call me Mr. Black down here in the labyrinth, because I've killed more creatures than the Black Mist ever has," he said, leaning in toward Elias' face. "They give all legendary warriors strange names down here."

"You're a Legend! But, if you're a Legend then why are you locked up in a nasty cell?" Elias blurted out.

"Once Mogdal the troll became ruler of Karl's Labyrinth, he put an end to the freedom for all Standing Heroes and Legends. He wanted to be the only Legend to walk freely among the people." Then Mr. Black's gnarled face turned near childlike, and he added a bit of sarcasm and a prissy tone to his graveled voice as if to mock Mogdal. "Or maybe he just doesn't want us to tell everyone that he sucks his fat thumb at night in fear of all the Legends breaking free and killing him. Or maybe his mummy didn't love him because he was so ugly his daddy slapped the wrong end at birth."

Elias snickered at Mr. Black's comments, and it helped him feel more at ease with the beastly man. "So, what do you do down here?" Elias asked.

"Well, mostly I sit here and wait until they open the cell door. Then I go topside and kill a few poor souls for the crowds in the arena. After that, Mogdal sometimes throws me or another Hero into one of the "Specials" just to keep things interesting." Mr. Black chewed at the scab on his right thumb as he spoke.

"Specials?" Elias wondered.

"Specials are battles between a Standing Hero and a Legend or a Legend and a winner or a Standing Hero and a winner or a mix match of whatever Mogdal chooses, but I digress. I'm tired of killing. I would be quite fond of sitting here reading a good book or something, but killing is all I know... and I'm *very good* at it." Mr. Black spoke with a devilish grin that forced Elisa to lean back slightly away from him.

Elias scratched the back of his head and asked, "So... have you read any good books lately?"

Mr. Black scowled and replied in his deepest graveled tone.

"There are no books down here, boy. This is the Labyrinth. Only pain and death await us both."

It was clear to Elias that Mr. Black was trying to terrify him, but Elias no longer feared death, and the man's words had no impact on him. When the man realized this, he sat back against the wall, and a strange gleam of wonder appeared on his face. "Humph, but you're not afraid of dying, are you, boy?"

ON THE OTHER SIDE OF THE LABYRINTH PRISON LAY THE Jackboot, the lost child, Ouranos; the chosen one of the Petinon people. His body was exhausted from the events triggered by Hex and his fire berry paste. Grundorph and Hex stood over him wondering if he was dead. Grundorph gave the Jackboot another tap with his massive index finger, and the Jackboot let out a simple groan.

"HE'S ALIVE!" Hex exclaimed.

"Barely," Grundorph said, nudging the man's body again. "Look! One of his boots is loose on his leg. It must be from the heat. I've seen this before with the bolts on my own head. Someone needs to tighten the boot down... like this," Grundorph smiled and gave one of the bolts on his skull a twist with his finger and thumb.

Hex grimaced at Grundorph's demonstration of skull maintenance. "Please, Grud...don't do that! It's disturbing."

"Well, it has to be done, and I can't do it. I might overtighten it and snap his leg off." Grundorph held his large hands up at Hex.

"Well, I can't do it either," Hex said, holding his clawed hands up at Grundorph.

"I guess we'll have to wait until he gets well, and maybe he can do it himself," Grundorph theorized.

A grave look of concern washed over Hex's face. "So, what

do we do with him? We can't leave him in here when the gates open, or the wolf hybrids will eat him."

"We're going to have to take him out with us."

"It's going to be difficult to protect a man in his condition."

"We don't have a choice, Hex."

Hex looked up at Grundorph's head with a subtle squint of his eyes and said, "We need to find a way to strap him to the top of your metal plate." He looked back at the Jackboot's boots. "We could turn the boots on, and that would secure his feet. And maybe between our clothes we can tear enough cloth to strap his body down to one of your skull bolts."

Grundorph smiled. "Uhmmm… I heard my father, Ogg the Murderous, once made a man-hat from a poor fellow who'd beaten him in a game of cards." Grundorph grabbed his large kilt by the edges and dipped slightly at Hex. "Shall I curtsy when I step out into the arena or just give a bow with my Jackboot hat?"

"THIS IS A SERIOUS MATTER, GRUND. This man might very well be the chosen one of my people. We must keep him safe."

"Alright, alright, don't get your feathers in a bunch. I was just having a bit of fun with it. It's not like I get many opportunities for a laugh down here. Especially with someone as emotionally constipated as you are, Hex."

"I am sorry, my friend, but I have never experienced anything like this day, and the significance of it is weighing heavy on me. I know I am right about this. I feel it in my bones. He must be the one."

"Well, then, let's get him strapped down to my skull plate before the next round begins."

A WORLD AWAY, DEEP INSIDE THE TREMBLING MOUNTAIN, THE remaining Whisper crew sat in the silence of their prison cell. Charlie's screams had ended, and all that remained of his agonizing transformation were strange smells and hot steam rising from his exhausted body. Izzy sat with her back against the dirt wall, twirling her baton with her mod-hand. The rest of the crew sat in a row to her right and did their best to cover their noses from the putrid smells emanating from Charlie's cell. Izzy pushed herself back deeper into the cool mountain dirt and grimaced enough to catch Gideon's attention.

"Izzy, is something wrong?" Gideon asked.

Izzy looked at him like he'd lost his mind. "What's that supposed to mean?"

Gideon rephrased his question when he realized the foolishness of his inquiry in light of their odd circumstances. "I'm sorry. What I meant...I was wondering about your back. Is everything okay with it? It seems to be bothering you a lot."

"It's just irritated from the burns." Izzy said with an off-putting tone, hoping to keep him quiet.

"What burns?" he asked.

"From the thing, Gideon, the thing in the streets," she snapped back at him, then realized he was unconscious during her strange moment of pain. "Sorry, I forgot you weren't awake. Something happened to me when they were bringing us to the prison. I fell down in the streets and felt like I was burning alive, but it stopped. I have a couple of burns on my back that are healing, so I'm just a bit irritated at the moment."

"Oh, I didn't know. Do you want Ava to take a look at it?" Gideon said in his most sincere tone.

"No, that's fine. She already did. I'll...I'll be fine. Just let me deal with it on my own, okay?" Izzy winced a bit. She wanted to tell her friends about what she'd learned from the queen, because she'd promised not to hide things from them anymore, but it just felt like bad timing. Her thoughts raced with so many things as she watched her friend Charlie lying in the next cell. Her problems felt small compared to his, but it wasn't like she didn't have major issues of her own to consider. *Oh, by the way, Gideon, I just learned my father, the Jackboot, is really the lost son of Queen Elehos and King Arkone. You know, the king I just killed, and well, he was my grandfather. Not a good one, I guess, but he was still something. Oh yeah, they might kill us all if my father doesn't get here soon and put a stop to this. Who am I kidding? I really screwed up. And these burns on my back are killing me right now.* She paused at the revelation of her own thoughts. *BURNS! But I shouldn't have been burned from fire berries.* Her heart raced in panic at the thought of eating another fire berry. What if something happened and she couldn't eat them anymore? Sweat dripped from her forehead as panic set in, and her back became more noticeably irritated from her thoughts. She felt as if she couldn't breathe, and a tremor shook her hand.

"Are you sure you're okay, Izzy?" Gideon asked as he noticed she suddenly looked very pale.

Izzy instantly stood to her feet gasping for air. "I-I-I think, maybe Ava should check... look at my back. I-I don't... I can't breathe. I can't breathe!" She grabbed her chest and began hyperventilating. Gideon and Ava quickly stood up and looked at her. They were yelling, but she couldn't hear them speaking as black circles closed around her eyes.

Moments later she came to, and she was lying on the floor. Ava was kneeling over her. "You passed out. I think you had a panic attack or something."

"Oh," she responded in a daze.

"I checked your back, because Gideon said you were complaining about it. Izzy, you have two large burns on your back, and they look terrible. You need help or they... they might get infected." Ava dabbed a cool rag on her forehead. "We've never seen you panic like that before. It really scared us."

"I-I don't want to talk about it right now." Izzy said, closing her eyes.

"Well, it's probably better if you don't right now anyway. That way you don't panic and it doesn't happen again," Ava reasoned.

"Is Charlie better yet?" Izzy asked.

"He's been moving some, but we can't see very well in here, so...I...I'm worried about him, Izzy."

"I'm worried about all of us, Ava. If my father doesn't get here soon... I don't know what they will do to us." Izzy sat up and got her bearings then scooted back into the cool wall again. "Ava," she said.

"Yes?"

"Something is wrong with me. I can feel it everywhere. In my whole body. My arms. My legs."

Ava placed her hand on Izzy's shoulder. "I think it was the berries, Izzy. You shouldn't have eaten them. Just because Elias can eat them doesn't mean that you can."

Izzy smiled. "Ava, you're one of the best friends I've ever had, and I never should have kept secrets from you. I blame my father for that way of thinking. Anyway, I've been eating the berries since I was four. It might be the berries, but this time it didn't feel like that at all. I don't know what's happened, but I feel different. I feel like my body is going to float away without me."

IN THE VALLEY OF BONES THERE REMAINED NOT A SINGLE BONE lying on the ground. Steam rose from the rich, black soil left behind from the tunnel rat's bone construction of the massive egg shaped Keep in the center of the valley. The sounds of work had nearly come to an end and only a few rats remained to complete their finishing touches on Cassandra's deliciously weird egg project. Rat 47 tightened bones with bolts around the inside of the larger hollow dome, while 44, 45 and 46 worked closer to the smaller egg-shaped dome in the center. The small, boney egg was about thirty feet in height and about twenty feet at its larger center part. Although their project was coming to a close, these remaining rats took great pride in the work they did for their Puppet Master, and they wanted him to be pleased enough to receive their due reward at the finish.

Rat number 44 was a portly rat, but very good at finish work. His whiskered snout tickled at the scent of something strange as he tightened a few bolts on the smaller egg with a goodly sized wrench. He then took a rag and polished a few of the bones he'd just completed for good measure. As he continued to inspect his handy work, he noticed Rat 45 had caught the scent of something as well and was giving a good sniffing at the bottom of their smaller egg. The strange scent was coming from some blackish goo that had slimed its way into a puddle at Rat 45's feet. Rat 46 noticed the problem and marched over to help troubleshoot the goo. Their lack of productivity must have angered Rat 47, who let out a disapproving hiss at them all. Brain-mods flashed and they all looked back at Rat 47 then back at the egg. Rat 47 soon joined them beside the wonderfully delicious goo oozing its way onto Rat 45's feet. For reasons unbeknownst to all of them, Rat 45's brain-mod gave no warning and red light of disobedience when he reached down with his claw and dipped it into the goo. Rat 45 sniffed his claw and then licked it. He looked back at his rat brothers in wonder at what it might be then, suddenly, without warning, he dropped down on all fours and began lapping up every bit of the goo.

This, of course, was quite embarrassing for all of them. Their brother rat was mysteriously defying their master's set commands and had turned from a sophisticated creature of good merit into a nasty goo-gobbler down on all fours. It was a disappointing turn of events for the day as they all knew what must be done with rats that defy the master's commands. Rat 46 blinked his eyes then un-holstered a large hand gun strapped to his side. He placed it against Rat 45's head and looked to his brother rats for their approval. They gave a nod and Rat 46 pulled back the hammer on his gun.

Suddenly, without warning Rat 45 stopped his disobedience and stood up. His eyes were on fire, and a horrible angry snarl was on his face. Rat 47 gave a sideways nod to Rat 46 to move ahead as planned and put Rat 45 down, but before he could do it, Rat 45 gnawed off 46's face. Rat 46 ran around in circles howling in pain and bouncing off the walls of the larger egg. Rat 47 drew his weapon then proceeded to put a bullet into Rat 45 but missed and he too was attacked and lost his right front claw almost instantly. Rat 47's weapon discharged and ricocheted around the large boney dome until it hit the smaller egg in the center and cracked it.

Out of pity for Rat 46 losing his face, Rat 44 decided he should put his brother down. Rat 46 was running in circles trying to find his eyes when Rat 44 stepped up next to him and cold cocked him on the back of the head with his wrench. Several blows later and Rat 46 was gone. When he turned around, Rat 44 noticed that Rat 47 was staring up at an opening on the top of the smaller egg. Black goo was running down the side of the egg, and a large hole was in the top. Rat 45, however, was nowhere to be found. Rat 44 stepped over next to Rat 47 and looked his work mate in the face. Rat 47 looked terrified. Rat 44 gave Rat 47 a nudge as if to say – *What the cheese happened to 45?*

Rat 44's brain-mod flickered with several lights, and Rat 47's lights responded in kind, then Rat 47 pointed to the top of the egg with his remaining claw. Rat 44 scratched his whiskered snout for a pondering moment, then suddenly a large creature rose out of the center of the egg and grabbed Rat 47 by the neck. It pulled Rat 47 up into the egg, and in the blink of an eye Rat 44 was all alone.

Rat 44 picked up Rat 47's gun that was still attached to the severed claw. He cleaned it and then quickly backed away from the egg until he was standing up against the inside wall of the larger egg. He waited for a time, but when nothing happened, he decided to investigate the problem. He snuck around the inside of the large circle until he could see the back side of the smaller egg. It had cracked all the way open, and a part of it had slid off the back side. Black goo was oozing everywhere, and Rat 44 wondered just how this day could have gone so terribly wrong for his crew. Then he spotted something over by Rat 46's body. Whatever took Rat 45 and Rat 47 was now eating Rat 46. Rat 44 unloaded his weapon into the creature, but all that did was draw its attention to him. The monstrous creature slowly made its way over to the trembling Rat 44, and with a quick snap of its mouth, Rat 44 and his entire construction crew were gone.

16

BROTHERS

Sunlight dawned carefully over Grand Fortune City as the Puppet Master's sons stood gazing at the newly modified Iron Weaver. The black train hovered about four feet off the surface of the dock tracks as blue bolts of lightning crackled and flashed underneath it. The large stack above the bull head seemed useless at this point as not a single puff of black smoke rolled from its cap. Its cars, now fully constructed to the engine as one whole vehicle, floated at the same level, and all moved as one. The Puppet Master had turned the locomotive into a fortified airship that needed no sails, hot boiler gasses, or hydrogen to fly. To the south of them, tunnel rats quietly loaded into four massive airships that were linked to the Iron Weaver with a long chain. The boys watched while their father stood on the steps of the hovering train and embraced their risen mother as she floated in the air next to him with her dark green umbrella. She kissed his glass head covering and gently brushed her gloved hand down the side of it. Merlin grimaced at the sight of it, and Jimmy still wondered if he should kill *IT* or *HER* or *WHATEVER IT WAS*. She waved goodbye to her sons and without delay, rose high into the sky for a destination unbeknownst to either of them.

Their father leapt off the side of the train and walked over to them. "James. Victor. I know it's difficult to understand the decisions I've had to make, but I promise you... I promise you, you will understand someday. It will all be worth it in the end," he explained.

Merlin sneered at him. "Where are you going? Who are you going to betray today, Father?"

Hans' leather gloves made squinching sound as he tightened his grip on his dragon's head cane to calm his response. "I am going to secure a kingdom for you, my son, and whether you like it or not, it is your destiny. I will create a lasting legacy for our family. One the world will never forget. Once this task is complete, I will have fulfilled my agreement with the witch, and she will no longer hold your mother's life over me."

"I can't believe you actually trust her. She's pure evil, Father. She'll never keep her word," Merlin warned his father in his most convincing tone only now, with his father's new face made of metal, it was difficult to tell if he was getting through to him.

"I've made... preparations," he said, looking over at James, "in case...she decides to betray me, but for now I must complete this task so she will finish her end of the bargain. Only then can I complete my final goal. My... my resolution."

"And what would that be, Father?" Merlin asked, but his father did not respond. Hans simply gave him an endearing brush on his shoulder then offered Jimmy a kind pat on his foot and stepped back toward the train. One of the rats inside lowered the train to within a foot of the tracks, and Hans climbed onboard. He waved goodbye to his sons then strolled toward the back car of his iron monster. As the last of the tunnel rats loaded onto the airships, their doors closed, and the Iron Weaver rose into the air with flashes of lightning crackling all around the bottom of its iron wheels. It momentarily blocked out the sun from the sky as it turned around in midair and faced the heavens. Bluish-green flames burst forth from two cylinders mounted to the sides of the Iron Weaver's boiler, and the train rocked sideways from the force of their thrust then suddenly stabilized and pulled slowly into the sky. The other airships rose into the air behind the Iron Weaver, and the train slowly accelerated, pulling the chain taunt. A deafening roar shook the buildings of Grand Fortune City as the train powered up to full strength, and with a violent blast from its ghoulish, flamed rockets, the Puppet Master's army shot out into the cold blue sky.

The two brothers were at a loss for words or action as they stared at the tiny black dot disappearing into the ether, but only moments later, the sound of an angry Ever-Wheel rumbling through the city streets caught their attention. It seemed poorly driven as it entered the dock area and stopped beside them. A small boy climbed off and removed his goggles. His entire face was covered in tunnel dirt and grime, and his teeth were filled with bugs as he smiled at the brothers. He powered down the Ever-Wheel so fast it let out a loud bang that sent muddy globs from it tires splattering onto the walkway of the docks.

"Henry?" Merlin asked in wonder.

"Yeah, it's me, Henry!" the boy joyfully said. "I have a message from Elias."

After waiting for a few seconds, Merlin wondered what the boy was waiting for and said, "Well, out with it. What is it?"

"You have to get Izzy. You have to get to the Whisper crew before your father does."

"WHAT?!" Merlin shouted.

"Your father has Flit. He's going to attack the bird people. Your father is going to get Elias' black heart for the witch. You know, his mother!"

The marvelous brain boy slumped to the ground, shaken by Henry's words. "He...he just left with an army of tunnel rats. I-I didn't know where he was going." Merlin looked back up at Henry and Jimmy. "It's too late now. We'll never catch him. At the speed he's traveling, he'll be there in three days. The Whisper's boiler is damaged, and it could never travel that fast even if it was working at full capacity."

"I know what we need," Henry said, placing his hands on Merlin drooping shoulders.

"What?" Merlin asked.

"We need a fast airship, and I know just the person who can help us." Henry grinned and then bolted through the docks, leaving the filthy Ever-Wheel behind. Merlin and Jimmy were clueless at the boy's plan, but after a quick glance at each other, they took off after him.

The boys bobbed and weaved around supply crates, cargo trucks, Ever-Wheels and even silent dock-bots with blank stares – waiting – motionless, for someone to give them a task. After a goodly amount of time passed, and thoughts of strangling Henry entered Merlin's mind more than once, the boy came to a stop in front of a finely crafted airship. It was sleek and shaped like a bullet and out the back was an oddly-fitted, almost rocket-like boiler stack. A name was written on the side that read, *The Bradley Dunbar.*

"WHAT? You've got to be kidding me." Merlin snapped out his complaint. "This guy is never going to help us save Isabella *or* Elias." Merlin pointed to the large scrape across the side of the ship. "You see that? Elias did that and Izzy... well, haha... Izzy... ah, never mind." Merlin could barely contain himself thinking of what Izzy had told him of Bradley Dunbar.

"Trust me. He will help us. I know his brother," Henry said, walking up to the door and giving it a good pounding with his fist. Moments later, the door opened.

"IRON JAW!" Merlin said in shock. "But..."

"Yeah, yeah, yeah. Bradley's my brother. Not that I claim him, mind you, but family's family. What are you gonna do, huh?" he said with a clack of his iron jaw. "Come on in, boys. I've been hiding out here ever since your father lost his marbles and decided to betray the Jackboot."

Merlin and Jimmy followed Henry inside with a bit of uncertainty, but at this moment Merlin was bankrupt of options, and Henry's swift moving feet had been faster than his quick-witted brain. Again, Henry surprised Merlin and took charge of the situation.

"Mr. Iron Jaw, sir. We need to get to the bird people's mountain before the Puppet Master—I mean, their father. Elias is worried something might happen to Isabella. Hans is going to steal Elias' black heart for the witch. I mean, his mom. You know what mean, right?" Henry's face was so dirty, and his clothes so covered in grime it almost sent old Iron Jaw into hysterics, but when Henry said, "the witch," old Iron Jaw's eye twitch went into overdrive.

"We'll leave right away," Iron Jaw said, grinding his iron jaw.

"But, what about him?" Merlin said pointing to Bradley, who had just entered the room with two oddly dressed servants at his side. Bradley was near hyperventilating from Henry's filthy clothes dripping muddy sludge onto his plushy fine bridge and so he instantly ordered his two servants to begin cleaning the floor where Henry was standing. Bradley raised his finger in the air to begin scolding his brother, but Iron Jaw stopped him before he could speak. "Brother, we're going on an adventure."

"WE MOST CERTAINLY ARE NOT!" Bradley howled. "THIS IS MY SHIP, AND I AM IN CHARGE HERE, NOT YOU, BROTHER!"

Iron Jaw kept his back to his brother. and with a wink and a grin he said, "Well, boys, I guess we'll just have to forgo all those rare delicacies you were telling me about at the Petinon Mountain."

Suddenly, Bradley appeared right next to them as if he'd conjured up some sort of teleporting spell from his oversized belly. "Did you say… rare delicacies?" The two servants kneeling on the floor looked up at Bradley and smiled. Their teeth were horribly rotten, and Merlin couldn't help but wonder if part of their salary included leftover delicacy scraps from Bradley's table.

"As a matter of fact, I did, brother." Iron Jaw closed his eyes and spoke as if he were pondering the taste of such wonderful foods. "In fact, I did, brother, but I understand if you'd rather not indulge yourself in the finer…" Iron Jaw felt a tug on his pant leg, and he opened his eyes. It was Henry. "Where'd Bradley go?" he asked, but in an instant the answer revealed itself to them all with a jolt as the airship began pulling away from GFC's docks. "Better get strapped in, boys. We're on our way," he said with a sly grin.

BOGAN REACHED THROUGH THE BARS OF CHARLIE'S CELL AND helped him sip from their water bowl. His brother's body was wrecked from the horrible transformation taking place, but he desperately wanted to reconnect with him in case the worse happened. As Charlie sipped the water, Bogan's mind wondered of his own struggles with a modified metal body and the terrors that consumed him. He imagined Charlie's odd metamorphosis would be even more difficult with mods and it gave him peace that Charlie no longer had any. Watching his brother's suffering change was difficult, but Bogan was determined in his heart to care for his brother to the end, the bitter end, if necessary.

It was an uncomfortable feeling to help steady Charlie's clawed hand while he drank the water, and it quickly brought back memories of his hatred toward his old hunchbacked friend. *Let go of him before I snap that ugly hump off your back. I kid you not, lumpy, you touch him like that again and I'll cut out your heart and feed it to Casper.*

Hunchy's words divided his guilty thoughts. *Only the blade of a friend will do.*

He's got to be the stupidest. I'm going throw him over the edge.

Only the blade of a friend will do.

I bet you're one of the smoke charmers the Jackboot talks about, aren't you? Prince of the hunchbacks. Ha, ha! Hunchy, Prince of the hunchbacks.

Only the blade of a friend.

The truth matters, Gideon. Charlie always said it, the truth matters.

Bogan, I sincerely apologize. Only the blade of a friend will do.

Uh, well, yeah, y-you should. I-I was right, wasn't I? I-I was right?

Yes, you were, Bogan.

I'm so sorry, mate. I-I didn't mean it. I-I never really would have done it.

Only the blade of a friend. Only the blade of a friend.

Give the man your blade, Bogan. Give the man your blade. The Jackboot's words echoed. *YOUR BLADE, Bogan! YOUR BLADE! GIVE THE MAN YOUR BLADE!*

I never really would have done it.

Only the blade of a friend

"Brother?" Charlie's voice shook him out of his entranced state of mind.

"UH? Oh, I'm sorry, brother. I was... just thinking about something. Are you feeling any better?" Bogan asked, trying to get a better view of his brother's condition.

"I don't know. It's different every time, and this time is was very different."

Charlie's voice was strange and almost Hunchy-like as he held up his once partially transformed hand; only now a fully formed claw. Gideon must have caught a glimpse of him, because he fired up the mod-light on his hand for a better view. The light exploded throughout both prison cells, and Bogan's breath was stolen away from his lungs. His claws wrapped around the cell bars and he pulled himself up. Gone were his feet and in their place, massive claws with terrifying talons. Charlie arched his back and unfurled two wings so enormous he couldn't fully extend them. The feathers covering his head were deep red, and his wings so brightly colored the feathers looked like flames licking his back when he shook. Charlie's eyes were sharp and fierce in their gaze, and his size dwarfed that of any Petinon they had ever seen with the exception of the Guardian by the great tree.

Charlie looked at Bogan and spoke. "Brother, I fear I am losing myself in this new body. Ava, Isabella, come closer." He motioned with his clawed hand, and they all stepped up next to the cell bars.

"Charlie, no… please. I can't lose you again." Ava whimpered and tears streamed from the others' eyes.

Charlie cocked his head to the right. "What's done is done, my beloved Ava. We can't stop this from happening. All we can do is hope that something good will come from it. There… there must be a… a purpose to my pain, but for the moment, that is hidden from me, from us. We must always prepare ourselves for change lest we be buried by it."

"Brother, can I ask you something?"

"Yes, Bogan."

"How did you get so smart?" Bogan wondered in amazement, and the Whisper crew all laughed sorrow-filled tears for the brothers.

Charlie reached his massive claw through the bars sideways and placed it on Bogan's shoulder. His talons draped down most of Bogan's back and he was careful not to injure him. "Everything I now know—the prophecies, the Petinon way, the way forward—was taught to me by Prince Enupnion. He was my friend. He was my prince, my brother."

17

THE CRUCIBLE

*E*lias sat, both hands on his chin, staring over the shimmering light of Mr. Black's candle. He watched the shadows crawl up the man's grizzled face as he listened intently to his nostalgic tales of battle. Mr. Black's cold, dark pupils were as captivating as they were terrifying, and the man stirred his emotions into an intoxicating frenzy of wonder so intense, Elias nearly forgot to breathe. The tiny flame seemed to cower every time Mr. Black's voice fell low and rise whenever his voice roared from the glorious theatrics of his battle flash-backs. The macabre story time was intensified all the more by the ongoing arena battle taking place, and the little flame hopped up and down whenever the earth shook. Mr. Black's stories were timed so well with every boom and cry of the battle, Elias wondered if he'd rehearsed his story many times beforehand with previous cell mates. His massive arms would swing wildly up and down as he acted out his skillful attacks and even his own cries of agony as if he was injured all over again. Elias had never seen such powerful story telling in all his life, and he savored ever moment of it with the great anticipa-

225

tion that his friends would someday be able to experience Mr. Black's stories.

"Like I was saying, it was Bog Bog that broke this hand." Mr. Black raised a gnarled left hand over the tiny candle flame. *"WORST CHEAT* of any standing hero anyone ever fought. I know, I know. There aren't any rules in the Arena of Heroes, but… there is a bit of a loose code among the legends. Standing heroes though, HA! Those guys just want to kill a legend so they can level up, but I digress. Bog Bog knew I'd just survived a hard-fought battle with Rokon, the mutated bear."

"A MUTATED BEAR!" Elias blurted out in shock. "WHO WON?" Elias immediately felt stupid after he asked the question, but he was pulled so deep into Mr. Black's tale he couldn't help himself.

"You see that large fur rug on the floor over there?" Mr. Black lifted the candle and smiled. Elias' jaw dropped, and he gasped so hard he nearly put the candle out. "I have indeed been through the crucible of pain and come out the other side victorious… forever changed." He looked down at his hands as if he were remembering something, a battle, perhaps. "Unlike the other legends, I no longer thirst for the kill. A nice book and a warm fire would suit me just fine."

"Who are the other legends?" Elias asked.

"Well, let's see… there's Mogdal, of course, but he no longer considers himself to be one of the 'legends' now that he's the ruler of Karl's Labyrinth. Either way, he still counts in my book. Outside of that, there is Agmar the Wretched and Gonon the Vile; both full breed tunnel trolls as well as their brother Krom the Cruel, whom I hope never to have to fight. Then there is Brynjar the Wolf Beast. Quite possibly the most terrify of all the legends, in my opinion, and also someone I hope to never fight. Then there's Nakar the Serpent or half troll-half winged serpent, a truly nasty creature that spits acid venom on his enemies. He doesn't really do any fighting that I've ever seen, he just spits venom on his enemies and they die. He shouldn't even be allowed in the arena, but I don't make the rules."

Elias looked puzzled and asked. "But you said there were seven, and Mogdal doesn't count anymore, so who are the other two legends?"

"Oh, right you are, boy, I forgot about Rat-Face. I... uh, wish I had a better name for him, but that's what they call him. Giant tunnel troll with a face like a rat." Mr. Black rubbed his large chin for a moment in deep contemplation. "To be right honest, I'm not really sure if he's a mutated troll with a tunnel rat head or if he's just ugly as sin. I'm not entirely sure how he's still a legend. He was never really any good at fighting. Maybe he's just lucky." He raised his large eyebrows and smiled a nefarious grin. "Oh, and then there's me. That's all seven of us. Unless of course there are more that I'm unaware of, but I do try and stay on top of things even down here."

"Wow! You're really a legendary hero? That's awesome!"

Mr. Black soaked in the admiration for a bit then went back to his story. "Anyway, like I was saying, Bog Bog was the worst cheat ever, and we fought for a full day. One of the longest battles the arena has ever seen, but Mogdal soon grew tired of our battle." Mr. Black stopped for a moment and listened to the battle above them.

"So what happened to Bog Bog?" Elias asked with bated breath, but before Mr. Black could answer him, the door to their cell suddenly slammed open. Elias looked at Mr. Black wondering what would happen next.

"It's time for battle, boy." Mr. Black said with a cold, stone gaze, then he stood to his feet and removed his filthy coat.

"I can't fight out there. I'll be crushed."

"You can't stay in here boy."

"Why not?"

"The giant Bryn-wolves will eat you. Sometimes they leave our cell doors open during the fight. Come with me. I'll look after you. Just stay on my shoulders, and maybe we'll make it through."

"But how can you be so sure?"

"I've never lost a battle, and besides that, I stand before you as living proof that I'm telling the truth." Mr. Black raised his hands toward his face revealing a hideous, death mocking grin.

"Okay, okay," Elias said, climbing on top of the man's back.

"Hold on to my earrings, and don't worry about hurting me. I can't feel anything anyway." He laughed a horrible laugh and burst out of the cell at a dead run for the ramp at the end of the hall. Mr. Black yelled and beat his body harder and harder as he roused his mind for battle. When they reached the top of the ramp, he leapt twenty feet into the air and landed with a powerful thud that jarred Elias off his back and left him dangling by an earring. The crowd let out a deafening roar of praise, and Elias quickly scurried back onto the man's neck. Mr. Black raised his hands into the air and soaked in the admiration of the crowd as he paraded himself around the arena, but something caught his eye. "It looks like Mogdal is finally going to open the arena to the outside," Mr. Black said, pointing up to the top of the arena dome where workers were welding large iron beams in place and others were mounting massive panes of glass between them. The dirt still covered the dome, and Elias wondered how they were going to remove so much dirt. He started to ask Mr. Black about it when something in the center of the arena pulled his attention away.

In the center of the arena lay a large body, and a giant Bryn-wolf was feasting on it. Mr. Black didn't seem to like the Bryn-wolf's presence, so he picked up a large bone from the arena floor and flung it at the Bryn-wolf. The bone struck it in the head, and with a loud POP, the beast fell over. He walked over to the body that was lying face down and kicked it over on its back. It was a horrible, three-eyed troll with a single tooth, and its head was caved in on the right side. The large troll smelled like a rotten, wet sock, and even Mr. Black winced at the odor.

"Well, boy... you wanted to know what happened to Bog Bog. There he is." Mr. Black's voice was sullen as he kicked the beast over once more.

"But I thought he was difficult to beat."

"He was very difficult to beat. It's a rare thing when someone kills a Standing Hero. Let's hope we don't have to fight the monster that did this." Mr. Black seemed sad that someone had killed Bog Bog, and Elias wondered if it was out of pity for the cheating troll or if Mr. Black was jealous that someone had beaten him to the task. Mr. Black picked up the bone he'd used to strike the Bryn-wolf with and a worried look overtook the monstrous man. "If anything happens to me, you should hide under Bog Bog's body and stay there until the final horn is blown. There are two horns in these one on one matches. Be ready for anything if you want to survive."

A loud bang sounded from across the arena, and one of the large doors began to open. A long blast from Mogdal's horn and the crowd roared with anticipation. Mr. Black bellowed out to Elias, "STEEL YOUR SOUL FOR BATTLE, BOY! WE'RE GOING TO WAR WITH A LEGEND!"

Elias looked out over the enormous theater of death as a strange troll journeyed out into the arena. He thought for certain he felt Mr. Black shiver as the man stepped into the light, and the crowd let out a blood-chilling roar of excitement. The tiny hairs on Mr. Black's neck stiffened, and Elias knew the man was worried, so he yelled over the noise of the crowd. "WHO IS IT?"

But Mr. Black did not respond.

"I SAID, WHO IS IT?" he asked again.

"IT'S BRYNJAR! THE WOLF-BEAST OF KARL KASS! THEY SAY HE'S IMMORTAL! WE'RE PROBABLY GOING TO DIE TODAY, BOY... READY YOURSELF FOR IT! FOR

IT WILL BE A GRAND DEATH FOR SURE!" Mr. Black laughed in glorious wonder at the prospect of his final hour, but Elias was astounded by Mr. Black's eagerness to welcome death. As Brynjar drew closer, Elias could see that he was an enormous mutated beast. His limbs glistened in the light of the arena, and it became clear to Elias that his body was painstakingly covered in metal plates. The left side of his head was partially mutated with an enormous eagle-like talon poking out of the left side his gnarled troll skull like a horn. The right side of his face was a mutated Bryn-wolf snout that didn't seem to fit properly to the front of his troll face, but several metal plates locked things in place. His right arm was a big bushy-haired limb with an oversized wolf paw for a hand. The other arm was a thick, meaty troll limb with iron plates bolted in strange locations as if to hold the arm together and large green veins popped out in different places. His teeth looked like something from the mouth of a wolf, and it was clear to Elias that the people of Karl's Labyrinth worshipped Brynjar, maybe because he was so terrifyingly and grotesquely built.

Suddenly, two giant Bryn-wolves rushed into the arena behind Brynjar, so Mr. Black pulled Elias from off his shoulders and stuffed him under Bog Bog's right arm. "STAY HERE, BOY! THIS JUST GOT INTERESTING." He laughed for a moment until Brynjar let out a blood-boiling howl that raised the hairs on his neck again.

"I CAN'T BELIEVE IT, GRUNDORPH. YOU CAVED IN THAT TROLL'S skull with your bare fist. *HOW?*" Hex asked, glaring in terrified wonder at his friend's strength.

"I never wanted to kill him, Hex. Bog Bog didn't deserve to die like that. No one does, but... I did it for my friends." Grundorph held his head down as if he were ashamed of his actions in the arena—ashamed of his fury.

"Well, I am grateful for it, my friend. You saved us, and I am forever in your debt."

"How's Mr. Iron Feet doing?" Grundorph asked, trying to divert the conversation away from his kill.

"He is doing much better. I think Bog Bog must have jolted him back to his senses. Although, you were right about that boot, we should have tightened it down. We should have tried. Did you see where it went?" Hex asked.

"No, but I felt it when it popped off after Bog Bog hit me in the chin. I thought we'd lost the man, but that other boot kept him locked down fairly good. I certainly am impressed at how this man... well, Petinon, can take a beating." Grundorph smiled as the Jackboot began to regain his senses.

"W-What happened? Where am I?" the Jackboot asked. "WHAT HAPPENED TO MY BOOT?" he cried out in horror.

"It's okay. We'll find a way to get it back. We had to fight in the arena again, and it popped off when Grundorph took a hit to the chin by another troll. He saved your life and mine, so the boot can wait," Hex said confidently to steady the Jackboot's anger at them. "You almost died after I put the paste on your body. How do you feel?"

"I feel... I feel better, I think." The Jackboot took a moment to check himself over, and other than the missing iron boot, he seemed to be whole and healed. "I feel different, though. I can't explain it. Something... changed. What did you do to me?"

Hex and Grundorph looked at each other.

"What? Out with it?" the Jackboot demanded.

"Well, Mr. Iron Boots, Hex believes you are like him. A Petinon, only without wings, so he put some red berry paste on your body to heal you and..." Grundorph was cutoff.

"Yes, yes. I've heard that all before from the last birdman," the Jackboot said.

"WHAT? What birdman? WHO?" Hex snapped at him.

The Jackboot let out a sigh. "His name was Prince Enupnion. He said I was a Petinon like him, but... seriously, look at me! How is that even possible?"

Hex was beaming with wonder-filled eyes at the Jackboot's words. "The Prince! You've spoken to him? You've seen him? How is he? Has the replanting begun?"

The fury of questions from Hex was so intense the Jackboot didn't have the time or the heart to tell him the prince was dead and that he'd put Enupnion's heart into his son's chest. "Yeah, well, Hex, you see there's a... it's a long story. How about we get out of here first and then I'll fill you in? What do you say?"

"NO! I must know everything. It has been so long since I've seen my people. I need to know what progress has been made. I need to know if the great season of planting has begun. And you, there's this whole thing with you, the chosen one. I can't wait to tell the prince I have finally found you. Or is that why you are here? Does he know? Did he send you?"

"Hold up a minute, Hex. I'm not sure I follow you. Look, I'm the Jackboot and no one sent me here. I was betrayed by my friend and my ex-wife. They stole my city and dropped me down here to die."

Hex grew angry and impatient with him, and even Grundorph seemed startled by his outburst. "I DEMAND THAT YOU TELL ME NOW! I'VE BEEN DOWN HERE FOR YEARS, AND I HAVE WAITED LONG ENOUGH! YOU WILL TELL ME!"

The Jackboot knew there was no way around it even though he'd hoped for better timing, and so he gave Hex his best run down of the situation. "I don't know what happened when you put that stuff on me, but I will tell you this much. That is not the first time I've seen or used the berries. I've fought for many years using them to destroy my enemies. Angus Grand even tried to kill my daughter and me by forcing us to eat them, but… something happened. We didn't die, we grew stronger. It even healed us and the voice…we heard a voice, and I'm sorry, Hex, but your prince… he's dead." The Jackboot stopped as Hex slumped down to the floor. At first the Jackboot thought Hex was distraught by the death of the prince, but then Hex raised his head from a humble bow and spoke.

"Then it is true. You *ARE* Ouranos, the chosen one of our people." Hex carefully proclaimed.

"Oh no, you must be talking about my son, Elias. Enupnion said he was the chosen one or something or other. I'm not really into all that prophecy stuff anyway. I'm just an iron weaver. I'm nothing, but my son… Oh let me tell you about my son. He is wonderful. He is…"

Hex raised his claw and stopped the Jackboot's boasting. "Your son cannot be Ouranos. He is far too young, and Prince Enupnion did not know what I know about Ouranos." Hex smiled at him with those strange Petinon eyes. "I am one of only four that know the truth about the lost child. Not even Prince Enupnion was told of you. He only knew of a lost, "wingless" Petinon, but he was never told he had a brother. It was for your safety that we were sworn to secrecy by your mother, but I am certain you are him. You are the one. You are the son of Queen Elehos and King Arkone, rulers of the Trembling Mountain and the great city of Pterugas, and I am saddened to hear of the death of my friend the prince, but I am even more heartbroken now to tell you that he was your brother."

The Jackboot dug his bootless stub into the dirty floor of the cave and pushed himself up against the wall. "I-I…" he wanted to speak, but his mind was locked in a battle with his past. All he could think of was the days of sitting in his tower watching the hunchback suffering down in the mine below him, living in squalor and being treated like a monster. Many days he'd considered placing a bullet in the hunchback's head, but every time he would hear that tormenting voice in his mind calling out to him, *Truth Matters – Darkness lies*. He wanted to tell Hex everything, but instead, he placed his head in his hands, distraught and overcome with grief.

MR. BLACK GRIPPED THE LARGE BONE IN HIS RIGHT HAND AND smacked it in the palm of his left as the two freakishly giant wolves charged at him. The first wolf leapt into the air directly at his head, and Mr. Black gave its snout a good ball-bat swing. With a loud *CRACK* the beast soared through the air and landed on top of Bog Bog's carcass. The wolf's long tongue slid out of its mouth and draped like a wet blanket over Bog Bog's face, and it let out a groan of air from its lungs. A glorious smile rose on Mr. Black's face as he noticed the bulbous end of his boney weapon had snapped off, leaving a sharp, pointy end on it like a bone knife.

The second wolf immediately halted his charge and ran around behind the body of Bog Bog, menacingly circling as it studied Mr. Black's every move for a chance to pounce. Elias kept still as he watched from underneath Bog Bog's armpit until the giant wolf hopped up on top of Bog Bog's body, nearly collapsing it and burying him under the troll. The monstrous wolf let out a howl of sadness for his brother wolf then brought his face down into a snarled growl. When Mr. Black checked behind him to make sure Brynjar wasn't sneaking up on him, the wolf sprang into action with an enormous leap into the air. The wolf landed on top of Mr. Black's back and sunk its powerful teeth into his shoulder. Elias was amazed that Mr. Black didn't cry out in pain or show some emotion of agony. He simply looked back at the wolf as if it were some minor inconvenience and cast it off his back in the direction of Brynjar. The wolf yelped and squirreled back to its feet for another charge. It foolishly leapt into the air, and Mr. Black ducked down and raised the sharp end of his bone-knife over his head. The wolf soared over top of him, and with a horrible ripping sound, he sliced its belly open. The mangy animal sprayed blood all over Bog Bog, covering Elias in a thick red coating of nasty wolf guts.

"THANKS!" Elias shouted, mortified by the grotesque predicament that Mr. Black had left him in.

Mr. Black simply turned and with a wink and a nod, he offered his reply. "You're welcome." Injured, he brushed off the wolf's bite and adjusted his neck with a pop then prepared himself for battle with Brynjar.

Elias watched as the two foes studied one another carefully for any signs of flaws that either of them might be able to exploit against the other. As Brynjar drew closer, Elias figured it might be best to scoot back into the safety of Bog Bog's armpit, although something was preventing him from getting himself the rest of the way under. It was caught under his right shoe, and he kicked at it and kicked at it until he finally pushed it back far enough to get himself in deeper and safer than before. Now, the only thing exposed was his head, and if the horrible, putrid stench of Bog Bog's meaty armpit didn't kill him, he might just make it through this round. It was at that moment; out of the corner of his eye, Elias noticed the Bryn-wolf's tongue hanging over Bog Bog's face was beginning to move. *WHAT! NOT DEAD?* He started to warn Mr. Black but suddenly realized his foot was now caught on the thing he'd tried to kick out of his way. He was trapped with his head sticking out from under Bog Bog's arm, a perfectly shaped wolf snack just waiting to be snapped off and eaten. All he could do now was to hope the wolf wouldn't see him.

The crowd seemed to be growing impatient with the two warriors and began to jeer angrily at them as they paced in a circle. Brynjar was much larger than Mr. Black, who was no small beastly man himself. However, Mr. Black seemed to have a better feel for the crowd's desires than Brynjar, or maybe Brynjar was just too hardened to care about such things. Either way, Mr. Black grew tired of the methodical circling and decided it was time to give the crowd what they'd paid to see, a fearless warrior welcoming his death. Suddenly, Mr. Black let out a loud cry and charged at Brynjar with his bone knife. However, Brynjar remained motionless. Still. Unmovable. Fearless. The crowd let out a roar of joy and began repeating Mr. Black's words back to him in a deafening chorus of exhilaration. They marveled at his brave charge towards Brynjar, toward glory, toward death.

Elias was also captivated by Mr. Black's charge at Brynjar. So much so that he'd forgotten about the giant Bryn-wolf, who was now standing over him with a limp, bloody tongue, oozing saliva on the ground in front him. He lost sight of the two warriors when the wolf tried to force its snout up under Bog Bog's armpit. Elias might not have feared death, but he was certain he didn't want to lose his head inside the mouth of a monster wolf. He tried harder and harder to get under Bog Bog's armpit as the wolf pushed its snout in and snarled its teeth at him, snapping, biting, and growling at him with a fierce vengeance for his dead wolf-brother. The wolf's long white fangs clacked together only two feet from Elias' face as it pushed with all its might against Bog Bog's arm, trying desperately to move it out of the way. Elias thought for certain he'd seen a skeletal hand wedged in between the wolf's massive molars and the good jolt of fright forced an extra effort of strength from him. Finally, Elias was able to free his foot from whatever he'd caught it on, and he quickly slipped deeper into the grungy crevice of the troll's armpit.

Bog Bog certainly wasn't the most hygienic troll, if there even was such a thing, but it was better than ending up a skeleton in a Bryn-wolf's molar. Elias could still hear the roar of the crowd as Brynjar and Mr. Black battled it out, and he hoped with all hope that Mr. Black was able to defeat the genetically altered beast. It was extremely unsettling to Elias that Karl's Labyrinth had created so many monsters, and he was reminded of all the things his false father, Sunago, had told him. Of all the things Sunago had lied about, he certainly didn't lie about the things that crept in the darkest parts of the black mist covered land. It was now evident to Elias that Sunago had been referring to the beasts that must have escaped from Karl's Labyrinth.

As Elias sat in the darkness of Bog Bog's armpit, he noticed a sparkle of light every time the wolf would push up on the troll's arm during its efforts to snatch a nibble at him. It was glimmering off the thing that he had caught his foot on. He crawled over next to it, and in the darkness, he felt around it. It was a strange shape, and half of it was buried in the dirt, so he dug around it until he could get a better feel for what it was. As he ran his hands over it, a picture formed in his mind. It was hard and intricately crafted in the shape of a boot. *A BOOT?* Not just any boot, but an iron boot. A jackboot. A cold wave of chills rushed down Elias' back as he felt something wet on the top of the boot's shaft. Blood or something else. He tasted it, and suddenly his eyes brightened with a soft red glow. Fear and anger struck his heart unlike anything he'd ever experienced before. Not fear for himself, but the fear his father might now be lying dead underneath the body of this terrible beast or that maybe he'd been eaten by one the Bryn-wolves. His blood boiled with such furious anger that he began to shake, and he wanted to punish someone, anyone, for hurting his father.

MR. BLACK WAS GOOD AND BLOODIED FROM BRYNJAR'S VICIOUS swipes with his wolf paw, but he wasn't dead yet. Mr. Black had taken such a powerful blow that it knocked him to the ground in a daze, and the wolf-beast of Karl's Labyrinth was pacing around him like an animal waiting to feast. Brynjar was mostly unscathed, however, there was so much of Mr. Black's blood on the wolf-beast that it was difficult to tell where or if he was injured at all. Mr. Black slowly got to his feet and was still getting his bearings when, from underneath the body of Bog Bog, came a terrible cry of anguish and heartbreak. It was so loud; the crowd removed their gaze from the two legends and looked over at the dead troll carcass in wonder if Bog Bog had suddenly come back to life.

The Bryn-wolf standing next to the troll's body slipped its tail between its legs and took a few paces backward in panic. Bog Bog's body shook and rumbled, and the back of his armpit suddenly caught fire. The wolf stepped back a few more paces, and the crowd let out a gasp of shock as a small boy crawled out from under the troll's flaming armpit. Elias was dragging a large metal boot, his eyes were on fire, and his body was nearly all red as if it were burning. When the wolf realized it was just the boy, he mustered up his courage again and bared his teeth with a bloody growl. The crowd was silent in wonder as the boy approached the monstrous beast, fearless and angry, dragging his metal boot. Even Mogdal stood to his feet in amazement, no doubt pleased with the boy's coming sacrifice for the joy of the crowd.

Mr. Black started to run over to the boy and save him, but Brynjar swung that nasty mutated wolf paw at him again and slammed him back to the ground. As Mr. Black lay with his face halfway in the dirty floor of the arena, he was filled with astonishment as the boy fearlessly strolled up to the wolf and stared it down. Time stood still for a moment until the wolf decided he was ready for a meal and lunged for the boy's body. Suddenly, the boy flung the metal boot into the wolf's teeth and shattered them. The beast yelped and cried out in agony as it ran around in circles. The boot fell to the arena floor next to several of the wolf's teeth shards and the boy picked it up again and held it, watching the toothless-wonder cry out in pain. Mr. Black made an effort to get back to his feet again, but Brynjar stepped his mighty troll foot on top of him and pushed him back to the ground. Mr. Black smiled a nefarious grin as he noticed a look of concern growing in Brynjar's eyes.

The Bryn-wolf circled a few more times, yelping, then seemingly decided it would fight through the pain for one last chance at the boy. So, it made a hard run at him. Elias flung the boot at the wolf's head and hit the wolf in the eye so hard it crushed the socket completely closed. Then the crowd roared with glee for a moment until the boy reached out his hand and the boot suddenly flew back to him. Mr. Black watched as waves of gasps rushed over the stupefied crowd at the boy's amazing power then instantly fell silent as if they couldn't believe what their eyes had just seen. This quickly captured Mogdal's attention as he never liked strange weapons being used in the arena, and this boy's boot was no exception. He reached out his hand for a spear, but his attendant was too captivated by what had just happened to pass anything to him.

Injured, the wolf hobbled around the arena for a moment then went in for another attack, but this time there would be no speculation as to what was happening. In a sudden, terrifying display of fury, the boy flung the boot back at the wolf and crushed its side. Elias reached his hand out again, and the boot soared through the air and back into his hands. Again and again he flung the boot at the wolf until the beast fell to the floor of the arena. Silent. Dead.

Mr. Black spotted Mogdal looking for his attendant who should have already placed a spear into his hand, but the attendant seemed too busy staring at Elias. In anger, Mogdal cast his attendant over the edge of the balcony, and with a crunch and a thud, the man fell dead. Mogdal stomped over to his spear rack and took one out. The spear was large enough to cut the boy in half if need be, and he smiled as he drew back his arm and loosed the spear with a powerful thrust.

"BEHIND YOU, BOY!" Mr. Black cried out.

ELIAS TURNED AROUND TO THE SOUND OF THE WHISTLING WEAPON soaring through the air at him, and he instantly flipped the magnetic switch on the side of the jackboot. It let out a deep humming groan, and he lifted it up at the incoming spear. The spear suddenly jerked and flipped end over end backward towards Mogdal's balcony, and it stuck right beside the monster troll's head. The crowd let out a horrified gasp of shock at the near loss of their beloved leader, and even Mogdal's face seemed to indicate a bit of concern growing inside him from his near-death experience.

"BRYNJAR, KILL THE CHEAT!" Mogdal cried out.

Brynjar gave Mr. Black a hard kick, sending him rolling over toward the edge of the arena wall then put his head down in a charging position. His large horns pointed straight at Elias as the wolf-beast ran toward him. It was unfortunate for Brynjar that the many repairs to his body had been done with metal bolts and plates, and though they were an intimidating feature for most, they were an unfortunate flaw against Elias' jackboot. As Brynjar's frightening charge drew closer, Elias let go of the magnetic jackboot, and it shot directly at the wolf-beast. It hit the metal plate on his side hard enough that it almost knocked him down, but he kept his footing and charged for a bit longer. He stopped quickly when he realized the boot was still attached to his side. He tried to pull it off, but the magnet was powerful.

"I can help you with that," Elias said, and he reached his hand out and called back the boot. The boot pulled hard on Brynjar's side until it broke free and pulled the metal plate with it. Terror struck the crowd, and Brynjar dropped to one knee to catch his breath. The injury was devastating, but he'd suffered worse and wasn't about to let this child beat him today. He got back to his feet and readied himself for another charge.

"Please. Don't do it," Elias warned, but Brynjar didn't listen. He ran at Elias again, and this time the boot hit the plate on his left arm, but Brynjar didn't stop. The wolf-beast continued to run at him, so Elias called the boot back once more and ripped the plate from Brynjar's arm. The wolf-beast stopped again to catch his breath from the injury, so Elias decided to take advantage of the moment and began beating Brynjar severely with his father's boot. Soon Brynjar fell to his knees, and Mr. Black rushed over to finish him off. Mr. Black aimed his sharp bone weapon at Brynjar's throat and was about to kill him when Elias stopped him.

"NO!" he hollered out and ran over to Mr. Black.

"He has to die, boy. It's the way the game is played," Mr. Black explained as he held the sharp bone to Brynjar's neck.

"Yeah, but it's not my way. I don't want to kill anyone."

The crowd began chanting for Elias to kill Brynjar. "BECOME THE HERO! TAKE HIS PLACE! TAKE HIS PLACE!" they cried out, but their words only deterred him all the more.

"It has to be done, boy. It's our way. If you can't do it – I will." Mr. Black said, lifting the weapon again.

"NO!" Elias said, raising the boot in the air. Mr. Black's eyes grew large with surprise at Elias' willingness to spare the monster, but their moment of contemplation was ended quickly with a blast from Mogdal's horn. A large door opened and the arena began filling with giant Bryn-wolves.

Mr. Black quickly scanned the arena and yelled, "RUN, BOY! RUN!"

Elias looked into Brynjar's terror-filled eyes, and he was struck with sorrow for the wolf-beast. "WE CAN'T LEAVE

HIM!" Elias cried out to Mr. Black who had already started to run toward the exit.

"WHAT? ARE YOU MAD, BOY? YOU CAN'T FIGHT THEM ALL!"

"TAKE HIM. YOU CAN DRAG HIM."

"HAVE YOU GONE MAD? HE'LL KILL US! LEAVE HIM BE."

"I'M NOT LEAVING HIM," Elias said as he lifted the boot into the air in preparation for the wolves' attack. Mr. Black let out a disgruntled groan and ran back to Brynjar. He grabbed the beast by his leg and began dragging him toward the tunnel entrance. Elias spun his father's boot in a circle around them as the wolves closed in. He clobbered a few in the jaw, and their yelping traumatized the others long enough for Mr. Black to get Brynjar back into the tunnel. As he backed into the tunnel, he could see the anger in Mogdal's eyes and how the crowd was no longer chanting his name with shouts of glory. He never wanted their admiration anyway. He only needed to find his father. He threw the boot up to the iron gate overhead and forced the bars down in front of the hungry wolves, then he walked back into the darkness of the tunnel.

18

TRIAL BY FIRE

*T*hunder shook dirt from the ceiling of their cave prison, and the strange marching sounds of Petinon warriors soon filled the hallway outside their cell. The Whisper crew stood to their feet with hearts pounding in their chests. They knew why the guards were coming. Ava took hold of Izzy's arm, and Bogan stepped in front of her as the torchlights filled the hall. A row of ten warriors marched in front of the cell and then ten more behind them and another ten behind that row. It was far more guards than Bogan and Gideon had figured from the sound of their marching, and their thoughts of escape vanished quickly.

Thunder crashed again, and a flash of light brightened Thumacheo's face as he stepped in front of the cell door. He glared at Izzy through several more flashes of light and crashes of thunder until she removed Ava's hand from her arm and stepped in front of Bogan.

"Izzy... no. Don't go," Ava pleaded softly.

"Iz, we're not going to let them take you," Bogan said, stepping back in front of her.

"It's okay. Really," Izzy said as she placed her mod-finger on

243

her lips to quiet their response, then she stepped over to the cell door. Thumacheo unlocked it, and two warriors took her by the arms as soon as she stepped out. Bogan lunged for the door, but it was a worthless effort. As the soldiers took Izzy away, she glanced back at her crew, and for hope sake, she winked at them and smiled her best sneaky pirate smile.

Stepping outside the cave, Izzy expected the ground to be soaking wet, but the rain had not yet made it to the mountain. In the distance, the sky was darker and more ominous than the light still shining through the forest trees. The dark threat of storm clouds didn't deter the small birds from their chirping, singing and fluttering about as the guards marched the king slayer down the dirt path toward the city. Izzy drew the cool mountain air deep into her lungs and breathed out a frosty cloud at Thumacheo to mock his judgmental eyes, but he ignored her. Soon, her back began to irritate her again, and she arched and lifted her shoulders, trying to scratch it with her jacket, but the soldiers thought she was trying to get away. One of them gripped her fleshy arm so hard it brought a tear to her eye, and she begged them to let her scratch her back or do something to help her with the discomfort, but no one helps a king slayer.

At the entrance to Pterugas, she noticed several Petinon's standing next to the small fountain where Queen Elehos had given her a drink. As she looked farther into the city, she could see the streets lined with Petinon people on each side. It was then she knew this was the day she would live or die. As she trudged through the rows of Petinon people, she could feel their judgmental eyes and haughty looks carefully dissecting her. For some time she held her head high and kept her gate strong, but it didn't last. Their sorrowed eyes for the loss of their king ate away at her spirit, and her head dropped toward the ground in shame. They didn't know what had happened. They didn't know her or the hard life she'd lived or how long she'd looked for her brother. They only knew that she had killed their beloved king, and they wanted justice for him.

As the storm drew closer, her eyes were drawn to a strangely shaped cloud forming over top of the city. Izzy stopped and the guards jerked at her arms and yelled at her, but she was too captivated by the strange, bull-shaped cloud. She dropped to her knees and gazed into the sky, smiling until the cloud completely disappeared. Her thoughts rushed back to the moments before Brom's last charge and how she'd walked him through her imaginary fields. As she looked out over the beauty of the Trembling Mountain, her eyes awakened to the realization of the descriptions she had lavished over the bull in his final hours. Here, on this great mountain, she was walking through paradise, even now, to her death or life. Either way, she knew she would never be the same again. Her heart had awakened, and for the first time she believed her life had a greater purpose than what the world of iron and smoke held for her.

Thunder rolled overhead as Thumacheo marched over, grabbed her by her hair and pulled her to her feet. "GET UP!" he snapped at her as fiercely and cruelly as he could, but his face lost all authority when she smiled back at him with the gentle face of forgiveness. It stunned him, and he stuttered out his words in an effort to recover some sense of pride in front of his soldiers. "T-The queen is waiting."

She followed them obediently through the rest of the city until they came to the place where the path lead up to the great trunk. Her back was hurting so bad she could hardly walk, and she finally gave in to the pain and collapsed. Thumacheo was growing tired of her disobedience, especially as the rain was starting to fall and everyone was getting soaked. He stepped over to punish her but stopped when he noticed the rain was turning to steam on her back. He ripped the back of her jacket open and winched at the terrible scars. "What's wrong with you?" he asked.

Izzy shrugged her shoulders and thanked him with a smile as she enjoyed the cool rain running into the tears of her leather jacket, cooling her back. A merciful look filled Thumacheo eyes, and he decided to end the formalities of shame-walking the criminal through the streets. He picked her up and flew her to the king's castle and into the great hall. The other warriors soon followed, and the Petinon people quickly sought shelter from the storm.

THUMACHEO LANDED ON THE BALCONY JUST OUTSIDE THE HALL leading to the king's court. He walked her to the large cedar doors and opened one for her as she was still struggling with the pain in her back. She stood in the doorway gazing into the room filled with the Elders of the Convocation and Queen Elehos. The queen was at the very end of the long hall and seated in the king's chair. She was adorned in her finest silver robes with gold strands accenting every edge. Her crown was different than before and was of a twisted, gold, rope design with a large red ruby in the center. Light glistened off the pearl-white talons that were interlocked through the twisted rope, pointing up toward her head, and she glowed with a powerful radiance about her. White limestone pillars lined each side, and on the right side were three rows of seats where the elders sat, and on the left side were seated the nobles of Pterugas adorned in their black robes of mourning.

A loud *CRACK* of thunder and flash of lightning gave the torchlit hall an ominous feeling of impending doom that suddenly filled Izzy's heart with dread. Gone was the loving grandmother from the walk through the forest, and before her sat a dark queen on the throne of judgment. Izzy's feet froze to the floor, and for some odd reason, her thoughts turned to her mother, Cassandra. How she longed for her on the Night of

Darkness, when in reality, her mother had been an evil witch bent on acquiring power. Staring down the long hall at Queen Elehos seated on her throne, Izzy wondered if the queen was like her mother—appearing to be kind and loving and yet, deep down, filled with darkness and lies. A shiver of cold took hold of her arms.

Finally, out of frustration, Thumacheo shoved her the rest of the way through the entrance. She stumbled to her knees but mustered up her strength to get to her feet. She adjusted her torn coat as best she could to feel presentable, but her clothes were drenched in rain. Thankfully, the rain had washed most of the king's dried blood from her mod-arm, but it didn't make her feel less guilty. She sloshed one foot in front of the other as she made her way down the long hall. Behind her, she could hear the full company of warriors slowly filling the royal throne room. There was no way out. Like Angus Grand's day of burning, she was traveling the path into the flames. Only this time, she had lit the fire herself.

Lightning crashed hard outside when Queen Elehos raised her hand in a halting motion as Izzy reached the place where she was to stop. The queen stood to her feet, and all the elders and nobles rose together with her. After several blasts from a warrior's horn, the queen spoke. "Standing before you, great nobles and wise elders, is the slayer of our king—King Arkone, one of the longest reigning kings our people have ever known. Today, we will try this child, Isabella Brock, for the murder of our king."

Izzy blocked the queen's words from her mind and focused in on the comfort of the rain beating the walls outside the castle. The crushing weight of her actions now pushed hard down on her shoulders. *Why did I do it? I didn't have to kill him. Maybe I could have just injured him, and things would be different. Maybe he would have accepted me and Elias. Maybe we could have been a family. Why do I have to ruin everything?*

The queen finished her speech then returned to her throne. Not long after, one of the elders began calling witnesses to speak before the queen, and even Thumacheo was called to speak. He told of the night he and the king spoke and how the king was simply following the laws of their people when he decided to remove Enupnion's heart from Elias' chest. Then others were called to speak. Petinon's that Izzy had never even seen before, accusing her of things she'd never done. Things that allegedly took place in places she'd never been to before. She began to feel their hatred wrapping around her like the vines her mother wrapped around her on the culling floor in the Valley of Bones.

The black mourning robes of the elders and nobles turned to apparitions of death in her mind, and the dark storm clouds pushed their claw-shaped shadows around the hall toward her. As the mood of the trial turned darker, several elders began shouting at each other in some sort of disagreement but stopped when Izzy collapsed to her knees. All of a sudden, lightning crashed hard outside and ended with a loud popping sound, and Queen Elehos rose from her throne. It caught everyone by surprise, and Thumacheo gave a sideways nod to one of his warriors to check it out.

The queen stepped over to Izzy, helped her back to her feet and raised her chin. "Be strong," she whispered.

"But why? Even my own grandmother wants to kill me."

"Excuse me! I beg your pardon," one of the nobles shouted as he overheard Izzy's statement. "Did you say *grandmother?*"

"I did," Izzy replied.

Queen Elehos closed her eyes in exasperation as if she'd planned better timing for such information. "I wasn't quite ready for that, my child." Izzy's face slumped in disappointment as she realized the queen must have been working on a plan to save her.

"The king slayer now claims to be the granddaughter of our great king. The very king she has slain," the noble scoffed.

Bebahyosis stood and spoke. "It is true. The child is the granddaughter of King Arkone and Queen Elehos."

"OUTRAGE!" the powerful noble cried out, and suddenly the whole court was cast into chaos as nobles and elders began yelling and even cursing at one another in an effort to make sense of the new information.

"It doesn't matter even if she is the granddaughter of the king. She is a wingless disgrace and must be put down, or she will bring shame to our people," the noble said, clinching his claw into a fist.

"I say we take a vote – NOW!" the noble demanded. "THERE IS NO NEED TO DELAY THIS ANY FURTHER! WE MUST VOTE!"

The queen nervously looked over to Bebahyosis with alarmed panic in her eyes, but the elder dropped his head as if he didn't notice her. The vote was quick and the verdict swift. *Guilty*. The sentence was to be carried out immediately, and so Thumacheo pulled his sword and stepped up next to Izzy. He pushed her back down to her knees and raised his sword in the air. Queen Elehos was speechless. She fell backward onto her throne and her face turned pale—frozen in time as her plan crumbled around her. In sorrowed failure, she glared into Isabella's eyes.

"Close your eyes," Thumacheo said. "It will be easier."

In the blink of an eye, the great door to the hall burst open. It was the warrior that Thumacheo had sent to check the lightning strike. "IT'S ON FIRE! THERE ARE CHILDREN INSIDE!" he tried to catch his breath.

"WHAT'S ON FIRE?" the queen asked, jumping to her feet.

"THE PTERATORIUM!"

Loud gasps burst forth from the elders and nobles.

"WE CAN'T GET TO THEM. THEY'RE TRAPPED!" The warrior's eyes looked lost.

Isabella quickly stood to her feet. "I CAN GET THEM! I DON'T BURN!"

"WHAT? MORE LIES!" the noble cried out. "SHE'S TRYING TO ESCAPE."

The queen smiled at Isabella. "Now how would she be able to escape? She doesn't have wings," the queen sarcastically snapped back. "I believe her. Besides, if she is lying, the worst that can happen is that she will burn alive with our children." Several elders nodded to each other in agreement at the queen's wisdom.

"Thumacheo, I demand you take her to the city at once!" Queen Elehos smiled at Izzy, but when Thumacheo didn't respond, she roared at him in anger. "NOW, THUMACHEO! BEFORE OUR CHILDREN PERISH IN THE FLAMES!" Thumacheo's sword rattled to the floor in fright when the mountain trembled from her command.

"WAIT! I NEED FIRE BERRIES!" Izzy exclaimed.

The queen reached behind her throne, pulled out a bowl of berries and rushed them to her. Izzy shoved a handful into her mouth, then an angry Thumacheo grabbed her and dove out the balcony window.

Thumacheo swooped down into the city toward the rising smoke. In the distance, behind them, Queen Elehos, the nobles, and the elders were emptying out of the castle windows. They could see the Petinon people throwing buckets of water onto the flames in a futile effort to put out the fire. The rain helped some but not enough to put down the raging flames.

"I'll be here to finish your death sentence if you make it out," Thumacheo warned.

Izzy looked back at him, and with a red smoky grin and flaming eyes she scoffed, "WHATEVER!"

It startled him so much that he nearly dropped her, but even before they landed, she started to become too hot for him to hold on to. He barely slowed down for the landing in hopes that he could let go of her before he burned his claws any worse. They hit the ground hard with a crack, and it sounded like Thumacheo might have broken something in his leg. The rest of the Convocation of Elders and nobles, as well as the queen, landed about the time she stepped up to the burning building. She took one look back at the queen, who seemed horrified that she'd just agreed to this plan, then Isabella stepped into the inferno.

THE SMOKE WAS THICK AND THE FIRE MUCH HOTTER THAN SHE remembered from the day of burning by Angus Grand. As flames licked at her body, Isabella hoped with all hope that she would not burn alive and that she might be able to find and save the children. She called out for them as she made her way through the building until she heard a faint cry for help in the heaviest part of the fire. At first, she thought there was no way around the flames, but she noticed a large wood beam overhead. She launched her mod-hand at the beam and pulled herself up over the thick flames then dropped down onto a clear area of the floor. The floor was weak from the fire and gave way underneath her feet, sending her crashing into the lower level. She tried to find something to grab with her mod-hand, but there were no more beams or anything visible through the smoke-filled chaos.

Isabella stood frozen in the fire, unable to escape the whirlwind as the flames engulfed the room around her. Burning timbers COVERED in furious flames raged around her in a tempest of chaos, and a sharp pain in her back struck her like a weapon. She fell to her knees and cried out with all her strength, and suddenly a terrible ripping sound came from her back and the pain instantly left her. She stood to her feet, surrounded by the same massive wings from the day of burning, only this time everything was clearer to her. The flaming wings surrounding her were coming from her own back. They wrapped around her body, instinctively protecting her from the fire, and the cries of the children quickly rushed into her mind.

No one needed to tell her who she was now, for she could see her true self as she was always meant to be, a Petinon, albeit a Petinon with wings of fire, but a Petinon nonetheless. Isabella leapt through the flames and into the air, rising above the inferno. She blasted through the top of the ceiling then back down to where she could hear the children. As she crashed through the wall of the room, she spotted them, huddled in a corner where the rain water had pooled, and she reached out her mod-arm to them. At first, they were terrified of her because of the stories their parents had told them about humans with mechanical parts, but a little girl quickly stood up and took her metal hand. Soon the others followed, and she wrapped her flaming wings around them and walked them through the destruction of the burning building.

Queen Elehos, the Elders of the Convocation, the nobles and all the people of the Petinon city watched as the final parts of the building caught fire and the last wall caved in. The flames burst through the gentle rain like an unstoppable beast, and the cries and screams of mothers began to fill the streets with sorrow.

"So much for your wingless granddaughter, Queen Elehos," the powerful noble sneered.

The queen was devastated and simply unable to reply to the noble's calloused mockery. Then, without warning, a scream echoed through the whole city as a Petinon woman pointed to a raging ball of fire moving out of the flames. It moved carefully, as if it were heading somewhere, as if something were guiding it, controlling it.

"STOP IT! BEFORE IT BURNS THE WHOLE CITY TO THE GROUND!" the nobleman cried out.

Thumacheo picked up a bucket of water and threw it at the raging flames, but nothing happened. The elders, noblemen and warriors stepped back in terror, but Queen Elehos stood her ground until the fireball stopped in front of her. In a shocking display of miraculous wonder, the flames opened up into the shape of giant flaming wings that licked at the air, and they seemed to be attached to the back of the queen's granddaughter. Twelve children instantly came running out and into their mother's arms, but the Petinon leaders lurched back in horror. Some of them dropped to their knees in homage and cried out the name Ouranos.

Queen Elehos and Isabella smiled at each other, but the queen dared not embrace her granddaughter, no matter how badly she wanted to at this moment. Instead, she raised her clawed hand and said, "BEHOLD, I GIVE YOU THE DAUGHTER OF OURANOS!" Many were astonished and bowed down, but others remained skeptical of the queen's statement. Then the queen stepped closer to Isabella, still keeping a safe distance from her flaming wings, but close enough to accomplish what she intended. "Bow before your queen, my child." Isabella looked at her in confusion but obediently dropped to her knees. Then the queen removed the crown from her head and placed it on Isabella's. "I crown you this day with the crown of the ancient kings. Arise, Queen Isabella, ruler of the ancient kingdom of Petinon's and the great city of Pterugas, Commander of the Convocation and ruler of the Trembling Mountain."

As Isabella stood to her feet, her grandmother bowed down

and looked up at her. "Now you can save your friends," she said with a smile, and Isabella's face lit up with joy.

"The queen has lost her mind," the powerful noble mocked with laughter. "She has made the death of our great king into a show for her own amusement. She is only doing this to prevent the execution of the king slayer. Who can believe this? Who can accept this? I demand a hearing of the Convocation of Elders. How can any of you allow this wingless..." he paused his words for a moment. "I mean... she's not one of us; I don't care if she does have... have whatever those things are. They're not Petinon wings. It's sorcery! That's what it is. Thumacheo, I demand that you finish your job and execute her."

"Let me remind you of our laws," Elehos said, "No one can strike the ruler of the Trembling Mountain, or they will face certain death. Let me also remind you that the ruler of the Trembling Mountain may strike down anyone they please... even the king. For no one has more authority than the ruler of the mountain."

The defiant noble was unwavering in his protest. "Did any of you hear the mountain tremble? I did not!"

"Then let her sit upon the throne and see if the mountain will accept her," Elehos replied. Silence fell on their lips as the elders pondered her words. Then one of the elders gave a nod, and soon they all agreed.

Elehos leapt into the air and hovered for a moment, staring down at Isabella. "Well, I assume you can fly with those things, so come with me." She smiled and motioned with her claw.

Isabella beat her wings of fire into the sky and followed her grandmother to the castle. They landed on the balcony outside the throne room, but her wings were still burning bright. "I can't go in there like this, I'll burn the whole castle down," she warned.

"I don't think so," Elehos replied. "I think you can control them more than you know."

Isabella stepped toward the opening of the great hall, and suddenly the flaming wings evaporated around her. She smiled and followed Elehos down the path to the throne then stopped and waited for the nobles and elders to arrive. Elehos finally hugged her and checked her back for injuries.

"It's truly astonishing. Your wounds have already closed," Elehos said.

"Well... it's still sore." Isabella laughed.

When the last elder and noble arrived in the great hall, Isabella climbed up the steps toward the throne. She took a deep breath then sat down carefully on the great throne – and the mountain trembled. The nobles, elders and warriors reluctantly dropped to their knees in homage, and Elehos looked back at them and asked, "Does anyone here disagree with the Trembling Mountain?" No one spoke. "Queen Isabella, go set your friends free from their prison. No one will stop you."

Queen Isabella ran to the window then paused for a second. She looked back at her grandmother and asked, "Wait, what if they don't work? Should I eat a fire berry first?"

"Couldn't hurt." Elehos smiled, and so, Queen Isabella tossed a fire berry into her mouth and jumped out the castle window. Her back burst forth with flaming wings, and she soared back down toward the city. The elders, nobles and warriors could hear the cries of jubilation erupting from the people as she landed.

Elehos walked down the center of the great hall, stopped at the door then spoke. "You can't kill her now. She's your queen, but even more so, when her father returns, you will all know the true ruler of our people, for he is my son, Ouranos... the chosen one."

GRUNDORPH AND HEX AWOKE TO THE SOUNDS OF SCREAMING agony as the Jackboot sat up, holding both hands on his head. Neither of them knew what had happened to him and wondered if he'd injured himself in his sleep. They tried to console him, but he jerked away from them both and buried his head into the dirty floor of their earthy cell until he finally passed out.

"Something has happened," Hex said, looking to Grundorph as if he might have some brilliant idea as to what just happened.

"I do believe that is quite obvious, my dear friend," Grundorph replied with a subtle smugness to his voice. "The real question would be, what is it that has happened?"

Hex knelt down next to the Jackboot and rolled him over. "I do not know."

"His head. Look at his forehead, Hex. He has a strange mark on it."

"It... it looks like a rope." Hex stood back up and looked at his troll companion. "I've seen this mark before. When one of our nobles wears their crown for too long it leaves a mark like this. Almost like... like he's been wearing a crown. Grundorph, how is that possible?"

"I don't know. I don't see a crown anywhere in our cell, so how could he have been wearing it?"

"I have a strange feeling things are about to change. Whether for good or evil, I do not know, but change is coming, and soon, my friend. Very soon."

19

VOLUNTEERS NEEDED

hree hundred Umbrella Charmers soared through the clouds behind her as Cassandra entered the boneless Valley of Bones. Her Charmer's black coats flapped behind them in the wind, and dark puffs of smoke rolled from their mouths as a cold wind carried them with an eerie swiftness. Only a few hours ago, Cassandra had been working tirelessly through the night to prepare the next phase of Sunago's transformation. She had nearly completed her work when a messenger arrived at her labyrinth lab with troubling news. Sunago had broken out of his second stage and eaten the rats working on the final cocoon. She was so dismayed by the news that she dropped her potion-filled beaker, ruining all her painstaking work. In anger, she instantly killed the messenger with a dagger of smoke through the heart then mustered all her Charmers together and explained they would need to sedate Sunago for the next phase. She warned them not to be afraid of him, and though he was extremely dangerous, even now, he was also very vulnerable. She cautioned her Charmers not to damage him in this state, or she would punish them severely. Even before they landed, they could hear him roar through the egg-shaped tower made of bone. One Umbrella Charmer tried to flee, but she struck him down with a spear of smoke as a final warning to other deserters.

When they touched down on the ground, the roaring from the egg suddenly stopped as if the beast inside had heard or felt them land. Cassandra turned around and faced her Umbrella Charmers. She closed her eyes as if she realized her mistake of landing and then raised her left finger across her lips as a warning. Her Charmers gave a subtle nod of agreement, then she raised her hand in a lifting motion, commanding them to return to the air. Blackest smoke rolled from their mouths as they quietly spoke their words of darkness, filling their umbrellas with the smoke and lifting their feet from the earth.

Once they'd returned to their hovering, Cassandra motioned with her hand for them to wait as she circled the large egg-shaped dome, inspecting it for any flaws that might be problematic for further containment. When she found no cracks, she motioned for her Charmers to meet her at the top of the dome. Once there, she drew a large needle filled with blackish goop from her coat then explained the plan to her Charmers. Ten of them would remove the top cap with hands of smoke to prevent from startling Sunago, whilst another twelve would go down into the egg with her. Though the offer for volunteers was met with silence, she quickly persuaded her minions by crushing one of them with a giant hand of smoke and tossing the remains several hundred feet across the valley. Two hundred and ninety-eight Umbrella Charmers instantly volunteered for the job, but that was far more than she needed, so she chose the most eager among them. *It's so hard to find good help these days,* she mussed.

The torch lights used by the worker rats had long burned out, so once the top cover was removed, Cassandra tossed three green globes of light down into the egg. Though it was still difficult to see, she sent her twelve volunteers down into the egg ahead of her, and from the sounds of their horrified screams, she figured Sunago might still have been hungry. After all twelve screams were silenced; Cassandra tossed three more globe lights down into the egg and spoke. "I need twelve more volunteers, but fear not, he will be full soon enough. I do apologize for our fellow charmer's deaths, but this is the price of victory. This is the price that must be paid to achieve our goals."

Twelve more reluctant Charmers floated out of the crowd, then Cassandra lowered herself slowly into the egg. "Oh, darling... my darling Sunago, I have something for you. I promise it won't hurt... much." She spoke in her most charming of voices as she moved through the air with graceful ease. "I see you've grown so much faster than I expected, but we've one more push to the end, my love. I can't tell you how excited I am for you. You're going to be so beautiful when we've finished, so marvelously beautiful."

She passed by the smaller egg in the center and noticed a dark shadow crouched in the east area of the egg. She motioned for her Charmers to go around the other side of the smaller egg, and she waited for him to notice them. She knew she had lied to them, but it was much easier to create more Charmers than it was for her to craft greatness. Her Charmers swooped directly into his path as Sunago took the bait and lunged at them. He swallowed two of them with one bite, and the others suddenly fell from the air, seemingly too terrified to remember their words of smoke that held them aloft. Sunago rushed after them, and Cassandra made her move on him. She dropped down behind the smaller egg, and as he circled around to eat her Charmers, she stuck him in the back with her needle. He let out a groan then staggered around the massive bone-crafted egg until he fell, face down, on floor. Cassandra knelt in front of him and brushed her gloved hand over his head. "Soon, my love. Soon. You're going to be amazing. Simply wonderful!"

When Cassandra rose out of the giant egg, she noticed that only half of her Charmers remained at the top. She smiled at them. "Ah... loyalty is so hard to come by these days, but I do appreciate each and every one of you for staying with me. I promise you, you will all be handsomely rewarded when we have finished out work. NOW! Replace the lid and remain here until I return with the yolk."

Two days passed and Cassandra returned in a massive airship, carrying a large payload underneath of it. She commanded her Charmers to lift the lid from the egg, and she quickly filled it with the greenish-black yolk then had them lock the lid down tight. The temperature of her blood cooled as she drew deep from her well of darkness, then she commanded all her Umbrella Charmers to move away from the egg. When she felt the power come on strong, she smacked her hands together and began speaking dark words of smoke. Lightning cracked and the wind rushed into the valley with such fierceness that it swept away some of her Charmers, but she gave the expendable minions no consideration. All light vanished around her, and the blanket of darkness was comforting while she worked. Soon the entire egg was engulfed in thick black smoke and not a single, white, boney part could be seen beneath it. A bright purple spark lit the area she was floating in, *suddenly*, with a CRACK of lightning, she was finished. Exhausted, she fell from the sky toward the valley, but a loyal Charmer caught her with a hand of smoke. In dazed weakness, she watched as they carried her back to the airship, back to Karl's Labyrinth.

THE GUARDIANS WERE THE LARGEST OF THE PETINON PEOPLE AND were more bird-like in appearance than the average Petinon. Though some of them had retained a few attributes of who they once were, most had long forgotten their old life. Every seven years the Petinon people would choose from among their own, seven, who had sought the old ways and desired to become guardians of their people. A Protector of the Petinon Realm or Guardians of Pterugas as they were called, and they answered only to the king, *or queen* as it were, of the Trembling Mountain.

It is said, that to become a guardian, one's heart must be pure before the fire berries grown on the Burning Mountain can be injected into their heart. If they were not pure of heart, they would die a horrible death. If they were pure of heart, it was still a very painful transformation, but they would survive and live forever on the Burning Mountain. As of late, there had been few who desired to undergo such risk or agony for the sake of tradition. However, once their transformation was complete, they became extremely powerful, not only in physical strength, but in wisdom as well, and their life expectancy was thought to be eternal. No one really knew if that was true, because no ordinary Petinon was allowed to go to the Burning Mountain to check up on them. From time to time, a guardian might return to the Trembling Mountain to take the body of a king for burial, or bring a message, but this was an extremely rare occurrence, so most believed the guardians simply died like everyone else.

A guardian would serve their people for seven years on the Trembling Mountain. When new guardians were selected, they would mentor their replacements for seven more years while they continued to serve. After fourteen years, their service was complete, and they would leave the Trembling Mountain and forever retire on the Burning Mountain with the other guardians. There had only been two volunteers to become guardians during the last Festival of Fire, and King Arkone did not want to be known as the king who forced his people to hand over their children to suffer for the sake of tradition. This action forced five guardians to remain in service for another seven years on the Trembling Mountain. Those five guardians who remained were disheartened by the king's decision and quickly became loyal to Queen Elehos. Four nights ago, under the cover of darkness, Gemenon freed Epekneia from the prison, and the two fled the Trembling Mountain on the backs of two loyal guardians. It was the first time Epekneia had ever ridden on the back of a guardian. She'd never imagined such a thing was even allowed.

The guardians flew nonstop during the four days, at altitudes of over ten thousand feet, much higher than Gemenon or Epekneia had been with their own wings. Gemenon had brought several large, woven bags filled with fire berries, which she used to keep the guardians strengthened during their trip, but now, four days and nights of flight was taking its toll on them, and their swiftness was faltering. The crisp wind in the high altitude swept around their bodies, and they did their best to keep themselves low on the birds' backs to help with aerodynamics. When Gemenon noticed her guardian beginning to struggle to lift his right wing, she cried out to Epekneia, "THEY NEED TO LAND, AND SOON!"

Wind rushed hard and cold around Epekneia's face as she nodded in agreement. Then she gave her guardian a pat on the neck. The giant creatures leaned left and began their descent toward the earth, but Gemenon's guardian continued to struggle until it finally lost all strength. The creature began a free-fall, and Gemenon dug her claws into its tail and used her own wings to try and slow the massive bird's decent. Epekneia dove off her guardian and out into the sky. She yelled out a strange screech, and her guardian dove after Gemenon's. Epekneia dove after them all but knew she wasn't strong enough to hold either of them up. By the time Epekneia caught up with them, it was clear to her that their landing would not be gentle.

When she realized Gemenon was not going to let go of her guardian, Epekneia decided to pull her free from him in hopes of saving her life. She dove hard and grabbed her around the waist. Gemenon was startled by the girl's swift maneuver and lost her grip on the guardian. The two giant birds spun madly out of control until they hit the ground, and a terrible, agonizing screech echoed beneath the black mist. Gemenon jerked away from Epekneia in anger then dove through the mist.

"WHAT?" Epekneia shouted out in confusion. "I WAS TRYING TO SAVE YOU!" She let out a scoffing grunt of frustration then followed Gemenon down into the mist. Gemenon was on the ground inspecting her guardian's wing, and it was obviously broken. Epekneia landed beside her. "Hey! What was that? I was just trying to keep you from getting crushed. There was no way you could have saved them. You would have died!"

Gemenon looked up at her with a scowl on her face as she held the guardian's broken wing. "This one is my brother... I mean; he used to be, before he volunteered. His wing is broken. He can't fly anymore." Gemenon brushed the creature's wing with care. "We'll rest here for now. Check your guardian, and I'll see if I can find a branch or something to brace his wing."

Epekneia rushed over to the guardian she'd been riding. His head was lying next to a large blood-covered rock. "Gemenon, he hit his head on a stone. He's dead." The two dropped their heads for a moment in sadness at the loss of the faithful guardian. "Gemenon, why don't you stay with him? I'll go find something to brace his wing," Epekneia said, and Gemenon agreed with a subtle nod then continued brushing her brother's wing with care.

A long dirt mound was only a few feet away from where they had landed, so Epekneia decided to check on the other side of it in case there were any trees or something that might work to brace the guardian's injured wing. The mound was about fifteen feet high, so she gave a small burst from her wings and landed on top of it. Instantly, she recognized the place. It was Mine Five where she and Elias had fought the malfunctioning steam bots and also where she'd first embraced him. Only now it was cold and dark and there were no workers or any signs of production taking place. The black mist now filled every level of the mine, and the creeping mold crawled up the sides of the bench walls and all over the mining equipment. With one exception, the mine was completely void of life, but that exception was extremely unwelcoming.

Giant Bryn-wolves—hundreds of them—were circling the bench walls. The wolves were eating the creeping mold from the ground as if it were common place for them. She tried not to move so as not to spook the beasts and bring their wrath down on her. Unfortunately, a crust of dirt from the mound she was standing on broke free under her feet and rumbled down the bench wall. In an instant, thousands of ghoulish green eyes caught her in their gaze. They looked hungry, starving, but not for mold, for meat. She froze for a moment and turned her head slightly back toward Gemenon, who was still holding her brother's wing. Her heart sank as her body burst into the air with a great blast from her wings. She landed directly beside Gemenon and grabbed her by the arm. "We need to go. QUICKLY!"

The desperation in Epekneia's voice took Gemenon by surprise and she shuddered from it. "What is it?"

"Bryn-wolves! Hundreds of them!" Epekneia had only finished her words when the wolves began pouring over the dirt mound. Many of them went straight for the dead guardian, but others began surrounding the three companions. Gemenon drew the king's sword and readied herself. Some of the wolves reared back, but most seemed too hungry to be concerned with injury or death. Two of the creatures quickly lunged at them, maybe to test them, and Gemenon quickly struck them down with the sword. The two dead were instantly pulled away by their brother wolves and eaten, but more took their place. They circled left for a while then right and then back left again as if to study the Petinons.

Epekneia placed her claw hand on Gemenon's shoulder. "It's

about eight to ten miles to Grand Fortune City from here. We can try to carry him." Gemenon said nothing in response but only brandished the king's sword in a circle around the three of them. A bone-chilling howl ripped through the mist around them, and their eyes were drawn to the largest Bryn-wolf they'd ever seen. Its coat was deep red, and from Epekneia's observation, it seemed to be the pack leader. The injured guardian stood to his feet and brandished his long talons. He looked at Gemenon and Epekneia but spoke no words with his mouth. However, his eyes spoke volumes to Gemenon.

"NO! We'll fight them, brother," Gemenon cried out.

"We'll die if we stay," Epekneia said, "and you'll never fulfill the queen's request."

"I-It's not fair. I-I'll lose him all over again."

Epekneia strengthened her resolve and looked at Gemenon with the softness of someone who'd known loss and heartbreak. "It's why he volunteered. He wanted to be guardian to make you proud. It's time for him to fulfill his duty to protect his people... to protect you. Don't take that away from him by sacrificing yourself to the wolves. Don't let your death be the last thing he sees. It would defeat his spirit."

The guardian let out a frightening screech in anger toward the wolves and then another back at Gemenon. She sheathed the king's sword and responded back to her brother with a cry of her own then burst into the air with Epekneia. They exploded through the black mist quickly, and Epekneia could hear her crying as they flew toward GFC. After a few moments of flight, an agonizing screech echoed underneath the black mist as the guardian fell to the wolves.

Isabella landed outside the entrance to the prison and in front of the guardian. At first the creature didn't know what to think of her flaming wings, and it let out of powerful, screeching warning in her face. Isabella cocked her head to the right and tapped the crown on her head with the end of her baton. The guardian glanced at it for a moment but still did not open the gate to the prison. She let out a sigh of frustration at the giant creature then gave him a tap on the beak with her mod-hand. "Hello in there, I'm the new queen so, um… do your thing and open the gate." She waved her hand at the gate. When the guardian still refused, her anger began to burn and her wings grew brighter, then suddenly, the mountain trembled. The guardian instantly looked up at her in surprise, and she smiled at him. A large clawed hand reached out from his cloak, and he pulled the lever for the gate to open. "Thanks!" she said, giving his staff a tap with her baton as she entered.

The two guards standing inside the entrance to the prison nearly fainted when she strutted through. They didn't seem to know if they should run or bow down or try to arrest her. The prisoner they had just taken up for trial had returned wearing the queen's crown, and the mountain trembled when she spoke. Not only that, but the guardian had obeyed her and let her in. She ran right between them, untouched, and started to run down the rest of the tunnel to get her friends but suddenly stopped and thought for a moment then turned around to face them. "You guys have to do what I say, right?"

"Um, well… we, uh. Who are you?" one guard asked.

"I'm the queen of the Trembling Mountain," she said, smiling, and the mountain trembled again. Both guards quickly fell to their knees. "Good!" Her smile widened. "Now, here's what I want you to tell my friends." She leaned in close to them and whispered her plans.

They gave a nod and said, "Y-Yes, m-my queen. We will do it." The guards left her presence and disappeared into the darkness of the prison, then Isabella went back outside and waited next to the guardian.

BOGAN, AVA, AND GIDEON JUMPED UP WHEN THE GUARDS CAME into view. "WHERE'S IZZY!" Bogan roared at them.

"Yeah! What did you do with her?" Ava snapped.

"Your, um, friend is well. However, we bring a message from the queen," one guard said then looked over at his companion with a wonky look in his eyes.

"Well... out with it!" Gideon said, grinding his teeth.

"The queen is in need of... um... volunteers for a... a special mission and has asked if you would be willing to undertake such a task for your freedom."

Gideon and Bogan instantly bounced closer to the cell bars, and Bogan was the first to speak. "Maybe... what kind of mission is it?" he asked, rubbing his jawline and pretending to be somewhat disinterested.

The guard looked at his companion again as if he didn't want to explain the mission, so finally, his companion spoke up. "The queen has asked that you join her in the great dining hall, and your mission is to help her... eat twelve plates of lobster tail." The guard squirmed as if he felt stupid for being forced to ask such a thing.

"WHAT KIND OF JOKE ARE YOU TRYING TO PULL HERE?" Bogan snapped. "Come on, Gid, these guys are a bunch of..."

The guard cut him off. "If you choose to accept this mission, there is one condition."

"OH, Yeah! And what's that? We have to dance on one leg in a circle or something, and then you guys laugh at us and walk away? Right... huh, we aren't fallin' for it, bub!" Bogan scoffed.

"You must bring your friend Charlie with you," the guard said, placing the key into the door. Then he unlocked it and opened it all the way.

Bogan looked at his mates in wonder if it was real then

suddenly, Ava bolted out of the cell. When the guards didn't stop her, he looked back at Gideon, who was standing there mystified with his jaw dropped open. Bogan gave him a quick punch to the arm, then both of them rushed out of the cell together. He grabbed the keys from the guard's hand and put them in his pocket, just in case they were trying to pull a dirty trick then backed away from them in a distrusting manor.

"Is this for real?" Gideon asked.

"Yes!" The guards nodded

Bogan quickly pulled the keys back out of his pocket. "Which one opens Charlie's cell?"

The guard reached for the keys, and Bogan jerked away from them. "WHAT? I don't think so, BUB!"

"No, I was just going to unlock it for you." The guard reached out his hand again, only much slower this time.

Bogan dangled the keys in front of the guard's face. "Point to it, and I'll unlock it for you." The guard checked the keys, then with a raised claw he pointed. "Thanks, mate!" Bogan quipped then stepped over to Charlie's cell door and unlocked it.

Bogan and Ava quickly rushed inside and helped Charlie to his feet as best they could, but it was only now that Bogan realized just how big he was. "Hey! You two brutes get over here and help us out," Bogan yelled. The guards reluctantly obeyed but finally took hold of Charlie, then they all made their way down the long dark tunnel toward the exit.

"I don't understand. What made the queen change her mind?" Ava asked as they neared the exit of the prison.

"I'm afraid you will have to explain that to us," the guard said.

"What do you mean?" Gideon asked.

The guard point toward the opening of the exit and said, "Because your friend is now the queen." The crew looked down the tunnel where Isabella was standing with flaming wings stretched out across the entrance of the prison and light blazing all around her.

"HA!" Bogan blurted out in victory then pointed his finger at the guards. "HA!" he did it again, then for some odd reason he pointed his finger at Gideon. "HA!" Then he grabbed Charlie by the clawed hand and began laughing with crazed joy. Ava smiled, and Gideon shook his head in disbelief.

"You really are one of them," Gideon called out.

"I'm something. I'm not entirely sure they even know what I am," Izzy said with a twinkle in her eye. Bogan ran up to her and circled around her several times, gazing in wonder at her flaming wings. "HA!" he yelled out again and clapped his hands together several times in celebration. Suddenly, with a loud whoosh, they vanished into her back.

Gideon lurched back, visibly startled. "WHAT HAPPENED?"

"AH! Figures, as soon as something good happens for us, we lose it." Bogan said dejectedly, dropping his head.

"I did that, Bogan," Isabella explained.

"Really?" Bogan's face lit up and his joy returned.

"But why?" Ava asked.

"Charlie's suffered enough, and I don't want to take away from his big moment in the sun." She smiled and held out a handful of fire berries. "These are for Charlie. They will help him heal." Ava handed them to Charlie, and everyone watched as he stepped out into the sunlight. He was bigger than the guardian standing next to the prison entrance, and his red wings, though filthy, were clearly shimmering with gold underneath the dirt and grime from the prison.

"Open them up, Charlie. Let's see what you've got," Isabella prodded him.

Charlie struggled out onto the forest path and let out a groan as he arched his back then flared out his enormous wings. He shook the dirt and stench from his feathered body, sending a cloud of filth and dust everywhere. Soon it became clear that Charlie's feathered wings were quite possibly the most brilliant of any Bogan had ever seen. Suddenly, the guardian at the entrance let out a loud cry, startling everyone, and then he gave a slight bow to Charlie.

"You must be important," Isabella said with a grin. "What do you say we all head up to the dining hall and eat some grub?"

"WHAT? You weren't kidding?" Bogan asked.

"Bogan, you big lunk, I would never joke about food." Isabella raised her mod-arm and started to slug him in the shoulder, and he lurched back. "Made you flinch!" She smiled and quickly stole a hug from him, then lead the way back into the city.

It seemed as though many of the guards and people of the city had not yet been informed of Isabella's coronation, and their looks of caution worried Bogan as Isabella lead them through the streets. Some of the guards even stopped them and began to question her, but she grew angry with them and let loose her flaming wings as a warning. When the mountain trembled, the guards dropped to their knees, and the people instantly changed their opinion of her.

Once they had made it back to the castle, they entered the dining hall and took their seats wherever they pleased, and soon the food was brought out. It was a time of great joy, and even Charlie seemed to make an effort at happiness. Elehos stood at the entrance to the dining hall, smiling at them all as they joked and laughed away the burden of their imprisonment. She seemed filled with more happiness than Bogan had seen from her before, and finally, out of compulsion, he motioned for her to come join them and so she did.

20

DAY OF THE RAT

*T*he Bradley Dunbar was a much faster airship than Merlin could have ever imagined. Crafted completely out of cedar and titanium, the ship was extraordinarily light weight. The ship's envelope was small and tight around the top as it followed the ship's bullet-like design perfectly. It was powered by a single turbine, natural gas engine and shot a light blue, coned flame out the back when running at full speed. Bradley's pilot, Hal, was a very skilled and accurate man, and his performance captivated Jimmy so much, the boy could hardly take his eyes off of him. However, Merlin couldn't stop checking the skies below them to see if they were gaining ground on his father's armada. Iron Jaw was on one side of the ship and Merlin the other, and both were using monoculars to scan the clouds for any signs.

"DO YOU SEE ANYTHING YET, IRON JAW?" Merlin yelled out with his eye still mashed into his monocular.

"In the last thirty seconds since you just asked me that, the answer is still no, boy." Iron Jaw grumbled in frustration at Merlin's impatience.

"Sorry. I just… we have to beat them. We have to warn Izzy.

My father has lost his mind. I'm afraid he's going to do something... something terrible." Merlin's heart was racing in his chest when Iron Jaw cried out to him.

"QUICK, BOY! OVER HERE!"

"WHAT IS IT?" Merlin bellowed out, rushing to the other side of the bridge, and nearly knocking Jimmy out of the air in the process.

"Hey, that wasn't very nice, Merlin," Jimmy complained as he spun around in a circle.

"Sorry, Jimmy." Merlin spun the floating boy back around to facing Hal again then stumbled his way quickly over to Iron Jaw. "What? What do you see?"

"Look!" Iron Jaw held his monocular tight against the window to hold his position steady for Merlin. "Down there, beneath the smaller clouds."

Merlin looked through the tiny glass, and his vision was instantly teleported down into the passing clouds. There, just below a patch of smaller clouds was the Iron Weaver. "I SEE IT! I SEE THEM! WE'RE PASSING HIM! WE'RE PASSING HIM! HA, HA! YES!"

Iron Jaw gave him a pat on the shoulder. "See, what did I tell you? I knew we would, boy."

Merlin's happiness quickly faded. "It's not enough. We need to gain ground on him."

"I can't push her too hard, or we'll burn our fuel reserves and not have enough to make it back to Grand Fortune City," Hal grumbled.

Merlin ground his teeth in disappointment, but he didn't dare tell Hal it might be a one-way trip anyway. He needed a way to get the pilot to increase his speed without explaining the purpose of their mission. He snugged his hat down tight to prevent his bright blue brain bolts from drawing attention then worked his mind into a lightning storm of calculations. When it came to him, he smiled and took off down the hallway toward

Bradley's cabin. He burst through the door to find Bradley eating some kind of chocolate éclair treat that had dripped onto his chest, and standing next to him were his two smiling servants with rotten teeth. Their white shirts were pressed and perfectly clean, and it was obvious that Bradley had not been sharing any treats with them today. The two servants seemed almost entranced by something—Bradley's appetite perhaps. Bradley looked angrily at Merlin and his mouth looked too full to speak. *Perfect timing!*

Bradley muttered incoherently at Merlin's untimely intrusion. "Mumb ful umbnr strunckten."

"Sorry, but this is very important. Your pilot must hurry if we are going to be able to eat the rare fire berries that grow on the mountain. They bloom only once a year and that time is the only time humans can eat them safely. If we don't get there soon, we will miss out on a once in a lifetime delicacy."

Bradley's eyes nearly popped out of his skull, then he sprang up and bolted down the hall. Merlin was astounded at how fast a man of Bradley's size could move and nearly got run over by him in the process. He could hear Hal arguing with Bradley about the fuel, but a few short moments later he felt the ship jerk forward with a powerful thrust. Merlin fell against the wall of Bradley's cabin and smiled. *I think I like this Bradley guy,* he chuckled to himself.

SEVERAL HOURS LATER, THE TREMBLING MOUNTAIN CAME INTO view on the bridge. The green colors surrounding the mountain captivated Merlin, but Iron Jaw and Hal were too focused on landing preparations to be concerned with the scenery. Hal was also not pleased in the least bit when Merlin explained how he would have to land on the ground in a clearing at the back of the mountain, because the Trembling Mountain had no airship docks. Bradley however, seemed curious about what kind of place he'd been taken to, but his mind must have been too wrapped up in his thoughts of wonderful delicacies to ask any questions.

"We'll need someone to guide us in for a landing. How do we let them know we're here?" Hal asked.

Suddenly, two Petinon warriors appeared through the clouds about a thousand yards out on front of them. "They already know we're here," Merlin said with a grin, but his smile quickly vanished when something else broke through the clouds in between the warriors. It was a terrifying Petinon he'd not seen before with flaming wings and a powerful presence. The strange Petinon shot out toward them like a rocket, and as it drew closer, his eyes where filled with wonder. *Isabella? How can it be?*

She landed on the forward deck of the Bradley Dunbar, and her wings disappeared into her back with a whooshing sound. Merlin stared at her for a moment, speechless, then burst through the door and out onto the forward deck. "ISABELLA?"

She smiled at him. "Hey, brain boy."

"But... how?" Merlin asked, gobsmacked by her new gift.

"I don't know. It just happened. A building was on fire, so I rushed in to save some kids and, well... long story short—these things popped out when I fell into the flames. Oh, yeah, and I'm the new queen."

"WHAT? Slow down a minute. One bombshell at a time! I-I can't believe it. You can really fly with those things, and, and what about the king? We were scared to death they were going to do something to you. Like, I don't know, put you to death. I don't understand."

"Me neither," she said, smiling. "So, where did you get this ship? This is really nice." Isabella was still admiring the ship when Iron Jaw stepped out onto the deck. Bradley was behind him, and she didn't spot him right away. She ran over to Iron

Jaw to give him a big hug right as Bradley stepped out from behind him.

Seemingly out of shock, Isabella's fiery wings uncontrollably exploded out of her back "BRADLEY DUNBAR!"

"ISABELLA BROCK!" Bradley screamed in horror and ran back into the ship.

"Izzy, it's okay. He helped us get here... ahead of my father." Merlin dropped his head down.

"What do you mean? Is there a race or something?"

"No. Izzy, he is coming here with an army of tunnel rats. He is coming for Elias' black heart. He's joined forces with your mother. He has..." Merlin stopped when he saw the look on her face.

She closed her eyes for a moment. "Then he's the one that I saw in my vision. He's the one who took over Grand Fortune City."

"Yeah, and he used Cassandra's dark power to turn my mother into an Umbrella Charmer. I guess my father had given up on finding a cure and decided to try things a different way."

"How much time do we have?" she asked.

"One, maybe two hours, at the most," Merlin explained.

"Take the ship to the back side of the mountain, then meet me at the castle. I'll have the guards follow you around."

Merlin's gaze was sure and unwavering as he responded to her. "I'm not waiting to park this thing. I'm coming with you, and right now." Merlin turned and looked at the others. "Jimmy, we're following Isabella. Iron Jaw, follow the winged guys around to the back of the mountain and wait for us." Iron Jaw gave a nod and motioned for Hal to turn the ship port side while Jimmy took Merlin, then the three of them shot off toward the castle.

Isabella and Merlin burst through the door to the dining hall where the rest of the crew was leaning over the table like overfed slugs. "We've got a problem!" Merlin announced.

"HEY, it's Merlin," Bogan groaned out. "Man did you miss out," he finished with a nasty burp.

"We don't have time for that right now, Bogan." Isabella said, and the look on her face caught Elehos by surprise.

"What's wrong?" Elehos asked.

"My father, the Puppet Master, is coming." Merlin said, trying to explain, but was cut off again by Gideon.

"Oh, that's great, Merlin. He's going to love this place." Gideon smiled.

"NO, GIDEON! IT'S NOT GREAT!" Merlin yelled in frustration.

"Whoa there, mate. Who shook *your* brain globe?" Bogan snickered.

"He's telling the truth," Isabella said, looking to Elehos. "Hans is not coming as Merlin's father or even as a friend. He's coming as the Puppet Master."

"What does that mean?" Elehos asked.

Merlin jumped in to explain things better. "My father made a deal with Elias and Isabella's mother. She's a powerful Umbrella Charmer. She saved my mother from Black Mist sickness using the creeping mold then turned her into an Umbrella Charmer. My father is not just coming with an army of tunnel rats, but he has modified the Iron Weaver to fly. He's coming to for battle or to conquer if need be."

Bogan nearly fell out of his chair, and Gideon's head-mod let out a blast of steam as Merlin continued. "You all know what kind of war machine the Iron Weaver is, and he's flying it here right now. He's probably only an hour away."

"But your father doesn't know where we buried the prince." Gideon added a bit of reasoning, but Merlin let him have it.

"That's true, he doesn't know, but how long do you think it

will take for him to spot the fresh dirt under the tree? Come on, Gideon, it's my father, the Puppet Master. He's a genius—a master mind—and if he doesn't spot it, he's probably already programmed one of the rats to track it down as soon as he gets here."

"What do the Petinons do when they are attacked? Do you have a procedure for this sort of thing or something?" Isabella asked, looking over at Elehos.

"Not really. No one has ever attacked our people, except during the great civil war, but that was our own people who rebelled. And maybe the wolves, I suppose, but I can't imagine anyone wanting to attack us. We've never done anything to anyone," Elehos replied.

"Grandmother," Isabella said, drawing a quick, wonky-eyed look from Merlin and a smile from Elehos. "In our world, you don't have to do anything to anyone to make them attack you. They just do it because they can. Hans, the Puppet Master, was a good man, and he saved my life several times, but if he is working with my mother... well, we are in grave danger and all the people on this mountain are as well."

Elehos thought for a moment and then spoke. "I suppose we could hide out in the caves of prophecy. They're located beyond the prison tunnels."

"WHAT? I'm not going back in the prison," Bogan snapped.

"We wouldn't be. We would just have to travel through the prison caves to get there. That's why the guardian stands guard outside the prison. He is there to guard the sacred caves of prophecy where all the books are kept. They were placed there after King Arkone forbade anyone to study them any longer," Elehos explained.

"So, how do we let everyone know where to go and what's going on?" Isabella asked.

"We could sound the warning horn we use for the wolves," Elehos said.

"We need to sound it now so everyone has time to get to the caves." Isabella had just finished her statement when a loud blast of a deep, bellowing horn vibrated the walls of the castle.

Elehos shuddered and Bogan let out a laugh and said, "Wow Izzy, that was seriously fast. How did you... oh, *CRUD!*"

"It's too late. He's already here," Merlin said.

THEY RUSHED TO THE WINDOW AND GAZED OUT OVER THE CITY. The Iron Weaver was hovering over Pterugas, and tunnel rats were pouring out of the airships behind it. The Puppet Master was standing out on the golden bull horns, holding his dragon's head cane in the air, conducting his symphony of doom. Green eyed tunnel rats with machine guns slid down ropes and quickly infested the city with terror. Many Petinons were flying away from the mountain while others were swept up in the attack. Thumacheo and his warriors quickly took flight with swords and spears, but their sacred steel was no match against the rat's guns. Brave Petinon warriors fell from the sky before her eyes, and something stirred with in her Isabella that she couldn't quite explain, but she knew in her heart she could no longer stand the sight of it.

"Gideon, take everyone and get as many Petinons to the caves as you can," she said, climbing onto the window ledge.

"What are you going to do?" Merlin asked.

"I'm gonna keep the Puppet Master busy for a while," Isabella replied.

"Now go! Get them to safety," she said, and shoving some berries into her mouth, she drew deep from the well of fire within her then leapt out the window. Her wings exploded out of her back with such force, it momentarily took her breath away. She swooped into the air and was instantly caught in the Puppet Master's gaze. It was difficult to tell when Hans was surprised, because his lidless eyes always made him seem like he was in a state of shock, but even more so now with his metal face. Either way, Isabella knew she'd made an impact on him when his mouth dropped open in surprise. He was so taken by her flaming wings that he nearly dropped his cane and lost his footing on the golden horns. She swirled into the sky, wrapping her wings around her as the rats unloaded their weapons at her, but the heat from her flaming wings was so hot the lead rounds instantly melted when they made contact. She swooped and dove at the rats and sent her baton at them in a fury as she kept watch on the castle to make sure her distraction was keeping the rats from noticing her friends.

Thumacheo and his men seemed distraught, but when they spotted Isabella's magnificent bravery and her raging wings of fire, they quickly reengaged in the battle. The Puppet Master seemed quite displeased with her emboldening the warrior's spirits, and with the wave of his cane, the Iron Weaver switched to war mode. Gatling guns emerged from the sides of the train, and his tunnel rats let loose a fury of metal toward Isabella and her Petinon warriors. Isabella feared that his brutal display of power from the Iron Weaver would devastate her warrior's moral to the point of retreat, but just as the Puppet Master seemed to be enjoying his slaughter, a voice from the sky threw him off his game and left him utterly shaken.

"FATHER!" Merlin cried out.

The Whisper crew was fleeing the castle and headed down the main road toward the city. Merlin's unmistakable brain globe was lit up with furious bolts of lightning, and Jimmy was rocketing toward his father. "CEASE FIRE!" Hans yelled out, stopping his rodent attack.

Jimmy rose up in front of the Iron Weaver, and in a rare moment of epiphany, he was struck with comprehension that clearly didn't come from his brain-mod. "WHY, FATHER? WHY?"

Thumacheo took advantage of the Puppet Master's moment of confusion, and his warriors slaughtered the tunnel rats as the bristly haired creatures stood lifeless, waiting for their master's command. However, the Puppet Master's moment of weakness was short lived. "You wouldn't understand, James, and you probably never will," he said to his floating boy, then with the wave of his cane, his rats unleashed their chaotic madness upon the city once more. The Puppet Master turned the Iron Weaver sideways, and his heavy guns burned bright red with rage at every moving creature and city structure. Even the trees were shredded from the tops down, and the sky grew dark with smoke from the Iron Weaver's guns.

Isabella cried out to Thumacheo and his warriors to save the people and get them into the cave. She spotted Merlin and the crew in the streets trying to make their way past a large force of tunnel rats, but they were pinned down behind one of Sunago's statues. Isabella shouted at Jimmy, who was still frozen in the sky, watching his father's destruction of the city. "JIMMY! HELP MERLIN! PROTECT, JIMMY! PROTECT!"

Jimmy looked down into the city streets at Merlin and his friends then after a slight hesitation of brain-mod processing, he rumbled to their rescue. He hovered in front of the rats, who instantly stopped firing their guns when the red lights flashed on their mod-hats, but just as quickly the lights turned green again, and they hammered Jimmy with their hot metal rounds. Merlin was appalled that his father had removed the protections for his sons, and as the rest of the crew ran toward the forest path, Merlin lay heartbroken against Sunago's statue. Jimmy didn't seem surprised at all by the rats' attack and quickly disposed of them with a fierce bolt of lightning, then he swooped over toward Merlin, cocked his head to the right and asked, "Are you coming, Merlin?" But when Merlin didn't answer, Jimmy picked him up, and in a thick cloud of black smoke, they roared off into the forest.

About the time Isabella felt comfortable enough to make her strike on the Puppet Master, she suddenly spotted eight tunnel rats already digging under Prince Enupnion's tree. The Puppet Master had already figured out where the black heart was buried, and his rats were digging up the grave. Isabella was now torn between stopping the rats from getting Elias' black heart or killing the Puppet Master. She quickly decided the black heart was of greatest importance to Hans, and figured, if she could get to it first, she would have an excellent bargaining tool to force his surrender. She was about to make her move when her attention was instantly diverted to three enormous tunnel rats rushing into the forest after her friends and the people of Pterugas. Their heavy guns hammered away at the trees, ripping the bark to shreds and strafing the ground all around the entrance to the cave. She could hear her friend's cries for help as the rats let loose a barrage of lead into the forest.

Out frustration from the heavy weight of her decision, she let out a scream that filled the sky over the city, and the mountain trembled. It startled the rats everywhere, and even the Puppet Master took notice. He commanded his army to focus their guns on her, and suddenly her moral dilemma was the least of her concerns. She wrapped herself up in her flaming wings as the rats unloaded everything they had at her. For a time, the lead rounds melted in the flames surrounding her, but she soon began to notice some of them weren't melting, and they almost reached her body. One fragment made it through and ricocheted off her mod-arm, but another grazed her leg and a shockwave of pain ripped through her. In agony, she shot up into the sky above the clouds until she was hidden from their sight, then she tore the bottom part of her shirt and wrapped her wound with it. She reached into her pocket and took out the last three fire berries she had and stuffed them into her mouth, then she made her decision and dove back down below the clouds and into the forest with her friends. The large rats were blasting away at every tree, and she quickly noticed her friends were trapped behind them. She landed directly behind the three overgrown rodents that towered over her. They were enormous beasts that hunched over, and she couldn't tell if it was from the weight of their guns or if these were some new breed of tunnel rat Hans had manufactured himself. Either way, she made them pay for trying to harm her friends.

She grabbed one of the rats' tails and set it on fire with her wings. The beast took off down the path toward Gideon and Bogan, and Bogan gladly stepped out and blasted a hole into the rat's chest. The other two instantly turned around, and she struck the one on her right with her baton, straight through the snout, while Gideon blasted the other one in the back when it turned around. Her strike on the large rat's snout wasn't enough to kill it, and the beast jerked its head and took off through the forest with Isabella still holding on to her baton. It pulled her for a ways, until she finally let go of her baton and tumbled over the ground. Her wings flamed out, but not before they set the ground on fire as well as several trees.

Once she got to her feet, she could see the overgrown tunnel rat charging at her. She snapped her mod-finger several times, but her baton was buried deep in the bone of the rat's snout and wouldn't come out. It lunged at her and landed on top of her, trying to take a bite, but her baton was preventing it from opening its jaws. Its breath reeked of foul tunnel rat grime, as if the creature had been eating its own kind, and it dripped rotten saliva all over her face. Strangely, the grotesque beast stopped its attack as if it were thinking. Its brain-mod lights flashed on and off several times, then suddenly the rat began striking at her face with her baton as it protruded out the bottom of its snout. Isabella was aghast at how fast the rat learned a work around to its snout problem, and she moved her head left then right with every strike, in an effort to avoid being punctured in the face. The rat stopped again, and its lights flashed on and off, then it looked down at her as if it had learned something valuable. It lunged at her for another chance, but it's hard-learned effort was quickly wasted when a large spear ripped through its head and the beast slumped over.

Thumacheo kicked the giant rat off her and reached out his claw to help her up. "I don't have to like you, but you are the queen now. Come on. We need to get into the cave." She could tell it was a difficult thing for Thumacheo to do, and she wondered if she would ever win him over.

"Thanks," she said, taking his claw and getting to her feet. Then she kicked the rat's snout, broke her baton free, and the both of them rushed back toward the entrance of the cave. Gideon, Bogan and Jimmy were holding off the storm of rats outside, and the forest was filling with more than they could manage. The guardian at the entrance to the cave was still standing by the gate and had clearly been wounded to the point of death, but he continued to fight with his last bit of strength. Isabella lit up her wings around Thumacheo as they ran through fire fight. The rat's rounds whizzed and zipped passed them until they made it across the dirt path, and she was appalled that Thumacheo didn't stop to help the guardian.

"WE CAN'T LEAVE HIM!" she yelled back to Thumacheo.

"HE'S DOING WHAT HE WAS MADE TO DO!" Thumacheo said, but when she refused to go into the cave, the guardian looked over at her and let out a powerful screech of a warning. She froze for a moment until Thumacheo called out to her.

"HE SAID GO! He's giving us a chance to live, so don't waste it."

She stepped back into the cave, and Thumacheo pulled down the iron bars and locked the gate. They rushed back into the prison, passing by the cell where she had been for so many days, and continued on through until they came to another tunnel. She paused for moment when a horrible screech from the guardian echoed back at them.

"THIS WAY!" Thumacheo called out.

When she didn't respond, Bogan grabbed her mod-hand and pulled her, but he was careful not to burn himself on her wings. As the four of them ran down the winding tunnel, they began to see a shimmer of light growing. The cave tunnel suddenly opened up into a massive, circular room filled with Petinons, and only a single torch held by Elehos was illuminating the grand room. Thumacheo was first into the room, then Gideon and Bogan, but Isabella stopped for moment and stood in the cave tunnel. *Queen for a few hours and I lost the whole kingdom. These people are going to hate me. Why do I have to destroy everything I touch?*

Elehos stepped into the tunnel with her, carrying the only light the people had and leaving the room pitch black. Children began to cry and the shuffling of people in the darkness filled the room. "Granddaughter… you are queen no matter what has happened today, but keep this in mind. You are not queen because of anything you did or the fact that you are my granddaughter. You are their queen because the Trembling Mountain accepted you when I placed the crown on your head. Nothing you do will change how they perceive you unless you give in to fear and the mountain stays quiet. So, go in there and light up the darkness for them." Elehos dropped the torch light on the ground and stomped it out, leaving only the light from Isabella's flaming wings. Then she stepped aside.

Isabella took a breath before stepping into the dark room. In an instant, the room exploded with light from her wings. The air inside the large dome filled with the hot, cinnamon smell of burning fire berries, and the cries of the Petinon children quickly quieted. Flames licked the air around her as she extended her wings as far out as she could, and they sounded like the rushing of water from a great waterfall as they burned.

As she gazed into the shattered faces and broken spirits of her friends and her people, thoughts of vengeance fill her mind, and anger burned in her heart for the Puppet Master and her mother.

She took a deep breath of air into her lungs, clenched her fists together at her sides and softly, quietly spoke into the darkness, "Darkness lies!" The Trembling Mountain rumbled and shook, then all the people of Pterugas dropped to their knees.

21

LOYAL FRIENDS

*G*emenon and Epekneia approached Grand Fortune City with heavy hearts, but Epekneia stopped Gemenon in midflight when she noticed the absence of smoke rising from the city. Also not lost on her was how oddly quiet the city docks were, and so she motioned for Gemenon to drop down on the edge of the mine to better evaluate things. She also considered Gemenon could use a few moments to gather herself together after suffering such a great loss. Epekneia knew the difficultly of such suffering and was still carrying the weight of loss from her father's death. She carried the weight of everything Gemenon had told her about Elias and Izzy and how they were the grandchildren of King Arkone and Queen Elehos. She spent hour upon hour thinking through how to explain this to Elias but hadn't a clue where to begin. At the moment, though, her mind was filling with questions about the emptiness of Grand Fortune City. She scanned the mine below and the city above for any signs of people, but as time quickly passed, her subtle concern turned into deep dread. She paced back and forth in front of Gemenon in hopes of getting her attention without seeming to be rude about her loss,

287

but she knew something wasn't right. *Where are the airships and the smoke? Why is the mine so quiet? Did Elias make it, or did he already leave? Something's not right. We have to keep moving.* As her thoughts wandered, her eyes were reminded of the battle against Sunago and the Umbrella Charmers. The city had been repaired for the most part, but it still bore the scars of battle on its iron tower, and her concern deepened quickly as she began to fear the worse. *Did the Umbrella Charmers return?*

Something in the mine startled Gemenon out of her sadness, and she sprang up from the rock she was resting on, quickly unsheathing the king's sword. "Do you hear that?" she asked.

"Yeah, I think it's coming from down in the mine."

"More wolves?"

"No! I don't think so," Epekneia said as her mind instantly began to think of the terrifying moles that had attacked the city before. "It could be something... something much worse."

Gemenon gripped the king's sword and prepared herself. "We should take flight. We'll be safer above ground."

"Not from him we won't," Epekneia said smiling as she spotted Casper swooping in and out of the mine tunnels.

"It's the great gray!" A subtle smile rose up on Gemenon's face.

"Look! He wants us to follow him. Casper and Elias were practically inseparable on the way to Pterugas. I am certain he will lead us to him," Epekneia said, gently taking Gemenon by the arm. "Take heart, this is a good sign."

"But the tunnels... I've heard there are... things, beasts down in them." Gemenon said as she slightly pulled away from Epekneia's grasp.

"There are thing down there. I've seen them and fought them." Epekneia hardened her gaze on Gemenon. "If I can fight them, then I've no doubt a warrior of your renowned can fight as well. Besides, once we find Elias, you won't have to worry about monsters."

Gemenon was taken aback by her words. "What do you mean?"

"Why don't we find him first and then you can see for yourself." Epekneia smiled and gave another tug on Gemenon's arm, then the two swooped down into the mine. Casper looped in circles for a moment, then once they were close to him, the eager owl shot back into the tunnel.

BRYNJAR THE WOLF-BEAST HOWLED AND GROANED AS ELIAS worked to patch his wounds as best he could. Anytime the man-beast reacted in a hostile manner, Elias would threaten to strike him with the jackboot. On the other hand, Mr. Black sat against the cold stone wall of their cell, staring at the jackboot, and grumbling about Elias' lost opportunity at becoming a Labyrinth Legend. Elias took off his jacket and removed his shirt. He tore a piece off his shirt and placed the strip into his pocket then turned the shirt inside out to the cleaner side and began dabbing Brynjar's wounds with it. The beast winced and howled when the boy touched his side and Elias lurched back away from him.

"See what I mean? He's a monster. He can't be trusted. All the Labyrinth Legends are monsters... even me." Mr. Black sneered and suddenly he noticed Elias' chest. "That scar. How did you get it?"

Elias thought carefully before he answered. He liked Mr. Black but was still unsure if he could trust him. "I was injured, but my father's surgeon saved me."

"Your father must be a very important man to have his own surgeon," Mr. Black said, leaning in closer toward Elias' face. And in the darkness of their cell he could see Mr. Black's face change, and his voice grew darker. "There's something that's been nagging at me for some time now."

"O-Oh yeah... um, what would that be?" Elias nervously asked.

"What the devil is a boy like you doing down here with us - *MONSTERS?*"

Elias held his breath; in the off-chance Mr. Black could smell fear on him. He thought his answer through carefully and figured a stronger response would be better than a timid one, so he leaned in closer to Mr. Black's face, nose to nose and said, "Maybe I'm a monster just like you."

Mr. Black's eyes looked over at the empty jackboot resting on the ground and then back at Elias. "Uhm, maybe... maybe so," he said, slowly moving away from Elias and leaning back on the wall. Mr. Black rubbed the lower part of his massive jaw with his calloused hands so hard, Elias imagined any harder and sparks would have popped from his whiskers. Then the man stopped and spoke loudly. "SO, TELL ME, BOY," he hesitated, looking at the empty jackboot again. "Who IS your father?"

Elias nervously diverted the topic. "Oh he's... um, nobody really... um, just a nobody... say, could I get a hand with him for a minute?" he asked pointing at Brynjar, who looked as if he were about to pass out from the pain.

"ANSWER THE QUESTION, BOY!" Mr. Black snapped.

"Why? Why do you care who my father is, anyway?" Elias asked with a suspicious look on his face.

"Because I want to know who he is, that's why."

Mr. Black seemed agitated, and Elias was growing tired of his questions. He figured he would give Mr. Black another brash response to calm him down, but suddenly, the sounds of someone struggling came from the jagged "S" shaped hole in the wall. Someone was coming. Elias and Mr. Black both squinted their eyes to see who might be trying to get through, and even Brynjar groaned in wonder as he lifted his head up to get a better view. It soon became clear to the three prison companions that whoever was trying to get in was having an extremely difficult time of it. They grunted and scoffed angrily, and soon the sound of voices echoed into the cell.

"Push! Push harder! I can't make it..." several grunting sounds later and the first person tumbled into their cell.

"EPEKNEIA!" Elias hollered out joyfully. "How did you find me?"

"Epekneia! Can you give me a hand?" the other voice asked, somewhat agitated by Epekneia's lack of assistance.

"Oh, sorry. Hold on a second, Elias," she said, going back to jagged "S" entrance. She pulled, mashed, and grunted until the next person tumbled through. They both landed on top of each other in a mess of feathers that seemed to startle Brynjar, but when the Petinons saw him they screamed. Brynjar growled and tried to scoot away from them as Gemenon quickly brandished her sword in panic.

"NO! WAIT! Stop for just a second, okay?" Elias stood between them to calm everyone down, and it was clear that even Mr. Black was startled by the Petinons. "No one is going to attack anyone here. No one is an enemy. This is Brynjar the Wolf-Beast. He's injured and I'm trying to help him recover. Over there is Mr. Black, and he helped me survive in the arena." Elias pointed to Mr. Black, who tipped an imaginary hat to the two ladies. "And for you guys, this is Epekneia and..." he stopped and shrugged his shoulders at Epekneia, who quickly introduced her guest.

"Oh, you remember Gemenon... from the castle?" Epekneia said.

"Oh, that's right, um, with the, uhm... with the sparrow and the whole crunch thing with the neck. Right? How could I forget that one?" he said, smacking his hand on his head. "You can, um... put the sword down now." He waved his finger up and down at the tip of Gemenon's sword, and it suddenly moved the sword in her hand. It startled her so much, she dropped it on the ground and stepped back away from him. "Sorry about that." Elias winced.

"Yeah, he's got a real gift with metal, doesn't he?" Mr. Black snickered in the darkness.

"HOW? HOW DID YOU DO THAT?" Gemenon gasped in shock.

"If you think that's something, he just *whooped* the snot out of Brynjar with that boot over there." Mr. Black grinned.

Epekneia tried to speak up and ask Elias about his father's boot, but she was cut off by Gemenon's questions. "YOU DID THAT? TO THAT THING, I mean... *HIM?*"

"Well, yeah. I mean, he was going to kill Mr. Black, and his wolves were going to eat me, so I just beat him with the boot until he stopped. I didn't mean to hurt him. I didn't want to. So, I had Mr. Black bring him back here so WE could help him. Even though SOMEONE didn't want to." Elias looked at Mr. Black with a disappointed glare for his lack of compassion toward Brynjar, but Mr. Black simply shrugged his shoulders with indifference. "HEY! Maybe you guys could help me with him. He has some terrible wounds from where I pulled the metal off his side." Elias could tell by the looks from both Petinons that they were horribly uncomfortable with the giant wolf-beast, let alone helping him. "Or, well... okay then, maybe you could just tell me what to do so I can help him."

"So, this Wolf-Beast thing wanted to kill you and now you want to help heal him?" Gemenon asked in confusion.

"He was only doing what the arena taught him to do," Elias said, but his words did not go unnoticed by Brynjar.

Gemenon searched her satchel for a moment then removed some herbs and a few strange bottles of salve. She handed them to Elias and explained how he needed to apply them for the best results, then she stepped back away from the Wolf-Beast. Elias was about to begin applying the medicine to Brynjar when

Epekneia pulled him aside. "Elias," she whispered, "isn't that your father's boot?"

"Yes," he said softly with a nod when he noticed Mr. Black leaning in to try and catch an earful.

"Is he... is he okay?" Epekneia asked.

"I don't know yet, but according to Henry, he is some-where...*here*, in the labyrinth. Hey, how did you find me?"

"Casper, he led us to you. He's a loyal friend, you know." She smiled at him.

"He is, isn't he?" Elias nodded in agreement.

"Look, Elias... there's something you need to know." Epekneia grimaced a bit as if she was holding in some sort of terrible news, and Elias quickly grew concerned.

"What? What is it?"

"It's about the... um, it's about the queen. Look, it's probably better if Gemenon explains this, besides, she's the one who told me, and I don't want to mess anything up," Epekneia said, motioning for Gemenon to come over.

Gemenon stepped up next to them and quietly asked, "What going on?"

"You need to tell him everything you told me. You know, about the queen, about his family," Epekneia said with a stern look in her eyes. For a moment Gemenon hesitated and looked back at Elias' nosey cell mate, but after Epekneia continued to prod her, she finally relented and explained to Elias who Queen Elehos was and why she'd sent her to protect him. At first it was a bit difficult for Elias to believe, but when he searched his heart, he knew deep down that it felt right. It was also helpful that Gemenon's infor-mation was extremely detailed and delivered with confidence.

Elias also knew all too well the burden of learning your parents weren't who you thought they'd been, so he explained to Gemenon and Epekneia that he should be the one to tell his father.

"Elias," Epekneia whispered. "Izzy and the whole crew are imprisoned back at Pterugas. We need to get back to them before... we need to get back soon."

"I KNOW THAT..." Elias accidentally blurted out, then he quickly returned to a whisper. "I know that, but I can't leave without my father. As soon as we get Brynjar patched up, we'll get out of here."

"How are we going to do that? These bars are thicker than that guy's arms?" Epekneia said of Mr. Black.

"I have a plan." Elias said, kneeling down next to Brynjar. "But let me take care of him first. Oh, and get Casper in here. We're going to need him."

While Epekneia and Gemenon stepped over toward the crack in the wall to try and entice Casper into their cell, Elias patched up Brynjar as best he could. When he finished, the Wolf-Beast startled him by reaching his massive wolf paw at him. It was terrifyingly large and horribly disfigured, and Elias imagined he was about to be shredded for his kindness, but the beast slumped over. *Passed out!* Elias breathed a loud sigh of relief that caught Mr. Black's attention.

"We might just live long enough to regret your act of kindness towards Brynjar." Mr. Black chuckled.

"I hope not," Elias said then stepped up closer to Mr. Black. "I need to you pull Brynjar as far away from the cell bars as you can. That corner over there by the bear skin will do."

"And why would I do that?"

"Because if you don't, he will die." Elias grinned. "We're getting out of here, and you're going to carry him or at least drag him out."

"And just how do you intend on breaking through bars that not even I can bend?" Mr. Black scoffed.

"I have a plan." Elias smiled a nefarious grin at him then approached Epekneia and Gemenon, who were finally getting Casper through the crack in the wall.

Elias spoke to them quietly for a moment. After Gemenon slipped a berry into his hand, he slid over toward the cell bars with his back hidden. He waited until Mr. Black, begrudgingly pulled Brynjar out of the way, and then he took the strip he'd torn from his shirt and wrapped the fire berry inside it. Once everyone had taken cover in the far corner, he placed the berry on the hinge of the cell door then let the tiny strip of his shirt hang down from the hinge like a fuse. Then he opened the side of the jackboot boot and out popped his father's pipe and matches. With a whoosh, he struck the match, lit the cloth, then ran through the cell with a giddy laughter and hopped into the corner with the others. "Hold your ears!" he yelled.

Mr. Black suddenly looked horrified. "BOY! WHAT DID YOU JUST DO?" he asked, using his body to cover Elias and the Petinons. Seconds later the fire berry lit with a BANG, and the cell door flopped down sideways.

When the smoke cleared, Mr. Black cautioned Elias. "You're much smarter than I gave you credit for. Just keep in mind, if Mogdal's horn calls for anther free-for-all, every one of those cell doors in this hall will open, and we'll have no place to hide from the beasts of Karl's Labyrinth."

"Then what are we waiting for? Let's get going!" Elias said with smile, but he only succeeded at making Mr. Black feel like he'd been played.

Strange, monstrous-shaped eyes glared through iron bars at them as they trekked through the halls of the prison in search for his father. Epekneia and Gemenon kept themselves in the very center of the isle way so nothing could reach out and grab hold of their wings, and Gemenon had even brandished the king's sword for fear something would attack them in the darkness. Mr. Black was dragging Brynjar on top of the broken cell door, and Elias was doing his best to keep up with Casper, who was swooping and landing wherever he pleased without a worry in the world.

"Henry told me that all these tunnels connect to the different sides and that once I was in, I should be able to find him," Elias explained.

"Find who, boy?" Mr. Black prodded again, trying to trick Elias into giving up more information.

"You'll know soon enough," he said then quickly turned right down another tunnel. "THIS WAY! Casper went this way." He followed the great gray down the dark tunnel as all manner of foul smelling, growling and grunting beasts reached at him through the iron bars. The owl finally came to a stop in front of a cell door closest to the arena exit and seemed to be admiring something inside. As Elias ran toward the cell, he began to hear the laughter of victory echoing down the cavernous prison hallway.

THE JACKBOOT OPENED HIS EYES TO THE STRANGEST OF SIGHTS AS he awoke from his pounding headache episode. Hex was kneeling before him in an overly dramatic fashion with his head bowed. "Hex, what exactly are you doing?" he asked, but Hex remained quiet.

"He thinks you're one of his Petinon nobles. Royalty of some sort... now that you've got that strange mark on your forehead." Grundorph snickered as he gave Hex a pat on the top of his wing.

"Royalty? HA! Far from it, metal head," the Jackboot scoffed. "Wait... what happened to my boot?"

"You lost it during our battle with Bog Bog the troll. He was... a difficult opponent, but Grundorph finally bested him," Hex explained.

"Well, that's going to be a problem," the Jackboot said.

"I'm certain we'll be able to get it back at some point, sire."

"That's not soon enough," the Jackboot grumbled.

Hex looked at him quizzically, "And why is that?"

"That boot had my pipe in it."

"If I might just add a bit of sensibility to your predicament. This might be a good time to put an end to that nasty habit you've got," Grundorph said. "I know I don't particularly care for it myself, and to be right honest, I don't think Hex does either."

"Or maybe it's a good time for you to stop mothering me and think of a way to get me out of here," the Jackboot sneered.

Suddenly, the three companions were drawn to a fluttering sound outside their cell door. Hex and Grundorph quickly stepped over to check it out, and Grundorph stated the obvious, "It's a giant owl."

The Jackboot hobbled on his one foot until he made it over to the cell door. "I know this bird. This is my son's bird. My boy, he has come for me," he proudly grinned.

"YOUR SON? He'll be killed out there," Hex replied in shock.

The Jackboot grinned at Hex and said, "You don't know my son then, do you?" And he began to laugh a haughty laughter of victory that echoed marvelously throughout the prison hall.

22

QUEEN FOR A DAY

Queen Isabella's wings burned bright, illuminating the large dome room deep inside the Trembling Mountain. A count was taken by one of the Elders of the Convocation, and it was determined that just a little less than half of the city had made it to the safety of the Prophecy Cave. The others had either perished under the wrath of the Puppet Master or remained hidden somewhere on the mountain. Thumacheo and his warriors did their best to maintain order in the crowded cave, but with nearly every step Isabella took, the mountain trembled terribly, and she soon took notice of how disturbed the Petinons were by her presence.

She eventually approached Elehos with her concern. "It's not my fault. I'm not doing it. I don't know why the mountain is shaking so badly."

"I'm not for certain myself, but it's quite possible the fire berries are...are igniting. Come with me. You're doing more harm than good in here." Elehos motioned and Isabella followed her to the walls of prophecy where the history of her people had been recorded.

The walls themselves were covered with many different

writings and pieces of art that described all manner of wisdom and tales of what might have been or would be to come. For Isabella, the entire experience was a grand enigma that didn't make much sense. However, Ava seemed intrigued and instantly took out her notepad and began copying everything she could. Bogan scratched his head in confusion while Gideon appeared to marvel at the whole thing with wondrous blasts of steam from his mod. Boxed shelves were carved out in the walls and were filled with scrolls and books and at the far end stood another great guardian. Great battles of old were depicted as well as battles that no one living had ever witnessed. Isabella followed her grandmother along the wall until they came to a picture of King Arkone. It was a strange picture that seemed to catch Elehos off guard. The dark, foreboding depiction of her husband looked as though someone had crafted it in a way to indicate great dishonor. "I've been down here many times, and I don't believe I've ever noticed this before today." She took a deep breath as she stared intently at the picture.

"Is everything okay?" Isabella asked.

"The colors used in this picture of your grandfather are the colors of a disgraced Petinon. And this!" She suddenly pointed to a picture of a wingless Petinon. "This one is one of the draw-ings the elders have always used to explain why wingless Petinon children are such a terrible disgrace, but... but now it has all been revealed to me." She looked back at Bogan. "Get some of the elders. And quickly!" she snapped.

"Alright, alright... don't get your feathers in a bunch. I'm going," Bogan grumbled under his breath as he stamped away. "Humph! Last I checked, Izzy was queen, not her. Give someone a crown and they'll always want to be in charge," he muttered under his breath. Moments later he returned with several elders, who didn't seem too pleased by the informality of being summoned by a human with mods.

"LOOK! Look at this!" Elehos demanded of the elders.

"Yes, yes. We've all seen the depictions of what shamed, wingless Petinons look like," one named Anakrino said.

"NO!" Elehos shouted at him. "This is not a depiction of what it means to be a wingless Petinon. This is a dark depiction of Sunago the Great. And LOOK! Beside him is our fallen king, my husband, King Arkone, and he is depicted as a dark terror on the wall," she said. Then pointing to the wingless Petinon. "See here! Above him is the sign of one who was cleaved. This Petinon once had wings, but someone removed them by force." Elehos' face was filled with fury. "All these years, you have been mistaken and needlessly slaughtered wingless children because you assumed the Destroyer would be born wingless, but in reality, his wings were removed by force." The elders grumbled amongst themselves for a time and couldn't come to an agreement on Elehos' new revelation.

Then Queen Isabella spoke up. "I know the person in this picture very well. I first saw him when I was a child, at the age of four, and again at the age of eight on the day my father hacked off his wings." Some of the elders gasped at her words, and one of them rushed over to the far end of the wall near the guardian. He pulled a torch from it, then ran back to the corner and rudely pushed the guardian out of the way—an act punishable by death, but the guardian strangely did not react to his offense. The elder held the torch up to the wall and ran his claw across it until he stopped and looked back at the rest of the elders.

"Come! Come quickly!" he said, and the other elders slowly made their way to the corner of the wall. After a few moments, they all looked back at Queen Isabella then back at each other. They spoke quietly and looked back up at the wall, then one of the elders left the group and stepped back over to where Queen Isabella and the Whisper crew were standing.

"It is said that when the Golden Guardian arrives..." he cleared his throat and gave a nod toward Charlie. For a second,

Bogan looked like he wanted to strangle the elder for not spitting it out. "When the Golden Guardian arrives, the time of Ouranos is near. The wall also depicts the dark, shadowy figure with silver feet sending forth his wings of fire to slay our great king. The dark, shadowy figure has always been known to the elders as the great evil; the Dark Voice of Destruction that would bring the Destroyer upon us all. Many of the elders standing here believe that is exactly what has happened to us today. Come, let me show you," he said, waving his claw and wing in unison with one move.

They followed him over to where the other elders were standing, and he pointed up toward the wall. On the wall was a shadowy figure with brightly colored silver feet, and from his mouth came wings of fire that attacked a great king on his throne. "See here, next to the depiction of the great shadow of death is the one who holds the dragon's head, just like the one who attacked our great city today. We all remember and agree that in his hand he held a dragon's-head cane which he used to command his forces of destruction."

Elehos seemed greatly disturbed by the elder's words and asked, "Who do you say the dark shadow is?"

"As you can clearly see, there is smoke rising from his mouth. He is a black mist speaker. He is the Dark Voice of Destruction who will bring great evil and terror upon us," Anakrino said.

"No, he isn't" Ava abruptly quipped.

"Excuse me!" the elder sneered in offense. "And who are you that you would know our prophecies?"

Ava shrugged at the Petinon. "Maybe nobody, but I know who your dark shadow is," Ava said, smiling as she kept her eyes on her paper, drawing furiously. Isabella carefully tried to get Ava's attention by kicking dirt on her boot to prevent her from revealing something that might have catastrophic consequences, but her efforts were useless.

"Really? Please, then… do tell, do tell, oh wise one," Anakrino mocked.

"He's Izzy's father, the Jackboot. Angus Grand cut off his feet, and Hans, the Puppet Master, forged the iron boots for him," she said proudly as she kept drawing. The elders gasped and stared at Isabella as if they'd made a terrible mistake.

"We have just crowned the fiery weapon of the dark shadow as our new queen!" Anakrino exclaimed in horror.

Ava kept her head down and continued drawing as she spoke. "Well, I don't know about that, but you're wrong on the whole Destroyer thing. Izzy's brother Elias is the Destroyer. Prince Enupnion said so himself."

The Elders of the Convocation were near hysterics as Ava continued to reveal to them the prophetic explanations they had all worked a lifetime to try to understand. "And that's definitely not Hans the Puppet Master holding that dragon's head. That's Elias and Izzy's mother, Cassandra."

"How do you know such things?" Anakrino asked with a dumbstruck look on his face.

Ava finally lifted her head for a moment and pointed up at the drawings on the wall. "Because, the person holding the dragon's head is carrying an umbrella, and Elias and Izzy's mom is the queen of the…" Ava suddenly stopped. Isabella shook her head furiously and glared at her with her best, most horrified, look of warning. But, for whatever reason, Ava finished her thought anyway. "Their mom is Queen of the Umbrella Charmers." She quickly turned her head back down to her paper and gulped so loud it echoed through the tunnel. Most certainly out of shameful embarrassment, Ava slipped behind the guardian and continued to draw in hiding.

"Ah HA! See here! This only confirms what we've suspected all along," Anakrino shouted.

"AND WHAT IS THAT?" Elehos screeched back.

"That these mechanical beasts are not of us and never were.

Your granddaughter is a false queen sent to us by the Dark Voice of Destruction to kill the king and bring the Great Destroyer upon us all." His voice shook with conviction.

"So, how do you explain the Trembling Mountain accepting her?" Elehos asked.

"It did so out of the fulfillment of prophecy and not out of the acceptance of her authority."

A wild look crept up on Elehos' face and Isabella's wings grew brighter as her anger rose with her grandmother's. "And who do you say the dark shadow is, then?" Elehos asked.

"He is the great evil as we've always suspected," Anakrino replied.

Apparently, Elehos' anger reached its zenith, and she roared into the elder's face with such fury that Thumacheo and his warriors rushed down the hall to them. "YOU FOOL! HE IS OURANOS, WINGLESS SON OF KING ARKONE!"

"That only confirms why our great king tried to have the Dark Voice of Destruction put down before he came to power. He is now fully justified."

Thumacheo quickly interjected but addressed Elehos as if she was still the queen. "Is everything okay?"

Anakrino pointed to the wall and quickly explained to Thumacheo what the elders had discovered then looked back at Isabella and asked, "Is it true? Is this a depiction of your father and mother?"

Her face grew hot, but she took a deep breath and held in her fury so as not to kill them all out of anger. But in the process, she stumbled all over her words. "It is, but... but I don't understand. My... my brother would never destroy you. He loved your people and this place. I-I don't understand what's happening. It all seems correct, but I don't believe it's true."

Anakrino looked over at Thumacheo and gave a nod. "Thumacheo, arrest these imposters."

Thumacheo started to grab Elehos, and Bogan snapped his

hand cannon from his mod-leg and shoved it in Thumacheo's face. Gideon quickly lifted his mod-hand, and the end opened up into a black hole of death in front of Anakrino's face. Suddenly, Isabella'd had enough, and her anger burned her wings so bright and hot it terrified Thumacheo and his warriors as well as the elders. "LEAVE US ALONE!" she thundered, and the mountain shook fiercely as she stepped in front of her grandmother. "I've had it with your confusing prophecies and laws. If you don't want me to be your queen, then find a new one." She took hold of the crown on her head and started to remove it, but when she couldn't get it off, Thumacheo looked strangely at her.

"Are you sure she is not our rightful queen?" he asked Anakrino.

"See for yourself," he said, pointing back to the wall.

"Yes, but she cannot remove the crown, just like King Arkone's father could not remove it. In fact, the only king I've ever known who could remove the crown was King Arkone." Thumacheo stared at Anakrino's awkwardness at the odd moment. "Wait, you knew this?" Thumacheo asked.

"She is an imposter queen and must be arrested. If you will not follow the orders of the Convocation of Elders, then we will have your *wings cleaved*," Anakrino warned and gave a haughty shrug of his shoulders.

Suddenly, the young Petinon boy, Makarios, came running down the hall toward them. "SMOKE! The tunnels are filling with smoke. The mountain is burning."

Anakrino seemingly tried to capitalize on the moment. "See! See what I mean? She has brought destruction upon us all. I demand that you kill them! Kill them, Thumacheo! Do it! Do it NOW!" Anakrino bellowed at him. So Thumacheo drew his sword and instantly ran it through Anakrino's chest, and the chief elder fell over dead.

Isabella and the others stared in shock at Thumacheo's

actions, but the warrior responded to their surprise. "He was too eager to kill you all. It just didn't feel right. King Arkone was the same way, always eager to kill others, but my father told me many stories of King Arkone's father and how he was always slow to judgment. King Arkone and Sunago were close, and I never liked or trusted Sunago. Something wasn't right. I felt it in my bones." Then he looked at the elders standing by Anakrino's body. "Besides, these guys have always gotten the prophecies wrong because they are arrogant." He speared the elders with a glare of death, and they stepped back from Anakrino's body as if to say, "We're not with him." Then Thumacheo turned toward Isabella and waved his claw. "Follow me. We need to get everyone out of here."

Elehos swiftly jumped up next to Thumacheo and hugged him. "I always knew you were a wise warrior. You never went on the hunts with my husband. You always stayed behind to protect your people. Above all else, they were always what mattered the most to you." She smiled.

"Yes, my queen. I mean, Lady Elehos," he said, correcting his mistake as he looked back at Isabella. She said nothing in response to him but simply smiled and winked.

"Come, quickly. There is a way out through the tunnel beyond the great room." Thumacheo motioned with his wing as he turned and led the way. They nearly forgot about Ava, who was still copying everything she could from behind the guardian, so Isabella sent Bogan back to pull her away from the wall.

"Come on, Ava! You've already worn that pencil down to the nub," Bogan quipped.

"What, seriously? There still so much left to copy," Ava complained, but she finally relented and went with him.

Isabella's wings lit the way for her people to flee the smoke-filled tunnels of prophecy, and she made certain that she was the last one to exit the cave after the old guardian. The smoke-filled sky rising over the Trembling Mountain made it evident to everyone what had been causing the overabundance of trembling, and Isabella felt a sense of relief that it had not been her. However, that moment quickly passed as she gazed upon the flames engulfing the Trembling Mountain. Every time the flames hit a large area of fire berries, the mountain rippled with explosions and shook violently. Isabella had Thumacheo and his warriors lead the people through the smoke-filled area on the back side of the mountain until they finally reached an overgrown path and could walk no further. After a short debate with Elehos, Isabella decided that everyone would take flight over the mountain and look for a place to regroup. She had Thumacheo's warriors take the Whisper crew, and with a loud commanding shout, she led her Petinon kingdom into to the sky over the Trembling Mountain. The sound of their wings beating the wind was like that of continuous thunder without end as they hovered over the burning city of Pterugas, but the devastation of the mountain was difficult for everyone to behold.

Suddenly, a swift warrior emerged through the thick smoke and clouds over the city. He should have kept the matter to himself, but apparently out of pure heartbreak, he shouted out to Thumacheo his assessment. "COMMANDER, ALL IS LOST! THE GREAT CITY, THE MOUNTAIN, ALL BURNED! AND THE FIRE BERRIES, MY LORD, GONE! ALL IS LOST! ALL IS LOST!" he cried. Soon, the sound of weeping and wailing rose above the power of their thunderous wings as the Petinon heartbreak for their wonderful city weighed heavy in the sky. The only thing that remained was the castle and the mighty tree trunk beneath it, but the great guardian lay dead at the entrance.

Because the grounds of the castle had not yet been harmed

by the firestorm, Isabella decided to have the women and children land there until a plan could be established. The warriors and royal guards would remain in the sky above them for as long as they could or until a plan was agreed upon. Since Charlie had never flown before and couldn't see where he was going anyway, Isabella had asked six warriors to carry him out of the cave. They were also allowed to land on the castle grounds with Charlie and were quite pleased to be free of his weight when they did. It was at that moment, when the warriors set Charlie down, that Thumacheo, Elehos, and the Elders of the Convocation seemed to notice his size, and it was instantly apparent that no one had ever seen a guardian like Charlie.

"It is the prophecy! The Golden Guardian has come," an old elder said pointing at Charlie. "Our destiny is forever before us. Now is the time for the true king to arise and deliver us. The King of the Burning Mountain will come to us soon. We must all go to the Burning Mountain and await his arrival with the guardians of old."

"I think we're already on the burning mountain, old fella," Bogan replied in his usual snarky tone.

Elehos shook her head at Bogan. "The Burning Mountain is where the guardians go to retire after their fourteen years of service. It is forbidden for anyone but guardians to go."

"Ah, yes... indeed. This is what King Arkone and his dark lords kept from our people. This is why he chose to put Sunago's plan into motion and allow the creeping mold to grow across the earth. He did not want the new ruler to come. He did not want Ouranos to rule on his throne, but you can't stop prophecy." He began to laugh in a high tone that didn't strengthen his viewpoint any better with Isabella or anyone else for that matter.

Elehos quickly backed up his claims in an effort to maintain the throne for her wingless son. "I agree with him, and if our queen agrees, then we should all go to the Burning Mountain until the true king comes." Elehos smiled and looked to Isabella for her agreement.

"That's all good and fine by me, but just so everyone knows, I'm leaving to find my father. I'm worried something has happened to him and my brother. Thumacheo can take the rest of the people to the Burning Mountain, but I'm going back to Grand Fortune City and there's my ride." She pointed up into the sky at the Bradley Dunbar as it circled the mountain above them.

Elehos seemed reluctant with her decision at first but finally nodded in agreement then reaffirmed her granddaughter's words since many still seemed to be struggling with Isabella's appointment as queen. "Queen Isabella has spoken. Thumacheo, you will take our people to the Burning Mountain and wait with the guardians until we return. I will be going with my granddaughter and her crew to find my son –our one true king- - Ouranos."

Thumacheo bowed slightly toward Elehos and Isabella, not wanting to offend either. "I will do as you've commanded, my queen, and will await your return."

Isabella gave a nod and looked at her friends and then back at Thumacheo. "Can we get someone to help my friends to that ship up there?" she asked.

"Certainly, my queen." Thumacheo gave a nod and motioned for several warriors to come down from the sky. "Take the queen's friends to their ship and remain with her. She is not to go unguarded while she is away. If she is harmed in any way, you shall never return to us out of shame."

"Yes, my lord." The warriors bowed in agreement. There were twelve in all that dropped down from the sky to take the crew to the Bradley Dunbar. But as soon as they started to leave, an argument broke out as to whether or not Charlie should remain behind or go with his friends. The old elder, whose name was Dikastes, spoke up again and demanded that Charlie go to the Burning Mountain with the Petinons so that he might fulfill the prophecy of the Golden Guardian. This only frustrated Isabella all the more, because none of it was sitting well Bogan and Ava, who both demanded that Charlie be allowed to return with them to GFC.

"Why do you have to keep him, HUH? HAVEN'T YOU HAD HIM LONG ENOUGH?!" Bogan yelled at Dikastes.

"He must fulfill his place among the Great Guardians," Dikastes explained.

"And why is that? If he is so great, then why did you treat him so badly?"

"We did not know he was here, and you did not know who he was until he was freed by our queen, just as the prophecies foretold." Dikastes smiled carefully back at Isabella.

"It's not right! It's not fair! You've kept him from me for far too long, and now I'm supposed to just give him up all over again? It's not fair, it's not fair, Izzy!" Bogan sniveled.

Finally, Charlie spoke up on his own behalf. "Brother... Ava, my wonderful Ava. I can't see, and even though I have wings, I don't know how to use them. I'll just be a burden to you all and even a risk on your own lives if I return with you."

"NEVER, BROTHER!" Bogan snapped back at him in anger as he made a valiant effort to come to grips with the waves of emotion taking hold of him.

"I will, and you know it. If you are pursued by anyone, who will carry me? How will you hide me if you must hide yourselves? Your lives will be at great risk if you take me. I *must* stay with the Petinon people for, now, I am one of them. Besides, we will meet again, I know it."

Isabella spoke up. "Charlie is right. He will be safer here. Besides, we don't know what we will encounter once we arrive at GFC, and if Charlie is as important as Dikastes says then it's better for him to remain here." She tried to hurry Bogan along, and after a few moments of difficulty with Bogan and Ava, everyone reluctantly agreed that Charlie would travel with the Petinons to the Burning Mountain. After a few difficult moments, they all said goodbye to their long-lost shipmate and the warriors lifted the crew of the Whisper into the air.

IN A FLASH, THE PETINON BOY NAMED MAKARIOS RUSHED UP INTO the sky with them. "QUEEN ISABELLA!" he shouted. "I found fire berries on the castle grounds. It's not many... but they might help you." He smiled and handed her the bag while they were still in the air.

"Thank you." Isabella gave a nod, and the boy's face lit up with joy. "Tell Thumacheo that the queen has requested that you be trained as a warrior. He will need more to fill places of the ones we've lost today, and you seem like a good candidate. Tell him I said so. Tell him the queen has ordered that he train you." She grinned.

"YES! YES, I will! Thank you, Queen Isabella. Thank you!" Makarios was beaming as he flew back toward Thumacheo, but the commander of the royal guard was not as enthusiastic when the boy knelt down in front of him. Isabella nodded at Thumacheo to make sure he understood her orders then turned to head up to the Bradley Dunbar.

Moments later Thumacheo and the boy appeared behind her, shouting for her to wait. Isabella glanced back toward them, waiting for them to catch up. "What is it now?" She groaned.

"Dikastes is going to lead the people to the Burning Mountain. I believe it might be safer for the queen if I accompany her into dangerous territory. Besides, the best way for the boy to learn how to be a warrior is firsthand experience." Thumacheo tilted his head slightly, in a confident manner, as if to indicate he wasn't going to accept no for an answer.

"FINE! Fine by me, but he's going to need your protection more than I will, so you better take him under your wing." She winked then quickly shot up to the ship.

Twelve Petinon warriors, Thumacheo, Makarios and Elehos boarded the Bradley Dunbar with Isabella, Gideon, Bogan, and Ava. Bradley, however, did not seem pleased in the least bit with the feathered mess they'd made on his ship. Rather than confront the problem, he must have decided that hiding in his cabin and grumbling to his rotten-teethed servants was far better than face the flame-winged Isabella. Hal, the pilot, was more than pleased to get on the move and didn't seem to care who was on board at this point. Although, he continued to grumble about his fuel reserves and being forced to wait so long in the sky over Pterugas. Several of the Petinon warriors stood next to him and watched in amazement as the human piloted the strange craft, and even though Hal had to slap their claws away from the controls more than once, he seemed to enjoy their fawning attention. Ava continued to console Bogan as much as possible, all the while keeping her head down as she furiously worked to document everything she could remember from the prophecy caves into her note pad. Elehos remained out on the forward deck of the Bradley Dunbar with Isabella in an effort to help her through the difficulties of ruling, but Isabella was distraught over the Puppet Master's destruction. "QUEEN FOR A DAY! I was queen for a day. ONE DAY... and I lost it all," Isabella lamented.

"You never could have known what would have taken place today. These events were beyond your control. They were prophetic," Elehos soothed, hoping to console her.

"Prophecy? HA!" Isabella scoffed. "What a joke. I suppose my mother being on that wall down there was also unavoidable?"

Elehos took a deep breath. "You sound like your uncle."

"WHAT'S BOBBY GOT TO DO WITH... oh... right." She grimaced. "Prince Enupnion. I'm sorry. I didn't mean to... I forgot that he... Uhm, is my uncle. You know, Enupnion was such a great friend to Elias. Our whole crew loved him. Even though I didn't trust him when I found out what he was, but he was so kind and forgiving of us. You remind me of him."

"Thank you for your kind words. He was an amazing son, and I loved him dearly, but remember, if not for his sacrifice, I would never have found you and Elias, and our people might never see their chosen ruler, your father – Ouranos."

"But we've lost all the fire berries. How will we ever fulfill Hunchy... I mean, Prince Enupnion's goal of replanting?"

Elehos lowered her head as realization finally weighed heavy on her. "I don't know how we will recover from the fire berry loss, but I'm hoping that once we find Ouranos, your father... I'm hoping that he will know what to do. But let me ask you something. Why do you keep calling Enupnion that strange name—Hunchy?"

Isabella winced. "Oh, sorry, we all called him Hunchy because he kept a cloak over his wings so no one would know who he was. You know, a Petinon. He was very sneaky like that, but I see now how wise he really was." Isabella smiled.

Elehos smiled back at her. "All he ever cared about was the prophecies and fulfilling them. He felt compelled to push harder than anyone from the very moment he learned that he was the 'Whispering Voice of Truth' for our people."

"What do you mean, whispering voice?"

"Oh, I apologize. I thought that maybe you already understood since Elias seemed to know so much."

"Elias never told me much of anything that he learned from Prince Enupnion. I think he was busy spending time with a certain Petinon girl on the way here." She snickered, and Elehos smiled knowingly as she continued.

"The prophecies say the one who hears the 'Whispering Voice of Truth' will be the one that will lead our people to replant the world with fire berries. Have you or your father ever heard this voice before?"

"On the Night of Darkness, we both heard a voice. My father heard, 'Truth Matters,' and I heard, 'Darkness Lies.'"

"And did Elias hear the same words that you did?" Elehos leaned in closer.

"I know he heard Darkness Lies, but beyond that I'm not sure what else he heard. But..." Excitement quickly filled her voice as he suddenly had an epiphany of realization. "But the name of my airship...I named it The Whisper! That's got mean to something, right?"

"It has to, doesn't it?" Elehos felt her face warm with joy.

"Then Daddy truly is Ouranos." Isabella's eyes grew large.

Elehos quickly pulled Isabella into her embrace and in elation said, "OH! I can't wait to meet him."

"Umh, yeah... about that. He's not exactly what I would call *approachable*. He is a very... what's the word? Difficult, yeah, he's a very *difficult* man." Isabella winched as if she were uncomfortable.

But Elehos simply smiled a strong, nefarious grin back at her. "I wouldn't expect anything less from the son of King Arkone, and trust me; I'm quite used to difficult men."

Isabella smiled back. "It's going to be an interesting family reunion, isn't it?"

"It certainly is," Elehos winked.

23

BLACK HEART

*O*n the wings of scientific wonder, the Iron Weaver sailed through cloudy skies toward the Valley of Bones. Back toward Cassandra with the final price of her demands, the dead, black heart of her son, Elias. With it, she would grant Hans what his heart had desired for so long, the ability to deliver his cruel revenge with unrelenting brutality upon the one person his blood boiled hot to punish. He pushed aside his nagging concern for James and Victor's heartbreak and wellbeing even though it was eating away at his soul like spiritual leprosy. The looks on their faces during his attack on Pterugas felt like needles in his eyes and knives in his brain, but he would make things right with them when his goal was complete. Once everything was brought to fruition, he would explain everything to them and they would understand. Their suffering would vanish into a forgotten vapor when his wrath was finally quenched and his vengeance complete. He knew they would understand, his wonderful boys, as soon as they had their mother back and they were all a family again. He knew they would understand why they had to suffer, why their friends had to suffer, and why he was forced to betray so many.

It would all be worth it in the end when, once and for all, he'd slaked his desire for revenge on that half-breed tunnel troll, Angus Grand, for destroying the life he'd tried to build.

As the Puppet Master gazed out into the passing clouds, the oblivion of revenge took hold of him, and he grew disappointed with the speed of his flying train. Although he'd lost a fourth of his rat army during his needless slaughter of the Petinon people and now one of his four ships was nearly empty, it was not enough load loss to speed his vengeful heart. He needed unfettered, unrestricted speed on his return journey, and so he summoned his rat commander so he might explain the need to lighten their payload to make better time.

Within moments a large, mutated tunnel rat knocked on the door of his room with its boney rat claw. It was a beastly creature with hollow green eyes. Hollow, but obedient and loyal like no other. It wore a large belt around its waist that was filled with ammo clips, knives, a miniature blow torch as well as a pair of pliers. It had a brain-mod with the number 10k on the top of it, and around its neck it wore a dragon's-head command module on a chain.

The beastly rat listened carefully to the Puppet Master's commands with flashing mod-lights and blinking hypnotic eyes as he explained his desire to cut two airships free from the Iron Weaver's tow. His rat-servant cocked its head left and then right as his orders downloaded into its brain-mod, then without question or disobedience; the rodent commander severed their link to half his warriors. The Puppet Master would enter the Valley of Bones with only two thousand rat warriors. It was not a decision he took lightly, because he had no trust for the witch Cassandra and her wicked wiles. However, it was a risk he was willing to take to speed his revenge.

The two severed airships jolted the Iron Weaver forward, and the cold feeling of resolve seized him, but as his ship moved forward, his mind traveled backwards in time to the day of

Angus Grand's first 'Sky Falling.' Back in time, when life felt normal and the future was still illuminated with the limitless possibilities of his great scientific mind. The day before his heart was changed forever from a loving father and husband to a blood-thirsty monster of vengeance. If only he'd listened to his beloved Emilia and turned their ship back toward Sullivan's Coast, their lives could have been so much different—better— but he'd invested everything he owned in the success of Grand Fortune City. His old regrets of the past weighed heavy on him, and as that day came rushing back, his darling Emilia's voice echoed powerfully in his mind.

"HANS! LOOK! LOOK! James is walking. His first steps, Hans, just look!" Emilia yelled at him until he finally pulled his gaze away from the horizon of the setting sun.

"Wonderful, darling! Simply wonderful," he replied, checking his tunnel rat pilot's progress as it steered the yoke of his ship homeward toward Grand Fortune City.

Emilia scoffed softly under her breath. "HANS! Is that all you can say? Come over here and show him how proud you are. Boys need that, Hans. They need to hear their father's encouragement."

He again checked his tunnel rat pilot to make certain the beast was on course, then ran over too little James, who was still holding himself up on the edge of a chair. He ruffled the boy's hair and knelt down a few feet in front of him. "Come on, son, walk your to Father," he said, motioning with his hands for the child to step towards him. The boy's face lit up with a bright, joyful grin, and he laughed a small, nervous chuckle at his father. "Come on, James! You can do it! You can do it!" He motioned again, and little James slowly lifted his hand from the safety of the chair and took a single step toward his father. "THAT'S IT! YOU CAN DO IT! COME TO ME, JAMES! COME ON!" The boy took a few more shaky steps toward his father and suddenly lost his balance. Little James fell flat on his bottom then tumbled over sideways onto Victor's block tower he'd worked so hard to construct.

The blocks scattered everywhere, and Victor was heartbroken by the loss of his hard work. "UH! DADDY, MY BOOMER TOWER! HE RUINED IT! JAMES RUINED MY BOOMER TOWER!" Victor cried out in frustration at his brother's clumsiness, and little James burst into tears at brother's harsh tone of voice.

"Come now, Victor. It was a mistake. James is learning to walk, and he needs to be encouraged. He's doing very well for his age," Hans said, trying to console his older son's heartbreak. Somehow, slapping a brain-mod on a tunnel rat seemed much easier than raising sons.

Suddenly, Victor sprang up and ran out of the bridge in tears. "YOU LOVE JAMES MORE THAN ME!" Victor cried out, only forcing more tears from James who was already upset with his failure.

"VICTOR! GET BACK HERE IMMEDIATELY!" Han grumbled, propelling James into a torrent of tears.

"HANS!" Emilia scolded.

"WHAT? WHAT DID I DO?"

"You have to be careful how you speak to them."

"WHAT? All I did was try to explain that it was accident and that James is still learning. Victor overreacted."

"It was your tone, husband. It was your tone of voice," Emilia said, bending down. Then she picked up the sobbing James to comfort him while she explained parenting skills to Hans. "They're very sensitive at this age. It's not just what you say to them, but how you say it."

"Look, I'm trying here, Emilia, okay? I'm trying, but sometimes I think it would be easier to make an army of these rats than it would be to raise more boys," Hans complained.

"HANS KLOPPENHEIMER! Shame on you! These are our sons, *not* your experiments," Emilia snapped.

"Now, see, that's exactly why I let you do the parenting, and I stick to science. Science, I understand, but parenting... I'm... I'm just not good at being a father, Emilia. I don't know how... You can blame my father for that. He was an emotionally constipated fool, and it seems to have rubbed off on me."

Emilia stepped over to him and placed her soft, gentle hand on his left cheek while bouncing little James in her right arm. "Hans, you can't command children like you do your rat. They have to learn to think for themselves, or they will never survive in this harsh world. And the only way they will be able to do that is if we encourage them through love."

He nodded his head and looked to the floor in disappointment. "You're right, it is a harsh world that we live in, Emilia. That's why I've invested everything we have in these brainmods. I want to create a world where our sons will want for nothing. Where they can craft great things with a simple command to a tunnel rat. I know they seem like useless, rotten creatures, but one day they will be servants in everyone's homes. It will change the world as we know it."

"Hans, darling. I don't want to dash your hopes, but I can't imagine the world will ever accept tunnel rats as servants in their homes or factories."

"Maybe you're right, but they might accept other creatures like cats or maybe some genetically modified dogs or, or, birds or even sea creatures, Emilia. *The possibilities are endless!* You just have to have faith in me... believe in me."

"Oh, my beloved, I do, I do. You're brilliant! Simply brilliant, Hans, and I know that you will lead our family into a wonderful new world with so many possibilities, but in your efforts to do so I ask this one thing. Please, don't forget to be a father to your sons, because when all is said and done, they are your true legacy. Not the rats or any other creature."

A loud squeak from his rat pilot quickly drew his attention away from her, and he rushed over to the forward window of his airship. Grand Fortune City was surrounded by airships all waiting to dock but motionless as if something was preventing them from doing so.

"What is it?" Emilia asked.

"I don't know. There seems to be smoke rising from the mine below. I wonder if… if maybe there was an airship collision or something."

"But why are all the ships still waiting to dock?"

"A gas leak, perhaps? I don't know. I'll see if we can pull next to one of the other ships and find out what's going on."

"Hans… I… I'm worried."

"It'll be fine. We'll be fine. They can't make us wait forever. Why don't you take James and put him down for a nap, okay?" he said as he motioned for his mod-brained rat to bring them in closer then snugged a hat down on top of its head to keep people from noticing a rat at the helm of his airship.

His rat pilot obeyed him instantly, so Hans stepped out on the forward deck of his ship. The rat pulled Hans in close to a much larger airship with a tall, slender man standing out on the deck.

Hans, being a very handsome and approachable young man, found it easy to strike up conversations with just about anyone and such was the case with this fellow. "Good evening, sir. What's the hold up with the docks?" he asked.

"It's that blasted Angus Grand's son, Eddie. He had some harebrained idea of a game, and his father decided he liked it as well. My name's Tom, by the way. Thomas Rand," the man said, twisting his mustache with great intensity.

"My pleasure, Tom. I'm Hans… but, I'm sorry, you said… game? I don't understand."

"He calls it the 'Sky Falling' game," the man said with a sneer. "No one gets to dock their airship until the torchlight is lit."

"WHAT?! Forget that! My family is on board, and we've traveled all the way from Sullivan's Coast. If we don't dock soon, we'll fall out of..." Hans realized the intent of the game as he stopped his words.

The man looked at him and nodded. "Exactly. That's the game. Sick, stupid game!"

"Well... we'll dock anyway. He can't stop us from docking," Hans said, grinding his teeth loudly.

Then the man warned him. "I wouldn't do that if I were you."

"Why's that?"

"You see that airship burning at the bottom of the mine? Angus Grand's men shot it out of the sky when they tried to dock. No one leaves and no one docks. That's the sick game he's playing. Sky Falling!" The man spit toward GFC in disgust. "A bit of advice, once this thing is over, you should refuel and get your family as far away from this city as you can. That's what I'm going to do. I'm going to refuel and get my family back to Gabriel's Harbor. This fellow here is a madman. I never should have invested in this city."

"But... I... everything I own is here. I... my factory, my home... I'll be bankrupt." Hans was utterly dismayed. "How can this be? I-I thought this was going to be a great place to be a part of."

"Not with a half-breed tunnel troll in charge, it won't be," the man scoffed. "Best cut your losses and get out while you can. At least you'll have your life."

Hans grew angry and beat his fist on the rail of his ship. "THIS PLACE IS MY LIFE! Why... why I've *wagered* everything on Grand Fortune City's success. WHY IS HE DOING THIS?"

"Like I said, friend, Angus Grand is a half-breed tunnel troll. People warned me he couldn't be trusted, but the cheap investment seemed too good to pass up. I should have listened to them, but like they say, nothing ventured, huh? Just be sure you don't let anger turn your heart black. It's not worth it, friend. Anyway, good luck to you." The man finished his thought then stepped back into his airship.

Hans rushed back into his ship and over to his tunnel rat pilot. He checked the steam pressure and it was lower than normal, so he ran down the hall toward the boiler room. He checked the pulverized coal hoppers and they were nearly empty. *Enough for one hour. Surely that's enough time for this madness to end!* He rushed back toward the bridge but calmed himself and slowed his gate when he spotted Emilia coming towards him.

"Hans?" Emilia asked in desperation as she looked out over the city lights. "I need to put the boys to bed, and we haven't even docked yet. What's happening?"

"Everyone is in a holding pattern for now. We're waiting on Angus Grand to relight the torchlight so everyone can dock."

"I don't understand, why can't we just dock now?"

"Foolishness, that's why. Be patient, darling. We'll dock soon enough," Hans said, making an effort to calm her nerves, but he knew their ship wouldn't last much longer. Purely for financial reasons, he'd planned the fuel for their trip to Sullivan's Coast so tight that he'd left no room for error; no room for the foolish games of a madman.

An hour passed quickly, and he knew their fuel was almost out. He rushed back down to check the hopper. *EMPTY! CURSE THAT MAN! CURSE ANGUS GRAND AND HIS SON FOREVER,* then he rushed back up to his tunnel rat pilot. "We're going to dock the ship. Take us in." His rat servant obeyed instantly, and their airship began to move toward the dock plate.

Emilia quickly ran to him. "HANS! What is going on? Please tell me?"

"We're out of fuel. We must dock now, and I don't know what's going to happen."

"What do you mean? Hans, tell me what's going on."

"Angus Grand's son has…" Before Hans could finish his words, their ship was hit with a loud blast from the guard tower, and a massive explosion erupted from the top of their envelope. "RUN! GET JAMES AND VICTOR!" he cried out as their ship began to fall from the sky.

Suddenly, the Puppet Master's trip down memory lane evaporated thanks to the incessant tugging on his coat by tunnel rat number 10k. "WHAT?! WHY HAVE YOU DISURBED ME?" he grumbled at the rat's thoughtless deed of stealing his moment, but the rat lift a square black case and sat it down on the desk in front of him. It had two latches on the front of it and a strange morbid air about it. "Oh… right. Thank you, 10k. Thank you. You may leave me now," he said, waving his hand for the rat to leave.

The rat gave a quirky nod of agreement that seemed to bounce its snout several times more than normal to ensure his master was pleased. As the door closed behind his brain-controlled servant, the Puppet Master slowly opened the left latch. It clicked with a loud, uncomfortable sound, and then the right latch clicked, sounding much like a thud from a deep base drum. His heart raced as he slowly opened the case and stared down into the dark box that held the lifeless heart of his friend's son. The heart was motionless. Dead and black. Black as the Night of Darkness, when he'd saved Owen Brock's life from Angus Grand, but also sinister looking in its small black casket.

Though the heart was cold and dead, it had a brooding presence about it that filled the room with evil as if it were attached to something beyond his understanding. What had the witch done to her son's heart to make it give off such a dark presence? He started to reach out and touch it but stopped quickly before his boney finger lay upon it. A faint voice of darkness began filling the room around him, and his thoughts quickly returned to that fateful day of the Sky Falling.

Though there were not many things he could remember after their ship crashed to the bottom of the mine, there was one thing he never could forget, and that was Owen Brock's voice. It was young then and undamaged by the terrible attack on his throat from the Petinon's claw.

Even now as he remembered it, the man's voice held a strange comfort to him. "I got you. Stay with me, friend. Stay with me."

"I-I…"

"Don't talk. You've been terribly burned. Look… I don't want to frighten you, friend, but if you speak, it might rip your skin from your face. Best keep quiet for now," the man said as he carried him through flames and smoke.

"Y-You… you walked through fire… h-how?"

"I think you're seeing things, friend. Don't worry about that stuff. We've got to get out of here before this thing melts your flesh off."

"N-NO! My wife… *sons*."

"Don't worry, I got them out. I'll get you some help. I know someone who can save you… and them. She has a… a gift for healing things. My name's Owen Brock. Just hang in there, friend. Hang in there. You're going to make it. I promise!" Owen said as he turned and covered Hans' body from a burst of flames. The fire roared around him like water, then Owen turned and leapt from the burning vessel.

Suddenly, the dark voice broke through his thoughts with a terrible, agonizing moan, and Hans quickly slammed the lid on the black heart's container. He fixed the latches down hard then set it on the floor near the door. As he stared at the dark case, he placed his hand on his own heart, and the words of Thomas Rand came rushing back to him. *Just be sure you don't let anger turn your heart black. It's not worth it, friend. Anyway, good luck to you.* Hans took a deep breath and called for Rat 10k to return the case to the front of the train, then he slumped down in the Jackboot's mole-claw chair.

BLACK MIST SLITHERED ITS WAY THROUGH THE VALLEY OF BONES ahead of him as the Puppet Master finally arrived at his destination. He stood out on the golden horns of the Iron Weaver for a better view like the Jackboot had done so many times before him, but Hans shouted for his rat conductor to stop when something caught his eye. Bright flashes and powerful explosions rumbled the earth deep into the valley, and with every flash of light, the inhabitants of the night sky became clearer to him. Thousands upon thousands of bat-winged serpents littered the darkness above the great, egg-shaped Keep in the center of the valley. A large force of Umbrella Charmers was also floating around the top of the structure that seemed to be struggling to hold in its contents. Floating in the center was Cassandra.

The Puppet Master cut loose his two remaining airships so they might stay hidden in the darkness of the black mist, then he motioned for his rat conductor to approach the evil coven with caution. Rat 10k stood out on the Iron Weaver's boiler behind him while his pilot-conductor guided the flying train through the very center of the valley. The sharp rocks that shot out of the ground over the valley rose above his ship, trapping his train underneath them and making him feel even more uneasy about the situation. It didn't take long before the bat-winged serpents began lining up beside the Iron Weaver on both sides. Their eyes gawked in lustful hunger at him, and their tails wriggled with an almost choking desire as they flicked venomous tongues and flapped rubbery wings like the sound of a million fleshy hands smacking together. For the most part, he ignored the serpent beasts, but Rat 10k seemed to be struggling with the pungent vapors of venom rising all around him. He commanded his rat-servant to mask up so that he might at least have an alert bodyguard standing behind him in case things took a rotten turn. The rat obeyed, and though the plague mask was far from a perfect fit to his oversized snout, he quickly recovered from the vapors and raised his mini-gun back toward the Umbrella Charmers hovering over the giant egg.

He knew Cassandra was aware of his presence, but she seemed preoccupied for some time until his train reached a point where she became uncomfortable, and suddenly vines began climbing in front of it like a wall. His rat conductor halted their approach and peered his head out the window as if to say, "What gives boss." Hans raised his hand so the rat knew this was no time for war, but when she didn't respond, he grew impatient and struck his cane down on the golden bull horns. A large bolt of lightning shot out from the top of his top hat and crackled across the sky into a bluish green spider web of electricity. It was enough to draw her attention to him, and he raised the black case into the air for her to see. In an instant, the vines withered and slumped back to the ground as if they'd died, then with a dark puff of smoke she floated over to him. Forty of more Charmers followed her through the sky and lined up on the left and right of the Iron Weaver. Rat 10k hissed his disapproval through his mask.

She hid her face as she spoke, and smoke poured from under her umbrella like a waterfall of death. He wondered if her face was still as beautiful as the day she'd performed her work on Emilia or if she was simply hiding it from him for intimidating theatrics. "Master of Puppets, I'm so pleased to see you've returned. I hope your mission was successful."

"It was a great success," he said, raising the black case again.

Her breath quickened, and the black smoke rushed through the air toward the handle on the case, but he gripped it tight with his gloved hand as she reached for it. Rat 10k hit the red switch on his mini-gun simply to increase the intimidation factor and the barrel spun momentarily, but he kept the ammo belt from feeding into it and mowing down a sky full of prissy Charmers. Then he dropped the first round into the top of the barrel and closed the feed latch to make his point clear: Don't touch the Puppet Master.

Cassandra pulled her smoky hand back away from the case and spoke. "My dear Hans, there is no need for violence. You're amongst friends here."

"Where is Emilia? You said she would be here when she finished her task at Sullivan's Coast."

"Yes, yes, of course, and she is almost finished, but I thought you would have other things to attend to once our exchange is complete."

The reminder of his long-awaited revenge took hold of him again. "That's correct. So, tell me where I can find him."

"Patience, Master of Puppets, patience," she said, looking down at the black case as if she could barely contain her own excitement. She raised her umbrella to show her face to him as a measure of good faith. It was truly remarkable, even more beautiful than before. It struck him odd that her Charmers always looked worn and rotten after speaking out the black mist, but the black mist never seemed to age her. In fact, it did just the opposite. "Tell me exactly how you plan to enact your revenge?" Cassandra prodded.

"What does it matter how I do it? That's none of your concern."

"Oh, but it is, my dear Hans. You see, there are certain things you should know before you fly off to attack a tunnel troll."

"He's a half-breed."

"Yes, yes, that is true, but he is still a tunnel troll at heart, and they can be very dangerous. So, tell me, how do you plan to enact your revenge upon Angus Grand?"

"I'm going to do to him what he did to me. What he did to my family. I'm going to burn him alive and record his screams so I'll have a constant reminder of his pain."

"Now you see there, that is exactly why you need me to help you."

"I don't need your help – *WITCH!*"

"Now that's not a very nice tone considering our past and how I helped save your life." Cassandra took a deep breath and floated in closer toward him. "Many years ago before your, um... terrible experience with Angus, he came to me and asked me to make him immortal."

"HA! I've no time for this foolishness," the Puppet Master scoffed.

"True, very true. Immortality is impossible, but Angus desired this above all things, and the payment he was offering was... very lucrative, to say the least. So, I did the next best thing for him. Let's just say that I... altered him in a way. This made him extremely powerful in the Arena of Heroes. Angus was able to walk away from many fights that most would have simply conceded and given in to death, but not him. That's how a half-breed tunnel troll became so dangerous, even to his own brothers who are much larger than him."

Hans tipped his hat up a little and looked into her eyes. "Will he burn? That's all I care about."

"Yes. He will burn, but there will be no screams for you to record. Only laughter. Laughter at you for not knowing his greatest strength. Mocking laughter. And though he may die, you will not receive the satisfaction that you've desired for so long. There is also the small possibility that burning him will not work at all."

"YOU DID THIS! YOU STOLE AWAY MY REVENGE! MAYBE I SHOULD BURN YOU INSTEAD!" Hans yelled out, and Rat 10k quickly readied his weapon for war, but his efforts were frustrated by a giant, misty hand enclosing around him.

"HOLD YOUR TEMPER!" Cassandra cried out, and the sky around them darkened with a powerful cloud. "This was done long before you were ever harmed by Angus. Long before he knew of you, or you of him. Besides, I have not ruined your chance for revenge, but in fact, I might have unknowingly sweetened it all the more."

The sound of metal teeth grinding together, vibrated his glass face cover as the Puppet Master's frustration grew. *"What do you mean?"*

"I have another option for you that should satisfy your need for real revenge, and of all things, this is something Angus truly deserves." Her eyes widened with wonder as she leaned in toward him.

"What are you proposing?"

Cassandra looked over toward one of her Charmers waiting beside her then held out her arm. The Umbrella Charmer floated over and placed a large, white, murky-filled needle into her gloved hand, and she held it up to him. "You could still burn Angus Grand alive, as you've no doubt dreamed of for so many years, and he would probably die. He would not suffer at all, but he would die and die laughing at you. Or, you could inject this into him, and he would die a slow terrible death. He may not feel it physically... however, mentally it would be devastating to him."

Hans leaned back slightly as her words disturbed him. *"What is that?"*

"As you know, tunnel trolls are genetically created beasts that Karl Kass crafted in his labs in the early days of the labyrinth when he was searching a cure to Black Mist sickness. Because of this genetic modification, they are very difficult to kill. This special formula, made by Karl Kass, is called Necrotroll and is the last of what was used to put down the first-gen trolls that caused so much destruction in the early days." She held it in front of him, and the moonlight cast a sinister glow around it that appealed to him. "It's a kind of tunnel troll leprosy, and he will not enjoy his last days on earth... *not for a single minute.*" She grinned.

"How long will it take to kill him?"

"Once you've injected him with it, there will be a few days of discomfort that will... be interesting. After that, he will begin to see the effects on his body, and the horror of what is happening will become clear to him."

"HOW LONG?!" he snapped.

She cocked her head slightly and breathed out her frustration at his impatience. "He might last six months, but every moment will be horrifying for him. The loss of his strength and limbs, everything he's put so much pride in will slowly be taken away from him. He will literally – fall apart." She ended her statement with a sinister laugh that echoed through the whole valley with great force.

A subtle grin rose on the Puppet Master's face. "Give it to me!" he demanded, so she placed it into his hand and picked up the case containing Elias' black heart.

"Finally!" Cassandra sighed then handed it to one of her Charmers who conjured a table of smoke for her to set it on. She unlatched both latches and peered down into the darkness of the case as if she were relishing a moment of victory. "Master of Puppets, you have truly delivered, just as you promised." She reached into the case and lifted the black heart out then raised it into the air for all her Charmers to see. The valley erupted with shouts and chanting of jubilation that filled the air around him with thick black smoke, but she had begun her celebration much too soon. She had not yet fulfilled her end of the bargain and he swiftly brought his complaint to her attention with a powerful blast of lightning from his top hat.

"WHAT IS IT NOW, MASTER OF PUPPETS?" she asked with a perturbed sneer.

"You never told me where I can find him. Where is Angus Grand?"

She swooped in close and placed her hands on the sides of his glass face cover, then, resting her forehead on the surface, she said, "You'll find Angus Grand in the darkness where the monsters live and in dungeons where Mogdal has imprisoned the Labyrinth Legends. He's been hiding there since he was overthrown by the Jackboot, and like this black heart; he goes by the name Mr. Black."

The Puppet Master said no goodbye but simply waved his hand, and his pilot conductor instantly began backing the Iron Weaver out of the Valley of Bones.

24

FRIENDS AND ENEMIES

"*F*ATHER!" A voice rang out through the cavernous prison.

"ELIAS, MY SON!" the Jackboot responded, waving his arm through the thick iron bars of his cell.

"DAD!" Elias hollered out and ran over to cell. He reached his arms through the bars and hugged his father as best he could and for a moment the burden of concern was lifted. However, the presence of a massive tunnel troll and a six-winged Petinon in the cell with to his father quickly caught him by surprise. "WHOA! Dad are you okay? Who are these guys?"

"Oh, the uhm… big, gray, ugly one with plate on his head is Grundorph the troll, and the uh… pretty fellow over there with six wings is… well, his name's too big of a mouthful, so we just call him Hex."

"Uhm… okay, nice to meet you both." Elias leaned in close to his father and whispered. "Are you okay? Are these guys friendly?"

The Jackboot answered his question openly. "I'm fine. These two are real stand-up guys. They've treated me really good during my prison stay and even saved my life in the arena. At least that's what they tell me," he said with a wink and a smile.

"And he saved mine as well," Hex added.

"Phew! That's great! I was worried that something might have happened to you when I found your boot under Bog Bog."

"YOU WERE IN THE ARENA?" the Jackboot exclaimed as Hex and Grundorph echoed his shock.

"Yeah. We must have come in right after you finished."

"Son, you could have been killed!" The Jackboot grimaced.

Elias held up the boot. "At least I got your boot back," he said with a smile.

The Jackboot laughed and looked back at Grundorph and Hex. "See, what did I tell you? My boy is something, isn't he?" Hex and Grundorph stared at each other in speechless wonder at how a small boy could survive a battle in the arena.

His father's attention was quickly drawn back out to the hallway when Gemenon and Epekneia approached. "Epekneia! It's good to see you again... and who might this lovely creature be?" he asked of Gemenon.

Gemenon cautiously approached the cell, but still kept her distance far enough that she must not have seen the troll or her fellow Petinon behind him. "I'm Gemenon, royal guard to Queen Elehos, and I have been sent by the queen to protect her..."

"Uh, yeah, to protect me and Epekneia!" Elias said, quickly cutting her off before she went too far with the information. The boy didn't want his father to know that his mother was the queen of the Petinon people and that Izzy had killed his father. He wanted to filter the information a little at a time so it wouldn't hinder the Jackboot's battle readiness. "Dad, there's a lot we need to talk about, but first we need to get you out of this cell."

"Of course, son," the Jackboot agreed, then he gave nod to

Gemenon. "Thank you so much for watching over my son. I truly appreciate it."

"You're welcome. It's the least I can do for..." Gemenon was suddenly interrupted by the large six-winged Petinon spoke up from behind the troll.

"Gemenon!" Hex called out from the darkness of the cell. "Come closer."

"WHO'S IN THERE?" Gemenon asked with great surprise.

Epekneia swooped over to grab a torch light from the wall and quickly returned. She raised it up in front of the cell, casting more light into it. "It is I, Hexpteroox."

"WHAT! Y-You're alive!" Gemenon was so filled with joy, she rushed over to the cell for a better look, but when the torch light illuminated part of Grundorph's face, she stopped suddenly in terror. "HEXPTEROOX! STEP BACK AND I WILL SLAY THIS FOUL BEAST!" she cried out.

"Ooo, I like her already," the Jackboot quickly interjected.

Grundorph raised his arm, turned his nose to his pit, and sniffed at it in wonder if he truly smelled foul. "Uhmph! A bit ripe, I suppose, but foul?" he shrugged his shoulder as if he was unsure. "Well, I have been down here for some time now. I would expect nothing less," Grundorph acknowledged.

"Wait, you're not afraid of him?" Gemenon asked.

"Um, by no means. Grundorph is our friend, and he has saved my life more than once down here," Hex explained.

"But... he's a troll."

"Yes, yes he is, and he is also a friend." Hex smiled. "He truly is a friend. I know he looks terrifying, but he's good to have around when things get ugly."

Grundorph crossed his eyes as he leaned his massive troll head closer to the light. "Too late!"

ELIAS ASKED FOR SOME PRIVACY SO HE COULD FILL THE JACKBOOT in on the events of their journey. Hex and Grundorph agreed and moved back into the darkness of the cell while Epekneia and Gemenon checked the hall to see what was taking Mr. Black so long. At first, Elias was uncertain about how to explain the problem, and he didn't want to startle his father. But how do you tell your dad that your sister, unknowingly, just murdered her grandfather, who just happened to be a king? *Little bits at a time,* he reminded himself.

"Where's Isabella? Where are the others?" the Jackboot asked.

"Let me just... okay, everyone is okay. I think."

"You're not exactly filling me with confidence here, my boy."

Elias recalculated his thoughts. "Look it's... Pterugas is a beautiful city, and the people are amazing. The queen was very helpful in so many ways, and everything is green. I know it's hard to believe, but there's no creeping mold anywhere near their mountain or on it. The city is wonderful, and the food is amazing."

The Jackboot cocked his head left and grimaced. "The alliance, son, what of the alliance with the king? Is it possible?"

"Well... about that... uhm, you see... the king was a very difficult person, but I did save his and the queen's life when the capstone almost fell on them."

"That's great! Good job, son! That's wonderful news, then. He will certainly want to make an alliance with us, and maybe he will help us take back GFC from Hans."

"Well, I'm not so sure."

"Why is that?"

"The reason Isabella and the others are not here with me is because... look, I want you to promise me you're not going to fly off and get mad, first. Okay?"

The Jackboot's only good eye was about to pop out of his skull in frustration, but he loved the boy, so he bit down hard on his tongue and answered with a nod and a bit of a painful grunting sound.

"Okay, good. I'm not sure if the alliance is dead yet, but the king certainly is."

"Why? What happened?" The Jackboot winced. "Was it Bogan? He's always been a bit of a hot head and I…"

"No, Dad. Izzy killed the king."

"WHAT! If they tried to hurt her I'll…"

"Hold up! Would you just give me a second to explain?" Elias grimaced at what he imagined might be running through the Jackboot's mind. "After the burial of Prince Enupnion, the king learned that I had been given his son's heart, and he grew angry and tried to remove it, but Isabella was in my room hiding."

"That's my girl." The Jackboot grinned and adjusted his eye patch.

"She struck him in the back with her baton and killed him. I don't know what happened to them after that, because Merlin opened the door and she forced him to get me out of the city. We decided to come and get you and Hans, but…" Elias shook his head in disappointment.

"But he betrayed me with Cassandra." The Jackboot rubbed the stubble on his face for a moment deep in thought. "How did you find me?"

"Henry."

"Ah…" The Jackboot smiled, "That boy's a good rascal."

"And fast, too."

"Do you think the Petinons will harm the crew?"

"I don't believe they will, but they do have a harsh way of dealing with things, and the king seemed very cruel to the queen. She was the one thing that seemed good and different. She also liked me and Izzy, A LOT. She fed us, and she really is a good person. I think there is still hope for something, but we need to get back to the Petinon kingdom as soon as possible. I can explain more on the way there, but…"

Everyone's attention was suddenly drawn back toward the far end of the prison hall where the sounds of someone dragging something and grumbling echoed all around. "Never would have thought I'd be... Uguh... draggin your whipped butt... grrrrah... all over hell's half acre."

"Who's that? Who's coming?" the Jackboot asked.

"Oh, that's probably Mr. Black. He fell behind us on the way here. We were cellmates when I got here and, well, he helped me battle Brynjar the Wolf-Beast in the arena," Elias explained.

"YOU BATTLED BRYNJAR THE WOLF-BEAST!" Grundorph asked in shock, accidentally revealing his eavesdropping.

"Yeah. I mean, I had my dad's boot to help me... and Mr. Black."

"I DON'T BELIEVE IT!" Grundorph exclaimed.

"Okay. Fine by me, but it's true and you'll see for yourself how badly he's injured when Mr. Black gets here," Elias shrugged.

"You didn't kill him?" Hex asked.

"Why would I do that? He was only following the rules of the arena, and I don't live by those rules." Elias squinted his eyes a little.

"Soooo... you didn't kill him, and you brought him... with... you?" Grundorph winced. "So, what do you plan to do with him, now?"

"I'm going to help him recover. I injured him with the boot much worse than I thought, and he's in pretty bad shape. He needs help."

"You know what he's going to do when he gets better?" Grundorph asked.

"What?" Elias asked.

"He's going to kill us all. That's what he's going to do," Grundorph growled at the boy's foolishness.

"Maybe he will, and then again, maybe he won't. We don't know what he'll do yet, but if he survives and decides not to attack us, then we've made a friend. If he decides to try and kill us, then I guess he will be an enemy forever. We won't really know until then, will we?" Elias leaned in closer to the troll's face as he spoke.

"Uhm?" Grundorph grunted and stroked his mighty chin. "Well said, young Elias. Well said."

A FINE CLOUD OF DUST SOON ROLLED PAST THE CELL AND FILLED the hall as the overly disgruntled Mr. Black pulled the beaten body of Brynjar toward the Jackboot's cell. The grumbling soon quieted as Mr. Black drew closer toward the light of the cell, and the Jackboot felt he should, at the very least, offer a kind word to the man that helped his son stay safe in the arena. "Mr. Black, sir, I would just like to extend a hand of gratitude for keeping my son safe out there."

Mr. Black grunted in acknowledgement. "You're welcome... friend." A slight chuckle was heard underneath Mr. Black's words as he spoke.

The Jackboot reached his hand through the cell bars as Mr. Black came into view but was suddenly struck with a horrified chill in his bones. "ANGUS GRAND!" the Jackboot cried out. "ELIAS, RUN! GET AWAY FROM THIS MONSTER! THIS MURDERER!"

"What happened to the 'hand of gratitude' that you were so quick to lend when you thought I'd saved your boy?" Angus asked with a grin.

"Y-You're Angus Grand?" Elias said in shock. "B-But Merlin said you tried to burn Isabella."

"That is true, my boy."

"HE'S NOT YOUR BOY, ANGUS." The Jackboot seethed with anger. "Your boy was a rotten murderer just like you."

"Yes, yes, Eddie was. I blame myself for that. I truly am sorry about this, my boy." Angus said to Elias. "I had no idea you were the Jackboot's son until you opened the side compartment on the boot and took out the matches." He laughed a snort. "And when you blew the gate with the berry, I knew for sure you were his boy. I see your father taught you well."

The Jackboot could barely contain his anger as he tried to look for a way to get his hands on Angus. "Why don't you come a little closer to the cell, and I'll show you a few things I haven't taught him yet?"

"Relax, Owen. I'm not going to hurt the boy. Even though I've killed more people than Black Mist, I'm not the same troll I used to be. I've been imprisoned down here since the war for GFC." He dropped Brynjar's makeshift gurney to the ground with a thud, and the beast let out a groan. "Just look, I'm still wearing the same orange coat that I wore during the battles." He tugged on his lapels with both meaty hands and the tattered coat cast off its dust into the air. "Prison has reformed me," he grinned.

"I don't buy it for a second." The Jackboot said, but was suddenly pushed aside by Grundorph.

"And neither do I, *brother*!" Grundorph scowled at Angus.

"GRUNDY! Well, well, well. If this isn't the biggest family reunion I've been to in a long time. And who would have thought, the Jackboot and a son of Ogg as cell mates? This just gets better and better. WHO BROUGHT THE ALE, HUH? HA, HA, HA!" Angus clapped his hands together as he laughed, and it sounded like two boards clapping against each other.

"You say that now, but when these gates open up you won't be laughing," the Jackboot seethed.

"When these gates open the next time around, you're going to need everyone you can get." Angus smiled knowingly.

"We won't need you, brother," Grundorph said.

"Oh, yes you will. Mogdal has called a Battle of Legends. First ever! Many will fall, and if you don't want to be one of them, then you better makes some allies, and fast," Angus warned with a firm tone. "Might be a good thing after all that the boy spared Brynjar. Maybe he will heal in time to fight with us or kill us."

"A Battle of Legends... it's unheard of. How can you be sure?" Hex asked.

Angus stepped closer to the cell. "Did you notice the frame-work above the arena? Mogdal is going to open it up to the ground above us. He's sent word to many of the other king-doms, and they've paid a high price to watch from the safety of their airships. It's really quite genius, if you asked me. Uhm, wish I would have thought of it when I ran the labyrinth. Anyway, he's going to clean out the old legends and usher in a whole new breed."

"How do we know you're telling the truth? You can't be trusted." The Jackboot gripped the cell bars tighter.

"You don't know if I am or not, but you will when that gate opens and the horn blows deep. Then you will know," Angus growled. "Now, maybe we should see if the boy is right about Brynjar and see if we can nurse him back to good health." Angus looked the Jackboot in the eye. "And stop worrying about your boy. I'm not going to hurt him. He saved my life in the arena, and I am bound to the code of battle. Once I save his life, my debt will be paid, and then we can work through our differences if you like."

"Nothing would please me more," the Jackboot said with a snarled grin.

GEMENON AND EPEKNEIA HELPED ELIAS WITH BRYNJAR'S INJURIES, out of concern that Angus Grand was right about the coming Battle of Legends, while the Jackboot, Hex and Grundorph argued in the darkness of their cell. There was no small amount of anger and yelling as Hex and Grundorph worked to convince the Jackboot of the need for someone like Angus for a battle such as this.

"I'm afraid I must agree with the Jackboot on Angus' trustworthiness, but I'm not sure we have much of a choice. Besides, if he is lying, you can have your revenge legally in the Arena of Heroes, and no one will question the ethics of your actions." Grundorph stretched his neck with a loud pop and smiled a nefarious grin at the Jackboot. "I might even give you a hand with that."

"No one will question my ethics even if I kill him now, because there are enough mothers and fathers in Grand Fortune City that lost their children to this monster that no one will care. In fact, they would gladly hold him down for me to finish him off, and that's what we should be doing right now. Kill him and be done with it," the Jackboot grumbled.

Hex soon stepped in and gave his view. "I know I am speaking from more of an outsider's viewpoint, not having ever known Mr. Grand, but if he has done the terrible things you say, then justice must be done. However, I see wisdom in what Grundorph is saying. If there truly is a fierce battle coming our way, then we will need everyone on our side to overcome the enemy. Besides, I have been down here long enough to have heard stories about the legends, and now we just happen to have two down here that might be willing to fight with us."

"Don't forget your new Standing Hero!" Angus yelled out.

"WHAT?" the Jackboot asked.

"That's right. You have two legends and one Standing Hero."

"Explain, brother," Grundorph demanded.

"The Jackboot's son just defeated Brynjar the Wolf-Beast in battle. Brynjar is a Legendary Hero, so by all rights, the boy will now rank as a Standing Hero during the battle."

"Seriously?" Elias blurted out.

"Don't let it go to your head, boy," Angus snapped out. The

Jackboot gripped his hands into fists at Angus' tone, desperately wanting to strike his old enemy down, but given his current predicament, all he could do was listen to the brothers speak.

"By my count, there are now seven Legendary Heroes and twelve Standing Heroes, or maybe more. This will most certainly be a terrible battle." Grundorph rubbed the plate on his head in deep contemplation then slumped down on the ground and leaned against the cell wall with a troubled look on his face.

Angus took noticed and stepped a little closer to the cell. He seemed to know what was troubling his brother and spoke to him in a gentle voice the Jackboot had never considered would come from the murderer. "Yes, my brother. They will be out there, Agmar and Gonon, our cruel brothers that beat your skull in for fun and... Krom, brother. Krom will be with them."

Grundorph raised his head quickly with a terrified look in his eyes. "I-I thought he was dead."

"Many did, but Mogdal captured him and imprisoned him here with the rest of the sons of Ogg. Well, except for the five that died during the tunnel war and the eight that escaped. Either way, we will certainly have to face Krom, Agmar and Gonon, but vengeance will be for the taking if you can overcome them," Angus said with a grin.

"Krom...*here?*" Grundorph moaned.

"Yes, he is, but take heart, brother. He *might* try to kill me first, I'm not for sure. I probably deserve it, though," Angus said, looking back at the Jackboot with a subtle grin. "I deserve death for many of the things I've done."

"Finally, something we can agree upon," the Jackboot sneered. "If you wouldn't mind stepping a little closer to my cell, I'll be happy to help you along."

Angus lunged at the cell bars and snapped out at him, "When I've fulfilled my duty to your son, then you and we can finish our war. I might deserve death, but you murdered my boy."

"It wasn't murder. It was justice and you know it." The Jackboot held his ground, but Hex pulled him back.

"Now is not the time for fighting. Tell us, how exactly *did* you all get out of your cell?" Hex asked.

Angus pointed to Elias. "The boy used a fire berry."

"Then we should do the same so we might escape before the battle begins." Hex smiled and gave a nod toward Elias.

"Sure, and let you all kill each other right here? I don't like that plan," Elias interjected. "Besides, the only way out is too small for all of you. Epekneia and Gemenon barely made it through because of their wings. I think our best option is to help Brynjar and get ready for the gates to open."

Angus looked over at the Jackboot. "I agree with the boy. Fix the wolf-beast and get ready for war, otherwise we might not see the light of day."

"Good idea. I don't want waste the fire berries just yet. I might not have enough to blow your head off when this is over," the Jackboot quipped.

"Ha! Funny thing... I still had an entire warehouse at Sullivan's Coast filled with fire berries when the war ended. Probably would have won if I could have gotten them back to the labyrinth in time." Angus stepped closer to the Jackboot as he rubbed his jaw in contemplation. "Probably all rotten by now... Huh, war's funny like that, isn't it? Nothing but a rotten mess," he grinned.

FROM HIS EARLIEST MOMENTS OF LIFE, BRYNJAR THE WOLF-BEAST had only known one thing, kill or be killed in the arena. Half Bryn-wolf and half tunnel troll, Brynjar, the wolf-beast of Karl's Labyrinth, was the only remaining creature that was personally crafted by Karl himself. No one truly knew how old the creature was, except perhaps for Brynjar, but he never spoke to anyone but Bryn-wolves. He only lived for the next kill in the arena and the adoration of the crowd. He'd never known the love of a mother or father and had never been given any consideration for his wounds in the arena. He'd simply licked them clean as a wolf would do to heal itself, and though his troll mind was as brilliant as that of Ogg the Murderous, his inner wolf-beast fought against the sanity of his mind.

As the winged woman and the boy patched his wounds, Brynjar lay in wonder of what kind of people they were. He knew nothing of kindness before this moment, and it felt strange to him that creatures who knew nothing of him would seek to heal his wounds. And of fear... he knew nothing of fear until now, until the boy with the boot delivered blow after blow of agonizing pain to his body. How strange that this same boy would seek to heal the wounds he'd personally dealt. They gave him water for his thirst and wrapped his wounds tight with cloth from their own clothes, and the boy washed his face clean from the dirt of the grimy arena floor. It was odd, uncomfortable, embarrassing, but above all things, it was kind.

After they had finished with his wounds, the winged woman pulled the boy aside and spoke quietly to him for moment. The boy returned, stood next to his head and explained, "We're going to try and give you something that might help heal you. If she does it wrong it will be very painful, but if she does it right, you might heal faster. Either way, it will hurt, but she thinks it will work because of the bird's talon you have sticking out of your skull. It works on birds or... bird people if that makes any sense. If you don't want us to do this we need to know, but I'm afraid if we don't, you might be killed when the gates open."

Brynjar peered into the boy's eyes, and he spoke. "Why are you doing this?" he asked. Suddenly, everyone looked over toward him in shock and not just at his voice, but no one had ever heard the wolf-beast speak. They'd certainly heard him howl, but most thought he was a mute because of his mutations.

"Because I didn't want to fight you in the first place, but you gave me no choice. Now I'm going to help you so you can help us in the arena. Mr. Black..." Elias looked over at Angus Grand, "or whatever his name is, says there's going to be a Battle of Legends, and if that's true, then we're going to need everyone we can get to help us fight. So, what do you say?"

Brynjar nodded. "I am willing to fight with you, and she may try the medicine, but please hold me down so I don't hurt them. They are... delicate butterflies, and I am filled with wonder from their touch."

"Well, well, well... I guess the old wolf-beast has a heart after all." Angus clapped his gnarled hands together, but his mocking was ignored.

Gemenon and Epekneia went to work with Hex for a moment on a mixture of paste similar to what Hex had used on the Jackboot, and when they'd finished, they explained how painful it might be. Angus dragged the makeshift gurney over toward the cell so Grundorph could hold his troll arm, while Angus took hold of his wolf arm. Brynjar gave nod and a grunt to the boy, and then Elias quickly began applying the red paste to his wounds. At first, it burned horribly, and he let out a terrible howl that frightened some of the other beasts in the cells across from them, but soon the paste began to work, and darkness closed in around his eyes.

He came to a few hours later to the sight of Epekneia washing his face again with water. She was smiling down on him like an angel with flaming wings, and though the wolf in him wanted to eat her at that very moment, his better nature won over, and he did his best to thank her. "You've been kinder to me than anyone I have known. I promise I will fight hard when the battle begins."

"I know you will," she said gently. "There's just one request... one favor I would like to ask of you."

"Whatever you ask."

"First of all, I know I look like a frail little butterfly that you could easily kill, but if you don't stop looking at me like you want to eat me, things are going to get ugly, and fast." She smiled as she warned him then continued to wipe his forehead.

Brynjar was utterly embarrassed that she was able to sense his savageness and stuttered through his words. "I-I... um, yes... I am truly sorry."

"Good." She snickered and continued wiping his forehead. "Now, about my favor... if we get out of this and help you get free from the arena, I want you do to something for my friend Gemenon over there. She's the one that helped heal you."

"Name your request."

Epekneia continued to wipe his head with water and said, "I want you to kill the red Bryn-wolf that leads the pack outside of Grand Fortune City. Will you do that for her?"

Brynjar seemed greatly troubled by Epekneia's request and was quiet for some time. Finally, he explained, "I'm afraid you do not fully understand the measure of your request. Ask me anything but this... for it is too costly for me. I cannot, nor will I, strike down the red Bryn-wolf."

"Why?" Epekneia scoffed.

"We are... connected," Brynjar said, turning his head away from her.

"Then you are useless to me!" Epekneia said as she threw the damp cloth down on the ground in anger and left him.

25

A STRANGE WIND

A strange westerly wind rose up against the Bradley Dunbar, and puffy, gray clouds passed quickly by as they sailed back toward Grand Fortune City. No one was more pleased to be on their way than Hal, the pilot. Hal was also quite pleased to enjoy the fawning adoration coming from the young Petinon boy, Makarios, who couldn't stop bragging about his piloting skills. At first Hal was annoyed by the winged boy's questions, but it quickly dawned on him how truly flattering it was to have a winged creature so enamored with his flying abilities. He imagined this would certainly level up his cred with the other pilots back at GFC and instantly began calculating the many ways in which he could humbly brag about himself. Besides, the boy would never know if he was mocked in the pubs, and what he didn't know wouldn't hurt him.

"It cuts through the sky like a swift arrow!" Makarios blurted out in excitement.

"Well… she's not a racing ship, but she is the fastest private airship in Grand Fortune City, there's no doubt about that," Hal said with twinkle in his eye.

"Racing ship?"

"You've never heard of the airship races? Wow, you really have been sheltered," Hal smirked.

"I've never even seen one. What do they look like? Are they big like this one? Do they have all these gauges and buttons and switches like this ship?"

"Whoa! Hold on a second there, fella. One question at a time, okay?" Hal cleared his throat and adjusted himself in his seat. "Racing ships are kind of like souped-up speeders."

"SPEEDERS! What are those?" Makarios yelled out.

"Alright, look, kid... there's no doubt I'm enjoying this um... mentoring moment, here, but if I'm going to be able to... if *we're* going to be able to enjoy the lesson, then you're going to have to give me some space to craft the right words." Hal brushed his dark black hair back with his hand and let out a frustrated sigh. He certainly enjoyed the boy's fawning, but it was beginning to feel like he was training a squirrel how to fly an airship. "Okay. I'm going to talk for a while, and I want you to sit in the other chair and just listen for bit. Deal?"

"Okay. Sorry, sorry." Makarios nodded, folded his wings in tight and sat down in the co-pilot chair with eyes as big as goggles.

Hal started by explaining the difference between airships, speeders, racers, cargo hullers, warships and many other types, but it was clear the boy was overwhelmed. Makarios' eyes darted all around the control panels then back to Hal's hands as he worked the ship's yoke, guiding it through the skies. It was very perplexing to Hal why a creature with wings would desire so desperately to be taught how to fly by a man without wings, but the real irony of it all only filled his flyboy ego all the more.

The conversation was smooth sailing for some time until Hal began explaining the throttle operation, and the boy's over-sized claw accidentally bumped the throttle up to full. The Bradley Dunbar lurched forward with a powerful blast from the thrusters, and a loud crash echoed back up toward the ship's bridge. Before Hal could grab the throttle to pull it back, the ship seemed to slow down. It struck him as odd, but before he could think it through, Iron Jaw came rushing to the bridge rubbing his head.

"What the devil is going on up here, Hal?"

"My apologies, sir. I was just instructing the boy on how to fly," Hal replied feeling his cheeks grow hot.

Iron Jaw gawked at Hal with a glazed, wonky-eyed look and suddenly burst out laughing. He strolled back down the hall and yelled out to all the Petinon warriors in the dining area. "NO WORRIES, LADS. HAL'S JUST TEACHING THE WINGED BOY HOW TO FLY! HA, HA, HA!" For a moment it was quiet, then a raucous laughter from the twelve Petinon warriors abruptly filled the ship.

"Maybe this wasn't such a good idea. I've got a reputation to uphold, and you don't really need to know how to do this anyway," Hal said to the boy.

"Oh, I understand." Makarios dropped his head and began to leave. "They embarrassed you, and you're afraid I will make you look bad."

Makarios' words cut deep and quickly began to eat away at Hal. As the winged boy neared the exit of the bridge, Hal called out to him. "I bet you could teach me a lot about flying as well." The boy stopped and turned around. His face was beaming.

"You really think so?" he asked.

"For sure! Your kind of a pilot in your own way, so, um... maybe we could... talk shop, so to speak," Hal said.

"What's that mean?" Makarios asked.

Hal chuckled. "Never mind. Get back here, kid, and let's fly this ship." The boy's face lit up as he ran back, swooped right over the co-pilot's chair, feet first, and plopped down next to Hal.

IRON JAW'S MOCKERY OF HAL'S FLIGHT-TRAINING GENERATED some much-needed relief for the battle weary Petinon warriors. Bogan must have decided he would capitalize on the cheerful moment as he suddenly sprang out of his chair and began raiding Bradley's refrigerator. However, as soon as Bogan opened the door to the large food cooler, Bradley caught the sound of his thievery with his keen ears and instantly came running into the ship's dining room.

"NO, NO, NO!" Bradley yelled. "I'll not be handing out my supplies to these stowaways, or to you, for that matter." Bradley slammed the door shut with his rump and grabbed hold of the plate of buttercream cupcakes still in Bogan's hands. "Let go of it this instant!"

"Come on, now. These guys just fought a terrible battle – even lost some of their mates. Surely you can give up a few of your cupcakes for 'em," Bogan reasoned.

"I traveled all this way for rare delicacies, only to be duped by my own brother... AGAIN!" Bradley said, looking over at Iron Jaw, who was leaning against the wall with his arms folded.

Iron Jaw shrugged his shoulders and winked at Bogan. "I had to find some way to talk him into letting us use his ship."

Henry was standing next to Iron Jaw with his eyes glued to every movement of the cupcake plate as Bogan pulled them one way and Bradley pulled them back the other. Henry's mouth slowly fell open as the battle of the buttercreams began. After several back and forth moments, a small, clear line a drool appeared at the corner of Henry's lower lip. His breathing began to grow heavy, and soon everyone in the room took notice, even Bradley Dunbar.

"What's... what's he doing? What... what's that look in his eyes?" Bradley asked in horror.

Iron Jaw knelt down in front of him with a wonky look of his own. "Oh, that's not good, Bradley. I've seen that look before when I was a young lad." Iron Jaw's words drew curios looks from the troubled Petinon warriors, who seemed to wonder if something strange had bewitched the boy.

"What? What look?" Bradley desperately asked.

"I think those cupcakes have stolen this boy's soul." Iron Jaw laughed, sending the Petinon warriors jumping back against the wall in fright. "Those buttercreams are not long for this world, brother. I guarantee it." Iron Jaw laughed again. It was a forced, maniacal laughter that only worked to frighten everyone except Bogan and Henry.

It was at that moment, during Bradley and Bogan's distraction, that one of the cupcakes slipped off the plate toward the floor. Henry launched himself forward as if a swift wind had suddenly caught his back, and in the blink of an eye, he grabbed the buttercream and sucked it right out of the paper shell. In a flash, Henry slid underneath the plate. Bradley and Bogan's eyes shot down toward the plate as Henry's right hand magically appeared and slipped another one off the top of the plate. The paper shell suddenly floated down to the ground, empty, and Bradley lost control of himself.

"STOP! THIEF!" Bradley hollered out as Henry grabbed another one and threw it to one of the Petinons.

Thumacheo seemed terrified of the dangerous, soul-stealing buttercream and threw it back at Henry, who had already snatched two more from the plate. He peeled a shell and shoved one into a Petinon's mouth. Then Bogan caught a glimpse of the warrior's smile and must have picked up on Henry's plan. Looking back at Bradley, Bogan asked, "What else you got in that fridge?"

"NO! PLEASE, NO! Oh, dear me... I-I feel faint. The room, the room, it's spinning," Bradley said as sweat ran down his brow and slipped from his large chin. Trembling took hold of him, and he slumped to the floor as Bogan open the door to the large refrigerator.

"My Petinon pals, this is what we call a smorgasbord of

physical and emotional healing, or as some might say, comfort food for the battle weary." Henry grinned as he leapt from the table and snatched the last cupcake from the plate right when the feathers began to fly.

AVA SAT ON THE FLOOR WITH HER BACK AGAINST THE WALL AND her art pad on her knees. She would finish one drawing and then turn the page back to her notes and start drawing another with furious passion. "UGH!" she moaned in frustration. "If only Flit had been with us when we were in that cave. I would have been able to get so much more than this." She looked up at Jimmy who was hovering about a foot off the floor and staring out the window at the passing clouds. "Jimmy?" she asked to see if he was paying attention, but he didn't respond so she dropped her head back to her paper and continued.

The Bradley Dunbar was traveling at a good rate of speed, but Jimmy didn't seem pleased with it. "We were moving faster last time," he said quietly.

Ava looked up at him to see if he was okay then put her head back down. "I don't know, this seems really fast to me. It's much faster than the Whisper, that's for sure."

Much to her surprise, Jimmy said, "No! Not really."

Ava looked him up and down to see if maybe he'd suffered an injury during the battle but could see nothing that would indicate a problem. "Maybe you just need some rest. You've been through a lot today."

"No. Something is wrong. The sky… the wind looks strange," Jimmy said, still gazing out into the clouds.

"Jimmy, you can't see the wind, so how can you tell if it's strange?"

It must have made him angry because he looked back at her

and firmly stated, "I do not lie. It is a strange wind." He turned and sputtered away down the hall.

"Jimmy! I'm sorry, I didn't mean to say..." Ava sighed and got up to look out at the passing clouds. The ship seemed to be moving at a good rate of speed, so she began to wonder if Jimmy was simply struggling with what his father had done. When she noticed something strange in her notes, she quickly sat back down and began to draw again.

JIMMY FLOATED DOWN THE MAIN HALL AND PAUSED OUTSIDE THE dining area where Bogan was passing out tray after tray of goodies. Without even asking Jimmy if he was hungry, Bogan stepped over to him, opened the door on his food processor and tossed in a whole cup of chocolate mousse. He gave Jimmy a pat on the head then went back to his entertaining of the Petinons. Several times he spoke up about the speed of the ship, but no one wanted to listen. He continued his complaint until Iron Jaw stepped over and corrected him.

"Boy, this ship is the fastest ship in GFC. Maybe you should have your brother take a look at your brain-mod to see if it's calculating properly." Iron Jaw gave him a pat on the back and quickly went back to nibbling on one of his brother's goodies. Jimmy cocked his head to the left and gazed upon them in perplexed wonder until he heard a faint sound. He couldn't tell where it was coming from or even what it was saying, but there was most certainly a sound.

Jimmy left the hungry warriors to their comforting feast and made his way up to the bridge where Hal the pilot was speaking with the young Petinon boy. The two were engrossed in a deep conversation about the aerodynamics of wings when Jimmy rudely interrupted. "Something is wrong with the ship," he said boldly. His statement was not meant to offend, but the pilot must have taken it that way.

"Excuse me?" Hal scoffed. "There's nothing wrong with this ship. Now, run along, robot boy. We're in the middle of something important here."

Jimmy imposed himself for a closer look at the airspeed indicator, and Hal quickly let him know he disapproved. "HEY! I SAID MOVE ALONG!"

"It is incorrect. Our speed is incorrect," Jimmy said, floating back out of the way. He started to question Hal's piloting ability when he heard the strange sound again, and he realized it was an odd voice on the wind. At that moment he knew he had to find Merlin and Izzy, so he shot back down the hall and began checking room after room for them.

MERLIN AND IZZY WERE IN THE LOWER PART OF THE SHIP, MOSTLY due to Merlin's request to speak with her alone. After careful consideration of his and Elias' conversation about his true feelings toward Izzy, he figured there was never going to be a perfect time to explain his heart to her, so he decided to just go for it.

"Look, uh... Queen Isabella," Merlin rubbed the top of his globe and winced at his own words. As if it wasn't hard enough to express his feeling before, now he had to call her queen.

"Please, Merlin... stop it. I don't need the mockery right now. This crown is so tight it's giving me a splitting headache as it is." She grabbed the crown and tried to remove it, but it had fixed itself to her head permanently.

"No... I wasn't trying to mock you. It's just... I don't even know how to address you now."

She reached over and knocked on his glass dome. "Hello in there, brain boy, it's Izzy. You can stop the whole queen thing.

Besides, I was only queen for a day, anyway, and I lost the whole Petinon kingdom. Some queen I am, huh?" she scoffed.

"It's not your fault. It's mine or... well, my father's fault. I don't know what happened to him, but he really lost it." Merlin stopped and quickly regrouped his thoughts. "Look, that's not what I want to talk to you about anyway. I have something important to tell you."

"Oh really?" She smiled playfully while still messing with the crown, but her tone of voice only served to make him feel like a goofy kid again.

"When we took Elias back to GFC... we, um, sort of got into a fight and..."

"WHAT? You better not have hurt him, Merlin," Izzy blurted out in anger.

"HUH? No, wait, that's not what I mean. It wasn't a real fight. It was just an argument about what happened back at Pterugas. Anyway, that's not the point." Merlin sighed a heavy, relieved breath.

"What exactly is your point, Merlin?"

He looked down at his white-knuckled hands clutched together. "I just wanted to explain how I truly felt about..."

Just then, Jimmy burst into the room. "Merlin! Isabella! There is something wrong with the ship."

"Seriously, Jimmy? Can't this wait?" Merlin complained.

Izzy looked up at Merlin with astonishment in her eyes. "Merlin, if there's something wrong with the ship, shouldn't we take a look?"

"Well, yes, but I was trying to explain something important to you." Merlin jumped up in frustration and went to the window. The gray clouds were flying by at a fast clip, and he grumbled. "There's nothing wrong, Jimmy. We're moving faster than ever."

All of a sudden, Jimmy rushed over to Merlin and grabbed him by the lapel of his coat. Much to Isabella's surprise, he slammed his brother against the wall of the ship, and for the first time ever, Jimmy yelled at Merlin. "SOMETHING IS WRONG WITH THE SHIP, BROTHER! WE. ARE. IN. DANGER!"

"JIMMY!" Isabella blurted out in shock and rushed over toward Merlin.

Merlin quickly raised his hand and shook his head at her. "IZZY, STOP! Don't come any closer." Merlin turned back to his brother and looked deep into his eyes. "Okay, Jimmy. Okay. Tell me what's wrong. I'm listening now."

Jimmy gave a nod and spoke. "The ship's airspeed is wrong. The clouds are lying, and no one is listening to me. No one is listening to the sound."

"Okay, brother. I'm listening. Tell me what the problem is," Merlin said gently.

"Look out the window." Jimmy said, and Merlin looked out at the passing clouds. "Do you see the mountain in the distance?" Jimmy asked.

"Yes. Yes, I see the mountain." Merlin nodded.

"It's been there for an hour. We are not moving. The ship's airspeed is incorrect." Jimmy gripped Merlin's lapel tighter. "Now listen and listen carefully." Jimmy's eyes fixed to Merlin's. "*Listen.*"

Merlin closed his eyes for a moment, and suddenly he heard it. It sounded like voices. Dark voices. He opened his eyes quickly and looked back out the window at the passing clouds. Gray, puffy clouds on an otherwise clear day, and Merlin grimaced. He looked back at Izzy, who was gripping the crown tight on her head as if she were in terrible pain from it, and he knew right away what was happening. "Come with me and quickly."

They made their way down the hall toward the dining area. As soon as they came to the door, Jimmy smashed it open, and everyone instantly looked over in shock. "Where're Bradley's servants? The two guys with rotten teeth?"

Bogan shrugged his shoulders. "Haven't seen em. Why?"

"I should have realized it. Bad teeth and Bradley wasn't even sharing his goodies with them. They're Umbrella Charmers," Merlin sneered. When Merlin realized the Petinon's didn't understand what he meant, he remembered what Prince Enupnion had called them. "You know, Black Mist Speakers." The Petinons jumped up in shock.

Jimmy raised a clinched iron fist in the air and said, "PROTECT! KILL! WAR!"

"Search the ship, inside and out. There are two of them. We must find them quickly," Merlin warned.

"How do you know?" Bogan asked.

"We're not moving. The ship isn't moving at all," Merlin explained. "It's all a lie." Merlin pointed out the window at the passing clouds. "That's not clouds, its smoke."

Bogan smacked his hand on his head in frustration. "AH, CRUD! Jimmy tried to tell us."

"Me, Jimmy and Isabella will check outside. Bogan, you take some warriors and check the ship. We have to find them both," Merlin ordered, and they all split up.

It didn't take long for Merlin to spot the Umbrella Charmer puffing the false clouds around the windows and he instantly sent Jimmy after him. The man rushed away in terror, but his umbrella powered flight was no match for Jimmy's chest turbine. Jimmy grabbed the man, ripped the umbrella from his hand, then dropped him down on the forward deck of the Bradley Dunbar.

At first glance, Merlin could tell Jimmy had been a bit harsh with his grip on the charmer's hand as it was horribly mangled and broken. Merlin looked up at his brother excepting to hear a processed word of "Protect" from his rat brain-mod, but, instead,

Jimmy simply gave a nod. It struck Merlin with both fear and hope that maybe something had happened to his brother back at Pterugas, but whether it was good or bad was yet to be determined. He made a mental note of it and decided he would investigate after he dealt with the rotten-toothed stowaways.

It wasn't long before Bogan arrived with the other charmer and he too was far from gentle with the man as he dragged him across the deck toward Merlin. The man was kicking and screaming for mercy and had obviously been clawed up a bit from the Petinons. "I got the other one. He was down in the engine room with some nasty smoke-hand wrapped around the fuel intake." Bogan punched the man in the face as he pulled him across the deck. "So, what are we going to do with them now?" he asked and kicked the man over next to his fellow charmer with the crushed hand. Bogan gave an odd look at the other one. "Hey, shouldn't he be in pain or something? What gives with this guy?" he asked. "You guys nearly ripped his hand off, and he's just sitting there, still mumbling like a fool."

Merlin looked down at the charmer and noticed he was still speaking some kind of dark words, and that's when he caught sight of it. Izzy was gripping the crown tight with her eyes closed and wincing in pain. The charmer was doing something to her, trying to get into her mind somehow, and Merlin was having none of it. He reached down and took hold of the man and lifted him to his feet. "JIMMY!" he yelled out, and Jimmy instantly shot back down to the deck and grabbed the man. "Get this trash off our ship," he ordered. Jimmy grabbed the man and threw him out into the sky, then in a shocking display of force, Jimmy let loose a bolt of lightning into the man's body and vaporized him.

Izzy instantly dropped to her knees in exhaustion, and Merlin rushed over to her. "Are you okay?"

"Wow. Much better, thanks. What was that?" she asked.

"I don't know, but I think he was doing something. That's

why you had such a terrible headache," Merlin said and looked back at Bogan. "Get rid of that one too."

"Are you sure? I mean, he might have some valuable information that we could..." but before Bogan could finish his thought, Jimmy grabbed the other charmer and pitched him overboard. The man's screams echoed through the cloudless sky then were silenced suddenly. "Well, alright then," Bogan said. "I guess you don't need any advice today, do you?" He huffed then stomped through the crowd of stunned Petinon warriors standing on the deck, and back into the ship.

With a sudden jolt the Bradley Dunbar began moving again, and Merlin knew they had lost valuable time. "Izzy, I need a few fire berries from that bag they gave you."

"What for?" she asked, still rubbing the crown on her sore head.

"I'm going to use them to make up for lost time. We tried it with the Whisper and it worked, so I'm going to use it for Bradley Dunbar as well."

"Are you sure? This ship is completely different. What if it doesn't work? You might blow the whole ship up."

"It will work. Trust me." Merlin smiled.

"I do trust you, Merlin. I really do," Izzy said, placing her hand on his cheek. "The bag is in my room. Go—do it."

Merlin helped her to her feet, and they rushed back into the ship. Taking hold of the ship's intercom mic from Hal, he cried out. "Everyone take hold of something! Brace yourselves! We're about to make up for lost time. Hal, back the throttle down to the lowest speed." Hal started to speak up against whatever Merlin's plan was, but the look on Jimmy's face quickly shut him down.

"Y-yes sir," Hal responded as Merlin disappeared down the hallway.

Silence filled the bridge as everyone waited for Merlin to perform his magical act of making up for lost time, but it was

Jimmy's response that made everyone extremely uneasy. The mechanical flying boy reached up his hand and took hold of one of the bracing beams on the bridge as if to ready himself for something powerful. That's when Bogan must have realized what Merlin was up to and looked over at Izzy, who was grinning from ear to ear. "Izzy... he isn't... IS HE?"

"You better believe he is!"

"Oh, crud!" Bogan muttered and grabbed a bracing bar just as the Bradley Dunbar launched forward from an enormous blast of its engines. Hal's head slammed into the headrest of his pilot's chair, and his hands gripped the yoke tight as the Bradley Dunbar was instantly turned into a fire berry propelled rocket ship. Henry fell backward and rolled up against the far wall of the bridge, smacking his head on it, but suddenly began laughing an infectious laugh that quickly changed the mood of the whole room. In no time, everyone began laughing, even the Petinons, although Hal's knuckles were white as bone as he tried desperately to hang on the controls.

26

THE GATHERING

*S*ullivan's Coast was the most lavishly built city in the west. On the outskirts of the city towers, where the sea raged its white, foaming waters against sharp rocks, was an enormous iron amphitheater. Its seats were covered with cedar planks, and the floor base was filled with sand from the beach about three hundred feet below it. This night, the skies above the Black Mist were clear, and the moon was full and filled with an ominous presence of madness. The theater was packed tight with strange, frowning spectators sitting with their backs perfectly straight and holding umbrellas on their laps. A ghastly moon-lit glow washing across their faces made the spectators appear corpse-like as they sat motionless in their seats. It was a macabre gathering that seemed more befitting a funeral than the sporting shows the amphitheater was used to, but as three floating Umbrella Charmers rose over the top and descended to the sandy floor at the center, the crowd stood to their feet and began to clap joyfully.

The green-robed charmer in the middle touched down first and then the other two moments later. She lowered her umbrella, then closed it, forcing a cloud of smoke out of its canopy and into the air around her, and she secured it with a metal clasp. She lifted her dark green top hat then peered into the stands silently as if she were waiting for something. The right words, perhaps. She looked up at the pale, cold moon smiling a sinister grin down upon her and then she spoke. "Tonight will be a night unlike any the world has ever known. For tonight, we shall all witness the coming of the great one, the leader that will bring all peoples together in glorious harmony and change the course of humanity forever."

The crowd suddenly stood to their feet and erupted with a loud roar of praise at her inspiring words, and when they finished, she continued her speech. "My name is Emilia and I have been sent to you so that you will be prepared for her arrival. She will come to us in a way no one has ever seen or heard of before, and we must ready this place for her anointing. We must ready this place to crown our new queen and ruler. I want her to be honored by our loyalty and filled with pride from the outpouring of love we will lavish upon her. For she is our queen! There is none like her! She will make the world livable again, and we will rule by her side."

The crowd thundered their praise again, and this time they began chanting a name. "THERE IS NONE LIKE HER! CASSANDRA, QUEEN OF THE WORLD! MOTHER OF ALL CHARMERS! RULER OF THE CITIES OF THE WORLD! CASSANDRA! CASSANDRA! CASSANDRA!"

Emilia looked over at the man standing next to her and said, "Forsythe, bring them in now."

"As you command." He gave a nod then waved his hand in the air. An Umbrella Charmer at the far end of the amphitheater turned, opened a door behind him and thirteen Umbrella Charmers trudged out onto the sandy floor toward Emilia. They were all barefoot, and in their hands, they were carrying flat, round stones. Once they had come within a few feet of her, they dropped their flat stones into the sand and stepped on top of them.

Emilia reached out her hand to Forsythe, and he placed a small, soft brush into it, then she knelt down in front of the first charmer standing on the stone and began brushing the sand from their feet. She also meticulously brushed the sand from their stone until, one by one, she had swept their feet free of all the sand. She rose back up, turned to the crowded theater and spoke. "These are the thirteen that have pledged themselves to purify this ground for our queen. Let us honor them now." Emilia knelt down in front of the thirteen sacrificial Charmers, and the crowd responded in kind.

After a short time passed, she rose back to her feet and began chanting dark words until a large sword of smoke appeared in the air above her. The ghoulish spectators began chanting along with her until their voices reached a pinnacle, and Emilia brought down the giant sword upon all thirteen at once. Every voice in the outdoor theater went silent. A chilling wind blew in from the sea, and the moon seemed to hide its face from them as the sky grew darker, but the night was young and their dreadful deeds had only just begun.

THE JACKBOOT'S CELL DOOR GROANED AS IT OPENED SLOWLY. Everyone expected the other doors to open and the halls to fill with all manner of beast ready to bring death and pain, but theirs was the only door that opened in the hall. Once it reached the top, it stopped with a deep thud, and the Jackboot limped, bootless up to Angus Grand. The half-breed troll towered over him, but he had no fear in his heart as he considered how marvelous it would be to strike down his enemy before the battle ever began. Grundorph stepped up next to the Jackboot and seemed to know what he was thinking as he spoke. "Now is not the time for killing, little boot man. My brother is not a good man, but for today and today only, he is our ally."

The troll finished his warning about the time the large gate at the end of the hall began opening. Light cast shadows down the hall, across their feet and slowly up their faces as the gate rose. The roaring voices from the arena echoed their blood thirsty cries down hall, and the Jackboot turned away from his enemy to face the sounds of joyful madness. The Jackboot peered down the tunnel, mesmerized by the coming battle, and his blood began to warm for the glory of war. A sly grin arose on his face, and it did not go unnoticed by his prison mates. Brynjar, Hex, Angus and Grundorph stood to his right while Elias and Epekneia were to his left. Gemenon was directly in front of him, with the king's sword drawn, and she was crouched slightly with her wings tucked tight around her back.

"Dad? Do you want your boot back?" Elias asked, but the captivating sounds of bloodlust filled his ears, and he didn't hear his son's voice. "DAD?"

"Huh? What is it son?" He quickly looked down at his boy standing next to him.

"Your boot? Do you want your boot back?"

The Jackboot looked down at his naked stump and thought for a moment. "Oh, yeah, I guess that would help wouldn't it?" He smiled and ruffled his son's hair, then taking the boot from Elias; he slipped his bare stump down into it and flipped a switch on the side. A blast of air shot out from a tiny hole in the boot, and suddenly his leg was locked tight inside of it. As he raised his head up, his eye caught sight of the light blasting through the entrance to the arena. The air rushing down the hall was filled with a strong odor he'd smelled before, but never as strong as it did at this moment. He sniffed the air then took a deep breath into his lungs. "Do you smell that?"

Gemenon looked over her shoulder at him as he gazed, awestruck, at the arena. She sniffed the air and replied, "Smells like blood to me."

He gave a slight nod to her. "I've never... it's never smelled so strong until today."

Then Hex looked to Gemenon, and with a nod he said, "He is Petinon."

Gemenon looked back at the Jackboot. Her eyes caught sight of the burn mark on his forehead, and she quickly looked over at Elias, then her face lit up with surprise. "Elias is the queen's grandson," she said.

"Yes, it's true then. This man is... Ouranos," Hex said.

Gemenon's eyes grew large as she stared at him, then she suddenly dropped to her knees in front of him and held up the sword. "This belongs to you, great prince. It was your father's sword."

The Jackboot looked down at Elias who winced a little from the guilt of not explaining everything to him. "Uh, sorry, Dad. I, um... I didn't want to unload all of that onto you yet."

The Jackboot raised an ever so slightly displeased eyebrow at his son then said to Gemenon, "You keep it. Besides, I've never used one of those things before. I wouldn't know where to begin." Then he smiled at her with a mischievously flirtatious grin. "If we survive this battle... maybe you can show me how to use it."

"It would be an honor, great prince," she said, not fully understanding his playful tone. As she stood to her feet, the sword lifted out of her claws and rose into the air in front of him. She gasped in shock, and everyone looked at Elias.

"Don't look at me. I'm not doing it," Elias said.

The sword hovered in front of him, and the light shining down the hall glistened off the blade with a glorious glow that lit up his face. Strange vibrations seemed to be emanating from the blade like it was calling him to wield it, calling him to war.

He reached out and took hold of it by the grip. It felt good and right in his hand as if it was made especially for him, then he held it up in front of his face and said, "Let's go to war."

"Finally!" Angus scoffed.

Grundorph snugged down the troubled bolt on his head and smacked his hands together, then he pounded his chest with a deep thunderous growl. "I AM READY!"

THEY WALKED DOWN THE HALL AND CLIMBED THE SLOPE UP toward the entrance of the arena. The roar of the crowd was deafening as they stepped out into the open, and Elias held his hands over his ears until he became numb to the noise. Just as Grundorph had suspected, Mogdal had opened the Arena of Heroes to the outside by replacing the dirt covered dome with enormous glass panels, and hundreds of airship lights speckled the sky outside the dome. A tiny airship sailed from ship to ship, taking bets on the coming battle, and Mogdal sat on his throne smiling proudly at his great achievement. Mogdal was seated to the right of the arena and in the center of the stands; six of the eight gates were opened, with the exception the east gate beneath Mogdal's throne and the northeast gate to his right. Directly across the arena, to the north of them, five Standing Heroes were entering the arena, and at the southwest gate to their left, five more stepped out onto the battlefield. In front of the west gate there were already ten Standing Heroes waiting. The northwest gate was still opening, and when it came to a stop, four massive beasts stepped into view. Even though Mogdal's announcer identified the beast as Rat-Face, it was obvious to Elias who it was because of the troll's unique facial features and Mr. Black's detailed description.

The announcer spoke again as the next troll stepped out into the arena. "I GIVE YOU THE LEGENDARY HERO AND SON OF OGG THE MURDEROUS, AGMAR THE WRETCHED!"

The crowd stood to their feet as Agmar entered the arena. He was unlike anything Elias could have ever imagined, and the crowd went full on mad at the sight of him. Agmar's skin was pure white as if someone had painted him, and out of his shoulder blades, on each side of his back, rose enormous horns that curved over top of his shoulders and came to a sharp point back towards his own chest. Large golden earrings hung from each ear, and golden arm bands wrapped around his forearms. His head was bald except for a long ponytail jutting out of the top, and the only clothes he wore were custom pants made of a strange, leathery material. His eyes were a solid, cold blue, and he cared not for the adulation of the crowd.

The announcer introduced the next troll as he stepped out, "I GIVE YOU THE LEGENDARY HERO AND SON OF OGG THE MURDEROUS, GONON THE VILE!"

Gonon must not have been that popular with the crowd because they sat back down and many booed his arrival, but much like his brother Agmar, Gonon cared not for their opinion of him. Gonon's skin was light brown, and he had a large iron nose ring through his septum, and at the bottom of it was a strange skull. His body was covered in dark scars, and he was missing the index finger on his left hand. His eyes were solid black, and he was about two feet shorter than his brother Agmar. He also wore strange custom pants like his brother, and they matched his skin tone so closely that he almost seemed naked in the light.

Both Agmar and Gonon were taller than Grundorph, and Elias could tell that Grundorph was nervous. "We can beat them," Elias said, looking up at the giant gray troll, but his words didn't seem to comfort the beast much.

The announcer's voice caught Elias' attention again as he

introduced the next legend. "I GIVE YOU LEGENDARY HERO AND SON OF OGG THE MURDEROUS, KROM THE CRUEL!"

This time the crowd went silent and stood to their feet as if royalty was entering the Arena of Heroes. The thunder of heavy footsteps shook the ground like a giant as he walked up the ramp. Gonon and Agmar stepped away from the entrance as their brother came into view. Krom had to duck slightly at the entrance to the arena, but once he cleared it, he stretched his arms out wide and cracked his neck from left to right then let out a loud groan. The crowd responded with wondrous elation, and Krom raised his hands up high and soaked in their admiration. His body was a deep red color, and his large ears came to a point at the top and drooped over a bit. Thick, black eyebrows rested over his solid gold eyes, and he wore a large iron chain around his neck. His ears were pierced with more gold earrings than could be counted, and large gold nose ring hung from his septum. On each of his arms, four black horns stuck out like weapons, and a large black horn rose out of the back of his bald head. And every one of his fingers were adorned with gold rings that were clearly larger than Elias' head.

When the monster troll caught sight of his brothers Grundorph and Angus, he made his way over toward them. Mogdal did nothing as he watched from his throne and seemed to want to know what Krom would do. Soon, Agmar and Gonon followed behind him, and Grundorph began to tremble. The ground of the arena shook like the Iron Weaver rumbling down the tracks as the trolls approached. Elias looked up at Grundorph and noticed how he was rubbing the metal plate on his head, and he figured maybe the plate was a cruel gift from his brothers.

Krom stepped intimidatingly close to them before he stopped at the Jackboot's threat. "That's far enough, horn head," he said in a grizzled tone. His father's mocking words struck

Elias' funny bone, and he almost burst out laughing at his father's threat. He held it in for the sake of the moment, but a tiny snort slipped out of his nose. It caught Epekneia by surprise, and she glanced over at him with fear in her eyes. Elias returned her stare, unable to crush his amusement at the realization his father wasn't afraid of anyone or anything, even the monsters of Karl's Labyrinth.

"Sorry," he whispered to her. "I-I get it. I do. I just... it reminded me of when I first met the Jackboot." He tried to reassure her that he was taking their situation seriously, but it didn't come out right."

In a deep, powerful voice, Krom spoke to his brother Grundorph. "Brother... how's the head?" he asked with a subtle chuckle in his voice. But Agmar and Gonon laughed loudly at his words, and Grundorph cowered ever so slightly.

"How cute!" Angus growled back at them. "Father should have killed you all for what you did to him. He didn't deserve to be treated that way. He is your little brother. You nearly killed him for fun, and why? Because he is smarter than all of you? You disgust me and that's not easy to do."

"Angus Grand!" Krom sneered. "How is it that you are still alive? You're a flea in a world of giants. Why father loved you the most, I'll never know. Maybe his mind was rotten from all the humans he'd eaten during your war."

"No. No, Krom. He loved me because I was better looking than you," Angus said with a sly grin as he was clearly the ugliest of them all, but he knew how vain Krom was.

Krom's face grew angry, and he looked down at the odd group of misfits standing with his brothers. "Just how long do you think these bugs will last in here tonight? Brynjar is the only one worthy to be here. Why don't you take your place with us, wolf-beast? You belong with the gods of the arena, not with those waiting to die." Brynjar simply responded with a low, growling disapproval at the troll's words.

Agmar took hold of his strangely curved horns and slid his hands down them gently. "Grundorph was never one of us, brother," he said to Krom. "We should've finished what we started that day and caved the rest of his skull in."

Gonon laughed. "Yes, brothers. Father was wrong for stopping us. Grundorph was the weakest of us all. He didn't deserve to be a son of Ogg."

Grundorph smiled a subtle but naughty grin at his brothers, knowing full well he would bring them to anger. "Dear brother, you think that my meekness was a sign of weakness, but we all know it was my intellect that drove you all to jealousy. I could have killed you many times in your sleep, but I learned to tame the beast within me. You, my brothers, were the weaker ones and gave in to your basic troll instincts. That is why Father respected me and loved me more than you."

Krom's open hand closed into a fist, and he raised it to strike Grundorph, but Mogdal must have grown tired of waiting to see if they would fight or argue. Mogdal picked up his horn and gave it a long blast, and the gate to the right of them slowly began to open. Krom, Agmar and Gonon stepped back and readied themselves for what would come out of the gate as Grundorph motioned for everyone to move back, then he stepped out in front of them. "Ready yourselves!" he warned.

THE PUPPET MASTER LOWERED THE IRON WEAVER BELOW THE Black Mist and brought it to a hover over the edge of Mine Five. Rat 10k stepped out on the back of the train and began beating a large drum made of Bryn-wolf hide, and moments later, Bryn-wolves began climbing over the edge of the mine and into his airships. On their heads they wore tiny brain-mod boxes that were impossible to see unless you were riding on their backs. This was by design, as he had no intention of someone discovering his long-term plans to gain control over the entire west.

Hans stood on the back of the train and watched as his Bryn-wolf army filed into the ships one by one in a perfect orderly fashion. There were no growls of anger or howls of discord as the wolves crawled over the wall of Mine Five toward the ship, and unlike men who might retreat from battle, these warriors were perfectly obedient, even unto death. The Puppet Master was filled with pride that he had been able to conquer them. He had lost many tunnel rat warriors during his campaign against the Bryn-wolves, and though their obedience was sealed in mind-altering brain-mods, wolves were still wolves and he took no chances with them. A large force of heavily armed tunnel rats lined both sides of the Bryn-wolves as they filed into a single line behind a giant red Bryn-wolf. The red Bryn-wolf that had caused him so much difficultly in the beginning stages of his campaign was now unable to refuse a single command, and he glared at the beast as a cruel ruler would look down on a conquered king. The beast bowed its head toward the ground in shame as it entered the airship, and its brother wolves followed quietly behind.

When he felt comfortable with the situation, Hans retreated to his room and changed his clothes. He'd always hoped this day would come, this day of vengeance upon Angus Grand, and he had requested a special, hand-crafted suit all the way from Sullivan's Coast for the occasion. Identical to the clothes he had worn on the first Sky Falling, he hoped to make a point with himself that he had accomplished his ultimate goal of revenge. His suit was solid black, except for the deep red breastplate, with three rows of golden buttons and a blood red cape. It took him some time to finish dressing, but once he had finished, he fixed the lapels on his coat and straightened himself as best he could, then he reached into his pocket and pulled out a handful of fire berries. On the table beside him sat the large syringe

Cassandra had given him, and in his hand he held his true desire for the half-breed troll.

I don't care if he laughs. I'll burn the monster anyway! Everyone in labyrinth will see what I have done to him.

HUNDREDS OF UMBRELLA CHARMERS SURROUNDED THE BONEY egg-shaped tower in the center of the Valley of Bones as their sorceress of darkness clapped her hands together and began to speak. In front of her, held by a smoky hand of black mist, floated the dead, black heart of her son, Elias. Beneath her, inside the massive egg-shaped structure, her beloved Sunago lay in darkness. His body, now mutated beyond recognition, was changing, going through a metamorphosis so drastic that only Karl Kass could appreciate. Strange gold lightning crackled around the black heart as she spoke, and purple lights flashed deep inside the boney egg. As her voice grew louder and darker, Black Mist rushed into the valley and swirled around the bottom of the cocoon.

Behind her, on a platform of smoke, stood the Dream Slayer, and beside him were five cloaked figures dressed in identical robes. Their hands were hidden inside the large sleeves of their cloaks, and their hoods covered every feature except their eyes which were glowing deep in the darkness of their hoods. At the command of their dark ruler, they all leaped on top of the egg with freakish speed and lifted the cap on the egg. They raised it over their heads and held it there while a foul-smelling steam rose from the boiling, black goo inside of it. Cassandra continued her chanting, and her Charmers soon joined her, until the black heart was glowing with a dark purple tinge about it. When it began pumping, she cast it into the boiling egg and commanded the Dream Slayer and his companions to close the lid. They locked it down with large clasps and then leapt back onto the smoke platform held by one of the Charmers.

As the egg began to shake, black lightning crackled around it, striking the ground and the sky. It even hit a few Umbrella Charmers, and they vanished into a dark puff of purple smoke. The ground shook violently from the power of the beast inside the egg until the egg began to crack. It started slowly at the bottom and quickly climbed up the sides of the weaker bone connections. Black slime oozed out the sides of the egg as the fracturing quickened, and the structure grew weak and unable to hold the beast inside of it.

Suddenly, in a powerful explosion of black lightning, bones and bolts, the creature emerged from its grotesque cocoon. It flung the black goo everywhere and covered many of the Umbrella Charmers with it.

As the beast let out a powerfully deep roar of strength, Cassandra smiled a wicked grin at the creature. She approached it slowly and with much caution, but she also carried herself with great confidence as she gazed upon the creature with the authority a mother might have toward her children.

The beast let out a roar at her as she came closer and glared its deep golden eyes at her as if it wanted to devour her. "You're hungry. I can see it in your eyes. Soon, my love, soon. But first you need to stretch your wings and show me the glory that I've returned to you. The glory that was taken from you so long ago. LOOK! See how I have given it back to you," she said, pointing to the creature's massive wings.

The beast turned its head and looked over at the enormous wings now stretching out of its back. It spread them out over the valley and the Umbrella Charmers moved away in fear. The beast looked back at her then raised its head toward the moon light and let out a powerful bellowing roar of victory that sent black flames towering into the sky. An eerie glow of green surround the flames as the entire valley lit up from his breath, and his powerful wings beat the air so hard that it brought down many of the Umbrella Charmers floating around him. Cassandra was filled with joy at her masterful mutation of Sunago, and the Valley of Bones echoed with the sound of her laughter.

27

BATTLE OF LEGENDS

*M*ogdal's powerful horn blast was so loud, it vibrated Elias' chest with a deep violent shaking that stole his breath away. His heart pumped fiercely, as if it knew something was wrong, and his body ached from the pressure building inside his chest. When the sound of Mogdal's horn ended, Elias knew it wasn't the horn that caused his chest to feel like it was going to explode, something else had happened. He felt as if a part of him had died, and suddenly his eyes lit up with fire. Epekneia kept her eyes on him the whole time and it gave him a sense of comfort, but everyone else's gaze was still held captivate by the southeast gate opening.

Epekneia leaned over and whispered in his ear, "Did you eat fire berries?"

"No, but I feel like someone just tore out my heart. It felt like my chest was going to explode and then it suddenly stopped and my... my eyes lit up. I didn't eat any berries, I promise." He looked at her with red tears rushing down his face. "Epekneia, I... I feel like I died. D-Do I look okay?" he asked.

"No, you don't. You're pale and... your eyes." She brushed her claw down his cheek, wiping the red tears away, then showed him her claw. "Your eyes are streaming with red tears. We need to get help." She grabbed the distracted Jackboot by the shoulder and gave it a powerful jerk. The Jackboot's mind was so fixed on battle at this point that he reacted forcefully and almost hit her in the face but caught himself just in time.

"WHY DID YOU DO THAT?" he yelled.

Epekneia tilted Elias' head up so he could see his son, and the Jackboot's face quickly lost all color. "SON! What happened?"

"I don't know. I was..." Elias started to explain but waited when the gate to the arena finally came to a stop with a loud boom. The warriors in the arena were captivated as they stared into the dark tunnel, waiting for whatever Mogdal was sending out at them, and the crowd-filled stands held their breath.

The Jackboot dropped the king's sword then scooped his boy into his arms and cried out, "HEX, SOMETHING IS WRONG WITH MY SON!" Grundorph, Hex, Brynjar and even Angus Grand caught notice of the boy's face, and the beastly creatures were instantly struck with concern for him.

"Was he injured by something?" Grundorph asked.

"No... I-I don't think so." The Jackboot looked at Epekneia who shook her head. "We don't know what happened."

"Whatever comes through that gate, we have to hold it off. We have to keep it away from them," Hex ordered as he brandished his talons.

Gemenon reached over and grabbed the king's sword from the Jackboot and swiftly struck the large chain next to Hex's foot, leaving the long end still attached to Grundorph's leg. The two prison companions looked at each other like she'd just severed their umbilical cord of friendship, but soon Grundorph had a gleam in his eyes as he seemed to realize she'd just given him a weapon.

Powerful thumping echoed from the darkness of the tunnel, and the sound of hissing caught everyone's attention. Agmar the troll yelled out. "IT'S NAKAR!" Krom, Agmar and Gonon rushed back toward the southwest gate, next to the five Standing Heroes, right about the time Nakar swooped out of the dark tunnel and into the center of arena.

Nakar, the serpent-troll, had two black wings on his back and the face of a serpent. His body was shiny, with black scales covering most of it and a bright red stripe down the center of his chest. His red tongue flicked between two large fangs that dripped white poison on the dirt floor, and a wickedly thick tail beat the ground as a warning. Nakar had no hands, but he did have arms that each came to a sharp claw point, and the claws were blade-like underneath. His feet were more stumps than feet, but his short wings and tail helped him to balance himself as he walked around on the ground.

Elias dangled helplessly in his father's arms as he watched the monster serpent-troll terrify even Krom and his brothers. However, Krom the Cruel quickly lived up to his name by grabbing one the Standing Heroes at the southwest gate and casting the warrior at the feet of Nakar. The hero didn't even have a chance to get his bearings before Nakar melted him with acid-venom. Agmar and Gonon laughed at Krom's cruel deed and decided to join in their brother's game by tossing a Standing Hero of their own for Nakar to punish. Nakar quickly responded with the same venomous attack on the next two, and the astonished crowd let out a gasp as if they expected more of a sporting battle instead of a bone-melting slaughter. The remaining two heroes at the southwest gate made for the safety of the western gate, but Krom smiled at his brothers as if he'd just forged a battleplan to deal with Nakar and the Standing Heroes. Suddenly, the three giant trolls ran toward the western gate.

"Krom is going to feed them all to Nakar!" Angus said with a sly grin on his face.

"They don't deserve to die that way, brother," Grundorph complained.

"Look at it this way, for every one they feed to that monster, it's one less we have to fight," Gemenon said, gripping the king's sword. Her words seemed to catch the Jackboot by surprise, and he looked at her with an odd glare of astonishment.

"There is no honor in this. It's a slaughter," Hex replied.

"What do you mean?" Angus asked curiously.

Hex explained as he pointed toward the ruler of Karl's Labyrinth, seated high on his throne. "Look at Mogdal. He is smiling. You believe this to be a Battle of Legends, but for Mogdal, this in an extermination."

About the time, Krom grabbed another Standing Hero and threw the poor soul toward Nakar, a weary Elias noticed Rat-Face had taken out on a dead run for the serpent-troll. Nakar quickly melted the poor Standing Hero into the ground when Rat-Face came up from behind him and leapt onto his back. Nakar let out a horrible hissing cry as Rat-Face gnawed off his right wing then jumped off his back and took off running with it. Rat-Face laughed as he beat the wing in the air, pretending to fly with it. The crowd let out a roaring laughter at Rat-Face's brilliant comedic attack on Nakar, whom most consider to be a cheat anyway. Even Krom, Agmar and Gonon began laughing as Rat-Face ran circles around the injured serpent-troll. But it was Nakar that had the last laugh. Rat-Face had become so caught up in the adulation of the crowd that he didn't realize he'd gotten too close to Nakar, and the serpent-troll hit him with a blast of acid-venom on the left side of his body. Rat-Face dropped to his knees in front the northeast gate as his left arm and the left side of his face began to burn away. Where most would simply melt away and die instantly from Nakar's venom, Rat-Face was a tunnel troll, and his flesh was thick and difficult to melt, so Rat-Face suffered greatly as he knelt there.

The eastern gate sat directly beneath Mogdal's throne while

the northeast gate was to his right, and neither had been opened yet. Though Rat-Face's hilarious wing-flapping had struck everyone as brilliant and comical, Mogdal seemed greatly disappointed with it, and he grabbed his horn and let out another blast. Moments later the northeast gate began to open and Legends and Heroes quickly looked at each other in wonder. Everyone they knew was already in the arena, and it suddenly became clear to many that Mogdal had planned something far grander for his Battle of Legends.

The pounding thuds shook the Arena of Heroes as Mogdal's surprise rushed through the darkness of the tunnel toward the opening of the northeast gate. Even the concrete stands shook, and it terrified the people sitting over the gate, but all of a sudden there was a massive crash deep inside the northeast tunnel that felt like an earthquake had struck the labyrinth. When it stopped, everything was quiet for a moment, then a great commotion in the crowded arena took place as everyone wondered what had happened. Even the suffering Rat-Face lifted his head toward the entrance of the tunnel, and the airships overhead moved closer to the glass for a better look.

Moments later, a bit of rumbling started, and the pounding thuds began to shake the earth again as if some creature had regained its direction and headed back down the tunnel. It drew closer and closer until finally an enormous troll stepped into the light under the gate. At first it looked lost, but as it stood there trying to enter the arena, it kept smashing its head on the top of the gate's entrance. Then it would back up and try again. Everyone let out a laugh, then something pushed the beast out of the hole. The crowd gasped as a giant troll fell to its hands and knees, and another one stepped out from the tunnel behind it. They were both wearing what seemed to be large diapers, and the one that had fallen on its hands and knees began sobbing like a hurt child. Then, without warning, six First-Gen trolls rushed out of the tunnel entrance and knocked down the other troll. They ran directly at Rat-Face, and one of them stepped right on his head, instantly crushing the Legend underfoot.

A deep laughter arose from Nakar while he watched the First-Gen trolls finish off Rat-Face as they ran over the body. They pushed and shoved each other and stomped Rat-Face into the ground as if he were a child's play thing, and then they turned their attention to Nakar, who seemed to welcome them toward him. The serpent-troll spewed acid venom everywhere at the massive beasts until he hit one of them on the leg, but Nakar was aghast when it barely even burned the beast. In one stunning move, a First-Gen troll grabbed Nakar and ripped him in half. A sense of stunned shock took hold of the Legends and Heroes at how quickly Nakar was dispatched by the monstrous beasts.

"What madness? Mogdal's remade First-Gen trolls? *WHY?*" Grundorph asked, smacking the plate on his head with his hand.

"Very hard to kill! This should be an interesting battle," Angus grinned.

ELIAS' FATHER PLACED HIM ON THE GROUND NEXT TO THE entrance of their tunnel then asked Epekneia and Gemenon to watch over him while they tried to fend off the child-like beasts. "Whatever happens, keep him away from those things."

"But what if we can't? What if something happens?" Epekneia asked with a terrified look in her eyes.

The Jackboot placed his hand on her cheek. "Try not to think about it, but if we're all going to die, make sure you do one thing above all others."

"What's that?" Gemenon curiously asked.

"Die well!" the Jackboot said with the cold, hard gaze of a warrior.

"Yes, my prince," Gemenon answered. The Jackboot look at her strangely then took the king's sword from her clawed hand and climbed on top of Grundorph's head.

Elias was nearly unconscious from the pain in his back, but he held on to Epekneia's claw-hand like a lifeline of hope. For the first time in a long time, he was truly concerned that death was reaching its way back to him. As he held her hand, all he could think of was living long enough to tell her how he felt about her. He knew that whatever was happening to him right now felt eerily similar to the night on the Whisper when his hands melted through the upper glass dome. Although, this time he hadn't eaten any fire berries. His mind rushed with all the possibilities of what could be happening, but no matter how hard he searched his thoughts, he could find no plausible answers to what was causing his pain.

Elias turned his head to the side and watched as chaos took hold of the arena, and his anger burned inside of him for not being able to help. He watched as Hex, Brynjar, Angus and Grundorph rushed to war with his father riding on top of Grundorph's head. As his father rode the troll into battle with King Arkone's sword, Elias couldn't help but think of what Hex had said of the Jackboot—that he was Ouranos. If his father truly was Ouranos, then his father was future king of the Petinon people, but even if he wasn't, the Jackboot certainly looked kingly as he charged off to war.

Epekneia had an epiphany and grabbed Gemenon by the arm. "I think we should give Elias some of the fire berries."

"What? No, I think that would be a bad idea right now."

"Why? It always helps him recover whenever something happens to him. We've done it many times before."

"Epekneia... look at him. He looks like he's dying. Has he ever looked like this before?"

"Well, sort of, but maybe not exactly like this." Epekneia

winched as she looked into his eyes. "Okay, but what if he is dying and we didn't try it? What then?"

"For now, I think we should wait—use it as a last measure. If we're not going to make it, then we can try it, but I don't want the prince to worry about him during battle." Gemenon gave a subtle nod, and Epekneia reluctantly agreed. Elias didn't even argue with them because he was in so much pain. He feared what would happen if he ate fire berries in his current condition, so he simply lay there staring out into the madness of the arena.

THE FIRST-GEN TROLLS WERE BRUTALLY STRONG AND SEEMED completely oblivious to their cruel actions, even to one another. Mindless brutes with childlike brains and unnatural strength, they pushed and punched each other and even knocked one another down by accident. They looked like a mass of pale green muscle tumbling around the center of the arena as the Jackboot charged at them. It quickly became clear to him that Krom, Agmar and Gonon had no intention of helping them deal with the First-Gen trolls as they stood at a distance with wickedly delightful grins on their faces. It wasn't that the three powerful sons of Ogg were completely terrified of the massive beasts, but it seemed more like a battle strategy to let others thin their numbers before they got involved.

As they charged toward the massive beasts, the Jackboot took measure of the battlefield and realized that most of them were captivated by Hex flying in the air. However, one of them was clearly not paying attention to his surroundings and continued to toy with the remains of Nakar. He cried out to Hex, who was inflight over top of him. "HEX! DISTRACT THE OTHERS WHILE WE PICK OFF THE DUMB ONE."

"WHICH ONE IS THE DUMB ONE?" Hex asked, looking

out into the mass of bumbling trolls. "THEY ALL LOOK DUMB TO ME!"

The Jackboot looked back out toward the beasts and realized Hex had made a very solid point. "RIGHT! GOOD POINT! WE'RE GOING TO PICK OFF THE ONE BEATING NAKAR'S BODY ALL OVER THE GROUND."

"AND JUST HOW DO YOU PROPOSE WE DO THAT, MY DEAR JACKBOOT?" Angus sarcastically asked.

"JUST FOLLOW MY LEAD, HALF-BREED, AND MAYBE YOU'LL LEARN SOMETHING ABOUT BATTLE!" the Jackboot quipped, but quickly returned his attention to the distracted troll in the center of the arena.

Hex went to work on captivating the others with fancy swooping and diving movements, as well as a few daring maneuvers between them, while Grundorph ran behind the troll that was currently beating Nakar's battered corpse into the arena floor. When the Jackboot felt he was close enough, he engaged his magnetic boots and launched himself off Grundorph's metal plate. He landed right on top of the First-Gen troll's enormous head and drove King Arkone's sword deep into its skull. He expected the beast to drop to the ground dead, but instead, the troll let out a moan and smacked at itself on the head several times, nearly crushing him.

Grundorph yelled out. "YOU MISSED THE BRAIN!"

"HOW'S THAT POSSIBLE?" he asked, in bewilderment.

"SMALL BRAINS!" Angus laughed as he pinched his finger and thumb together 'til they almost touched.

"TRY WIGGLING THE SWORD AROUND IN THERE. MAYBE YOU'LL HIT SOMETHING!" Grundorph hollered as he worked to distract the beast from knocking the Jackboot off.

The Jackboot tried to move the sword around in the beast's head, but the skull was too thick, so he pulled the sword out and began striking it into the troll's head to see is he could hit something. This only seemed to anger the monster more and forced it to strike at him with both hands. The troll finally hit him with its left index finger and knocked the wind out of him, but it also hit the sword and drove it deeper into its own skull. The beast stopped instantly and stood as motionless as a tree as it stared out into the crowded stands.

"HA! GOT IT!" The Jackboot wheezed, catching his breath then reached down to pull out the sword, but when his hand took hold of the grip, the beast jerked and began running in circles. It flung him off, and he nearly hit the ground, but Brynjar caught him and tossed him back on top of Grundoph's head. The sword must have hit something vital enough to cause a malfunction in the beast's brain, because it continued to run around in circles until it drove itself, head first, into the side of the arena wall right next to the northeast gate. Unfortunately, the malfunctioning troll had caught the attention of his fellow First-Gen brothers, and they no longer seemed interested in Hex's airshow. They slogged over to the body of their brother and began poking and grunting at it to see why he wasn't moving.

"ONE DOWN!" the Jackboot cried out and gave Grundorph a victory tap on his metal plate, but it was short-lived. The crowd let out a subtle, mocking laughter at the beast's clumsy death stroll, but the troll's brothers didn't find it comical at all. They quickly turned and faced the Jackboot, and in unison they let out a powerful, threatening roar and charged at him.

"Now you've done it!" Angus groaned. "They're going to have us for lunch, thanks to you."

"RUN, GRUNDY! RUN!" The Jackboot yelled, and Grundorph took off toward Krom, Agmar and Gonon with Brynjar and Angus not far behind them. The monster trolls followed clumsily but quickly after them, and the crowd let out a cry of laughter that seemed more like a cry of bloodlust than joy.

The twelve Standing Heroes that were behind Krom and his brothers fled the coming freight train of troll flesh headed their way. Some went south and others north, but Krom, Agmar and Gonon just stood there as Grundorph ran at them with a giant, nefarious grin on his face. Suddenly, the Jackboot realized he'd lost his sword inside the dead troll's skull when he reached for it. "GRUNDY! MAKE FOR THE DEAD TROLL!" he yelled, but Grundorph clearly had another plan in mind.

"NOT YET, MR. IRON BOOTS! NOT YET!" he roared back up to his tiny battle commander.

The Jackboot looked ahead of them, and from the look on Krom's face, it became terrifyingly obvious what Grundorph was planning. "Oh, you can't be serious? GRUNDY!"

"HANG ON TO YOUR BOOTS, MR. JACKBOOT!" Grundorph cried out as he lowered his shoulder and rammed the center of his brothers, knocking Gonon into Krom and Agmar. The Jackboot launched himself into the air just before impact and landed on the edge of the arena wall, momentarily facing a crowd of bloodthirsty labyrinth folk. The loud collision of troll flesh echoed through the area as the brothers collided together in a terrible crash and Grundorph toppled over his brothers but thankfully rolled off to the side and out of their grasp. When Grundorph finally got back to his feet, the Jackboot jumped back on top of his friend's head then Grundorph set out on a hard run to retrieve the sword from the dead troll's skull.

ANGUS WAS HALF THE SIZE OF GRUNDORPH, SO HIS STRIDE WAS shorter than his brother's, and Brynjar had not fully recovered from his wounds to handle such a hard run. By the time they figured out Grundorph was leading the First-Gen trolls toward his brothers as bait, they didn't have much time to get out of the way. Angus was able to dive out of the way before being crushed underfoot, but Brynjar was much too large to move out of the way and ended up in the massive troll pile by the eastern gate.

Brynjar the wolf-beast quickly maneuvered himself into an attack position against one of the First-Gen trolls and tore the monster's arm off with several swipes from his powerful wolf claw. The bloodthirsty crowd went completely out of their minds with glorious shouts of death as Brynjar went to work on the First-Gen troll as only the wolf-beast of Karl's Labyrinth knew how. It was brutal work, but it was all he'd ever known, and he had no intention of letting anyone get near the boy and the winged girls that healed him. In his mind, they were the only creatures that had ever shown him kindness and every cruel strike filled him with purpose. His attack was terrifying and ferocious in nature, and he howled and snapped his teeth at the creature until the massive troll picked up its own severed arm and struck him hard across the chest with it. It sent him soaring to the center of the arena, and he lay motionless as the crowd raged their depraved cheers of glory for the troll who'd struck him. No one could tell if Brynjar was dead or simply unconscious, and given the circumstances, no one had time to check on him.

THE SINGLE-ARMED TROLL SPOTTED ANGUS, WHO WAS NOW ON the run toward Grundorph and the Jackboot, but the massive beast quickly caught up with him. For some odd reason, it seemed like it was blaming him for the loss of its arm by Brynjar as it pointed to the bleeding stub and roared at him. Angus tried to reason with the monster, but it was too stupid to understand anything except the basic instincts of pain, rage and hunger.

Unlike the other sons of Ogg, Angus didn't seem afraid of the giant troll as it accused him of stealing its arm. Instead, Angus laughed at the beast then ran at it. It tried to grab hold of him as he went between its legs, but he grabbed the beast by the finger and pulled its own arm between its legs until the troll lost its balance and fell face first to the arena floor. Angus ran up on its back and began pounding the dumb brute in the head until a loud pop echoed throughout the arena as he cracked its skull. The beast lay motionless, and the crowd was stunned that such a small, half-breed troll could beat a First Generation troll to death with his bare hands. Angus stood up on top of the troll's head and raised his hands in the air for the crowd, and they leapt to their feet with glorious shouts of victory and adulation for his success. Even his old foe, Mogdal, stood and clapped for Angus Grand.

KROM, AGMAR AND GONON QUICKLY WENT TO WORK ON THE First-Gen trolls that had piled on top of them, and they proved their titles with shocking swiftness. Gonon the Vile bit all the fingers off one of the First-Gen's hands then shoved the beast's thumbs up its own nose before the creature knew what had happened. The crowd roared with laughter, and Agmar the Wretched provided even more glee to their evening by smashing all the teeth from another First-Gen's mouth. The two childlike giants ran away from them as fast as they could, weeping tears of sorrow around the edge of arena walls as they tried to climb out. The crowd enjoyed a bit of sport with them by firing their guns into the faces of the monsters, but it only seemed to agitate the beasts.

Krom the Cruel had no time for games like his brothers. Krom instantly struck down the First-Gen that had landed on top of him with the sharp horn in the back of his head. He reared his head back into the troll's chest, striking it directly in the heart, and the beast was dead before it could ever dig itself free from the pile. Krom then went to work on another First-Gen with the spikes jutting out of his arms, and before his brothers could even start on another troll, Krom had slain two First-Gen trolls by himself.

The brothers all worked together on the next one with such amazing skill, it was if they had planned and choreographed their every move before the battle had ever begun. The beast swung at Agmar and hit the curved horns that protected the front of his chest. Agmar was knocked to the ground, but he laughed at the beast as it held its hand, crying in pain. Gonon quickly climbed up its back and covered its eyes with his hands while Krom began pummeling the beast's leg with his horned arms, then Agmar crawled behind the troll and tripped the beast. It hit the ground hard, and the three brothers finished the troll with such terrible cruelty, even the bloodthirsty crowd went silent from their deeds as the creature wailed and cried out like a child.

The Standing Heroes saw the two remaining, injured, First-Gens as a perfect opportunity to level up to Legendary Hero status, and they all blitzed the disoriented trolls and began beating them. However, the one that got away from the sons of Ogg rushed upon the Standing Heroes and began tearing into them as punishment for their heartless actions against his brothers.

WHILE KROM, AGMAR AND GONON WERE DUSTING THEMSELVES off from their slaughter, the Jackboot was busy digging the sword from the first First-Gen that had fallen. "You're going to have to go in there and dig it out. We don't have any other options. Or did you not see how fast my brothers dispatched the other ones?" Grundorph asked.

"I'm not crawling into this nasty troll's skull to dig out that sword," the Jackboot complained.

Hex swooped down next to them and offered his take on

their predicament. "The sons of Ogg are not going to be easy to kill, and that weapon is the most powerful thing we have. You must retrieve it."

The Jackboot sneered at his cell mates in disgust but finally crawled inside the First-Gen's skull where King Arkone's sword had fallen after the beast hit the wall. The hole in the beast's skull was plenty big enough for him to climb in, but he didn't have to go in very far before he spotted it. Much to his shock, when he reached out his hand to grab the weapon, it shot out of the troll's brain and straight into his hand. *WHAT? How could this be?* He dropped the sword back down on purpose then reached for it again and the weapon jumped back into his hand. A glorious smile crept up on his face as he crawled out of the troll's head with the sword and trudged over to Grundorph.

"Well, you sure put on a nasty fit about climbing in there to be stepping out with such a wondrous smile on your face," Grundorph said. "Now let's get you back up top so we can get ready for my brothers." But the Jackboot ignored him and walked out toward the First-Gen troll now terrorizing the Standing Heroes by the northeast gate.

"WHAT ARE YOU DOING?" Hex cried out, but the Jackboot continued walking toward the massive First-Gen. Krom, Agmar and Gonon took notice as did Mogdal and the crowded arena. People soon began yelling and pointing at him as he closed in on the beast, and their reaction caught the troll's attention. The First-Gen turned around to see what everyone was yelling about, and he quickly spotted the Jackboot coming at him. In each hand the giant troll held a Standing Hero. One was missing its head, but the other was screaming in agony. When the gleam from the Jackboot's sword caught the troll's gaze, he discarded the two heroes over the back his shoulders like a child discarding old, broken toys for a shiny new one.

The troll let out a goofy laugh at him, and the crowd rose to their feet to watch the beast crush the tiny man's body into the dirt, but he stunned the crowd into gasps of astonishment when he took off on a hard run toward the beast. The troll reared back slightly in curious surprise at him, then he flung the weapon at it and struck the beast in belly. The sword went clean through the creature, and it let out a horrible, moaning cry of pain.

His weapon soared through the air toward the crowd for a few seconds until he reached out his hand for it, stopping it in midair. He opened his hand wide, and the sword felt his call to return and it shot back towards him. He caught it about the time the troll grabbed its enormous gut wound with one hand and swung at him with the other. The beast's hand scraped a massive cloud of dust into the air as it swiped towards him, and he leapt into the air to avoid its grasp, but its massive finger caught the edge of his boot and sent him tumbling through the dirt cloud. It knocked the same faulty boot off his leg, and he had no idea where it went. After the dust cleared, he got to his one boot and saw Hex, Grundorph and Angus yelling and pointing above him. When he looked up, a giant troll was staring down at him with a slobbering grin on its face, but this wasn't the beast he had been fighting. This was the troll that had all of its teeth knocked out by Agmar. Either way, it looked hungry, and he'd been caught off guard. *OH! NOT GOOD!*

He dropped the sword as the beast took hold of him and lifted him up to its mouth for a juicy Jackboot bite. The beast's grip was so strong he thought he might pass out from the crushing pressure. Its breath smelled like dead, bloated tunnel rat as it opened its mouth, and in one shocking bite, the beast swallowed the Jackboot whole. The crowd was disturbed, but the sons of Ogg let out a blast of laughter infectious enough for Mogdal and the crowd to join in with them. Their joyful laughter was short lived due to a blood chilling scream from the other side of the arena.

Through blurred vision and constant waves of pain, Elias watched in horror as the First-Gen troll swallowed his father. The mocking laughter of the crowd burned his anger hot, and he reached for Gemenon's satchel of fire berries, grabbed a handful and shoved them into his mouth. Epekneia and Gemenon had been so captivated by the troll's swallowing of the Jackboot, they had no idea what he had done. When he stood to his feet and strolled out in front of them, they were astounded, but much to his surprise, the berries didn't seem work this time. Although they did help with the pain, he felt no connection to Izzy or his father and no healing or strengthening in his bones. He felt alone, terrified and angry. Very angry! His entire back throbbed in terrible agony, and he felt as if he was going to explode into flames as red smoke rolled out of his nose and mouth. Epekneia reached out and took him by the arm to stop him and instantly burned her claw, but Elias didn't look back as he continued out toward the center of the arena.

In the distance, Elias looked like a red beacon screaming "HELLO" at the center of the arena, and the three First-Gen trolls quickly caught sight of him. They took out after him with such joy, they didn't notice that Brynjar was waking from the powerful blow he had suffered, and he reached out and tripped the first one that passed by him. The First-Gen trolls tumbled over one another, and the crowd doubled over with gut-busting laughter again as the bulky beasts fell into a twisted pile. By the time they got back to their feet and started out for him again, Elias had spotted his father's faulty boot shining on the ground behind them, and he reached out for it. Brynjar quickly dropped back to the ground as the boot passed over him, and suddenly the crowd began to shout, "BOOT BOY! BOOT BOY! BOOT BOY!"

Elias swung the boot back toward the one Agmar had bitten

the fingers off of and struck it hard on one of its knees. A loud crack echoed through the arena, then the troll groaned and grabbed its knee as it fell to the ground. The one the Jackboot had stabbed in the belly was moving slowly and still holding its wound when Elias struck the beast in the back of the head and knocked it face first into the dirt. Then he turned his attention to the one that had swallowed his father. Elias brought the boot right into the troll's rump with a swift blow and knocked it to its hands and knees. The beast began sobbing, as if he'd wounded its pride more than he injured its bottom, and the crowd roared with glee at his disciplinary punishment on the creature. The beast began rubbing its bottom to sooth the injury when it suddenly stopped and grabbed its enormous belly then fell over on its back, writhing in pain. He groaned so loudly that even his injured troll brothers crawled over to check on him.

Suddenly, over by the northeast gate, the Jackboot's sword began to vibrate on the ground, then it shot across the dirt floor of the arena, drawing a line of dust until it hit one of the trolls in the foot. The sword popped up into the air and flipped end over end all over the place, as if it had no sense of direction, then, in the blink of an eye, it felt back to the ground, motionless. The First-Gen troll let out a fierce, nasty belch that seemed to make it feel better for a moment, so it sat up. The troll looked around, rubbed its tummy and smiled, then out of the blue it let out another belch, and then another, until it began to groan in pain again.

The Jackboot's sword quickly bounced back up in the air and shot straight at the troll, disappearing into it the troll's gelatinous gut. The beast leapt to its feet and began hopping up and down, screaming in pain so much that it terrified the other two First-Gen trolls, and they fled from their brother in fear until the beast stopped. It stood motionless, gazing up at the airship lights speckling like stars through the glass above the arena. The troll began to sway as a tree would before it falls to the ground; subtle at first, but then it went back too far and collapsed on its back – *dead*.

For a moment, the troll's belly shook, then, without warning, the Jackboot's sword ripped through the belly of the beast, and Elias' father climbed out on top of the creature. The crowd was silent for a moment in utter shock then let out cries of adulation and praise for the Jackboot and his son. But Mogdal seemed extremely unhappy with the loss of nearly all of his First-Gen trolls. Mogdal grabbed his horn and let loose a long, angry blast over the arena. Moments later, labyrinth guards began handing spears to everyone in the crowd. The Jackboot climbed down from the troll and hobbled his way over to Elias, who by now was completely exhausted, and his face was so red he looked like he was about to explode. "What's happening to you, son?" he asked.

Elias' breathing was labored, but he was still able to stand as he spoke. "I-I don't know. I feel like there's a fire inside of me, and it's trying to get out. I don't know how much longer I can take this. I don't know what's happening to me." Epekneia and Gemenon dropped down next to him, cautiously in hopes of helping him, somehow.

Hex, Grundorph and Angus approached, and Angus asked, "Do you see this? No one's going to survive this. We can't hide from thousands of spears."

"They can't reach us if we stay in the center of the arena." Grundorph explained as he looked out over the crowd.

The Jackboot pointed at the gate with his sword and said, "Hex was right, this is an extermination." He'd barely finished his words when the Standing Heroes rushed toward their group at the center of the battlefield. The Jackboot's group readied themselves for a terrible attack from some of the best warriors the labyrinth had ever produced, but no attack came. The game had changed, and it had become clear to every Standing Hero in the arena that the Jackboot was no ordinary man, and this was no ordinary battle. The Standing Heroes dropped to one knee in homage to the Jackboot as Krom, Agmar and Gonon began to work the crowd into a bone-chilling frenzy.

AIRSHIP LIGHTS BLURRED THROUGH THE GLASS DOME ABOVE THE Arena of Heroes like distorted yellow eyes as waves of pain crawled across Elias' back. Kneeling on his hands and knees, he clinched his fists tight from the pain, while the muffled sounds of Krom whipping the crowded arena into chaos echoed all around him. He tried to focus on Epekneia's comforting voice to help guide him through the pain, but it was too faint from the ringing in his ears. Everyone had encircled him to protect him from the coming attack, although nothing could protect him from the fire that was burning inside his body, and his thoughts returned to that night in the Valley of Bones.

He grabbed his chest where his heart-mod had been installed as he remembered the fire escaping from his heart when it exploded on the culling floor, but this was different. This time, the painful heat was radiating from his back, not his heart. He looked at Epekneia and tried to explain to her what he thought was happening, but the sound from the crowd was deafening, and she couldn't hear him over their cries of bloodlust.

The spectators raised their spears in unison with Krom, Agmar and Gonon as the Legendary Heroes lifted their arms up and down to encourage their adulation until suddenly, they stopped. The crowd brought the spears to their sides with the points toward the ceiling and began pounding the ends of them on the floor in a perfect drum beat together.

"What's happening? Why are they doing that?" the Jackboot asked as he sensed something was coming.

They looked around for a moment until Hex spotted the empty throne in the stands. "Where's Mogdal?"

The sound of heavy footsteps filled their ears, and Angus pointed to the open gate under Mogdal's throne. A giant, shadowy figured stepped into view, and Angus' face turned pale. "I'm afraid we're all in for a terrible beating."

"*Mogdal!*" Grundorph exclaimed in astonishment. "But... why? Why would he fight in the arena?"

"Because he can, Grundy. Because he can," the Jackboot replied with a snarled look on his face.

"We're all going to die, aren't we?" one of the Standing Heroes added, but no one wanted to respond to his assessment except Hex, who lifted his head and let out a terrible, screeching cry. Epekneia and Gemenon looked at each other and nodded in agreement to the giant Petinon's call about the same time the crowd erupted with wondrous joy at their leader's entrance into the games.

Mogdal stepped into the light of the arena wearing fierce armor made from troll bones, and in his right hand, he dragged behind him a large war hammer carved from the trunk of a tree. Mangled iron spikes jutted out of each end of the hammer, and his fingers gripped its blood-stained grip hard enough to leave an imprint on it. A double-horned helmet made of black iron covered most of his face, and his skin looked like fleshy bark with coarse hair growing out of it. In his left hand he held his curved horn, which he raised into the air above his head several times to ready the crowd for his command. They shouted back at him until he placed his horn to his mouth and let out a long, powerful blast. When Mogdal's sounding command ended, the crowd let loose their spears into the arena with all their might, and the airship lights above them disappeared as the cloud of death covered the sky.

Suddenly, Hex took hold of Elias and Jackboot in his massive claws. "WHAT ARE YOU DOING?" the Jackboot yelled out.

"You are Prince Ouranos, I swear on my life that I will not let you or your son perish." Then Hex shot up through the middle of the spears toward the dome. Epekneia and Gemenon followed quickly behind them as the spears fell upon their companions in the center of the ring. The last thing Elias saw was Angus Grand grabbing one of the Standing Heroes and snapping his neck. The heartless killer lifted the dead hero over his head like a shield as the spears fell upon them all.

Once the spears landed, everything was silent for a moment, and the crowd waited to see the outcome of their attack. Fortunately for Grundorph and Brynjar, the arena spectators were a terrible aim and not strong enough to wield the weapons effectively. Most of the spears missed their targets, and those that did hit had lost a great deal of the force needed to successfully penetrate the center of the arena. However, five Standing Heroes lay dead, and Grundorph and Brynjar had taken a few hits of their own. Brynjar had four spears in his back, which Grundorph removed along with the three in his own left arm. The spears were small compared to their massive troll bodies, but wounds were still wounds, and Grundorph's brothers seemed happy to have weakened their brother and the wolf-beast. Angus, on the other hand, cheerfully crawled out from under the dead hero he'd used to protect himself. The half-breed dusted himself off and stood up with a smile as if he'd used that tactic several times before in other arena games.

Krom and Mogdal seemed extremely displeased with the outcome of the crowd's participation and decided to give them a demonstration on spear throwing. They both grabbed spears lying on the ground and flung them at the Petinon's soaring overhead. Two spears struck Hex directly in the back, and he let out a terrible cry as he fell back toward the ground. Elias and his father both slipped from Hex's grasp and flipped wilding through the air, but Epekneia was close enough to catch Elias. Gemenon dove for the Jackboot and was able to slow the descent, but the Jackboot was too heavy, and they hit hard and tumbled across the arena.

Grundorph let out a bellowing groan of anguish as he saw his good friend hit floor of the arena, and he shoved his way past the wall of Standing Heroes then ran over to where Hex had landed. Both spears had punctured all the way through his friend's chest, and from the sound of Grundorph's heart-wrenching moan, it was clear to everyone that Hexpteroox was dead. Grundorph pulled both spears from his friend's body and charged at his brothers. At first Agmar and Gonon laughed at their brother as he rushed them, but their amusement quickly died off as he drew closer. Chaotic fury was in his eyes and vengeance was in his hands. He flung both spears at his brothers, but they easily deflected them. So, he tried for a more direct approach and hit Gonon with a bare fist, knocking him to the ground, then he grabbed Agmar by the curved horns around his chest and threw him at Gonon, sending them both tumbling. He went for Krom next, but he his anger was no match for Krom's strength. Krom grabbed him and began beating Grundorph with the spikes on his arms.

"I'LL CAVE YOU SKULL IN AGAIN, BROTHER!" Krom laughed as he beat Grundorph.

The Standing Heroes saw this as a good opportunity to strike at Gonon and Agmar, and they rushed at them while they were still recovering from Grundorph's attack. Brynjar and Angus squared off against Mogdal while Gemenon and the Jackboot ran over to check on Hex about the time Epekneia and Elias landed next to his body.

"WHY?" Gemenon cried out at the crowd. "HE NEVER HURT ANYONE! HE DIDN'T DESERVE TO DIE LIKE THIS!"

The Jackboot gripped his sword tight in anger. "I'll make them pay for this, I promise," he said to Gemenon. Then he turned around and headed for Mogdal. The crowd roared with laughter and shouted for more blood as the Legends battled each other to the death, but everyone's attention was quickly captivated by a bright flash and a loud thudding explosion outside the glass dome. An airship had exploded overhead. The crowd thought maybe Mogdal had done this for greater theatrics, and they cheered as another one next to it exploded. As the fire and sparks rained down on top of the glass dome, the jubilation of the crowd quickly died out.

Everyone turned toward Mogdal to see if this was part of his glorious plan, but from the surprised look on his face, it was clearly not his doing. Moments later, a long shadow stretched out over the dome, and the loud blaring of a train's horn ripped through the sky. The Jackboot's mouth dropped open as the Iron Weaver smashed through the glass dome at the top of the arena. Glass came crashing down on the spectators, and the arena battle instantly came to a stop. Krom halted his beating of Grundorph, and Mogdal, who was in the process of crushing Angus' windpipe as he held off Brynjar, stopped in dumbstruck awe at the destruction of his beautiful glass dome.

28

BITTER REVENGE

*T*he Iron Weaver circled above the stands while Hans' airships entered through the opening. Within moments, hundreds of heavily armed tunnel rats began sliding down ropes and landing on the floor of the arena. The rats quickly encircled the side walls and some pointed their weapons at the crowd while others pointed their guns toward the Legends and Heroes. Another ship landed directly on the arena floor by the northeast gate, and a burly tunnel rat stepped out and kicked the side door open, then he smacked his claw on the side of the door several times. A few seconds later, giant Bryn-wolves began filling the arena and instantly surrounded everyone on the ground. Frozen shock took hold of the warriors as they watched tunnel rats and Bryn-wolves quickly take control of the Arena of Heroes. Even the two remaining First-Gen trolls cowered by the northeast gate as if they were begging Mogdal to open it so they could flee back to their cell.

The Puppet Master had conquered the Arena of Heroes so fast that Mogdal looked baffled and speechless from it all. It seemed he didn't know whether to fight or stand in shocked amazement at what he was witnessing, but the Jackboot knew who their conqueror was right away. Though he had not seen the modified Iron Weaver, the Jackboot was wise enough to know that only the Puppet Master could forge such a marvelous flying machine. Hans stepped out on the rear deck of the train car and took measure of his swift and successful attack. As he spoke, a loudspeaker on the front of the Iron Weaver projected his voice throughout the arena with a god-like echo that seemed to chill the people to their bones. "I want to make this perfectly clear. I am not here for war, and I do not wish to turn this into a blood bath. The outcome here will be entirely up to you."

"THEN WHY ARE YOU HERE, OLD FRIEND?" the Jackboot scoffed.

"I'm here for Angus Grand, or Mr. Black, as he calls himself down in the labyrinth."

Mogdal was still holding Angus by the throat when Angus responded to Hans facetiously. "Figures. Everyone wants a piece of me these days, don't they?" Mogdal tightened his grip on Angus' throat a little more.

The Jackboot grinned and shook his head. "Yeah... yeah, that makes sense," he said as he finally remembered Hans' betrayal. "ALL THIS FOR REVENGE? WHY DIDN'T YOU JUST ASK ME FOR HELP? I WOULD HAVE GLADLY HELPED YOU TRACK ANGUS DOWN AND KILL HIM."

"It's deeper than that – *Jackboot*," Hans said mockingly. "Your wife has given me something neither you nor I could ever accomplish. She's given Emilia a chance at life."

The Jackboot quickly looked over at Gemenon while he corrected Hans' statement as if he wanted to make sure she knew he was very much available. "EX-WIFE, HANS! EX-WIFE! AND YOU SHOULD NEVER TRUST A WITCH! SHE'LL MAKE YOU REGRET IT."

"I don't have time for you, Owen. Like I said, I'm here for Angus Grand." Hans turned and directed his words toward Mogdal. "All I want is the half-breed. If you hand him over to me, I will leave and take my army with me, but if you don't, I'll destroy everything here and leave your city in ruins."

"There's plenty of me to go around. No reason to... uh... fight over me," Angus gagged out and some in the crowd next to him let out a laugh.

It was at that moment the Puppet Master realized how wondrous it would be to burn Angus Grand in front of the entire stadium, and he was filled with joy at the prospect of it. "Give him to me now and I'll burn him alive, right here in the arena, for everyone's enjoyment."

Mogdal took measure of the situation for a moment, then looked back at Angus, whom he was currently choking. "Well... I'm busy beating on Angus at the moment, so how about you check back with me tomorrow and I'll let you have what's left," he said, his laughter mocking the Puppet Master.

In anger, the Puppet Master raised his cane in the air, and the sound of a thousand guns ratcheting a round into the chamber echoed through the arena. "I AM IN CONTROL OF THIS SITUATION, NOT YOU!"

"We'll see about that," Mogdal muttered under his breath, then with a wicked smile, he released his grip on Angus' throat. Angus slumped to the ground, and twelve large tunnel rats quickly surrounded him. Mogdal subtly strolled over toward something on the arena floor, reached down and picked it up. When he turned around, his battle horn was in his hand, and he let out three long blasts from it. Hans' tunnel rats and Bryn-wolves quickly looked up at him as if they were waiting on a command, but the Puppet Master had momentarily stepped inside the train to retrieve something. Hans burst back out the door at the sounding of Mogdal's horn only to see every gate in the arena opening. Mogdal had released the terror of the labyrinth upon him, and every grotesque, genetically altered beast was now on its way into the arena circle. Howling moans and shrieking cries filled the tunnels as the monsters rushed toward the open gates. The Puppet Master quickly redirected some of his forces toward the openings in an effort to hold off the coming attack long enough to get Angus Grand, but within moments the freakish beasts exploded through the tunnel openings. Madness and chaos took hold of the arena, and many in the stands began to flee as tunnel rats opened fire on everything that came out from the tunnels. The rats gave no measure of mercy, even to the spectators in the stands as their bullets zipped, popped, zinged and splattered in every direction with raw abandon.

Giant boars with frightening tusks, wild Bryn-wolves with oversized heads, deformed trolls and genetically altered men with six arms, two heads and no mercy in their eyes; all mindless beasts without an understanding of rules or morality, hungry creatures that were never meant to be freed from their cells, and they encircled the massive arena like a pack of wild dogs. The Puppet Master's forces backed away from the arena walls as the creatures ran the edges and forced them into the center with the Legends. Wild boars squealed as they skewered the Puppet Master's tunnel rats and flung them in every direction, some into the stands and others back toward the center of the arena. Bullets flew in every direction as tunnel rats went flying through the air with their fingers still holding down the triggers on their guns after the boars had launched their bodies into the air.

Hans was filled with fury at Mogdal's act of defiance and decided he would change battle tactics by forcing his Bryn-wolves into sacrificial mode. At the click of a button on his dragon's head cane, the Puppet Master's wolves were set free with abandon. They charged wild boars head on, and some were impaled instantly on their tusks, but others attacked with heroic fearlessness and ripped the boars apart. In a matter of minutes, the dirt floor of the arena became saturated in the spilled blood of battle. Hans could see his rats still had Angus in their possession but were having great difficulty getting their prisoner through the messy slaughter taking place around them. What made matters worse was the look on Angus Grand's face. The half-breed monster seemed to be enjoying the chaos as the tunnel rats blasted everything that came at him just to keep him alive long enough for their master to satisfy his own measure of revenge.

The Puppet Master watched his rats maneuver his prisoner through the onslaught from high above the battle in the safety of the Iron Weaver, and with every second he grew desperately concerned they would never make it back to the train. Four of the twelve rats he'd sent to retrieve Angus had already been picked off by wild Bryn-wolves, so he moved his own mod-controlled Bryn-wolves in a circle around them. However, his tunnel rats and Bryn-wolf forces were quickly being swallowed up in the horror below him, and he felt his chances to savor a sweet revenge on Angus were slipping through his grasp. To make matters worse, Mogdal's two remaining First-Gen trolls had climbed a mass of corpses and were now in the arena stands throwing anyone and everything at the Iron Weaver in an attempt to bring it down. For some reason, the dumb beasts were annoyed by the train hovering over them, and though Hans had directed several rats to fire upon the brutes, their lead rounds did more to anger the monsters than it did to curb their attacks.

His anger burned hotter with every impact of the First-Gen trolls' projectiles pounding against the Iron Weaver, so he hit the beasts with several blasts of lightning from his top hat. The trolls seemed unfazed by the powerful shocks on their meaty hides and roared back at the train like disobedient children when they didn't get their way. What's more, even if his rats were successful at getting Angus back to the Iron Weaver, the glory of burning Angus alive in front of everyone was now gone as many of the spectators were fleeing the arena. Those that were trapped at the crowed exits were currently being slaughtered by some of the monsters that had hopped into the stands. The entire arena was a cluster of madness as multiple battles raged in every corner and crevice with a deafening roar of chaos. When he spotted the First-Gen trolls ripping apart his Bryn-wolves and tunnel rats, he began to feel the sweetness of his revenge taking a bitter turn, and he decided it was time to deal with things on a more personal level. Hans stepped back inside the Iron Weaver and grabbed the syringe Cassandra had given him as well as two large pistols loaded with special fire berry rounds then stepped back out on the deck. Locking his feet onto a flat, circular hover platform, he flicked a switch on his belt, igniting tiny thrusters that lifted him into the air over the arena, and he went straight for the First-Gen trolls.

The Puppet Master's hover platform sent black smoke billowing over top the arena as he rushed toward the stands where one of the First-Gen trolls had just picked up a Bryn-wolf. Suddenly, a six-armed man stepped out in front of his hover craft and launched six spears directly at him. He weaved his way around the soaring spears then fired both pistols directly at the freakish man, and the man evaporated at the center, sending his six arms flinging wildly through the air in every direction. By the time he reached the First-Gen troll, it had already torn his Bryn-wolf in half and was still holding both pieces. The troll was holding one part of the severed wolf in its left hand and the other part in its right hand and seemed confused as to which part to start nibbling on first. Hans reloaded his fire berry pistols and helped the beast decide by blowing its right arm completely off. The troll barely flinched at the loss of its arm and looked down at the severed limb in stupefied wonder as to why its arm was now lying motionless on the arena stands. The Puppet Master was aghast by the beast's unusual tolerance of pain and figured it would be best to put the monster down immediately, so he fired his other pistol at its chest but missed when it bent down to pick up its lost arm. Hans began reloading his pistols until the troll suddenly swung the severed arm at him. He flipped end over end but managed to keep his feet firmly attached to the hover platform and finally regained control just in time to see the beast leap from the stands toward him.

The First-Gen troll tried to grab him as it soared through the air but missed and plunged toward the airship his tunnel rats had left parked on the ground. The giant troll collapsed the ship's envelop and fell all the way into the main fuel hold. The ship exploded with such force it scattered troll parts in every direction and the beast was completely obliterated by blast. Unfortunately, the massive explosion also took out every one of his Bryn-wolf and tunnel rat guards surrounding Angus Grand, and for a moment he lost sight of his prisoner. Hans shot through the smoke and flames of the blast and scanned the battlefield until he spotted the half-breed over by the eastern gate, and he took measure of what he saw.

Angus Grand was on fire from the airship blast, and just as Cassandra had warned, he was unfazed by the flames. The half-breed dove into the blood-covered ground and put out the fire covering his body then stood to his feet, covered in the grimy blood from the arena battle, and went about slaughtering anything that stood in his way. At that moment, Hans decided he would simply shoot Angus with his guns and blow the half-breed troll to pieces. So, he went straight for the monster as his hatred rushed through his blood like fuel for vengeance. *This is for you, Emilia, for you, James and Victor! This night, that cruel monster will pay for what he did to us. Angus Grand will pay for the lives he ruined. He might not burn but he will DIE! HE WILL DIE!*

He approached Angus from behind with great speed and fired both barrels at the half-breed's shoulder blades. Just then an enormous explosion rocked the arena, and for a moment Hans was unable to see what happened to Angus. *Gone?* he wondered to himself, looking down at his pistols. *Evaporated into nothingness?* A glorious euphoria washed over him as he felt the culmination of his hatred fade away into a cloud of red fire berry smoke in front of him. Yet, as the battle raged around him, a subtle feeling of emptiness crept up inside him, and he wondered what purpose his life would have now.

A FINE CLOUD OF DIRTY, RED MIST ROSE ABOUT THIRTY FEET OVER the Arena of Heroes as the battlefield reached an absurd level of gore. Krom, Agmar and Gonon had lost sight of Grundorph in the fog of battle and had become so over whelmed by the onslaught that they could barely keep their heads above the fray. The Arena of Heroes had become so cluttered with dead trolls, tunnel rats, Bryn-wolves and other beasts that no one could move more than a few feet in any direction. No one, that is, except for Grundorph, who brutally made his way over toward the Jackboot by flogging everything in his path with the chain attached to his leg. He cleared tunnel rats, Bryn-wolves, wild beasts and strange men with massive swipes in front of him, and the Jackboot could hear his raging fury as he drew closer and closer to their location.

The Jackboot struck down everything that came at them while Epekneia tried to reason with Gemenon about the body of Hex. Gemenon didn't want to leave him to be devoured by the wolves, but they needed to get Elias out of the arena as soon as possible. When Grundorph finally made it over to them, he cleared a massive circle around them with several swipes from his chain, then he picked up the body of his friend to carry him out.

"YOU'LL NEVER MAKE IT WITH HIM!" the Jackboot warned.

"WE CAN'T JUST LEAVE HIM HERE. HE DESERVES BETTER!" Gemenon pleaded.

"IN CASE YOU HAVEN'T NOTICED, THE GIANT TROLL CAN'T FLY. THEY'LL EAT HIM ALIVE BEFORE HE EVER MAKES IT TO THE TUNNELS!" The Jackboot struck down a wolf that was lunging at her, then Grundorph finished the beast by crushing its head into the bloody grime of the arena floor.

Epekneia reached out and yelled at him, "WE NEED TO GET ELIAS OUT OF HERE! LOOK AT HIM! HE NEEDS HELP, PLEASE! WE CAN'T WAIT ANY LONGER!" She pointed toward the opening in the glass dome. Her eyes were filled with tears, and she moved aside so the Jackboot could see his boy. Elias' eyes were solid black as if there was no life left in him, and steam was rising from his body. He was lying in the muck of slaughtered wolves the Jackboot had slain, but he was no longer moving.

The Jackboot's heart sank in his chest. In the heat of battle, he'd forgotten what was happening to his son. "TAKE HIM NOW, EPEKNEIA! GET HIM OUT OF HERE! GO! GO NOW!" he cried out. Epekneia turned and reached for Elias, but before she realized what was happening, the giant, red Bryn-wolf grabbed Elias in its mouth and disappeared into the crowded warzone. She screamed for the Jackboot, but he couldn't hear her. In shock from the loss of his son, he collapsed to the bloody arena floor. Gemenon grabbed the sword from his hand and took a defensive position around them, while Epekneia shot up into the air as fast as she could in hopes of spotting the red Bryn-wolf that had carried Elias away.

Grundorph was stunned motionless, and before he knew it two Bryn-wolves snatched the body of Hex from his back and fled. When Grundorph turned around and saw that Hex was gone, he instantly lost control of his fury, and madness took hold of him. He rushed out into the battle with his chain swinging in all directions until it was so drenched in the blood of beasts that it slipped from his hand. After which, he proceeded to pummel everything he could with his bare fists, crushing Bryn-wolves' heads into the ground and ripping tusks from wild boar's snouts. The crazed troll moaned and wailed for the loss of his friend's body, and he punished everything in sight for it. He ripped the snout of a twelve-tusked boar completely off then proceeded to wield it as a weapon, striking down anything that came within the reach of his deadly circle. His battle cries caught the attention of his cruel brothers, and by the looks in their eyes, they'd clearly lost the fortitude to toy with their little brother at this point.

AS THE PUPPET MASTER HOVERED ABOVE THE BATTLEFIELD, HE seemed bored by the events taking place around him and was about to head back to the Iron Weaver until something caught his gaze. About 100 yards out from where he'd shot Angus, something was moving beneath the red smoke. "ALIVE? IMPOSSIBLE!" He quickly reached his hand inside his long coat and took out the syringe Cassandra had given him, then in one swift move; the Puppet Master swooped down on Angus and jammed a needle into his neck. Hans emptied every drop into him, but Angus instinctively thought some tunnel rat had tried to claw him and swung around and hit the Puppet Master with all his might, sending him flying backward into the raging battle.

The Puppet Master's hover platform flipped madly around the arena, landing somewhere out of sight, but when Angus realized who he'd hit, he was surprised and rushed over to Hans, who was about to be gored by a giant boar. Angus grabbed the beast by the tail and pulled back on it. The boar turned on him, and he smashed its snout with his fist. The boar

squealed and lunged at him, causing him to slip on the bloody
ground, and the beast went right over top of him. As he lay
under the boar's stomach, he felt one of the stray spears from
the crowd lying next to him. He pulled it from the bloody muck
and jammed it into the beast's belly. It let out a terrible squeal
then fell over sideways, wriggled for a moment, then died.
Angus got to his feet and towered over the Puppet Master as he
lay speechless in the slaughter.

"WHY?" Hans asked, but Angus' attention was quickly
drawn away toward three wild Bryn-wolves that surrounded
them.

"These don't look like yours," Angus said, as he beat back
their snarling attacks.

"STOP! STOP THIS NOW! WHY ARE YOU DOING
THIS?" Hans cried out furiously at him as he beat back the
wolves, but Angus ignored his enemy and continued his work.
He crushed one wolf's snout, shattered its teeth to the ground
then picked up the sharp, boney teeth and struck another in the
eye. The last one he clobbered with a right hook so hard the
beast instantly fell over dead, then he turned back to Hans and
held out his hand.

Hans' protective glass was cracked, and he was covered in
the mess of the bloody grime of the battlefield. His dangerous
top hat was gone, and his modified skull was a horrible sight to
behold, at least from Angus' perspective. "I sure did a number
on you, didn't I, Puppet Master?" Angus said, still holding out
his hand.

"WHY ARE YOU DOING THIS? LEAVE ME BE!" Hans
demanded.

"If I leave you here, you'll be killed in no time."

"I'd rather die than be saved by you."

"Well, I can't have that now, can I? I might not figure out
what that nasty concoction was that you stuck in my neck.
Besides, who said anything about *saving you*?" Angus laughed as

he grabbed the Puppet Master, slung him over his shoulder and began carrying him through the battle. But when Mogdal spotted them, he began clearing a path toward them with his giant war hammer. Nothing stood in his way as he swung it to the left and the right in front of him, annihilating everything in his path.

ELIAS AWOKE FACE DOWN INSIDE THE ENTRANCE OF THE northeast tunnel with something large breathing down the back of his neck. Though his body was racked with pain, he mustered the strength to check what was behind him, only to see a giant, red Bryn-wolf sniffing his body. Its mouth was covered in blood from the battle, and its breath reeked of rotten tunnel creatures. The wolf's eyes were a deep, shiny green and seemed void of life as it sniffed at him. Elias ached so terribly from the burning inside him that he figured it might be for the best if the wolf just finished him off, and so he goaded the beast in an effort to end the horrible pain radiating from his back.

"Go ahead! Do it! Get it over with," he moaned.

The wolf sniffed his body several times as if it was looking for something, almost as if was trying to sniff something out of him. Then the wolf lowered its snout all the way down toward his face and let out a deep, low growl.

"WHAT ARE YOU WAITING FOR? GET ON WITH IT!" Elias yelled with all his strength. Red, misty smoke rushed out his mouth at the wolf, who snapped at him and pulled back in fear, but when Elias collapsed back to the ground, the wolf regained its courage and came back. The red wolf crouched low as it approached him and nudged his body with its snout. When he didn't move, it let out a snarled howl then planted its paw directly on Elias' back and ripped at it. His leather jacket tore as the beast's claws sliced his back open, and a blast of heat suddenly escaped from the two claw wounds the wolf opened up. Suddenly, a massive burst of fire erupted into two wings, and the red Bryn-wolf lurched back against the tunnel wall. It let out a yelp as the flames hit it on the end of the nose.

Elias stood to his feet in shock, and his body quickly began to recover now that the heat was able to escape through the wounds. He took several deep breaths, and in amazement he admired the wings, then he looked back at the Bryn-wolf with a sneaky grin. At first, he wanted to kill the beast, but when the beast lowered its head in a cowering posture, he noticed something shiny on the back of its neck. He approached the wolf slowly as it snapped and growled at him, but he snapped back at it with a fierce yell that caused his wings to grow larger and brighter. He hemmed the wolf in on the left and the right with his wings so it couldn't run, and then he ran right up its snout and onto its back. *A BRAIN-MOD!* Elias smashed the mod with his boot, and it let out a loud pop and electrical crackling sound. Finished, he hopped off the back of the wolf.

He watched as the bright green hue of the wolf's eyes slowly faded away into two solid black pearls gazing back at him. He'd freed the wolf from the Puppet Master's grip, and the call of battle from the arena quickly stirred the creature's blood. The red Bryn-wolf rushed out of the tunnel and jumped on top of a pile of dead tunnel beasts. For a moment, the wolf gazed out over the chaos that gripped the battlefield, then it raised its head and let out a powerful, howling cry that stopped the wild Bryn-wolves in their tracks. Another howling cry from across the arena caught the wolf's attention, and it quickly answered with another bone-chilling howl that was answered by all the wild Bryn-wolves in the arena.

The red wolf ended its call to war with a powerful leap back onto the battlefield, and Elias rushed to the opening of the tunnel to see what the wolf was up to. He spotted the wolf biting the necks of the Puppet Master's Bryn-wolves. At first, he thought it was attacking the wolves, but he quickly realized it was smashing the brain-mods on the backs of their heads. The red Bryn-wolf's actions were surprising to him until he spotted Brynjar standing on the edge of the arena wall, sending out commands to the red wolf.

I'm sure glad I didn't kill that guy!

As Elias caught sight of the battlefield, he was appalled by the devastation. He'd been so overwhelmed by the pain in his back, that he'd lost sight of how the battle was transpiring. When he looked out over the Arena of Heroes, the shock of it all felt like a punch directly to his heart. The arena was filled with mayhem, gore and death on all sides, and dead tunnel rats were strewn everywhere as well as Bryn-wolves, wild boars and tunnel creatures of all sorts. At first, Elias didn't know what to do or where to engage until he spotted Epekneia in the air. She was watching the red Bryn-wolf with fury in her eyes, then she quickly dove down to where Gemenon was fighting and stole King Arkone's sword from her hand. She rose back into the air and instantly disappeared down into battle.

Though he'd never flown with wings of his own, his heart knew what to do, and so he leapt into the air and spread his flaming wings as if he'd always belonged to the sky. Like a burning rocket shot into the air, Elias rose above the battle with daring fearlessness. His presence caught the gaze of almost everyone on the northeast end of the arena, and for a moment the battle-weary creatures seemed frozen by the fire in the sky. Elias spotted Gemenon grabbing his distraught father by the arm and pointing up toward him, and his father quickly leapt to his feet.

The Jackboot seemed instantly revived by the sight of Elias with flaming wings, and he raised his fist in the air and began to laugh victoriously. Suddenly, an odd metal disc shot over top of the Jackboot's head and into the ground behind Gemenon. The Jackboot ran around behind her and began digging in the muck of dead tunnel rats until he emerged with the Puppet Master's hover platform in his hands. He grinned and locked his boots down to it then fired up the thrusters. Within moments, Gemenon and the Jackboot met Elias in the air.

"SON! YOU'RE ALIVE!" the Jackboot said with a gleam of joy in his eye. Gemenon was speechless as she watched the flames from his wings lick the air around him.

"Where's Epekneia?" Elias asked.

"S-She was... I think she was going after the red Bryn-wolf. I think she's going to kill it," Gemenon stuttered out.

"We have to stop her! The red wolf is on our side," Elias said. They quickly scanned the battlefield until the Jackboot caught sight of her.

"THERE SHE IS!" he yelled, pointing over toward by east gate.

By the time they reached her, Epekneia was midflight over the red Bryn-wolf and looking for a chance opportunity to strike at the beast when Elias called out her name. "EPEKNEIA, NO!" She nearly dropped the sword down into the raging battle as she turned around. "ELIAS?" she asked in shock, unsure if it was truly him.

He smiled at her. "Yes, it's me." His face no longer looked pale like death, and his eyes were a deep red, with misty flames rolling out of them, but she seemed much more captivated by the flaming wings rolling out of his back and could hardly take her eyes off them.

"But... the red Bryn-wolf. I-I thought you were..."

"Dead? No. I'm not dead. AND LOOK!" Elias pointed down at the red wolf as it attacked the brain-mods on the Puppet Master's wolves. "See how the wild Bryn-wolves are following the pack leader?" Then he pointed at Brynjar. "The red wolf and Brynjar are working together. Come on! Let's help them smash the brain-mods and free the wolves." Elias quickly dove down into the raging torrent of blood and gore while Epekneia tossed the sword back to the Jackboot. Then they quickly followed after Elias.

At first, Epekneia struggled to reach the mods on the back of the Bryn-wolves' necks, but when she spotted Gemenon hopping on the back of their necks and crushing the mods with her claws, she quickly copied the method. The Jackboot simply swooped down on the hover platform, struck the mods with the sword then swiftly moved on to the next one. Elias preferred a more daring method of collapsing his flaming wings. Shutting off the flames from his back, he would simply drop out of the air onto the backs of their necks, crushing the mechanical brain contraptions with his boots. It certainly wasn't the safest way, but at least it was in keeping with his current moniker of "boot-boy" the labyrinth people had bestowed upon him. It was also the only way to prevent his wings from setting the Bryn-wolves on fire. They went to work as fast as they could, but Elias knew from number of wolves that it was going to be a long night.

ANGUS GRAND BEAT HIS WAY THROUGH THE BATTLEFIELD WITH HIS bare fists, making short work of the foolish beasts that got in his way, all the while carrying the battered Puppet Master over his shoulder. Mogdal was coming. Angus knew if he could make it to the east gate, he might have a chance to escape, but out of the corner of his eye he began to notice tunnel rats closing in around him. He only took a moment to check behind himself, but when he turned his head back, a massive tunnel rat had slid down a rope from the Iron Weaver and landed in front of him. The bristle haired, goggle eyed creature had the number "10k" stamped on its brain-mod, and it was holding a mini-gun in its claws. Rat 10k was half the size of Angus, but the creature held no fear in its eyes, and its demeanor was not very welcoming.

"I'm friendly, see!" Angus said as he carefully slid the Puppet

Master off from his shoulders and onto the ground in front of Rat 10k. Then Angus raised his hands in the air as if to surrender. "Now, hold on... just be careful, now. I was only helping him. See, I could have killed him already, but I just needed to know what that stuff was that he put in my neck."

The Puppet Master got to his feet with the help of Rat 10k, and the rat hooked a cable onto his master's belt then pushed a button on his arm band. As the Puppet Master rose into the air, back toward the Iron Weaver, he gave Angus Grand his answer. "10k – kill him!"

"BUT I SAVED YOU!" Angus yelled out.

"No! You destroyed me and my family, and you deserve to die. If the witch was right, it's going to be a terrible death. My only regret is that I won't be here to witness it," Hans replied.

Rat 10k and several other tunnels rats lined up to follow the orders of their Puppet Master, but in the reflecting glass of Rat 10k's goggles, Angus caught sight of something. Mogdal was there, and his hammer was coming directly at them. Mogdal swung the massive hammer through the crowed battle zone like a tornado wielding a giant tree. He swiped through every creature all the way to where Angus and the rats were standing. The hammer cut half of them down instantly and just slightly nicked Angus on the shoulder, sending him to the ground. Rat 10k had already let loose the fury from his mini-gun by that time, and his rounds splattered Mogdal's armor like angry metal hornets pelting impenetrable iron. The rounds bounced off in every direction and even killed some of the tunnel rats standing next to Rat 10k, then Rat 10k's gun jammed. Mogdal raised his hammer over his head to crush him, but his attention was drawn away by the terrible battle cry coming from the approaching Grundorph.

"MOGDAL! YOU MURDERER! I'LL SPLIT YOUR SKULL WIDE OPEN!" Grundorph yelled as he cleared a path toward the giant troll with his prison chain. Mogdal didn't have enough time to react before the freight train of a troll hit him and sent him flying over top of Angus, who grinned at Mogdal as he watched him soar overhead. The stunned look on Mogdal's face filled Angus with pride for his little brother Grundorph. *Ah, I could have suffered through ten battles like this if I knew I would have seen that look on Mogdal's face just once.*

By the time Mogdal landed, Grundorph was already there and began pummeling the giant troll with his bare fists. Angus looked around for Rat 10k, but he was gone. So, he got back to his feet, dusted himself off and scanned the battlefield. He took a deep breath and savored the moment as he watched Grundorph beat Mogdal's face into the arena floor.

Angus laughed at Mogdal as he stood over them watching Grundorph pummel the troll. "Ahhh... it warms my heart to watch my little brother follow in his father's footsteps. Such craft he learned from Ogg the Murderous, such wonderful craft!" It brought a smile to his face until he heard Krom call out his name. Angus turned around to see Krom, Agmar and Gonon completely covered in the slaughter of the arena and grinning from ear to ear.

"Right about now, I'll bet he's wishing he joined us. Wouldn't you say so, brothers?" Agmar said with a snarled upper lip.

"Come now. It's never too late for brothers to make amends. What do you say we just put it all in the past, for the sake of the old Dad, huh? Or have you forgotten... this is where they found his body. Right here in the area."

"And this is where they'll find yours, brother," Krom replied.

Angus tried to reason with them in hopes Grundorph would soon finish with Mogdal and come to his aid, but his hopes were quickly dashed when Grundorph went flying past him, landing right at the feet of Krom. Krom stepped over top of Grundorph and approached Angus, reaching down, Krom took him by the throat and lifted him high in the air. "Today is the day you die, brother." Then Krom threw Angus to the ground and began to beat him mercilessly. The last thing he could see was Mogdal standing by as Agmar and Gonon went to work on Grundorph.

Hans awoke on the floor of the Jackboot's office, inside the Iron Weaver, and Rat 10k was standing over him. He didn't know how long he'd been out, but he knew the brutal hit from Angus Grand had broken several ribs, and he was struggling to breath. The faithful Rat 10k handed him his top hat but must have been unable to find his cane with the dragon's head control module on it. *It's time for this battle to end. Time to move on.* Rat 10k helped him to his feet, and he snugged his top hat down over the cracked glass dome on his head. He started to walk but fell against the desk. Rat 10k handed a spare cane to him, then Hans hobbled his way out of the office and down the hall.

His rat servant followed close behind his master and listen to his commands carefully. "Come... come with me, we're going to the front... the front of the Iron Weaver and..." He took a moment catch his breath. "... and the lever, we'll pull the lever – 'War Mode.' Have the train crew stand by for guns. We're going to..." He stopped. Something outside the window caught his eye. *Surely not! How could it be?* He opened the window and peered down onto the battlefield but saw nothing. Just as he was about to cast aside his vision as a faulty apparition of pain brought on by the powerful hit from Angus Grand, a bright blast of red flames rose up through the battle and into the air. *THE JACKBOOT'S SON! WINGS OF FIRE!*

Elias was diving down onto the Bryn-wolves and smashing the mods on their heads. The Puppet Master watched as his entire Bryn-wolf army was quickly being handed over to Brynjar the Wolf-Beast, and the mutated troll was sending them directly at his tunnel rat army. When Hans realized that the battlefield was turning against him; he gave in to the darker side of himself. "10k... KILL THEM ALL!"

The rat cocked its head sideways in confused wonder at his master's command; as if to ask in rat speak, "What the cheese did you just say, boss?"

The Puppet Master looked back at Rat 10k and wondered if the beast didn't hear him correctly. "DO I HAVE TO DRAW YOU A PICTURE, YOU STUPID RAT? I SAID THEM! KILL EVERYTHING DOWN THERE! YES, EVERYTHING!"

Rat 10k's snout bounced nervously up and down several times, then he rushed to the front of the Iron Weaver and pulled the war lever. Gatling guns shot out of the sides and the tops of the train and several rats took their places behind the weapons. The Puppet Master yelled out his command, and suddenly the train let loose a hail storm of lead down upon the whole northeast side of the arena. His tunnel rat crew gunned down their own rat brothers as they pinned the Jackboot and his feather friends behind a wall of Bryn-wolf and tunnel rat corpses.

"CUT THROUGH THE BODIES! CUT THROUGH THEM!" Hans cried out to his crew, and they quickly directed all their firepower into the wall of dead beasts. Some of the Puppet Master's tunnel rat soldiers were confused by the Iron Weaver rounds hitting their own brothers and stood there stupefied as their fellow brothers in arms gunned them down in cold blood.

29

CHILDREN OF THE PROPHECY

*H*ot lead rounds burst through the mangled pile of dead beasts as the Jackboot and his son lay crouched down in the bloody muck of the arena floor. It was far worse for Epekneia and Gemenon, whose wings had become so saturated in the slippery grime of the battle slop that they feared they wouldn't be able to fly away if things got any worse. The Puppet Master's guns pounded their makeshift wall of dead things until the bullets soon began to penetrate the wall of bodies.

"We're going to die if we stay here!" Elias yelled at his father.

"Look at our wings! We can't fly out of here!" Gemenon said, grabbing Epekneia's wing and shaking it in Elias' face.

The Jackboot nodded in agreement and after a moment of pondering said, "We only have to hold on long enough for Brynjar to finish what we started. I'll create a diversion. It's the best chance you have to get out of here. And when I do, I want everyone to run into the northeast tunnel. Do you understand?"

"NO! You can't! You... you could be killed!" Gemenon blurted out, and Elias and Epekneia looked at each other with a wonky-eyed gaze. "Well... I mean, you're Ouranos, the Prophecy of our people and..."

"Well, I um... I appreciate your thoughtfulness, Gemenon." The Jackboot smiled. "But we're out of time, and I can't let my boy die. I'll use the hoverboard and head toward the south end of the arena as a diversion. Trust me; he'll point the guns towards me. There's no good outcome for him if I survive this, and he knows it."

"Okay, but... be careful. Y-You're very important... to our people, I mean," Gemenon said, dropping her head and doing her best not to seem overly affectionate toward the Jackboot, but it was quickly becoming clear to Elias and Epekneia that the two were drawn to each other.

Epekneia rolled her eyes at Elias and whispered, "Yeah, right!" Elias tried not to laugh, given the seriousness of the moment, but a tiny snicker slipped out of his nose.

The Jackboot ignored his son's childish mockery and said, "Good! It's a plan then." He locked his boots back down on the hover platform, positioned himself just right then fired it up. He ruffled Elias' hair and gave a nod to Epekneia and Gemenon then shot up above the wall of dead rodents and wolves. He was instantly hit with a round in the left shoulder and then another on his right hand, and multiple rounds ricocheted off his boots as well as the hover platform, knocking him out of the air and back onto the mound of dead beasts.

Elias quickly grabbed him and pulled him back down behind the dead wall and scolded his father. "Fine plan that was, Dad!"

The wounded Jackboot grinned.

"What?" Elias asked with an odd look on his face.

"You called me 'Dad;' I like the sound of that." The Jackboot winced as Gemenon applied pressure to his wounds, but a grave look washed across her face when she noticed a round had hit him in the side. Soon, a sense of dread took hold of them all as more bullets began to zip through their protective wall of dead beasts.

"I don't understand. What happened to Grundorph? That giant metal plate on his head would sure come in handy about now," Elias grumbled.

The Jackboot gave a subtle nod of agreement when, suddenly, Epekneia screeched out a terrible sound of pain and grabbed the top of her left wing. "NO!" Elias cried out and grabbed the wound tight. "We're not going to make it, are we?" he asked his father.

The Jackboot wanted to tell his son that everything would be okay, and that, somehow, they would get out of this, but he just couldn't lie to him. "I-I don't think so, son. I really don't." He'd just finished his crushing situation report when the Puppet Master's guns went completely silent.

"What happened?" Gemenon asked.

"Maybe he ran out of bullets," Epekneia said.

"Ha! Not likely on my train. It's got to be a trick. He's trying to draw us out," the Jackboot warned.

"Maybe not. We have to check. We have to know for sure," Gemenon said, looking down at his wound.

"NO! Don't do it!" he warned, but she didn't listen.

Gemenon crawled up the pile of dead tunnel creatures, then moments later she returned. "It's an airship!"

"A battleship? Ah, Thomas Rand has come to us help out!" the Jackboot said.

"No! Not at all. It's a finely craft airship. A beautiful one. I didn't see any guns on it at all," Gemenon explained.

The Jackboot's head dropped down for a moment. "I don't understand; why isn't Hans firing at it?" he asked.

"I don't know," Gemenon replied. "I'm going back up for another look." She was gone for several minutes then returned with a strange look on her face.

"What? What is it?" the Jackboot asked.

"It's the iron boy. He's hovering next to the train and talking to the dark man or, um…the Puppet Master guy."

"Ah, Jimmy! That's a good sign, I think," the Jackboot said with look of hope in his eye.

"There's something else."

"What?"

"You're not going to believe this, but it's your daughter, Isabella."

"WHAT? Is she okay? What is it? Tell me now!" the Jackboot yelled.

"She's… like him," Gemenon said, pointing to Elias. "She's flying next to the iron boy and… with flaming wings."

Elias and the Jackboot looked at each other in shocked surprise. "Get me up there! Get me up there, now," the Jackboot demanded.

Elias quickly jumped at the chance to see Isabella. "Gemenon, I'll help him. Take care of Epekneia for a minute. If anything happens, head for the tunnel." Gemenon nodded in agreement, then the Jackboot and Elias crawled up the mound of dead beasts and peered out above the battlefield. Just as Gemenon said, Isabella was hovering next to Jimmy with flaming wings, and they seemed to be trying to reason with the Puppet Master. Suddenly, the Puppet Master began yelling at Isabella and ordered his rats to open fire on her. She spun wildly in the air as the guns erupted, and then she exploded into a giant fireball before their eyes.

"NO!!" the Jackboot cried out and stood to his feet on top of the dead beasts. "HANS!" he screamed in anger at the Puppet Master, but he was even more astonished when the fireball stopped spinning, and Isabella unwrapped herself from the protection of her wings.

"What?" Elias said in shock. "How did she do that?"

The Jackboot smiled at his son. "I don't know, but I think this war is about to turn in our favor."

THE PUPPET MASTER SEEMED DISMAYED BY HIS FAILED ATTEMPT on her and turned the guns back down toward Elias and the Jackboot. When he opened fire on them, Isabella spotted them on the mound and shot down toward them. She wrapped her wings around them as she landed and the lead rounds melted into the flames. "It's okay! The rounds can't get through my wings. I learned this when he attacked Pterugas," Isabella said, smiling at them.

"Ah, Isabella. You look magnificent." The Jackboot said with a gleam of pride in his eye.

"Thanks Daddy. I've been worried sick about you. I had a vision. I knew something wasn't right, but I never imagined that Hans would betray you. I'm so glad you're okay."

"HEY! What about me?" Elias blurted out.

Izzy quickly reached up and ruffled the hair on his head. "Of course, I was worried about you. Maybe not as much so cause you're so awesome with your metal moving thing."

"That's not all. Guess what?" Elias asked her.

"What?" Isabella asked with a smile.

Elias grinned and let his wings explode out of his back. He wrapped them around her and their father making them look like a giant ball of fire on top of a dead rat wall. "I got wings too," he said.

"ELIAS! THIS IS AWESOME!" Isabella was overjoyed and ruffled his hair again with her mod-hand.

"It really stinks!" he said, much to her surprise. "I didn't know that was a thing. You know... the fireball thing with the bullets thing. If I'd known that I could have gotten us out of this mess sooner... I guess I'm still new at this."

"Hey, me too. I only learned by accident when the Puppet Master tried to shoot me down during the battle of Pterugas. Merlin and Jimmy came back to warn us of their father. Elias...

the Puppet Master destroyed the whole city—even the mountain and the fire berries. The Petinon people suffered many losses during the battle."

"What?" Elias was devastated by her news. "Why? Why is he doing this?"

"He came for your black heart that we buried with Prince Enupnion... and he got it," Isabella explained.

"Before you arrived, Hans mentioned something about a deal with your mother. Something to do with bringing Emilia back. Maybe he needed Elias' heart to do that. Oh, I almost forgot, Isabella there's something you need to know. There's someone..." The Jackboot was about to explain but he was cut off by Elias.

"HANS NEEDS TO PAY FOR WHAT HE'S DONE! For what he did to the Petinons," Elias said, clinching his fists.

"I don't disagree with you, son, but I'm not prepared to kill someone who's been such a good friend for so many years. Hans saved my life many times on the battlefield, and I his, and I would like to..." The Jackboot's attention was suddenly drawn to something on Izzy's head. "Darlin', why are you wearing a crown?" he asked.

"Uhm... it would be better if I let your mother explain that."

"My mother?"

"Queen Elehos. She's the real queen of the Petinon's. She only crowned me queen to prevent the Convocation of Elders from cutting off my head."

"WHAT!"

"NO! It's okay. It's... it's complicated. Hey, can we get out of this mess first, okay?" Isabella was about to figure out a plan when she noticed her father's wounds. "DADDY! You've been shot. You need fire berries. We have some on the ship. Wait here and I'll..."

"No. Gemenon has some," he explained. "She's just below us, and Epekneia is too," the Jackboot said.

426

Isabella and Elias helped their father back down the mound as the Puppet Master's rounds melted around them. After a short update on their current circumstances, Gemenon gave the fire berries to the Jackboot, and after he'd eaten them, everyone waited for something amazing to happen. Although his body healed quickly, no flaming wings came out of his back, so he decided he would be just as happy battling on the hover platform. Gemenon stayed with Epekneia to nurse her wound while Isabella, Elias and their father readied themselves for battle with a small family pep-talk and a simple plan of attack.

ELEHOS STEPPED OUT ON THE DECK OF THE BRADLEY DUNBAR against the better judgment of Thumacheo. More than anything, she wanted to see her son, Ouranos. Too many lost years and missed moments haunted her thoughts and dreams, and she was determined to see him above all else. Neither the Puppet Master, nor the terrors of this strange place, nor pain of death would stop her now as she stared out over the battlefield. The great gray owl landed next to her on the railing as she watched the Puppet Master's guns blazing away at the pile of dead beasts on the ground. The owl was a comfort to her as she listened to the freakish creatures of the labyrinth roaring, moaning and howling in the distance. Soon, Thumacheo and the others stepped out on the deck to join her, but she was oblivious to their presence while her claws gripped the railing tight, peering hopelessly into the madness of war below them. Thumacheo placed his claw on her shoulder to comfort her, but she instantly jerked away from him.

"Sorry, majesty. I…" Thumacheo quickly shut his mouth and stepped back away from her. She noticed Ava standing next to Gideon, and she was still scribbling away on her notepad, while the glass brained Merlin and the beefy Bogan seemed desperate to join the battle. At the moment, almost everyone's focus was on the iron boy out in front of the flying train, trying desperately to convince his father to stay his madness, but to no avail. She lowered her head and terrible thoughts of loss filled her mind as she waited for some signs of life, but somehow, deep down, she knew they were safe. She could feel it in her bones and hear it. Yes, she could hear it. A faint voice in her mind. She raised her face back up toward the battlefield, and her heart was filled with joy. Before her eyes, the children of the prophecy came exploding up from the battleground below, into the sky with blazing wings and they rushed toward the Puppet Master's train.

Behind them, a strange man on a metal platform rose into the air. A black eye patch covered one eye, and just as Isabella had told her, he wore large iron boots made from the sacred fire. In his hand was the sword of King Arkone. Elehos watched with the pride of a mother as her lost son, Ouranos, sent forth his father's sword at the Puppet Master's guns. The blade struck the barrels on the rats' weapons and instantly destroyed them. Shards of metal exploded into the air, and he miraculously recalled the blade back into to his hands. His children showed the rats no mercy as they set the beasts on fire with their wings and rushed head on into battle with uncommon fearlessness. The rats did their best to shoot them down, but her grandchildren outwitted them at every turn by simply covering themselves with their flaming wings.

Then, Ouranos approached the train with his sword in hand. Her heart nearly stopped when a large rat with a 10k on its head stepped out on the train carrying a strange gun, but the Puppet Master suddenly stopped the beast when Jimmy quickly moved in front of him.

"JAMES! GET OUT OF THE WAY!" the Puppet Master demanded, but the boy refused to move.

"No, Father. I must... 'PROTECT,' they are my friends," Jimmy said.

"DON'T MAKE ME DO THIS, JAMES, PLEASE!" the Puppet Master begged with a sorrowed voice.

"You would cut down your own son just to kill me? What happened to you, friend? Stop this madness. It doesn't have to be this way." Ouranos pleaded with the Puppet Master, but he ignored the Jackboot's efforts for unity.

"James, come with me, son. We'll be a family again. Your mother has returned to us just as I promised she would." He motioned with his hand for the boy to come aboard the ship, but the metal boy refused.

Then Jimmy spoke in a plain, uncalculated tone that visibly stunned the Puppet Master. "That was not my mother. It was thing. A dark thing."

The Puppet Master seemed wounded by Jimmy's words, and he turned to his oldest son, standing on the Bradley Dunbar. "MERLIN! Come with me, son, my wonderful boy. Come, be with your mother and father, and we'll be a family once again." But Merlin simply shook his head in disgust at his father. A devastated countenance fell over the man from the harsh assessment brought on by his sons.

"Hans, look! Your army has been decimated, and Brynjar has seized the battlefield. You've been defeated. You've failed."

"No, you're wrong, *JACKBOOT!* I have completed what I came here to do. My years of suffering and loss have been avenged." The Puppet Master finished his words then flicked a switch on top of his cane and flashes of lightning crackling all around the bottom of the train. Bluish green flames lit up the Arena of Heroes, and with one powerful blast of lightning, the train shot off into the night sky, and the Puppet Master was gone.

Elehos didn't wait for the battle to end to see her son face to face. She leapt from the airship and flared out her wings to join them. At first glance, her son looked terrifying to her. He was covered in blood from the arena battle, and the scars traveling down his neck were exactly as Isabella had described, but she was determined to greet him in the air. When she reached them, she didn't know what to say or how she was going to say it and was greatly pleased that Isabella spoke first.

"Father, I would like to present to you, your mother, Queen Elehos. Well, I guess I'm the queen now, but you get the point. Elias, I present your... I mean 'our' grandmother. Wow! I'm really bad at introductions, aren't I?" Isabella said.

Elehos approached Ouranos carefully until she was close enough to embrace him. She stared at him for a moment and desperately wanted to embrace them all, but suddenly the sound of howling Bryn-wolves rose up from the battlefield. A horrifying troll resembling a Bryn-wolf was motioning with his paw for her son to join him, and behind the monster was an army of Bryn-wolves. So, she took a deep breath and said the only thing she knew to say to the son of a king. "Victory belongs to you this day, my son. Go! Take your place on the battlefield." Her son smiled at her, and her claws began to tremble from the joy inside her heart, but she contained it as he moved closer toward her until they were almost nose to nose. He looked deep into her eyes as if he was investigating her then gave a subtle nod and backed away. Her son and two grandchildren instantly dropped back down to the battlefield next to the beast and spoke for a moment then they marched toward the south end of the arena. They'd spoken to the monster as he were a friend, and it was then that Elehos realized her lost son had bridged that gap between their worlds. But she couldn't help but wonder to herself as she looked out over the arena. *The world of Iron and Smoke is terrifying!*

AGMAR AND GONON HAD BEATEN THEIR LITTLE BROTHER SO HARD they'd loosened the bolts on his skull plate, and they continued until Grundorph's face was so badly damaged, he was hardly recognizable to even them. Things went very well for the cruel sons of Ogg for several minutes as they punished their brothers, until Angus said the strangest thing Krom had ever heard someone say during a beating.

"WHAT THE DEVIL IS THAT?" Angus muttered. Krom seemed completely caught off guard by Angus' odd statement and halted his beat-down for a moment.

"It's called a beating, brother. HA, HA!" Krom laughed. "Don't tell me it's your first, because I know first-hand that would be a lie!" He laughed some more.

"No, you thick-skulled pea brain! WHAT'S THAT?" Angus motioned with his head toward the sky.

As Krom looked up from his brutal work, his face suddenly froze, and he quickly called out to his brothers. "Agmar, Gonon... look," he said, but his brothers paid no attention as they enjoyed their punishing work on Grundorph. So Krom yelled at them in his most powerful troll voice, "LOOK, BROTHERS!"

The three trolls had been so busy beating on their brothers that they hadn't noticed Brynjar's army of wolves had taken control of the battlefield. Mogdal, Agmar and Gonon looked up and spotted Elias and Isabella coming toward them. They were in flight over an army of Bryn-wolves, and the Jackboot was hovering beside them on a platform with his sword in hand. Jimmy was to the right of the Jackboot, and Brynjar was riding the giant red Bryn-wolf. Angus laughed as the army quickly surrounded them.

Isabella did not speak but merely spun her baton in her hand as she stared down the cruel trolls. However, Elias warned them, "Those are my friends you're beating on."

"Let them go!" the Jackboot demanded.

"You can have them when we're finished. Might not be much left by then, but you have my word, whatever is left, you can have it." Mogdal laughed at him and picked up his hammer, but Krom, Agmar and Gonon weren't laughing. Their eyes were frozen on the flames coming out of Elias and Izzy's backs, and it was obvious they were intimidated by the fire. Elias forced the flames out of his back, stretching his wings to a hotter, brighter and larger span for greater theatrical impact. His intimidation tactic brought a grin to the Jackboot's face.

"I'm going to ask one more time, and if you don't let them go, things are going to get ugly," the Jackboot said with a snarled lip.

"No need to ask again. I have no intention of giving them up." Mogdal raised his hammer to the ready. "All this fighting and I've yet to find a worthy opponent today."

"Who said anything about a fight?" the Jackboot grinned at the massive troll.

Mogdal looked confused by his statement and seemed as though he was wanting to barter for something. "I see. You're looking to make a deal then?" he asked.

"No. I'm not here to make a deal, either."

Mogdal grew impatient with the Jackboot. "Well, what do you want then?"

"I just told you what I want. I want you to let my friends go."

"Maybe you weren't listening, but I said you can have them when I'm done with them." A low-tone growl rose inside Mogdal's throat as his anger began to boil.

The Jackboot lifted his sword and pointed it at the troll. Mogdal smiled. "So, you do want to fight then."

But the Jackboot did not respond to him. He simply pointed the sword at the arena walls. Isabella slowly rose into the air above them as her wings raged with bright, hot flames, and her eyes turned dark red, then she shot off toward the edge of the arena and began setting the cedar walls on fire.

"If you don't let them go, my children are going to burn your whole city to the ground," the Jackboot warned. Mogdal suddenly looked as if he'd been outwitted, and Mogdal the Magnificent never liked it when someone got the upper hand on him. When he didn't respond, the Jackboot pointed with the sword to the other side of the arena and Elias took off to join Isabella in setting the cedar walls on fire until they both met in the middle. Once they had finished, the walls of the arena were engulfed in a massive, circular fire.

Mogdal became furious and swung his mighty hammer at the Jackboot, but in one swift slice, the Jackboot severed Mogdal's hammer head completely off. Mogdal stared at the broken hammer shaft for a moment and smiled. "Finally, someone worthy of killing!" Then he lunged at the Jackboot with the hammer shaft, but the Jackboot swiftly cut it in two. Mogdal kept swinging until suddenly he realized the Jackboot had sliced off his arm. The four monstrous trolls were dumbstruck at how swiftly the Jackboot had removed Mogdal's arm with the sword, and they took off running toward the south tunnel. The howling sounds of Mogdal's defeat echoed back into the Arena of Heroes.

Angus Grand stood to his feet and began cleaning bloody grim from his mangled face while Brynjar and the Jackboot helped Grundorph to his feet. Although Angus Grand's face was severely battered, it didn't take long before Isabella seemed to recognize something unique about his voice. "Do I know you?" she asked.

The Jackboot suddenly looked up from helping Grundorph and turned his gaze directly back on Angus. His eyes seemed filled with the stunned realization that no one had told Isabella who they were saving. Angus quickly improvised. "The name's Black. Mr. Black."

Isabella began looking him up and down as she circled around him. Her eyes investigated his whole face from his earrings to his bald head with long strands of hair on the back and his tattered orange coat. The girl cocked her head to the left and then the right until suddenly her eyes grew large and she had an epiphany. "I know who you are."

"Oh?" Angus winced.

"YOU'RE ANGUS GRAND!" she yelled and grabbed him around the back of the neck, shoving her baton against his throat.

"IZZY DON'T!" Elias pleaded. "We can't kill him!"

"You don't know him, Elias. You don't know the things he's done. More than anyone, Angus Grand deserves to die."

The Jackboot stood up to reason with her. "Isabella, you said the fire berries are all gone. Burned up from the attack on the Petinons?"

"What does that have to do with anything?" she complained.

"Angus has a warehouse filled with fire berries," the Jackboot explained. "Look, darling... I know how badly you want to punish him, and trust me, I feel the same way, but we need him alive."

Angus figured he would add his own take on the situation. "I don't blame you for wanting to kill me."

"SHUT UP!" Izzy snapped back.

"Of course," Angus agreed quietly.

Elias approached her carefully. "Izzy... Merlin told me about how Angus tried to burn you alive, and I don't blame you for wanting to kill him."

"Thanks a lot, kid!"

"SHUT UP!" Elias snapped.

"Absolutely," Angus muttered.

Izzy's baton pushed harder at his neck. "Please, Izzy. If all the fire berries are truly gone, then we will need whatever he has to replant. We could help restore Pterugas and the Trembling Mountain, but if you kill him, we might never find the berries. After we find them, then maybe we'll figure out what to do with him." Izzy raised her baton into the air as if she were about to strike Angus, but she simply screamed out her frustration and pushed him away.

Angus took a deep breath and cracked his neck, rubbed it for a moment, and then spoke. "As I was trying to say, I fully understand why many of you would like to see me punished or kill me yourselves. And while I don't mean to disappoint you, I believe the Puppet Master has already beaten you to the task."

"What do you mean?" the Jackboot asked.

"I don't know what it was, but during the battle, the Puppet Master injected something into my neck. At first, I didn't feel any different, but while Krom was beating on me I began to feel different. For the first time in many years I felt pain."

"GOOD!" Izzy blurted out.

"I know you don't believe me, but I am not the troll I used to be. I've grown tired of killing. Although I did what I had to for survival while in the arena, I have changed."

"None of that matters to me, Angus. You've killed too many innocent people in your life, but you can redeem yourself in some way by helping us find your warehouse," the Jackboot said, grinding his teeth.

Angus nodded in agreement. "Then I recommend we get moving right away. I've no idea how long I have left."

30

—————

UNDER A PALE MOON

*A*bove the Black Mist and under a pale moon, the Bradley Dunbar sailed toward Sullivan's Coast with Angus Grand onboard. Brynjar remained behind to care for Grundorph, who was much too large to fit onto the airship, not to mention Brynjar himself. Besides that, the Arena of Heroes was filled with a massive pile of dead tunnel rats for Brynjar's wolves to do what Bryn-wolves do with a fresh kill. The two-hour ride to the coast was somewhat quiet due to the exhaustion of battle for the Jackboot and Elias, but for the others, it was more so from the exhausting break-neck speed of their return journey from Pterugas.

Before they left, the Jackboot had placed Angus Grand under guard with Thumacheo and the twelve Petinon warriors, but the half-breed seemed too exhausted to care about who or what was guarding him at the moment. Isabella, however, didn't trust Angus Grand even under heavy guard and decided to keep watch on the troll from across the hall with Merlin, who jumped at the chance opportunity to be alone with Izzy. Merlin's brain was on overload as he worked up the nerve to explain his feelings for her, but after a minor slipup in their

437

conversation, he spent most of his time apologizing for damaging the Whisper's boiler and leaving it at GFC. She was quick to forgive him and figured he would want to talk about his father's betrayal, but deep down all Merlin could think about was her brown curls bouncing while she spoke. By the time the Bradley Dunbar reached Sullivan's Coast, Merlin had finally worked the conversation back around to where he felt comfortable with her mood again, but suddenly Hal shot the whole thing down.

"WE'RE HERE!" Hal called out over the intercom.

Izzy leapt to her feet, drew her baton and pointed it directly at Angus's heart. "Don't try anything stupid."

Angus slowly opened his eyes. "Could you at least let me open my eyes before you run that wand through my heart?"

"Through your heart! Good idea! Now why didn't I think of that?" Izzy sneered.

"Because you're not a killer like me, that's why." Angus grinned.

"Oh, I'm a killer alright."

"Now, Izzy, don't say something..." Merlin tried to stop her, but she wasn't listening.

"I struck down your father, Ogg the Murderous, on the floor of the arena five years ago and let the rats eat him alive."

"...you'll regret." Merlin closed his eyes as he finished his sentence.

Angus Grand stood to his feet. "So, it was you! I should have known when we all watched you ride Brom the Bull through the battle and especially after you killed Nom the troll." Angus adjusted his tattered, orange coat by the lapels then clinched his fists together, but he backed off quickly when Elias and the Jackboot entered the room.

"What's going on in here?" Elias asked.

"Your crazy sister murdered my father," Angus growled.

"IZZY!" Elias exclaimed in shock.

"Oh, I didn't murder him. I just paralyzed him and let the tunnel rats finish him off," Izzy said, winking at the Jackboot, who smiled back at her.

"Good job, darling!" the Jackboot said.

"So, you're no better than me, are you?" Angus grinned as if he'd won some sort of victory over her.

"EXCUSE ME! Your father had just eaten a man, and he attacked us as if it was our fault. He was practically still nibbling on the guy's innards when we came across him." Izzy's eyes suddenly lit up with flames.

"Whoa there darling," the Jackboot said. "We don't need to catch the ship on fire. It's the only one we've got. Besides, we need him alive."

"Fine!" Izzy grumbled and stepped back from Angus.

"We'll take some people with us and head into the city. A small group. I don't want to attract too much attention, especially with Angus tagging along." He turned and faced Angus. "Once you've shown us where the warehouse is located, you can be on your way and be glad we don't kill you." The Jackboot motioned for Elias and Izzy, and after a brief conversation about who would go with them; he decided that each would select someone from the crew to accompany them to the warehouse.

By the time the Jackboot and Gemenon stepped back onto bridge, the entire team of spies was standing next to Angus Grand and Thumacheo. Henry and Epekneia had also joined them. "What happened to this being just a small group?"

"About that... um one thing led to another, and this is kind of what we ended up with." Elias smiled then pointed at Gemenon. "I suppose she's going, too?"

"Well, I just... um... I thought that since she had been so instrumental during the battle that she should accompany us to the warehouse." He winced a little as Elias and Epekneia smiled and winked at each other.

"Oh yeah, of course… why not?" Elias smiled an excessively large grin at his father.

AFTER A BRIEF PLAN WAS DISCUSSED AND THE PETINON'S WERE forced to cover up with "Hunchy" style cloaks, the Jackboot and his new spy crew set out through the city of Sullivan's Coast in search of Angus Grand's fire berry warehouse. The cloaked Petinon's began to grumble about their cloaks for the first couple of city blocks as a gentle rain began to fall upon the city, rumpling their wings inside the heavy garments. They became even more frustrated when Angus Grand suddenly stopped to get his bearings.

"Could you hurry it up, please?" Izzy tapped her foot in a puddle on the street and flung her dripping hair back into Merlin's face. He didn't seem to mind, though.

"You have to give me a minute, here. I was in the labyrinth prison for a very long time," Angus snapped.

Elias' body still seemed hot from his flaming wings during the battle, and Izzy smiled at him as she watched his mouth open to let the rain fall in. He closed it quickly after just a short taste and retched on it. "Ugh! You would think Sullivan's Coast would have cleaner rain, being so close to the ocean, but that was the worst." Epekneia giggled a bit, but it was obvious that everyone was growing frustrated with Angus Grand's poor memory as they waited on the troll to figure things out.

"AH HA! Now I remember, it's this way!" he said and suddenly took off running down the street. He turned down an alley then back across a cross street and into another alley. He stopped next to a window, wiped the misty rain from the glass then motioned with his hand for everyone to join him. The Jackboot's crew rushed through the alley, and Henry was first to the window, but he wasn't tall enough to see inside. Angus picked him up and held the boy for a moment, but Izzy was having none of his pretense at kindness.

"Put him down! Put him down right now!" she demanded, instantly releasing her baton from her mod-arm and pointed it at him.

Angus quickly set the boy down and grumbled, "Come on, now! I wasn't going to hurt the boy."

"I don't believe anything you say," she exclaimed.

"Why? Because 'Darkness Lies'?"

His reply caught her off guard. "Well... y-yeah. T-That's right... and... and you're darkness, just like Eddie!"

"I don't need you to remind me of my evil deeds. I remind myself every night, especially on nights like these," the troll said, pointing at the dreary weather falling down on them.

"Good! You deserve the worst!" Izzy said.

"You're right, I do." Angus winked at her.

Suddenly, the Jackboot smashed open the door to warehouse with his boot and ran inside. He cracked open one of the containers and yelled out, "He was telling the truth! Fire berries, the containers are filled with them. I don't know how, but they're not even rotten. They're preserved in some kind of jars." Everyone rushed in out of the rain and stared at the hundreds of crates filled with fire berries.

"Yeah, but how do we get them out?" Henry asked, and for a moment everyone looked clueless as the Jackboot closed the crate back up.

"Wait! What are you doing?" Gideon asked.

"We'll come back for them," the Jackboot said.

"WHY?" Thumacheo asked as his face was lit up with excitement. "Why don't we take them now?"

"Because we don't have any way to get them out of here," Izzy explained.

"We need a train. We need to get my train back!" the Jackboot said with a smile.

"Now how are we going to do that?" Merlin scoffed.

"How else? We'll steal it." The Jackboot grinned.

"From my father? HA!" Merlin laughed a single, mocking laugh, and Izzy almost punched him in the arm.

"You're going to steal the Iron Weaver from the Puppet Master?" Henry said in shock.

"We don't have a choice. We'll ask Thomas Rand for support. Come on. Let's get back to the ship," the Jackboot ordered, and the crew closed the warehouse up and swiftly made their way back through the city.

THE RAIN POURED DOWN ON THEM AS THEY TURNED DOWN THE road leading back to the docks, and out of nowhere, they were nearly run over by a crowd of people rushing down the center of the street. The Jackboot was furious and yelled at them, but they just kept going as if they'd done nothing wrong. The crew started to head out again, but another crowd rushed by and knocked Gemenon to the ground. The Jackboot helped her back to her feet and complained, "Can you believe it? I didn't realize there were so many rude people in Sullivan's Coast."

"Mr. Jackboot, sir!" Henry called out but was ignored as Bogan spoke over him.

"Rich snobs, that's what it is, sir. Filthy, stinking snobs." Bogan nodded.

"I suppose you're right, Bogan," the Jackboot agreed.

"Mr. Jackboot, sir!" Henry said again but was cut off by Ava.

"It was always that way when I lived here. It's kind of a rude city by nature. You know, coastal folk," Ava said, huddling under Angus Grand's giant arm to keep the rain off her hair.

"Mr. Jackboot, sir!" Henry asked again.

"YES, HENRY! OUT WITH IT ALREADY!" the Jackboot snapped back at the annoying boy.

"They all had umbrellas, sir," Henry pointed out.

"That's because they're smarter than we are, boy," Angus added.

Henry dropped his head and looked down at the ground like a fool then muttered softly under his breath. "Sorry, sir. It's just that their feet weren't..."

"Wait! What did you say, Henry?" Elias asked in shock.

"Nothing. I'm... I'm sorry. I talk too much, anyway."

"No. It's okay. Tell me what you said," Elias asked again.

Henry muttered to himself for a moment then said, "Their feet... their feet weren't touching the ground." The Jackboot's crew stood in the falling rain, frozen by Henry's words, when suddenly another large crowd of Umbrella Charmers swiftly floated by them.

"Sullivan's Coast is filled with Umbrella Charmers!" Elias exclaimed.

"But... how? Why?" Izzy asked.

"I don't know, but we need to find out. Come with me," the Jackboot said as he motioned for his crew to join him, then they hurried across the street and into the alley.

They only had to wait for a few minutes before another group promptly glided by, and they took off after them through the murky streets. They kept up with them for a time, but the Umbrella Charmers were much faster than they anticipated, and the crew momentarily lost them in the rain. When they spotted some bright lights coming from the west part of the city, the Jackboot figured that must be where they were heading. He had Gemenon swoop on top of a building so she could guide their way through the streets, and when they were almost there, she dropped back down with the rest of the crew.

"There's a large gathering in an amphitheater just one street over," Gemenon said, struggling to get her wet cloak back over her soaked wings.

"Large? How many?" the Jackboot asked as he straightened the back of the cloak.

"I'm not sure."

"Any idea what they were doing?" he asked.

"Chanting or something. Very strange people," Gemenon said.

The Jackboot took a deep breath. "Okay, we stay low and come around to the far end of the street and keep our distance."

The Jackboot stopped the crew at the corner of a cross street with a large awning so they could watch from the shelter of the rain as well as remain somewhat out of sight. From their location, they could see the back side of the amphitheater and hear the loud chanting from the Charmers. The Jackboot held his finger across his lips and shook his head. Everyone gave a nod of approval and watched as wave after wave of Umbrella Charmers poured over the top of the outdoor theater, while others entered from the street entrances. This continued for some time until Gideon quietly spoke up. "The whole of Sullivan's Coast is infested with these things."

"This is not good. We need to get out of here and fast," Merlin said.

"I agree." The Jackboot nodded, but before they could lift a single foot to head back, a sky thundering roar broke out over the city.

"What the devil was that?" Angus asked, but no one answered him, because turning to look at him they stood frozen, staring into his eyes, eyes filled with foreboding uncertainty. The sound echoed through the sky again, and the message from Angus Grand's eyes translated to fear, and it was enough to shock even the Jackboot to his core. As Angus gazed up into the sky in search of the cause, he said, "In all my days in the Arena of Heroes, I have never heard a creature sound like that."

"Me either," the Jackboot said.

"Okay, Dad, you're starting to scare me a little. Can we just go?" Izzy tugged at his arm about the time another blasting roar ripped through the sky overhead, and suddenly a large shadow covered the city above them. The beast let out a roar so loud this time that it felt as if the creature was directly above them, and everyone crouched together under the perceived safety of the awning. The shadow soared over the amphitheater for a moment then dropped down in the center.

"Did you see it? Could anyone see it?" Elias asked with blood red tears streaming down his cheeks, but no one replied as they stared into his eyes. "I have to know. I have to see it," he said and suddenly took off across the street and through the entrance. Everyone was stunned motionless for a second, then all took off after him. They found him just inside the entrance, and from their location they could see a massive, winged beast in the center of the amphitheater.

"What? What is it?" Bogan whispered.

"I know what that is," Henry said in a matter-of-fact tone.

"Well… out with it, boy!" Angus grunted.

"That's a dragon!" Henry smiled.

"Nah! Dragons aren't real, kid. That's some kind of… giant… bat-winged s-serpent thingy," Merlin said in a scoffing but uncertain tone. His assessment was instantly shut down by the sound of a powerful roar from the beast. It shook their bones and rattled their teeth so bad that one of Angus Grand's front teeth suddenly fell out of his mouth. The half-breed looked horrified, but with a shrug, seem to chalk it up to Krom's brutal beating on his face.

All at once, Izzy jerked the Jackboot's arm and almost shouted, but she quickly caught herself. "Daddy! Look! It's Momma!" She pointed out toward the beast's head, where a woman dressed all in black was riding on top of the creature. The Jackboot dropped his head and shook it in disgust. The crew glared, gobsmacked at the sight of Cassandra riding the monstrous creature, and for a time they were frozen. Then the beast let out a deep growl, raised its head toward the murky sky, and under a pale moon it let loose a mighty, bellowing roar that was followed with a violent blast of black fire.

"Yup! Dragon!" Henry said, poking Merlin in the chest with his finger.

"He's right," Ava said, much to everyone's surprise. She pulled out her notepad and quickly turned to a page with one of her drawings from the caves of prophecy. The picture was that of a small boy turning into a great winged beast and destroying the whole world. "Izzy, that's what Cassandra was doing with Elias all those years. She was making the Destroyer."

"HUH! That's why the prince was so upset about Elias' vision at the tree! I remember how heartbroken he was, but I didn't understand why. He thought he'd found the prophesied child, but what he'd really found was the Destroyer," Epekneia blurted out shock.

"But that's not Elias. He's right here," Izzy said, pointing at him.

Ava thought for a moment as she looked at her drawings. "True, but maybe it was supposed to be. If Enupnion hadn't given Elias his heart, then that dragon might have been..."

"ELIAS!" A sudden epiphany came over Izzy, and she quickly finished Ava's words. "Just like she did with Eddie when she trapped him inside of Brom. That dragon would have been Elias! I mean... it would have been Elias and Sunago, or something like that."

"Then our prince has conquered the Great Destroyer," Thumacheo said proudly.

Merlin quickly rebutted Thumacheo. "Not so fast, bird Commander! What do you think that thing out there is? That thing is a Destroyer."

"It's a black fire dragon!" Henry said with eyes as big as dinner plates.

"That's why she wanted the Puppet Master to bring her my heart." Elias somberly dropped his head. "That night in the Valley of Bones… all she wanted was my heart. She didn't even care if I died. All she wanted to do is create another monster."

"Sounds like her," Angus said with a smirk as the dragon let out another violent, flaming roar into the sky.

"Yeah," the Jackboot said. "Yeah it does." He shook his head in disappointment. "Come on. Let's get out of here." The crew agreed and they quickly snuck out of the entrance and back down the drizzling streets of Sullivan's Coast.

AFTER MAKING GOOD TIME THROUGH THE RAIN, THEY'D ALMOST reached the road back to the docks when Angus Grand suddenly stopped under a street lamp and stared down at his hand for a moment. The pale moon almost looked as if it were weeping tears of sorrow as the Jackboot's spy team waited on Angus to get moving again. The half-breed was now practically motionless as he stood in the rain under the eerie street lamp looking down at his hand.

"AH, COME ON! This again! Can we just get out of here?" the Jackboot complained as the rain poured down on the monster for several minutes.

"What's wrong with him, anyway?" Bogan asked as he winced while adjusting his mod-leg.

Angus turned around slowly, and he was holding something in his hand. "Justice, that's what's wrong with me. Ironic justice." The half-breed lifted the item into the light of the street lamp.

"Is that a thumb?" Izzy asked.

"Yes. It's my rotted thumb." Angus said. "I now know what the Puppet Master injected into my neck. I didn't think it still existed. Only the great, great granddaughter of Karl Kass could have manufactured more Necrotroll."

"Necrotroll? What's Necrotroll?" Elias asked with a concerned tone that seemed to irritate Izzy.

"It's a sort of troll leprosy. It's lethal, and there is no cure," Angus replied.

"Okay, so who's Karl Kass?" Elias asked.

"Karl Kass was the founder of Karl's Labyrinth," the Jackboot quickly interjected.

"Not only the founder, but the creator of all the tunnel trolls, even the First-Gen trolls that we fought in the arena," Angus said with sinister glare.

"And his great, great granddaughter made this stuff? So, who is his great, great granddaughter?" Isabella asked.

An odd look came over Angus Grand for a moment, then he looked at the Jackboot and reared back his head. He turned to Izzy and glared into her eyes until he suddenly began to laugh a powerful laughter that echoed through the city streets. "You don't know? HA, HA, HA, HA, HA! None of you know! HA, HA, HA!" Isabella folded her arms in disgust as the half-breed shook his head at them all, then he looked directly into Izzy's eyes and said, "She's your mother! HA, HA, HA, HA, HA!"

Suddenly, Angus looked at the stunned Jackboot as the rain rushed down his face. "You didn't know who she was, did you? HA, HA, HA, HA, HA! The almighty Jackboot didn't know that he married the great, great granddaughter of Karl Kass, the founder of Karl's Labyrinth? Karl Kass, the creator of Bryn-wolves and tunnel rats, the father of all the tunnel trolls and First-Gen juggernauts as well as all manner of terrifying beasts that now lurk in the darkness of this Black Mist covered land. Oh, Karl would be so wonderfully and gloriously proud of his great, great granddaughter. Mother to two flame-winged freaks and the creator of the greatest beast to ever grace the skies, a Black Fire Dragon! HA, HA, HA, HA, HA! You didn't know. You didn't know."

AFTERWORD

Thank you, good reader, for joining this adventure. If you enjoyed Revenge of the Puppet Master, an honest simple review would be greatly appreciated. Your opinion is very important to me.

The adventure continues in Book 4: War of the Black Fire Dragon. For more information goto Joseph A Truitt: Tales of Iron and Smoke on Facebook or visit JosephTruitt.com.

Made in the USA
Middletown, DE
29 October 2020